D0011019

FROM POCKET BOOKS AND JAYNE ANN KRENTZ

JAYNE ANN KRENTZ WRITING AS JAYNE CASTLE

Praise for
Jayne Ann Krentz
and her marvelous bestsellers

FLASH

"ROMANTIC SUSPENSE OF THE HIGHEST ORDER . . . [told with] wit and intelligence. . . . As always, Krentz pairs two equally strong people, endowing them with just enough quirks to make them real, and provides plenty of plot twists to keep her story humming."

—Amazon.com

"*FLASH* GLITTERS AND GLOWS with all of Jayne Ann Krentz's patented humor and spice."

—*Romantic Times*

"ANOTHER WINNER. . . . The sparks fly. . . . Krentz entertains us with her own brand of magic."

—*Rendezvous*

"KRENTZ DELIVERS . . . a compelling plot with equal parts romance and suspense, and a surprise denouement."

—*Publishers Weekly*

"With superb style and skill, Krentz creates a series of false trails that cloak the identity of the threat. . . . Th[e] element of suspense, plus Krentz's trademark family squabbles and strong characters, will thrill her fans."

—*Booklist*

JAYNE
ANN
KRENTZ

FLASH

POCKET BOOKS

New York   London   Toronto   Sydney   New Delhi

Pocket Books
An Imprint of Simon & Schuster, Inc.
1230 Avenue of the Americas
New York, NY 10020

This Pocket Books paperback edition September 2020

POCKET and colophon are registered trademarks of Simon & Schuster, Inc.

For information about special discounts for bulk purchases, please contact Simon & Schuster Special Sales at 1-866-506-1949 or business@simonandschuster.com.

The Simon & Schuster Speakers Bureau can bring authors to your live event. For more information or to book an event, contact the Simon & Schuster Speakers Bureau at 1-866-248-3049 or visit our website at www.simonspeakers.com.

Manufactured in the United States of America

10 9 8 7 6 5 4 3 2 1

ISBN 978-1-9821-3881-3
ISBN 978-1-4391-2013-2 (ebook)

First Prologue

Eight years earlier . . .

Jasper Sloan sat in front of the fire, a half-finished glass of whiskey on the arm of the chair beside him, a thick file of papers in his hand. Page by page he fed the incriminating contents of the folder to the ravenous flames.

It was midnight. Outside a steady Northwest rain fell, cloaking the woods in a melancholy mist. The lights of Seattle were a distant blur across the waters of Puget Sound.

In the past his Bainbridge Island home had been a retreat and a refuge for Jasper. Tonight it was a place to bury the past.

"Watcha doin', Uncle Jasper?"

Jasper tossed another sheet to the flames. Then he looked at the ten-year-old pajama-clad boy in the doorway. He smiled slightly.

"I'm cleaning out some old files," he said. "What's the matter, Kirby? Couldn't you get to sleep?"

"I had another bad dream." There were shadows in Kirby's intelligent, too-somber eyes.

"It will fade in a few minutes." Jasper closed the half-empty file and set it on the wide arm of the chair. "I'll get you a cup of warm milk."

The dozen books on parenting that Jasper had consulted during the past several months had given conflicting advice on the subject of warm milk. But the stuff seemed to be effective on Kirby's bad dreams. At least there had been fewer of them lately.

"Okay." Kirby padded, barefoot, across the oak floor and sat down on the thick wool rug in front of the hearth. "It's still raining."

"Yes." Jasper walked into the kitchen and opened the refrigerator. He took out the carton of milk. "Probably stop by morning, though."

"If it does, can we set up the targets and do some more archery practice?"

"Sure." Jasper poured milk into a cup and stuck it into the microwave. He punched a couple of buttons. "We can do a little fishing, too. Maybe we'll get lucky and catch dinner."

Paul appeared in the doorway, yawning hugely. He glanced at the file on the chair. "What's goin' on out here?"

"Uncle Jasper's getting rid of some old papers he doesn't want anymore," Kirby explained.

Jasper looked at his other nephew. Paul was a year and a half older than Kirby. Instead of the overly serious expression that was Kirby's trademark, Paul's young gaze mirrored a hint of his father's reckless, aggressive approach to life.

Fletcher Sloan had bequeathed his deep, engaging blue eyes and his light brown hair to both of his sons. In the years ahead, when the softness of youth would give way to the harsher planes and angles of manhood, Jasper knew that Paul and Kirby would become living images of the dashing, charismatic man who had fathered them.

He also had a hunch that, given the strong forces of their two very different personalities, there would be problems as both boys entered their teens. He could only hope that the parenting books he was buying by the pallet-load these days would guide him through the tricky years.

Jasper was relying on the books because he was only too well aware of his inadequacies in the field of parenting. His own father, Harry Sloan, had not been what anyone could call a strong role model.

Harry had been a devout workaholic all of his life who had had very little time for his sons or anyone else. Although ostensibly retired, he still went into the office every day. Jasper sensed that the day Harry stopped working would be the day he died.

Jasper poured a second cup of milk for Paul. He would have to take things as they came and do the best he could. It wasn't like there was much choice, he reminded himself. Fortunately, there were a lot of books on parenting.

He watched the digital readout on the microwave as it ticked off the time. For a disorienting moment, the numbers on the clock wavered and became years. He counted backward to the day, two decades earlier, when Fletcher had entered his life.

Flamboyant, charming, and slightly larger-than-life, Fletcher had become Jasper's stepbrother when Jasper's widowed father had remarried.

Jasper had few memories of his mother, who had died in a car crash when he was four. But his stepmother, Caroline, had been kind enough in a reserved fashion. Her great talent lay in managing the social side of Harry's life. She was very good at hosting dinner parties at the country club for Harry's business associates.

It had always seemed to Jasper that his father and stepmother lived in two separate universes. Harry lived for his work. Caroline lived for her country club activities. There did not appear to be any great bond of love between them, but both seemed content.

Caroline's only real fault was that she had doted on Fletcher. In her eyes her son could do no wrong. Instead of helping him learn to curtail his tendencies toward reckless irresponsibility and careless arrogance, she had indulged and encouraged them.

Caroline was not the only one who had turned a blind eye to Fletcher's less admirable traits. Six years younger than his new brother and eager for a hero to take the place of a father who was always at work, Jasper had been willing to overlook a lot, also.

Too much, as it turned out.

Fletcher was gone now. He and his wife, Brenda,

had been killed nearly a year ago in a skiing disaster in the Alps.

Caroline had been stunned by the news of her son's death. But she had quickly, tearfully explained to Jasper and everyone else involved that she could not possibly be expected to assume the task of raising Paul and Kirby.

Her age and the social demands of her busy life made it impossible to start all over again as a mother to her grandsons. The boys needed someone younger, she said. Someone who had the patience and energy to handle children.

Jasper had taken Paul and Kirby to live with him. There had been no one else. He had committed himself to the role of substitute father with the same focused, well-organized, highly disciplined determination that he applied to every other aspect of his life.

The past eleven months had not been easy.

The first casualty had been his marriage. The divorce had become final six months ago. He did not blame Andrea for leaving him. After all, the job of playing mother to two young boys who were not even related to her had not been part of the business arrangement that had constituted the foundation of their marriage.

The microwave pinged. Jasper snapped back to the present. He opened the door and took out the mugs.

"Did you have a nightmare, too, Paul?" he asked.

"No." Paul wandered over to the fire and sat down, tailor-fashion, beside Kirby. "I woke up when I heard you guys talking out here."

"Uncle Jasper says we can do some more archery

and maybe go fishing tomorrow," Kirby announced.

"Cool."

Jasper carried the two cups to where the boys sat in front of the fire. "That's assuming the rain stops."

"If it doesn't, we can always play Acid Man on the computer," Kirby said cheerfully.

Jasper winced at the thought of being cooped up in the house all weekend while his nephews entertained themselves with the loud sound effects of the new game.

"I'm pretty sure the rain will stop," he said, mentally crossing his fingers.

Paul looked at the closed file on the arm of the chair. "How come you're burning those papers?"

Jasper sat down and picked up the folder. "Old business. Just some stuff that's no longer important."

Paul nodded, satisfied. "Too bad you don't have a shredder here, huh?"

Jasper opened the file and resumed feeding the contents to the eager flames. "The fire works just as well."

In his opinion, the blaze worked even better than a mechanical shredder. Nothing was as effective as fire when it came to destroying damning evidence.

Second Prologue

Five years later . . .

Olivia Chantry poured herself a glass of dark red zinfandel wine and carried it down the hall toward the bedroom that had been converted into an office. She still had on the high-necked, long-sleeved black dress she had worn to her husband's funeral that afternoon.

Logan would have been her ex-husband if he had lived. She had been preparing to file for a divorce when he had suddenly jetted off to Pamplona, Spain. There he had gotten very drunk and had run with the bulls. The bulls won. Logan had been trampled to death.

Trust him to go out in a blaze of glory, Olivia thought. And to think she had once believed that a marriage based on friendship and mutual business interests would have a solid, enduring foundation. Uncle Rollie had been right, she decided. Logan had needed her, but he had not loved her.

Halfway down the hall she paused briefly at the thermostat to adjust the temperature. She had been feeling cold all day. The accusing expressions on the faces of the Dane family, especially the look in the eyes of Logan's younger brother, Sean, had done nothing to warm her. They knew she had seen a lawyer. They blamed her for Logan's spectacular demise.

Her cousin Nina's anguished, tearful eyes had only deepened the chill inside Olivia.

Uncle Rollie, the one member of Olivia's family who understood her best, had leaned close to whisper beneath the cover of the organ music.

"Give 'em time," Rollie said with the wisdom of eighty years. "They're all hurting now, but they'll get past it eventually."

Olivia was not so certain of that. In her heart she knew that her relationships with the Danes and with Nina would never be the same again.

When she reached the small, cluttered office, she took a sip of the zinfandel to fortify herself. Then she put down the glass and went to the black metal file cabinet in the corner. She spun the combination lock and pulled open a drawer. A row of folders appeared, most crammed to overflowing with business correspondence, tax forms, and assorted papers. One of these days she really would have to get serious about her filing.

She reached inside the drawer and removed the

journal. For a moment she gazed at the leather-bound volume and considered the damning contents.

After a while she sat down at her cluttered desk, kicked off her black, low-heeled pumps, and switched on the small shredder. The machine whirred and hummed to life, a mechanical shark eager for prey.

The small bedroom-cum-office with its narrow windows was oppressive, she thought as she opened the journal. In fact, she hated the place where she and Logan had lived since their marriage six months ago.

She promised herself that first thing in the morning she would start looking for a bigger apartment. Her business was starting to take off. She could afford to buy herself a condo. A place with lots of windows.

One by one, Olivia ripped the pages from the journal and fed them into the steel jaws. She would have preferred to burn the incriminating evidence, but she did not have a fireplace.

The zinfandel was gone by the time the last entry in the journal had been rendered into tiny scraps. Olivia sealed the plastic shredder bag and carried it downstairs to the basement of the apartment building. There she dumped the contents into the large bin marked *Clean Paper Only*.

When the blizzard of shredded journal pages finally ceased, Olivia closed the lid of the bin. In the morning a large truck would come to haul away the contents. The discarded paper, including the shredded pages of the journal, would soon be transformed into something useful. Newsprint, maybe. Or toilet tissue.

Like almost everyone else who lived in Seattle, Olivia was a great believer in recycling.

1

The present . . .

Jasper knew that he was in trouble because he had reached the point where he was giving serious consideration to the idea of getting married again.

His attention was deflected from the dangerous subject less than a moment later when he realized that someone was trying very hard to kill him.

At least, he *thought* someone was attempting to murder him.

Either way, as a distraction, the prospect was dazzlingly effective. Jasper immediately stopped thinking about finding a wife.

It was the blinding glare of hot, tropical sunlight on

metal reflected in the rearview mirror that got Jasper's attention. He glanced up. The battered green Ford that had followed him from the tiny village on the island's north shore was suddenly much closer. In another few seconds the vehicle would be right on top of the Jeep's bumper.

The Ford shot out of the last narrow curve and bore down on the Jeep. The car's heavily tinted windows, common enough here in the South Pacific, made it impossible to see the face of the person at the wheel. Whoever he was, he was either very drunk or very high.

A tourist, Jasper thought. The Ford looked like one of the rusty rentals he had seen at the small agency in the village where he had selected the Jeep.

There was little room to maneuver on the tiny, two-lane road that encircled tiny Pelapili Island. Steep cliffs shot straight up on the left. On Jasper's right the terrain fell sharply away to the turquoise sea.

He had never wanted to take this vacation in paradise, Jasper thought. He should have listened to his own instincts instead of the urgings of his nephews and his friend, Al.

This was what came of allowing other people to push you into doing what they thought was best for you.

Jasper assessed the slim shoulder on the side of the pavement. There was almost no margin for driving error on this stretch of the road. One wrong move and a driver could expect to end up forty feet below on the lava-and-boulder-encrusted beach.

He should have had his midlife crisis in the peace

and comfort of his own home on Bainbridge Island. At least he could have been more certain of surviving it there.

But he'd made the extremely rare mistake of allowing others to talk him into doing something he really did not want to do.

"You've got to get away, Uncle Jasper," Kirby had declared with the shining confidence of a college freshman who has just finished his first course in psychology. "If you won't talk to a therapist, the least you can do is give yourself a complete change of scene."

"I hate to say it, but I think Kirby's right," Paul said. "You haven't been yourself lately. All this talk about selling Sloan & Associates, it's not like you, Uncle Jasper. Take a vacation. Get wild and crazy. Do something off-the-wall."

Jasper had eyed his nephews from the other side of his broad desk. Paul and Kirby were both enrolled for the summer quarter at the University of Washington. In addition, both had part-time jobs this year. They had their own apartment near the campus now, and they led very active lives. He did not believe for one moment that both just happened, by purest coincidence, to find themselves downtown this afternoon.

He did not believe both had been struck simultaneously by a whim to drop by his office, either. Jasper was fairly certain that he was the target of a planned ambush.

"I appreciate your concern," he said. "But I do not need or want a vacation. As far as selling the firm is concerned, trust me, I know what I'm doing."

"But Uncle Jasper," Paul protested. "You and Dad

built this company from scratch. It's a part of you. It's in your blood."

"Let's not go overboard with the dramatics," Jasper said. "Hell, even my fiercest competitors will tell you that my timing is damn near perfect when it comes to business. I'm telling you that it's time for me to do something else."

Kirby frowned, his dark blue eyes grave with concern. "How is your sleep pattern, Uncle Jasper?"

"What's my sleep pattern got to do with anything?"

"We're studying clinical depression in my Psych class. Sleep disturbance is a major warning sign."

"My sleep habits have been just fine."

Jasper decided not to mention the fact that for the past month he had been waking up frequently at four in the morning. Unable to get back to sleep, he had gotten into the habit of going into the office very early to spend a couple of hours with the contents of his business files.

His excuse was that he wanted to go over every detail of the extensive operations of Sloan & Associates before he sold the firm to Al. But he knew the truth. He had a passion for order and routine. He found it soothing to sort through his elegantly arranged files. He knew few other people who could instantly retrieve decade-old corporate income tax records or an insurance policy that had been canceled five years earlier.

Maybe he could not control every aspect of his life, he thought, but he could damn sure handle the paperwork related to it.

"Well, what about your appetite?" Kirby surveyed

him with a worried look. "Are you losing weight?"

Jasper wrapped his hands around the arms of his chair and glowered at Kirby. "If I want a professional psychological opinion, I'll call a real shrink, not someone who just got out of Psych 101."

An hour later, over lunch at a small Italian restaurant near the Pike Place Market, Al Okamoto stunned Jasper by agreeing with Paul's and Kirby's verdict.

"They're right." Al forked up a swirl of his spaghetti puttanesca. "You need to get away for a while. Take a vacation. When you come back we'll talk about whether or not you still want to sell Sloan & Associates to me."

"Hell, you too?" Jasper shoved aside his unfinished plate of Dungeness crab-filled ravioli. He had not been about to admit it to Kirby that afternoon, but lately his normally healthy appetite had been a little off. "What is it with everyone today? So what if I've put in a few extra hours on the Slater project? I'm just trying to get everything in order for the sale."

Al's gaze narrowed. "It's not the Slater deal. That's routine, and you know it. You could have handled it in your sleep. If you were getting any sleep, that is, which I doubt."

Jasper folded his arms on the table. "Now you're telling me I look tired? Damn it, Al . . ."

"I'm telling you that you need a break, that's all. A weekend off isn't going to do the trick. Take a month. Go veg out on some remote, tropical island. Swim in the ocean, sit under a palm tree. Drink a few margaritas."

"I'm warning you, pal, if you're about to tell me that I'm depressed . . ."

"You're not depressed, you're having a midlife crisis."

Jasper stared at him. "Are you crazy? I am not having any such thing."

"You know what one looks like, do you?"

"Everyone knows what a midlife crisis looks like. Affairs with very young women. Flashy red sports cars. A divorce."

"So?"

"In case you've forgotten, my divorce took place nearly eight years ago. I am not interested in buying a Ferrari that would probably get stolen and sent to a chop shop the first week I owned it. And I haven't had an affair in—" Jasper broke off suddenly. "In a while."

"A *long* while." Al aimed his fork at Jasper. "You don't get out enough. That's one of your problems. You lack a normal social life."

"So I'm not a party animal. So sue me."

Al sighed. "I've known you for over five years. I can tell you that you never do anything the usual way. Stands to reason that you wouldn't have a typical, run-of-the-mill midlife crisis. Instead of an explosion, you're going through a controlled meltdown."

"For which you recommend a tropical island vacation?"

"Why not? It's worth a try. Pick one of those incredibly expensive luxury resorts located on some undiscovered island. The kind of place that specializes in unstressing seriously overworked executives."

"How do they manage the unstressing part?" Jasper asked.

Al forked up another bite of pasta. "They give you a

room with no phone, no fax, no television, no air conditioner, and no clocks."

"We used to call that kind of hotel a flophouse."

"It's the latest thing in upscale, high-end vacations," Al assured him around a mouthful of spaghetti. "Costs a fortune. What have you got to lose?"

"I dunno. A fortune maybe?"

"You can afford it. Look, Paul and Kirby and I have already picked out an ideal spot. An island called Pelapili. It's at the far end of the Hawaiian chain. We made the reservations for you."

"You did *what*?"

"You're going to stay there for a full month."

"The hell I am, I've got a business to run."

"I'm the vice president, second largest shareholder, and the chief associate in Sloan & Associates, remember? You say you want to sell out to me. If you can't trust me to hold the company together for a mere month, who can you trust?"

In the end, Jasper had run out of excuses. A week later he had found himself on a plane to Pelapili Island.

For the past three and a half weeks he had dutifully followed the agenda that Al, Kirby, and Paul had outlined for him.

Every morning he swam in the pristine, clear waters of the bay that was only a few steps from his high-priced, low-tech cottage. He spent a lot of time reading boring thrillers in the shade of a palm tree, and he drank a few salt-rimmed margaritas in the evenings.

On days when he could not stand the enforced tranquillity for another minute, he used the rented

Jeep to sneak into the village to buy a copy of the *Wall Street Journal*.

The newspapers were always at least three days old by the time they reached Pelapili, but he treasured each one. Like some demented alchemist, he examined every inch of print for occult secrets related to the world of business.

Jasper thrived on information. As far as he was concerned, it was not just power, it was magic. It was the lifeblood of his work as a venture capitalist. He collected information, organized it, and filed it.

He sometimes thought that in a former life he had probably been a librarian. He occasionally had fleeting images of himself poring over papyruses in an ancient library in Alexandria or Athens.

Cutting himself off from the flow of daily business information in the name of relaxation had been a serious mistake. He knew that now.

He still did not know if he was in the midst of a midlife crisis, but he had come to one definite conclusion: He was bored. He was a goal-oriented person, and the only goal he'd had until now on Pelapili was to get off the island.

Things had changed in the last sixty seconds, however. He had a new goal. A very clear one. He wanted to avoid going over the edge of the cliff into the jeweled sea.

The car was almost on top of him. On the off-chance that the driver was simply incredibly impatient, Jasper tried easing cautiously toward the shoulder. The Ford now had room to pass, if that was the objective.

For a few seconds Jasper thought that was what

would happen. The nose of the Ford pulled out into the other lane. But instead of accelerating on past, it nipped at the fender of Jasper's Jeep.

Metal screamed against metal. A shudder went through the Jeep. Jasper fought the instinct to swerve away from the Ford. There was no room left on the right-hand shoulder. Another foot and he would be airborne out over the rocky cove.

The reality of what was happening slammed through him. The Ford really was trying to force the Jeep over the edge of the cliff. Jasper knew that he would die an unpleasant but probably very speedy death if he did not act quickly.

The green Ford was alongside the Jeep now, preparing for another nudge.

Jasper forced himself to think of the situation as a business problem. A matter of timing.

His timing was really quite good when it came to some things.

He slid into that distant, dispassionate state of mind that came over him whenever he concentrated on work. The world did not exactly go into slow motion, but it did appear in very sharp focus.

The goal became crystal clear. He would not go over the side and down the cliff.

The path to that goal was equally obvious. He had to go on the attack.

He was intensely aware of the physical dimensions of the space around him. He gauged the distance to the upcoming curve and the speed of his own vehicle. He sensed the driver of the Ford had nerved himself for another strike.

Jasper turned the wheel, aiming the Jeep's bumper at the Ford's side. There was a shudder and another grating shriek of metal-on-metal. Jasper edged closer.

The Ford swerved to avoid the second impact. It went into the next curve in the wrong lane. The driver, apparently panicked by the thought of meeting an oncoming vehicle, overcorrected wildly.

For an instant Jasper thought the Ford would go straight over the edge of the cliff. Somehow, it managed to cling to the road.

Jasper slowed quickly and went cautiously into the turn. When he came out of it he caught a fleeting glimpse of the Ford. It was already several hundred feet ahead. As he watched, it disappeared around another curve.

The driver of the Ford had obviously decided to abandon the assault on the Jeep. Jasper wondered if the other man, assuming it was a man, had lost his nerve or simply sobered up very quickly after the near-death experience on the curve.

Drunken driving or maybe an incident of road rage, Jasper told himself. That was the only logical explanation.

To entertain for even a moment the possibility that someone had deliberately tried to kill him would constitute a sure sign of incipient paranoia. Kirby would have a field day. Probably drag Jasper off to his psychology class for show-and-tell.

Damn. He hadn't even gotten the license number.

Jasper tried to summon up an image of the rear of the green car. He was very good with numbers.

But when he replayed the discrete mental pictures

he had of the Ford, he realized he did not remember seeing a license plate.

A near accident. That was the only explanation.

Don't go paranoid on me here, Sloan.

He spent most of the warm, tropical night brooding on the veranda of his overpriced, amenity-free cottage. For a long time he sat in the wicker chair and watched the silver moonlight slide across the surface of the sea. He could not explain why the uneasiness within him increased with every passing hour.

He had put the incident on the island road firmly in perspective. He knew that it was illogical to think for one moment that anyone here on Pelapili had any reason to try to murder him. No, it was not the brush with disaster that afternoon that was creating the disturbing sensation.

But the restlessness would not be banished. He wondered if he was suffering from an overdose of papaya, sand, and margaritas. The problem with paradise was that it held no challenge.

At two in the morning he realized that it was time to go back to Seattle.

2

The following morning Jasper called his office from Pelapili's tiny, open-air flight lounge. The connection was scratchy, but he had no trouble hearing Al.

"What the hell do you mean, you're on your way back to Seattle? You're supposed to stay there for a full month."

"There's been a change of plans, Al." He was already feeling better, Jasper thought. Just the thought of getting back to the real world was doing wonders for him.

"Look, we had a deal. You're supposed to stay out of the office for a full four weeks."

"I don't have time to discuss this. The plane leaves

in forty-five minutes. There's only one flight a day off this rock. If I miss it, I'll be trapped until tomorrow."

"So much for your vacation." Al sighed heavily. "I was afraid this wasn't going to work."

Jasper covered his free ear with his hand to block the roar of a small, private plane that was revving up for takeoff. "Listen, Al, has anything happened while I've been out of town?"

"Nothing significant. I would have contacted you if there was anything you really needed to know."

"How about anything insignificant?"

"Just the usual stuff." Al's tone conveyed a shrug of unconcern. "The Bencher deal is coming together nicely. I should have everything tied up by the time you return. We've got an interesting application for funding from a small firm that specializes in sound wave technology. Worth a look."

"It's your decision now, Al. You're going to own the company as soon as we get the papers signed. Anything else I should know about?"

"Nothing serious. None of our clients has gone bankrupt or anything like that. Hang on, I think there were a couple of phone calls from a lawyer."

"Which lawyer?"

"Just a second, I'll ask Marsha."

Jasper drummed his fingers on the small shelf beneath the phone while he listened to the muffled exchange between Al and Marsha.

After a moment, Al came back on the line. "Okay, here it is. The lawyer's name is Winchmore. He wants you to get back to him at, and I quote, your earliest convenience."

"Winchmore." Jasper swiftly sorted through some mental files. "That doesn't ring any bells. Wait a second, is that Winchmore of Winchmore Steiner and Brown?"

There was another short pause while Al communicated with Marsha.

"Right. Something about wanting to notify you of the death of one of your clients. But the name wasn't in the files. Marsha told him you were out of town until the end of the month."

Outside on the island's single runway, the small plane launched itself into the air with a noisy whine. Jasper pressed the phone more tightly against his ear. "What was the name of the client?"

"I didn't recognize it, and like I said, we couldn't find a record. Must have been someone you dealt with before I came on board." Al paused to converse again with Marsha.

Jasper watched the little plane climb into the endless blue sky.

"Here we go," Al said finally. "Roland G. Chantry. Marsha said the story was a bit sketchy. Apparently Chantry and a friend named Wilbur Holmes were both killed in a sightseeing balloon crash while on a photo safari in Africa three and a half weeks ago."

"Damn." Jasper had a sudden, vivid mental image of a vital, silver-haired, debonair man in his early eighties. Rollie Chantry had been a savvy businessman with an unquenchable enthusiasm and a zest for life. "You're certain he's dead?"

"According to Winchmore, he is." Al's voice shaded with concern. "Sorry. Was Chantry a close friend?"

"No, but we did business together. I liked the guy. He owned a company called Glow, Inc., there in Seattle."

"I've heard of it. Designs and manufactures high-tech and industrial lighting fixtures?"

"Right. Chantry came to me for venture capital funding two years ago, just before you joined Sloan & Associates. He wanted to expand the R&D side of his business. No bank would touch him because of his age."

"So you backed him?"

"Sure. He obviously knew what he was doing, and he looked pretty damn healthy to me. Played tennis three times a week. From my point of view, Glow has always been a money cow, but now it's set to become even more profitable."

Assuming the company was properly managed during the tricky transition period ahead. Jasper considered the problem. The loss of the founder and sole owner could easily deal a devastating blow to Glow, Inc., at this particular juncture.

"Why isn't there a file on him?" Al asked. "You're infamous for your files."

"There is one, but it's in my personal files at home. I made a private arrangement with Chantry."

"Private? You mean this was not a Sloan & Associates deal?"

"No. Just me and Chantry."

There was a short pause before Al asked delicately, "Mind if I ask why?"

"I saw it as an opportunity for a personal, not a company investment."

It was as good an explanation as he could come up with. The truth was, Jasper thought, he did not really know what had made him sign that contract with Chantry. It had just seemed the right thing to do at the time. When it came to business, he always followed his instincts.

Now it looked as if he had unwittingly made an investment that would change his future.

"I see." Al thought for a moment. "Glow is a closely held firm, isn't it?"

"You can say that again. Chantry owned all of the stock."

"What did he use for collateral?"

"The company, itself, of course," Jasper said.

"You did a contract that gave you controlling interest in the event things went sour and he was unable to repay the loan?"

"Sort of."

"What did you take?" Al asked with professional curiosity. "Fifteen or twenty percent ownership and a seat on the board of directors?"

Al's assumption was a logical one, Jasper knew. A controlling interest and a voting seat on the board were common enough hedges for a venture capital firm seeking to secure its investment.

"My arrangement with Glow was a little different than the ones we usually set up with Sloan & Associates clients," Jasper said. "Chantry needed a very large infusion of capital to carry out his plans. He also wanted to be sure that the future of the company would be protected in the event that something happened to him. He didn't want it sold off or merged."

25

"What are you saying?"

"Chantry did not want an investor, exactly. He wanted a silent partner. Someone who would care about Glow if he was no longer around."

"Silent partner? This is getting downright weird. What's the bottom line here?"

Jasper exhaled slowly. "The bottom line is that I now own fifty-one percent of Glow, Inc."

There was a short, sharp pause on the other end while Al digested that. "Interesting," he said cautiously. "And just who, may I ask, owns the other forty-nine percent?"

"Rollie told me that, although he employs any number of shade tree Chantry relatives, the only other person in the family who has a head for business is his niece. He said he intended to leave the forty-nine percent to her."

"What's her name?"

"Her last name is Chantry, too, but I'm not sure about her first name. I think it begins with an O. Ophelia or Olympia, maybe. It's in my personal files."

Al chuckled. "Yeah, I'll just bet it is. Kirby told me just the other day that he's starting to worry about your obsession with files."

Jasper decided to ignore that. He was still trying to recall the first name of his new junior partner. It snapped into his head with dazzling clarity. "Olivia. That was it. Olivia Chantry."

"Why does that name sound familiar?" Al mused.

"Rollie told me that she runs her own business there in Seattle. One of those event production companies."

"You mean the kind of firm you hire to stage a large function like a fancy charity ball or a political fund-raiser?"

"Yes." Jasper rummaged around in a few more mental drawers and came up with another name. "Light Fantastic. I think that's the name of her company."

"You're kidding?" Al whistled softly. "I'll be damned. It all comes back to me now."

"What comes back to you?"

"We are talking about Olivia Chantry of Light Fantastic, right?"

"Yes." Jasper noticed that a small line was forming near the departure gate. "Why?"

"If you weren't such a philistine when it comes to art, you'd know who your new partner is."

"Rollie never said anything about her being an artist."

"She's not," Al said patiently. "But she was married to one for a while. Logan Dane, no less. Even you must have heard of him."

"Dane." Jasper watched the gate. It looked like the plane was loading early. He did not want to risk missing the flight. "Sure, I've heard of him. Who hasn't? He's dead, though, isn't he? Got killed in an accident in Europe or something a while back?"

"Three years ago the man ran with the bulls in Pamplona," Al whispered reverently.

"Probably drunk."

"For God's sake, Sloan, is there no romance or passion in your soul? Didn't you ever read Hemingway? Running with the bulls is the ultimate challenge. Man against beast."

27

"I take it the beast came out on top in Logan Dane's case?"

"Yeah." Al's voice resumed its normal tenor. "Some say it was suicide. Legend has it that his wife, your new partner, was getting set to divorce him. Dane went a little mad at the prospect of losing his wife, his business manager, and his muse all at once and took off for Pamplona."

"His wife was all of those things rolled into one?"

"So they say."

"Where did you get all that, Al?"

"Don't you remember the article in *West Coast Neo* magazine last year?" Al asked.

"Hell, no. *West Coast Neo* is one of those slick, glossy rags that caters to the arty-literati set, isn't it?"

"Yep."

"I don't have time to read that kind of stuff."

"You know, Jasper, some day you really ought to try reading something besides the *Wall Street Journal* and *Hard Currency*. You'd be amazed at how much more well-rounded you'd become. People might start inviting you out. You could even develop a social life."

"Skip the lecture on how I don't get out enough. What else do you know about Olivia Chantry?"

"Just what I read in the *West Coast Neo* piece. Crawford Lee Wilder called her Logan Dane's Dark Muse."

"Who the hell is Crawford Lee Wilder?"

"Damn, you are a troglodyte when it comes to culture, aren't you? Wilder works for *West Coast Neo*. He's very big in the journalism world. Got a Pulitzer a while back when he was working for the *Seattle Banner-Journal*. He did an investigative reporting series on one of those big motivational speaker firms. You know, a company that gives seminars on how to motivate employees."

That clicked. "I remember the series. I read it."

"Congratulations," Al said dryly.

"He did a solid, in-depth analysis. Showed that the company was operating a scam."

"The firm he profiled later filed for bankruptcy because of the article."

"How come Wilder called Olivia Chantry Dane's Dark Muse?" Jasper asked.

"Wilder credited her with being the marketing genius behind Dane's career. He also hinted strongly that she was Dane's artistic inspiration. That he could not paint without her. When she threatened to leave him, he went nuts. Ms. Chantry, however, made out like a bandit after Dane's death."

"What do you mean?"

"Apparently she inherited all of the Logan Dane paintings that had not been sold. Since the market for Dane's work has done nothing but explode straight into the stratosphere in the past three years, I think you can assume Ms. Chantry is sitting on a fortune in art."

"Interesting."

"We may get to see some of her private collection at the end of the month." Al's voice was suddenly infused with enthusiasm. "The Kesgrove Museum of Modern Art is putting on a Dane retrospective soon."

"That's nice," Jasper said absently. He noticed that the line at the departure gate was starting to move. "Look, I've got to go, Al. I'll talk to you when I get back."

"You're sure you don't want to finish out the month there on Pelapili?"

"Not a chance. I'm suffering serious fax-withdrawal already. No telling what will happen if I stay any longer."

Jasper replaced the phone, but he did not take his hand off the receiver. For a moment he contemplated the view through the open walls of the flight lounge. Palm trees shuddered in a sluggish trade wind. The sparkle of sunlight on blue water would have been blinding if not for the dark glasses he wore.

His entire future had been altered by the deal he had done with Roland Chantry. Fifty-one percent of Glow, Inc., was now his.

He released the phone and picked up his flight bag. There was something to be said for a tropical vacation after all, he decided. True, until yesterday, the trip had been a crashing bore. But things were finally looking up.

For the first time in months he had an intriguing project on which to focus his considerable powers of attention and energy. He had a goal.

He not only owned a new business, he had a new business partner. That meant that a wide assortment of problems awaited him back in Seattle. They were the kind of problems he was good at handling.

The fleeting thoughts he'd had concerning a second marriage vanished. Just as well, he thought cheerfully. He was not very good at marriage.

He was, however, downright brilliant when it came to business.

He was whistling under his breath when he walked

on board the plane a few minutes later. When the cabin attendant offered him that day's edition of the *Wall Street Journal,* Jasper decided that life was good.

He immersed himself immediately in a piece on corporate tax strategies. He did not bother to look out the window to watch Pelapili disappear.

3

Bolivar waved his hands in exasperation. "Know what your problem is, Olivia? You've got no romance in your soul."

Hands on her hips, Olivia glared up at her cousin, who was perched on a stepladder. "I'm not looking for romance. I'm after a few cheap thrills. I want chills down the spine. A nice creepy feeling."

"This is supposed to be Merlin's Cave." Bolivar stabbed a finger at the looming entrance of the life-sized model of a cavern. "You're dealing with a romantic archetype. The fog will enhance the atmosphere, trust me."

Olivia pushed her glasses more firmly into place on

her nose and scowled at the mammoth structure that occupied a large portion of the Light Fantastic studio. It was one of her company's most ambitious projects. The walls of the artificial cave, inside and out, were painted a distinctive, eerie dark turquoise. The same odd color, a sort of futuristic medieval shade, was being applied to every prop scheduled for the Camelot Blue software launch event. It was Camelot Blue's trademark hue. All of the company's products were boxed and wrapped in it.

"You're supposed to be studying to become a physicist, a hotshot fiber optics type," she said to Bolivar. "A man who gets turned on by cold light technology and electroluminescence. What the heck do you know about romantic archetypes?"

"A lot more than you do, apparently." Bolivar hopped down from the small ladder. There was a soft thump as his running shoes hit the bare wooden floor.

Bolivar was twenty-one years old. He had the sharp, aquiline features, dark auburn hair, and gray-green eyes common to many in the Chantry family tree.

He frowned as he absently shoved the trailing tail of his plaid shirt back into the waistband of his faded jeans. "I'm telling you that if you want special effects that will really wow the guests at the Camelot Blue event, you'll go for a romantic touch with the fake fog."

"The guest list is riddled with teckies, bean counters, and high-level corporate execs. I doubt if any of them would recognize a romantic touch if it bit them on the throat."

"Just because you're obsessed with business doesn't mean everyone else is."

Olivia hesitated. The Camelot Blue event was an important contract for Light Fantastic. Alicia and Brian Duffield, cofounders of the company, belonged to Seattle's new class of young, smart, affluent techno-wizards. They had hired Olivia's event firm to produce the software launch event because she had convinced them that Light Fantastic could provide the high-tech flash they wanted to promote their products.

The dazzle-and-glitter part was easy, Olivia thought. Thanks to her family connections, she had access to the state-of-the-art industrial lighting equipment and fixtures produced by Glow, Inc. Her resources had grown even more bountiful recently with the completion of the company's new research and development lab. She raided it at will whenever she was in search of new special effects.

She could handle flash, all right, she thought. But the archetypal romantic stuff worried her. Bolivar had a point. She was not very good at that kind of thing.

"I still can't figure out why they insisted on naming the company Camelot Blue," she grumbled. "It doesn't provide what you'd call a high-tech image."

"It's a teckie thing," Bolivar explained. "Comes from playing all those fantasy games."

Olivia nodded reluctantly. She was well aware that Camelot Blue's first product had been a software game, a futuristic version of the Arthurian legend. It had sold like gelato in August. The company had been growing in quantum leaps ever since that first trip to market. Now it was set for another big push with a new line of products.

"Believe me, Olivia, you want to go with the

romance of the Arthurian legend on this." Bolivar's expression brightened as he looked past her. "Ask Aunt Zara. She'll tell you I'm right."

Olivia glanced over her shoulder and saw her aunt walking toward them across the scarred wooden floors of the old factory loft. Olivia hid an affectionate smile.

A former soap opera actress, Zara still knew how to make an entrance. Today she was a vision in a silver-studded denim jumpsuit and a pair of strappy, high-heeled sandals. She had put on some weight since her retirement from the long-running daily drama *Crystal Cove*, but she managed to look voluptuous, not plump.

Zara wore big shoulders and big hair with an aplomb that awed Olivia.

Her years in Hollywood had endowed her with a fine eye for flashy design, which had proven invaluable to Light Fantastic.

Olivia saw that Zara carried two plastic-covered latte cups decorated with the logo of Café Mantra. The tiny, hole-in-the-wall coffee shop and espresso bar occupied premises on the first floor of the building.

"You're a life saver, Aunt Zara." Olivia seized one of the latte cups and ripped off the lid. "I hope you made mine a triple?"

"Yes, dear, just as you requested." Zara handed the second cup to Bolivar. "Although I really do think you're drinking a little too much caffeine these days."

"Are you kidding? It's the only thing that's keeping me going. You try sorting through Uncle Rollie's business affairs and keep track of things at Glow while running this operation."

Zara frowned in concern. "You've been pushing yourself much too hard since Rollie died."

"Not like there's any option." Olivia took a healthy swallow of the triple-shot espresso-revved latte. "Until my so-called silent partner decides to return from his summer vacation, I'm stuck. Everything is in limbo until he shows up."

"Be careful what you wish for." Bolivar gave her a troubled look. "This Sloan guy owns fifty-one percent of Glow now. Who knows what he'll want to do with it?"

Zara nodded in somber agreement. "Rose says that everyone at the firm is speculating Sloan will want to sell or merge Glow. That would be a disaster."

Olivia had been dealing with her family's fears about the future of Glow since an hour after the news of Rollie's death had reached Seattle. Everyone's first reaction to the prospect of having a stranger at the helm of the family firm had been instant panic. Not without reason, she reminded herself. One way or another, most of the Chantry clan had a strong, personal interest in Glow.

She took another sip of the latte and prepared to give Zara and Bolivar the same reassuring patter she had given all the other Chantrys who had besieged her lately.

"Sloan's a venture capitalist," she said mildly. "He arranges startup and expansion capital. He doesn't actually run the companies in which he has a stake. All he'll care about is getting his money out of Glow. Don't worry, I'll arrange a way to pay him off and get rid of him."

Zara sighed. "I certainly hope you're right."

"Trust me on this," Olivia said. "I may not know much about legendary passion and romance, but I do know business."

"Speaking of romance and legend," Bolivar said deliberately. "What are we going to do about the Camelot Blue fog?"

Zara looked at Olivia. "Bolivar's absolutely right, dear. You must go with the romance and passion angle here. This is King Arthur. The Round Table. Knights in shining armor. It cries out for a dreamy, atmospheric feeling."

Olivia eyed Merlin's Cave. "You're sure?"

"Positive," Zara said.

"Okay, okay," Olivia said. "When it comes to that kind of thing, you know I rely on your opinion, Aunt Zara. Let's punch up the romantic angle for the whole event."

Bolivar grinned. "Good plan."

"I still say we should be going for creepy, not romantic," Olivia said.

"Don't worry," Bolivar assured her. "The new cold light fibers I've installed inside the cave will give you both an eerie and a romantic quality. The whole thing will really pop when we crank up the fog machine."

Olivia set her cup down on Zara's drafting table. "Let's try it."

"You got it." Bolivar went to stand at the control panel.

Olivia walked to the six-and-a-half-foot-high entrance of the blue cave and peered into the depths of the plastic foam construct. The fake cavern walls shimmered with a weird blue light.

"Give me the full range of special effects, Bolivar. Lights, sound, and the stupid fog. I want to see the whole show."

Bolivar flipped switches on the panel. "Here we go. I give you Merlin's Cave."

Olivia stepped into the artificial cavern. She was quickly enveloped in the futuristic blue light. The strange glow turned hazy as the fake fog swirled from concealed jets.

"Creepy enough for you?" Bolivar called.

"Pretty eerie, all right," Olivia admitted. She moved deeper into the cave.

The imitation stone walls had been painted by one of the freelance artists who contracted with Light Fantastic. The woman specialized in faux and trompe l'oeil finishes.

Olivia was pleased with the final result. The stone-textured surface of the interior of the cave was satisfyingly rocky in appearance.

A short distance past the entrance, the cavern curved abruptly, cutting off the view of the studio outside. Olivia studied her surroundings with a critical eye.

It was not Hollywood or Disneyland, but it was good, she decided. The client would be pleased

The mist thickened, and the light grew more ominous. She looked at her hands and noticed that the strange glow had turned her skin an otherworldly color.

She walked around another corner and stepped into the center of the cave. On the night of the event a half-dozen computer stations would be installed to allow guests to experiment with the latest versions of Camelot Blue wizardry.

"Give me the storm sequence," Olivia called.

"Here goes." Bolivar's voice was muffled by the cave walls.

Haunting electronic music swelled. Wind blew. Thunder drummed in the distance. Arrows of blue light crackled overhead and underfoot. The hazy mist thickened. It reflected the glow, intensifying the aura of sorcery.

Olivia was engulfed in the special effects. The dancing lights pulsed with the electronic music in a dazzling, intricate pattern that had a mesmerizing effect.

"Well, shoot," she muttered. "I'm going to have to give Bolivar and Zara another raise."

Bolivar had gone a bit overboard on the fog, she decided. It was getting noticeably thicker by the second. She waved a hand to clear away some of the misty stuff.

"Turn off the fog, Bolivar. I can't see a thing."

There was no response. She realized he could not hear her above the music and the sounds of the gathering storm.

"*Bolivar, shut off the fog.*"

The vapor grew denser. The lenses of her glasses misted. She realized that she could no longer make out the outlines of the fake rock walls.

She removed her glasses and wiped the lenses on her sleeve. When she put them back on they immediately clouded over a second time. It was like being trapped inside a blue cotton candy machine, she thought. Everything around her was concealed in a fuzzy, dark turquoise mist.

The music soared, a high-tech electronic symphony with strong Celtic themes.

Irritated, she groped her way toward the exit. At one point she flung out a hand and made contact with a wall. Her knuckles scraped against the rough surface.

"Ouch." She winced and shook her bruised fingers. Gingerly she made her way by touch along the twisting corridor that led to the mouth of the cave.

She rounded a corner.

And froze when she saw the dark figure looming in the glowing mist.

"Bolivar?"

But she knew it was not her cousin. Even with vapor-shrouded glasses she could see that whoever he was, this man was too tall, too broad across the shoulders, too overwhelming in every way to be Bolivar.

Please don't let him be a potential client. The runaway fog would not make a good impression, she thought. Belatedly it occurred to her that he might be from the Camelot Blue publicity department come to check on progress.

Her business instincts surged to the fore. She rallied swiftly.

"A small problem with the fog machine," she said in her most reassuring tones. "Nothing to worry about. We'll have it adjusted in no time."

Blue mist swirled around the man as he moved toward her. "I'm told there's a mechanical problem. The young man at the controls asked me to come in and guide you out. He said that by now your glasses would be fogged up."

Perhaps because she could not make out his fea-

40

tures, she was acutely conscious of his voice. It was imbued with a deep, dark resonance that vibrated along her nerve endings. He spoke softly, but she could hear him quite clearly through the ancient music.

Instinctively she removed her glasses again. She batted impatiently at the seething mist. It parted just long enough to reveal a magician's enigmatic eyes and severe, ascetic features.

Merlin had returned to his cave.

"Who are you?" she demanded.

"I'm Sloan."

A strange shiver shot down her spine. The glowing blue vapor seemed to intensify. She waved her hands frantically to clear her view.

"Darn it, I told Bolivar it was a mistake to go for the romantic atmosphere," she said.

"It usually is."

He gripped her arm with powerful fingers and led her out of the mist-filled cavern into the light of day.

4

He had done business with plenty of women in the past, but he knew in his gut that this time things would be different. This woman was different.

Jasper paused briefly in the doorway of Olivia's small office. He barely managed to suppress a groan.

The desk was piled so high with papers, notebooks, and invoices that he could not see the surface. There were more papers on top of the computer.

On the other side of the room a file drawer stood open. The folders inside were crammed willy-nilly with documents. More folders, apparently waiting to be filed, were stacked perilously high on top of the cabinet. The air of busy clutter made him want to grind his teeth.

Without a word he made his way through the crowded space. He went to stand at the glass window that looked out over the studio.

The fact that his new business partner had no respect for order and organization was the least of his problems, he told himself. Of far more immediate concern was this intense, edgy awareness that arced through him. The office seemed very small with the two of them in it. He felt as if he stood in the center of a small electrical storm. Invisible energy crackled in the air.

Behind him he heard Olivia close the door. He glanced over his shoulder and watched her circle around behind her desk. As far as he could tell, she appeared blithely unaware of the sizzle in the atmosphere.

He had to fight the urge to watch every move she made. Something about her fascinated him. Probably the fact that she owned forty-nine percent of his new company, he thought grimly. *This is business, not sex. Get the right message to the hormones before they do something really, really stupid here.*

It had been sheer curiosity as much as his innate desire for information that had led him to stop at the Seattle Public Library before making his way to Light Fantastic today. He had found the year-old edition of *West Coast Neo* magazine and read the piece Crawford Lee Wilder had written about Logan Dane and his so-called Dark Muse.

Wilder had got it all wrong, Jasper decided. Olivia Chantry was not an arrogant, imperious, ball-busting Amazon with predatory marketing instincts. She was a

43

sharp, intelligent, vital woman who gave off sexual sparks.

He swiftly reviewed the facts in the magazine article and compared them with the flesh-and-blood woman in front of him. He concluded immediately that Crawford Lee Wilder had probably been secretly intimidated by Olivia. The strength in her had obviously been more of a challenge than Wilder could handle. The journalist had taken his revenge by turning her into a notorious part of the Logan Dane legend.

She was tall, Jasper noted. In a pair of heels she would look him straight in the eye.

Her height and slender figure did interesting things to the long lines of her fluidly draped menswear-style trousers. The pale lime green linen shirt fell elegantly over small, firm breasts.

The sculpted line of her shoulders and spine, together with the easy, energetic way she moved, hinted at the benefits of a regular physical fitness routine. She might be careless about her filing habits, he reflected, but she looked as though she was highly disciplined about her workout.

Goal-oriented. Like himself, he thought.

Her interesting, fine-boned face was framed by glossy red-brown hair that she wore in a casual twist. The sleek designer frames of her glasses emphasized the perceptive awareness in her wide hazel-green eyes.

Jasper sighed. He knew only too well that it was his dangerous lot in life to be attracted to intelligent women. The older he got, the more pronounced the taste had become.

"Sorry about the greeting you got when you arrived.

We're a little busy at the moment." Olivia waved a graceful hand to indicate the busy scene on the opposite side of the windowed wall. "We've got four major events coming up in quick succession. One of them is a reception for Camelot Blue investors and clients."

He inclined his head. "That explains the giant glowing blue sword-in-the-stone and the fake cave."

"Uh-huh." She sprawled lightly in her chair. The casual pose belied the glint of wary assessment with which she watched Jasper.

"What else is on the schedule?" he asked politely.

"Let's see." She held up one hand and ticked off items on her fingers. "We've got the annual Silver Galaxy Foods Night event, which will be an overnight cruise this year. A fund-raiser for Eleanor Lancaster—"

He raised his brows. "As in Eleanor Lancaster, the candidate for governor?"

"One and the same."

That event had to have been a major coup for Light Fantastic, he thought. The conventional wisdom and virtually every newspaper pundit in the state were busy predicting that Eleanor Lancaster would easily win the election. The event firm that produced her fund-raisers would be in a very nice position when the client became Governor Lancaster.

"I'm impressed," he said.

"Don't be." Olivia gave him a cheerful, conspiratorial grin. "I've got an inside track. My brother, Todd, is her policy consultant and speechwriter."

"Convenient."

She raised one shoulder in an elegant shrug. "Business is business."

He wondered how far she took that bit of philosophy. What exactly *had* she done with the fortune in Logan Dane paintings that Crawford Lee Wilder claimed she had inherited after Dane got run over by a bull?

"I think I've got invitations to every event you've mentioned so far," he said.

"Planning to attend any of them?"

"No. I don't get out a lot."

Olivia looked amused. "You'll probably be invited to the last big production on my list this summer, too."

"What is it?"

"The annual Glow, Inc., company picnic."

He smiled slightly. "You're right. I expect to be on the guest list. And I will definitely attend that event."

He turned back to the view out the office window. There was a fair amount of purposeful activity taking place in the studio, he noticed. An array of tools, art supplies, and electrical equipment littered the floor. The young man who had been introduced as Bolivar Chantry was deep into the guts of the control panel that had recently gone awry.

Zara Chantry was busy at the drafting table. Her wealth of golden blond hair glowed in the light that filtered through the huge factory loft windows behind her. Jasper wondered why she looked vaguely familiar.

Two androgynous figures, both artistically thin and terribly trendy, were at work in one corner. They appeared to be constructing huge foil flowers for a large silver foil vase. Jasper recalled that the pair had been introduced as Bernie and Matty. He was not positive which name went with which person, though.

Maybe when he figured out which was the male and which was the female he'd get that part straight.

"Have a seat," Olivia said behind him.

"Thank you." Jasper turned to survey the one unoccupied chair in the office. It was heaped with a variety of vendors' catalogs.

Olivia followed his gaze. "Sorry about that." She started to get to her feet. "I'll clear those off for you."

"Never mind. I'll handle it." He picked up the stack of catalogs and hesitated briefly while he considered his few available options. There was no place to set his burden.

"Just put them on the floor," Olivia said carelessly. She held up her latte cup. "Coffee? This came from the café downstairs, but I can make some for you, if you like."

He glanced at the gleaming black industrial-sized coffee machine in the corner as he sat down. "No thanks. I had some earlier."

"So did I." She took a deep swallow and set the cup down. "But I've been mainlining the stuff lately. The past few weeks have been murder."

For some reason Jasper had a sudden vision of his battle for life on the Pelapili cliffs. "An interesting choice of words."

"You know what I mean."

He watched her lean back in her chair. She propped both feet on the edge of her desk and stacked her heels. The cuffed legs of her trousers fell gracefully away from her slender ankles. He hoped she would not light up a cigar.

"Yes," he said. "I know what you mean."

47

A cool, critical gleam lit her eyes. "Ever since we got the news about Uncle Rollie and Wilbur, I've been swamped."

"I apologize for not getting back to Seattle more quickly. I only got word of your uncle's death a couple of days ago."

"Your office said you were out of touch."

"Sort of. I was supposed to be on an extended vacation."

She did not appear to be appeased by that explanation, but she let it go. "It was a shock."

"The deaths of your uncle and his friend? Yes, it was."

"Rollie and Wilbur Holmes were more than friends. They were together for nearly forty years. Absolutely devoted to each other."

"I believe your uncle once said something about Wilbur Holmes owning an art gallery?"

"That's right. Wilbur sold it last year, though." Olivia sighed. "He and my uncle planned to do more traveling."

"I see."

"I'll miss them both." She picked up her coffee cup and raised it in a small salute. "They were a couple of the good guys."

"I never met Wilbur Holmes, but I got to know your uncle a little. I respected his business skills and his sense of the market. He was a valuable client."

"Yes, I imagine he was." She smiled a little too sweetly. "Glow's profits have started to climb again in recent months. But I suppose you already know that."

"I'm aware of that fact, yes."

"All that money Uncle Rollie poured into research and development a while back is finally starting to pay off. Glow is poised to move out of its regional niche. It's on the brink of becoming a major player in state-of-the-art light technology."

Olivia's lecturing tone told him that she had decided to cast him in the role of the outsider who needed to be brought up to speed. The tactic was a not-so-subtle one designed to put him firmly in the role of the junior partner in this relationship.

He decided it was time to flex a little muscle.

"It was my money that good old Uncle Rollie used to finance Glow's R&D expansion." He smiled slightly. "But I guess you already know that."

She narrowed her eyes. "You mean, it was your company that lined up the investor financing for the expansion."

"No," Jasper said very deliberately. "That's usually the way I work, but in the case of Glow, I was the sole investor."

"What do you mean?"

"It was my own, personal money that went into the R&D expansion."

Her answering smile was as bright as a highly polished rapier. "Tell me, is it customary for a venture capitalist such as yourself to arrange to inherit half of the client's company in the event the client dies?"

"Venture capitalism is just what the name implies. Capital for high-risk projects. People come to us when they can't get funding from mainstream banks and lending institutions. Loan repayment arrangements vary. I try to be creative."

She raised her brows. "Your arrangement with my uncle was certainly creative. You wound up owning half the company."

"I should probably point out that I did not inherit *half* of the company," he said very evenly. "I inherited fifty-one percent. Controlling interest. For all practical purposes, I own Glow."

"So Winchmore said." She drummed her fingers on the arm of her chair. Her jaw tightened. Her cool smile, however, did not waver. "Well, *partner*, you'll need a quick rundown on the status of the situation at Glow, Inc."

He was amused by the new attempt to establish herself in the driver's seat. "Thanks, but that won't be necessary. I stopped by the Glow offices before I came here today. I told all of my managers that I'll want an initial status report by tomorrow morning."

"I see." She studied the toes of her stylish silver-gray oxfords. "I realize you'll want to cash out as quickly as possible. No problem. I've already talked to Melwood Gill, the chief financial officer at Glow. He says we can put together a generous offer to repurchase your shares in Glow."

"I've already spoken to Gill. I told him that it won't be necessary to waste any more time structuring a buy-out offer."

She went very still. "I beg your pardon?"

"I'm not open to an offer," he said gently. "I don't want to sell my fifty-one percent of Glow to you or anyone else. I intend to take Rollie's place as president and CEO of the company."

Her mouth opened, but no words came forth. She

closed it again. Briskly she removed her oxford-shod feet from the desk and sat up straight in her chair. She folded her hands in front of her. "I naturally assumed you'd want to be bought out."

"You assumed wrong. Naturally. Don't worry about it. A lot of people make that mistake with me."

"But you can't possibly be interested in running a company like Glow."

"Why not?"

"Well, because—" She unclasped her hands and spread them wide. "Because it's not what you do. You're a venture capitalist. You don't run businesses, you arrange financing for them."

"I've been doing venture capital for over a decade. I'm bored with it. I'm selling my company, Sloan & Associates, to my vice-president. I'm ready for something different."

She stared at him. "You're telling me you want to take an active role in running Glow?"

"I'm telling you that I own controlling interest in Glow, and I will be calling the shots," he said very patiently. "Is that clear enough for you?"

"But that doesn't make any sense."

"It does to me."

She glared at him. "Venture capitalists are all gamblers at heart. You get your kicks from taking risks on wild-card investments."

"I'm ready for a change. On the plane trip back here to Seattle I had the opportunity to give the problem of Glow's future a lot of serious thought."

She gave him a thin smile. "How nice for you."

He ignored the sarcasm. "The company is at a very

vulnerable stage. It's in a different position now than it was two years ago because of the R&D commitment. But it has not yet carved out a new, stable market niche."

"Glow is poised to do extremely well."

"One misstep during the next two years and the company will implode. If that happens, you and I won't be sitting around discussing who's going to be in charge. We'll be hiring bankruptcy lawyers."

She stiffened. "Things aren't that precarious. You're trying to scare me into agreeing to give you full control."

"I'm not *asking* you for permission to take charge of Glow," he said. "I'm telling you that I have already taken control of it."

"Glow has been a family-held business for nearly fifty years. You have no right to just walk in and take over."

"Correction. Glow was not a family-held business. It was owned by one man, Rollie Chantry. The fact that he employed most of his relatives at one time or another, is beside the point. None of them own any shares in the company."

"Correction," she retorted smoothly. "I now own half of Glow."

"The last time I checked my calculator, forty-nine percent did not equal half of anything."

"Let's get something straight here, Mr. Sloan—"

"Good idea." He leaned forward and rested his elbows on his thighs. He linked his fingers loosely together and watched her very steadily. "You're a businesswoman, Ms. Chantry. Try to step back and look at the situation logically."

"Whose logic do you propose we use? Yours or mine?"

He sighed. "Look, you know as well as I do that in order to take advantage of the recent expansion, Glow will need experienced management and guidance from a CEO who has a long-term vision for the company and a knowledge of the marketplace in which it must compete."

She gave him a politely skeptical look. "You?"

"Me."

She hesitated, obviously searching for another tactic. Jasper knew the instant she found it because a glint appeared in her eyes.

"There's no reason that we can't arrange to share the responsibilities of management," she said crisply. "You might be very useful. After all, I am pretty busy with my responsibilities here at Light Fantastic . . ."

"Forget it. I don't believe in consensus management. Only one of us can be in charge of the day-to-day operation of the firm. You already have a full-time job running your own company."

"While you, on the other hand, are conveniently free to take over Glow," she retorted.

"Not only am I free to assume the task of leading Glow, I'm better qualified than you are to do it. I've had more than ten years' experience overseeing technology companies as they moved through periods of growth and expansion."

"I've had a great deal of experience in business, myself."

"Is that a fact?" He raised his brows. "Let's take a look at your qualifications for running Glow, Inc. I've done some checking. Your sole business experience appears to be limited to owning and operating Light Fantastic."

"So?"

"So, your expertise is confined to running an event production company. Basically, Ms. Chantry, you put on very large parties."

Outrage had an interesting effect on the color of her eyes. They turned very green. He watched, intrigued, as she quickly regained her self-control.

Very coolly she removed her glasses and set them on the desk. "There is a vast difference between putting on a party, as you term it, Mr. Sloan, and producing a major event for several hundred or several thousand people."

He gave her his best shot at an innocent expression. "Is there?"

"The logistics of dealing with everything from city permits and health regulations to crowd control and public relations would challenge any CEO," she said through her teeth. "To say nothing of coordinating vendors and suppliers. And then there is the artistic and design side of the business."

He shrugged. "I'll take your word for it. But even if what you say is true, your background, extensive though it may be, is in a somewhat different field than my own. To put it bluntly, I've had a lot of direct experience with high-tech firms. You haven't."

Her eyes were no longer cool. They were cold. "Let's get to the bottom line here."

"Fine by me."

"Uncle Rollie fully intended that Glow should

descend down through the Chantry family. He left as large an interest in it as possible to me because he wanted me to take care of it for the sake of the present and future generations."

"I understand. Rollie was always very clear about his plans for Glow. I realize that he thought of it as a Chantry family asset."

"Exactly." She brightened. "My uncle never intended that you would take over Glow. He planned to pay you back and get you out of the picture."

"That's the funny thing about life, isn't it? It often doesn't turn out the way you plan it." He sat back slowly. "I don't want to argue about this."

"Really?" She shoved her glasses back on her nose and gave him another steely smile. "You seem to be doing a very good job of it."

"I realize your chief concern is that I will sell or merge Glow. I give you my word that I have no intention of doing either."

"Your word?" she repeated in a very neutral voice.

"Yes. Ask around, Ms. Chantry. Anyone who has ever done business with me will tell you that my word is my bond."

She was silent for a long moment.

"I don't have a lot of options here, do I?" she asked eventually.

He shrugged. "You could fight me every inch of the way, but I don't advise it."

"Fight you?" She looked briefly interested.

He smiled faintly. "If you take a strong, vocal stand against me, you could probably stir up some trouble at Glow, especially among your relatives and longtime employees. But if you force my hand in that way, I will probably end up firing the very people you're supposed to protect."

She studied him with her assessing eyes. "You play hardball, Mr. Sloan."

"Only when I'm pushed into a corner."

"I'm the one in the corner.

He did not dispute that. It was true. He was betting that she was a savvy enough businesswoman to realize that she had been outmaneuvered, at least for the moment.

She fixed him with a cool, warning look. "I want to be kept in the loop. I don't care how small the issue, I want to know about it. I own forty-nine percent of Glow, and I have a right to know what is going on at all times."

Jasper recognized a tactical retreat when he saw one. He relaxed slightly. He had won.

"As far as it's practical to do so, I'll keep you informed."

"I have a responsibility to the company."

"I understand."

"Do you?" She held his gaze. "There were eight Chantrys in my parents' generation. Uncle Rollie was the oldest. Seven of his brothers, sisters, and cousins, including my father, worked full-time for Glow for years. They have all retired on Glow pensions, and they depend on them."

"I'm aware of that."

Olivia did not pause. "At one time or another, nearly all of the kids in the family, including myself, had summer jobs at Glow."

"I see."

"Some of my cousins, Bolivar, for example, plan to work for Glow when they graduate from college. In addition, there are a great many people employed at Glow who have been there for many, many years. Loyal, hardworking people. I don't want them hurt."

"I appreciate your concern. Like I said, I'll keep you in the loop. I'll consult with you whenever possible before I make major decisions that affect the future of Glow."

"How do I know you mean that?"

He smiled. "Guess you'll just have to trust me."

5

*T*he chess player considered the pieces on the board. A mistake had been made. A lack of sufficient information in advance had made it difficult to devise appropriate tactics.

The opponent was proving to be unpredictable. But there was no reason that the original strategy would not work in the long run.

The key was to stay focused.

The game was about power. There had been so little of it in the early years, but now there was more than enough to do what must be done.

6

At eight o'clock that evening Olivia found her younger brother Todd at his desk in the back office of the Lancaster campaign headquarters. Lately, she could count on finding him there, she reflected. He lived and breathed the campaign.

The Lancaster team operated out of a storefront located on Second Avenue in the trendy section of downtown Seattle familiarly known as Belltown.

Through the glass window that separated Todd's office from the main room Olivia could see the campaign volunteers gathered around their leader. Eleanor Lancaster was holding a staff meeting.

"I hate to admit it," Olivia said, "but we're trapped. Sloan is in charge of Glow. At least for now."

Todd regarded her with serious green eyes made even more somber by his choice of eyewear, a pair of round, gold-framed glasses. "I don't like the situation, Olivia."

"No one does. But we've got to play the hand we've been dealt."

The troubled look in Todd's gaze deepened. He had always had a serious, idealistic bent, Olivia reflected, even as a child. He was an academic at heart. But underneath the studious, intellectual mien, there had been, until recently, a strong vein of humor that had nicely complemented the strength in his well-cut features.

Unfortunately Todd had become depressingly more pedantic in the past few months. The change had started when he left his post in the political studies department of a local college to accept a position at the Allenby-Troy Institute.

The institute was a small, prestigious, political policy think tank located on a pricey stretch of Lake Washington shoreline. Many of the papers it produced were published in influential magazines, journals, and newspapers around the country.

No one admired Todd's intellectual abilities and his professional accomplishments more than Olivia, but privately, she wished he'd stayed in academia. He might very well have developed this same tendency toward pomposity there, she thought, but at least he wouldn't have fallen in love with a politician.

Todd had been introduced to former state representative Eleanor Lancaster a few months ago when she had contacted the Allenby-Troy Institute.

She had just resigned from her position in the state legislature to run for governor. She had sought the Institute's professional assistance in crafting a coherent political platform that would appeal to the widest possible cross-section of voters.

Todd had been one of the policy developers who had worked with her. They had hit it off immediately.

Within days after she had kicked off her campaign, Eleanor had become the darling of the media.

Olivia reminded herself that she should be grateful. After all, Light Fantastic had gotten the contract to produce the huge campaign kickoff event, and now it had one for the big summer fund-raiser.

Nevertheless, she was still not quite sure how she felt about having a politician in the family, even one as dedicated, sincere, and hardworking as Eleanor Lancaster. She worried that Todd had been swept off his feet, not by true love, but by the potential of seeing his political theories put into action by a dynamic campaigner.

"This afternoon I went on-line to get some information about Sloan," Todd said.

"And?"

"There was surprisingly little. The man keeps a very low profile. But I found enough citations and references in the business news journals to tell me one thing."

"What's that?"

"To put it in a nutshell, you're a little outclassed here."

"Thanks a lot for the vote of confidence," Olivia muttered. "I can handle Jasper Sloan."

"There's no point even pretending you could protect Glow if he decided to sell or merge the company."

"He gave me his word that he intends to keep Glow a closely held family firm."

"Damn it, fifty-one percent of it is now owned by someone who is *not* family."

Olivia flushed. "You know what I mean. Sloan said he wants to fulfill Uncle Rollie's vision for Glow."

"You can't rely on a thing he tells you. The man's a venture capitalist. His every instinct is to go for the brass ring, the big payoff. You know as well as I do that the quickest way for him to turn a profit would be to sell or merge Glow."

"I offered to arrange to buy him out. He refused."

"Probably because he thinks he can get more if he fattens up the company and then sells it."

"He can only sell fifty-one percent of it," Olivia reminded him. "Anyone who buys his shares would still have to deal with me." She grinned. "That should be enough to discourage most prospective buyers."

Todd hesitated. Then the corner of his mouth twitched. He finally smiled reluctantly. "It would certainly make most smart people think twice."

"Thank you. I think. You know, I honestly don't believe that Sloan wants to sell or merge." Olivia recalled the look of unwavering determination she had seen in Jasper's eyes. He was a man with a goal, and as far as she could tell, that goal was to make Glow work.

She understood goal-directed behavior. She would not go so far as to say that she therefore understood Jasper Sloan, but she thought she had a handle on him.

The two of them had a few things in common, she thought.

"There's another factor to take into consideration here," she added slowly. "Glow was vitally important to Uncle Rollie. He wouldn't have taken a risk with its future. He would not have done business with a man he did not trust."

Todd reflected briefly on that. "You've got a point."

A good one, Olivia assured herself. Her natural optimism kicked in as she warmed to her own logic. "Uncle Rollie was obsessive about acquiring information before he acted. He would have researched Jasper Sloan very thoroughly before he did a deal with him."

"I suppose so."

"If Rollie trusted him, it's probably safe to say that we can trust him."

She broke off to help herself to a handful of chips from a bowl that sat on a nearby counter. She suddenly realized she was ravenous. She loved good food. Mealtimes however had been hit-and-miss lately. She enjoyed cooking, but she had not been able to spend any time in her own kitchen for days.

She dunked the chips in the bowl of salsa, and put a large number of them into her mouth. Munching enthusiastically, she glanced through the window into the outer room. The campaign workers, mostly young and practically vibrating with eagerness, were still grouped around Eleanor.

Outside, the street was still lit with the long light of the late evening summer sun. The sidewalk teemed with a mix that included the young and the restless, the terminally trendy, and others who, like Olivia, lived in the nearby condominiums and apartment buildings.

Some of those ambling along the street were on their way to the tiny fringe theaters that filled many of the nooks and crannies of Belltown. Others were headed toward the taverns and restaurants that were scattered liberally in the vicinity. The rest were engaged in stylish loitering, their only aim to see and be seen. Green hair and nose rings gleamed in the late light.

Sometime during the past three years downtown Seattle had come to feel like home, she thought. This was her neighborhood, and she thrived on its energy. She rarely even thought about the small, gloomy apartment she and Logan had shared for such a short time.

"I hope you're right about Sloan," Todd said.

"Don't worry." Olivia realized she was feeling more confident by the minute. "I'll keep an eye on him."

Todd cocked a brow as he helped himself to the chips. "What good will that do?"

She smiled. "I realize, dear brother, that Jasper Sloan looks like Godzilla in this partnership. But I'm not exactly Winnie the Pooh. If I don't like the way he operates at Glow, I can make life a living hell for him."

"Hmm." Todd grinned, looking slightly abashed. "I probably shouldn't tell you this, but that's more or less what I told Eleanor."

Olivia frowned. "What's Eleanor got to do with this?"

Todd shrugged. "Nothing. It's just that she knew that I was worried about what was going to happen at Glow. We talked. When I told her that if anyone in the family could handle Sloan, it would be you, she laughed and said I was right. Eleanor has a lot of respect for your flair for business."

Olivia chuckled, pleased in spite of herself. "Nice to know that the future governor of this state admires me. Speaking of which, how goes the campaign?"

"Brilliantly, if I do say so myself." Todd's gaze lit with fervent enthusiasm. "Eleanor is right on message. She's got incredible energy. The response at the rally in Spokane yesterday was amazing. Donations poured in this morning. The phones never stopped ringing."

"Great."

"The Stryker campaign is starting to panic." Todd broke off, his glance shifting to the outer room. "Here come Eleanor and Dixon. The staff meeting must be over."

Olivia looked over her shoulder and watched Eleanor rise to her feet. The volunteers clustered around her for a few last words of encouragement.

Tall and statuesque, her jet-black hair pulled back in a sleek knot, Eleanor Lancaster was a commanding presence in any room. She had a strong, stunning profile that would have looked good on an ancient gold coin. She also had a way of focusing the attention of those around her. *Charisma* is the word you're looking for, Olivia told herself. Eleanor pulsed with it.

Olivia felt Todd's eyes on her. "What?"

"I know what you're thinking," Todd said. "You still don't like the idea that Eleanor and I have a relationship, do you?"

"What do you want me to do, lie?" She turned her

head to look at him. "I just don't want you to make the same mistake I made. Don't get yourself into a classic marriage of convenience. You and Eleanor have a lot in common, but don't mistake your mutual interest in her career for something deeper."

Todd's jaw tightened. "Damn it, Olivia, don't try to big-sister me. I'm not your little brother any more. I know what I'm doing."

He was not her little brother these days, but he would always be her younger brother. She decided not to point out that fine distinction. Instead she summoned up a smile.

"You're absolutely right. I'll do my best to keep my mouth shut." She paused. "It won't be easy, you know."

Todd relaxed. He grinned briefly. "Yeah, I know."

In the outer room, Dixon Haggard left his boss to the gaggle of volunteers and walked toward the inner office. He was in his shirtsleeves.

Olivia smiled at him through the window. She had met him several times since Todd had gone to work for the campaign. Haggard was a narrow-faced, high-strung man in his mid-thirties. His light brown hair was thinning rapidly. The skull that was in the process of being revealed was as narrow as the rest of him. He carried his tension in his shoulders, and he was always tense.

He opened the door, nodded at Olivia, and headed straight for the coffee machine in the corner. He consumed coffee the same way she did these days, Olivia noticed. By the gallon.

"Thought we'd never get finished with that meeting," Dixon said as he poured himself a cup of the thick, dark brew. "You know how Eleanor is, Todd. Hard to stop when she's got an agenda."

Todd's eyes glinted with satisfaction. "One of the things that makes her a born winner."

"True." Dixon gulped coffee. "How's it going, Olivia? I hear you've got some problems at Glow."

"I don't know where you got that impression." Olivia shot Todd a warning glance. "Things are under control. The transition is going very smoothly."

She knew Dixon was only displaying friendly interest in her affairs, but her instincts toward Glow, Inc., were rooted in years of lectures from Rollie. Glow was a family business. Its problems were to be discussed only within the family.

There was one glaring exception to that rule now, she reflected. Jasper Sloan.

She gave Dixon her best I'm-in-charge-and-everything-is-under-control smile. He seemed to accept it, perhaps because he'd had a lot of experience with being on the receiving end of the same sort of smile from his boss. Eleanor was very good at giving the impression that she was in command. A natural leader.

Todd had told Olivia that Dixon Haggard had been Eleanor's campaign manager from the start of her career. Six years ago he had helped orchestrate her first run for the state legislature. He had been with her ever since.

Dixon was devoted to Eleanor Lancaster. There was something fervent in his voice whenever he said her name. Olivia sometimes wondered just how deep his feelings for her went. Occasionally she thought she caught a glimpse of resentment in his eyes when he looked at Todd.

She nudged the bowl of chips and salsa toward Dixon. "I just dropped in to say hi to Todd. He tells me that everything's going well with the campaign."

"Nothing can stop her now." Dixon gulped more coffee. "The money is starting to really roll in. Everyone wants to back a winner."

"That doesn't surprise me."

"Patricia Stryker is our only real competition, and in a month she'll be a distant second. By the way, Olivia, I've got a couple of things to discuss with you concerning the fund-raiser. I want to get a better idea of how the lighted flag concept will work."

"It's going to be fabulous," Olivia assured him.

In the other room, Eleanor dismissed her volunteers and started toward the small office. Dixon reached for the coffeepot.

"She'll want another cup," he said.

His proprietary air was not lost on Todd. Olivia saw her brother's jaw tighten, but he said nothing.

She glanced back at Eleanor, who had paused to speak to one lingering campaign worker. The young volunteer's eyes glowed with excitement.

"People can't help responding to her," Todd said softly. "Eleanor represents the future, not only of this state but of the country. They're going to be talking about her as a candidate for the oval office in a couple of years."

Olivia thought that he watched Eleanor with an expression that was closer to heroine worship than love. But what did she know? she asked herself silently. She had never been very good at love.

Eleanor eventually made her way into the small office. It was Dixon who pulled out her chair.

"Hello, Olivia. Nice to see you again."

Olivia smiled. "Hello, Eleanor." *Wow*. She was on a first-name basis with the woman who would very likely be the next governor of the state, she thought. A first-name basis with the woman who might well become president. "I was just about to leave. I know you folks are busy. I only stopped by to talk to Todd for a few minutes."

Eleanor smiled her easy, charming smile as she took her seat. "Todd tells me your new business partner finally arrived in town this afternoon. I understand he's very big-time and low-profile. That's usually a dangerous combination. What's the verdict?"

Olivia mentally crossed her fingers behind her back. "No sweat. I can handle him."

7

"**W**hat the hell do you think you're doing, Jasper Sloan?" Olivia slammed the door of Glow's executive suite and whirled to face him. "How dare you fire Melwood Gill? He's run the Glow accounting department for longer than I can remember."

Slowly, deliberately, Jasper put down the marketing report he had been examining. He set it aside. It was the only document on his otherwise pristine desk.

It had been three days since he had met Olivia at the Light Fantastic studio. Nothing had changed, he decided. If anything, the impact she made on his long-dormant libido this time around was stronger than it had been the last time.

Maybe it was the temper, he thought, trying to be analytical. It did things to her hazel-green eyes, made them even more vivid. It affected her cheeks, too. They were flushed. She glowed brighter than the new generation of experimental electroluminescent devices he had examined that morning in the new R&D lab.

The overhead lights danced on the red in her auburn hair. She wore another pair of flowing menswear trousers, gleaming oxfords with chunky stacked heels, and a rakish pinstripe jacket. She looked as though she had just stepped out of a 1930s gangster film. Fortunately he could tell from the fit of her jacket that she was not wearing a concealed shoulder holster.

Energy crackled in the air. He wondered again if Olivia was oblivious, or if she was just very good at concealing her reactions.

"I did not fire Gill," Jasper said. "I transferred him to a different position within the department."

"But he's always been the head of accounting and the chief financial officer. Transferring him to a lower-level position is the same as firing him."

"No, it's not the same thing. He'll know he's fired if he finds himself on the street looking for another job."

She gave him a fulminating glare. "He'd never find one at his age. You know how much discrimination there is against older workers."

"Relax. I'm not letting him go. Not yet, at any rate. But I want someone else running that department."

She came to a halt in front of the desk and crossed her arms beneath her high breasts. "Why? What's wrong with Melwood?"

JAYNE ANN KRENTZ

"Sit down, Olivia."

She made no move to take the chair he indicated. "Rollie used to say that no one knew Glow the way Melwood did."

"That may have been true at one time. But things change." Jasper opened a drawer and removed one of the financial printouts he had ordered from the accounting department. "From the looks of these, I'd say they started changing around here about three or four months ago."

She tapped her fingers on her arms and shot a wary glance at the printout. "What do you mean?"

"I'm referring to the fact that these reports from accounting are out of date and somewhat less than accurate."

Her eyes widened. "Are you accusing Melwood Gill of incompetence?"

"I'm not accusing him of anything." Jasper decided not to mention the suspicions that were beginning to take shape in his mind. "I'm saying I need someone in charge down there in accounting who can give me more accurate information."

"Did you talk to Melwood?"

Jasper dropped the report onto the desk. "Of course I did."

"Well? What did he have to say for himself?"

"He says that the switch to the new accounting software a few months ago created a lot of problems for his staff. He says they're only now starting to recover."

"So he had a good explanation." Triumph sharpened Olivia's eyes. "Perfectly reasonable. There's always a

72

certain amount of confusion after a major software change, especially in an accounting department."

"Is there?"

"Sure. Everyone knows that." She unfolded her arms and leaned forward to flatten her palms on his desk. Her voice softened to a confidential tone. "Look, between you and me, poor Melwood had a brush with cancer a few months back. It really shook him. Aunt Rose says he hasn't been himself since."

"Aunt Rose?"

Olivia angled her chin toward the closed door that led to the outer office. "Your secretary."

"Is she the one who called to tell you about Gill's transfer?"

"Yes."

"I see." He propped his elbows on the desk and steepled his fingers. "Out of curiosity, how many other Glow employees report to you instead of to me?"

The high color in her face intensified. "Aunt Rose is not one of my spies, if that's what you mean."

"Who are your spies?" he asked with great interest.

She took her hands off his desk, straightened abruptly, and glared at him. "We're a little off the topic here."

"Yes." He exhaled slowly. "We are. Look, it isn't just the reports from that department that worry me. There are some basic management problems."

"What kind?"

"The kind you get when the person in charge is not paying attention. Were you aware that both of the senior accountants handed in their resignations two months ago?"

Olivia frowned. "No. Uncle Rollie was still here at that time. No reason he would have told me."

"Gill's obviously in over his head." That was putting the nicest possible spin on it. The alternative explanation was far more sinister, but Jasper did not mention it. He did not yet have any proof of his darker suspicions. "If Rollie had not gone off on that month-long photo safari, he would have realized by now that he had a problem in that department."

Olivia sighed. "If he had not gone off on that safari, he'd still be here running Glow and none of us would be in this mess."

Jasper hesitated. When it came to business, he relied on his innate sense of timing. But with this woman he was wary of trusting his instincts. They were giving him dumb instructions. For example, right now he wanted to sink his fingers into her hair to see if the buried red fire there actually gave off heat. Logic told him it would be an extremely bad move. But everything that was male in him was urging him forward to disaster.

There was too much going on beneath the surface of his own reactions. Stuff he did not yet understand. A potential firestorm. An accident waiting to happen.

For a heartbeat, instinct warred with common sense. Instinct won. Which only went to prove that modern man was not nearly as evolutionarily advanced as he liked to think, Jasper decided.

Still, some small portion of his brain was working well enough to search for safe camouflage.

"This is not a good place to talk about such a, uh, sensitive matter," he said.

She slanted him a faintly derisive look. "Have you got a better place than the offices of Glow, Inc., in which to discuss Glow company business?"

He held onto his patience with an effort of will. "I've got a meeting with the R&D people in ten minutes. I'm sure you have a busy schedule today, too. Why don't we conduct the rest of this conversation over dinner tonight?"

She blinked a couple of times, as if he had just suggested that they take the next shuttle to the moon.

"Huh?"

Not the most flattering of responses, Jasper admitted. But for some reason it gave him hope. Maybe she was as unsure and cautious about what was going on between them as he was. Maybe she wanted to tread warily.

Then again, maybe she was totally unaware of the silent thunder and invisible lightning that he saw snapping in the air between them.

At least it was not an outright rejection, he told himself. He sensed that he had better move quickly.

"A business dinner. A restaurant won't work. We need some space. I've got a lot of paperwork you'll want to see. Reports and printouts. That kind of thing. How about my place on Bainbridge?"

"Your place?"

He was moving too fast. He could see the deer-caught-in-the-headlights expression in her eyes.

"No" He tried to appear as if he were mulling over the practical aspects of the situation. "Forget Bainbridge. Your office would probably be best. I'm going to be working a little late this evening."

"So am I," she said very quickly.

"Fine." He nodded once. Another executive decision made and executed. "I'll pick up some take-out and meet you at your studio."

"A working dinner?"

"You said you wanted to be kept in the loop, didn't you?"

"Yes, but—"

"In the meantime, I would appreciate it if you would keep your concerns about Melwood Gill's transfer to yourself. I'm sure you understand that it's absolutely essential that you and I present a united front to the employees of Glow, Inc."

She blinked again. "A united front."

He got to his feet and made a show of glancing at his watch. "Sorry to rush you out of here, but I can't put off the meeting with the R&D people." He smiled. "You know how it is."

"Oh, sure. Right." Like an automaton, she turned toward the door.

"I'll be at Light Fantastic at seven," he said again, very softly. "That will give us plenty of time to go over those reports."

She glanced at him over her shoulder. He saw immediately that the disoriented look had vanished from her eyes. In its place was a sardonic gleam.

"I'll check my calendar when I get back to my office to see if I'm free this evening," she said coolly. "I'll give you a call sometime this afternoon and let you know."

She sauntered into the outer room and closed the door very quietly but very firmly behind her.

* * *

Dinner with Jasper Sloan. Her hand froze on the doorknob for an instant. For some reason she found the basic concept hard to grasp.

A working dinner.

Okay, she could handle that. She knew how to do a business dinner with a man. On a good night she could even do a social dinner with a man, although she did not do a great many of those these days.

She gave herself a small, mental shake. *Snap out of it. We're talking take-out here, not the end of civilization as we know it.* She made herself let go of the knob.

Rose looked up as Olivia went past her desk. "Well? How did it go? Is he really going to fire poor Melwood?"

Automatically, Olivia gave her aunt a reassuring smile. "Of course not."

"Hmm." Rose narrowed her eyes, not entirely convinced. She slanted a long glance at the closed door of Jasper's office.

Olivia had great respect for her aunt's instincts when it came to this sort of situation. Rose had commanded her desk for nearly a decade. She was fifty-three years old and attractive in the typical Chantry manner, with red-brown hair and smoky-green eyes.

There was a comfortable, maternal roundness about Rose. Olivia knew it often misled strangers. They tended to overlook her razor-sharp instinct for the rumors, gossip, and other forms of unofficial information that flowed through Glow. Rollie had called her his weathervane. *She could have made a fortune working for one of the tabloids,* he'd said.

He had explained to Olivia that he relied on Rose to give him early warning of everything from impending births, divorces, and office romances to low-level grumbling among the staff.

Never, ever underestimate the value of information, Rollie had added. *You can never have too much of it.*

Rose sighed. "It's true that poor Melwood hasn't been himself lately. That brush with cancer, you know. He's going to be all right, but it gave him a terrible scare."

Olivia hesitated. "What kind of cancer was it?"

"Basal cell carcinoma. A type of skin cancer." Rose rattled off the diagnosis with the smooth precision of a dermatologist. "Rarely fatal if caught early. But Melwood was badly shaken."

"The word *cancer* has that effect on people."

"True. And Melwood is something of a hypochondriac." Rose eyed the closed door again with a foreboding look. "I'm afraid his problems may be only the beginning around here."

"What do you mean?"

"There's change in the wind," Rose muttered ominously. "I can feel it."

"Don't panic," Olivia said crisply. "I'm still here, remember? And I own darn near half the company. I can handle Jasper Sloan."

"I hope so," Rose said.

"I've got to run."

Rose's gaze sharpened. "By the way, I assume you've heard about your cousin Nina? Beth says it looks as if she and Sean Dane are getting very serious."

Olivia was proud of herself. Her smile did not flicker by so much as a millimeter. "I heard."

"Life is strange, isn't it?" Rose mused. "Who would have thought that Nina would have fallen in love with Logan Dane's brother?"

"Go figure. See you later, Aunt Rose." Olivia fled past her and escaped into the relative safety of the hallway.

What in the world was the matter with her? she wondered as she walked swiftly toward the elevators. It certainly wasn't the gossip concerning her cousin Nina's growing relationship with Sean Dane that had produced this funny hot-cold feeling. She had heard the rumors days ago.

It was Jasper's invitation to dinner that shook her. She was acting as if he had suggested an affair instead of a working dinner.

An affair. Now there was a concept.

If social dinners with interesting men were rare events in her life, the number of affairs she'd had fell into the vanishingly small category. There had been no serious relationships at all since Logan had died.

She refused to count those brief months with Crawford Lee Wilder a year and a half ago. That had been a mistake, she thought, but not an affair, thank God. Some sense of intuition had made her resist his slick, polished attempts to get her into bed.

She was aware that some of her relatives, Aunt Rose, for example, feared that she was secretly carrying a torch for Logan Dane. Olivia knew that was not the case, but she also knew that she did not want to look too closely at the real truth.

The harsh reality, she thought, was that she had lost her nerve when it came to love. Give her a good, convoluted, complicated business crisis any day. Business she could handle.

Which was why it was imperative that the problem of Jasper Sloan stay under the heading of business.

It would be a *working* dinner, she thought. Just keep repeating that over and over. A working dinner.

She came to a halt in front of the elevators and stabbed the button.

"Hi, Olivia," a cheerful voice called. "How's it hanging?"

"Hey, Olivia," another voice said a little too loudly. "Come to save Glow from the big bad wolf?"

Olivia stifled a groan. She turned her head to see her cousins Quincy and Percy ambling toward her down the hall. The twins were attired in their usual jeans, short-sleeved, nerd-pack-equipped sport shirts, and running shoes. They both wore thick-framed glasses. As usual, they had soft drinks and candy bars in their hands. The geek look, they frequently assured her, was trendy.

"Hi, guys." She glanced at the soda and snacks. "Break time?"

"You got it." Quincy glanced past her down the hall toward the executive suite. His brows bounced above the frames of his glasses. "So, are the rumors true? Is Sloan really going to fire good old Melwood?"

"No," Olivia said.

Percy cast a quick look around and then leaned in close. "What's all this stuff about a merger?"

"Nothing to it." Olivia stabbed futilely at the stubborn elevator button. "Wish I could hang around and chat, but I'm really busy today."

"Yeah, sure." Quincy stuffed half a candy bar into his mouth. "Me and Percy have to get back to the lab. Sloan's putting the pressure on. He wants all kinds of task updates ready by five o'clock."

"Guy doesn't cut any slack," Percy said cheerfully. "You oughta see what's on the schedule for tomorrow's staff meeting. He wants all of us there, not just the managers."

"Word is, he's going to push the new electroluminescent development project hard."

Olivia took a close look at Percy and Quincy. Neither appeared offended or anxious by the shakeup in the tech labs where they worked. If anything, they seemed to be excited. There was an energetic enthusiasm about them that she had not noticed when Rollie had been in charge.

"That's great," she said. She punched the elevator button a few more times.

Percy started past her. "Hey, you hear about cousin Nina and Sean Dane?"

Olivia tried not to stiffen. "Yes."

"Somethin' else, huh?" Quincy took a huge bite out of his candy bar. "Who'd have guessed that she and Sean would get together? Mom says she thinks they're going to get engaged soon."

"That's nice," Olivia said blandly.

"See ya."

"Ciao, cuz."

Mercifully, Percy and Quincy moved off down the hall.

The elevator doors finally opened a moment later. A short, bald little man with a pinched face stepped out. He was dressed in a neutral suit that blended into the neutral wall and the neutral office carpet.

"Mr. Gill." Olivia stepped back quickly. She always had the uneasy feeling that she might accidentally step on Melwood Gill. He was the kind of person you barely noticed unless he was right in front of you.

"Ms. Chantry." Melwood moved hastily out of the way and gave her his shy, apologetic smile. "So sorry. I wasn't paying attention."

"My fault, Mr. Gill." No one, so far as Olivia knew, not even Uncle Rollie, had ever called him Melwood to his face.

"No, no, it was my fault." Melwood made an obvious effort to straighten his thin shoulders, but they slumped forward again almost at once. "My mind was elsewhere." He glanced down the corridor to the door of the executive suite and seemed to shrink in on himself. "I expect you've heard the news?"

Instinctively, Olivia opened her mouth to tell him that she knew about his recent demotion and that she fully intended to defend him that very evening.

But something made her hesitate. She thought about the printouts on Jasper's desk. What if there really was a problem in the accounting department? Jasper's words slammed through her head. *It's essential that you and I present a united front. . . .*

Maybe it would be best to pretend for the moment that she knew nothing at all about Melwood's predicament, Olivia thought. There were times when taking the coward's way out was the only way to avoid painting oneself into a corner. In management-speak it was known as finessing the situation.

"Please excuse me, Mr. Gill." She stepped briskly into the elevator and pushed the button for the first floor. "I'd love to chat, but I've got to rush back to Light Fantastic. We're absolutely swamped this month."

"I'm so pleased to hear that business is good for you, Ms. Chantry," he whispered dolefully.

"Couldn't be better." She winced as a flicker of guilt shafted through her. It was unkind to rub poor Melwood's nose in her success on the very day that he had been demoted.

Fortunately the elevator doors closed quickly. Olivia sagged against the wall as the cab descended six floors to street level. She had not handled that small, uncomfortable scene well at all, she thought. Perhaps she should have talked to Melwood about the situation.

. . . a united front . . .

The memory of Melwood's sad, resigned expression stayed with her as she walked down Western Avenue toward the Light Fantastic studios.

She told herself that it wasn't acute depression she had seen in Melwood's eyes, just the perfectly normal unhappiness one would expect in a man who had been transferred to a less important position in his company.

She was still pondering what to do about Melwood Gill when she walked into the studio a few minutes later and found it deserted except for Zara.

Olivia's concerns about Melwood were instantly submerged beneath a far more pressing problem.

Her aunt was perched on the high swivel chair at the drafting table, crying quietly to herself. Olivia knew at once that something gravely serious had occurred. Zara was sobbing just the way her character, Sybil, had on the episode of *Crystal Cove* in which she had learned that she might have to have brain surgery.

"*Zara.*"

Olivia rushed across the studio, threading her way through the maze created by Merlin's Cave, five massive silver-foil flower arrangements, several boxes of red, white, and blue banners and a stack of electrical cords.

Zara straightened quickly and dabbed wildly at her eyes with a tissue. "I didn't hear you come in, dear."

Olivia halted on the opposite side of the drafting table and surveyed the mascara that ran down Zara's cheeks. "What on earth is wrong?"

"Nothing, dear." Zara's smile was the same brave smile Sybil had given Nick the day she told him that she might not survive the brain operation.

"Don't give me that," Olivia said. "You know damn well I won't buy it. Tell me the truth."

"I'm just feeling a little blue."

"Zara, please, this is Olivia you're talking to. Tell me what is wrong."

With her uncanny knack for positioning herself in the most flattering light, Zara raised her chin and tilted her head. The profile she gave Olivia was the one Sybil had turned to the camera on the episode in which she had told Nick that she was leaving him for his own good.

"There is nothing you can do, my dear." Zara blotted her eyes once more. "There is nothing anyone can do. I am doomed."

Olivia's stomach clenched. "Oh, God, Zara. Is it a

medical problem? A real one" She grasped her aunt by the shoulders. "You have to tell me."

Zara's eyes widened. "Good grief, no, it's not a medical condition. I'm perfectly healthy."

"Thank heavens." Olivia's insides untwisted. "Let's have it. I'm not going to walk away and pretend I didn't find you sobbing like Sybil in the episode where she discovered that Nick had an affair with her best friend, Alicia."

Zara tensed. Then she heaved a sigh and slumped in the chair. "I suppose I'll have to tell you everything now. In my heart, I knew that sooner or later, somewhere, someday, it would all come back to haunt me."

"What would come back?"

"I knew I wouldn't be able to bury it forever."

"Bury what?"

"He only wants a few hundred dollars this time. I can scrape that together." Zara plucked another tissue from the box. "But it will be more next time, won't it? That's always the way it is with this sort of thing. Eventually he'll bleed me dry."

Olivia stared at her, stunned. "Zara, are you trying to tell me that you've got a drug problem?"

"Drugs?" Zara looked suitably scandalized. "Of course not."

"Then what is it?"

"Didn't I make it clear? I'm being blackmailed."

8

Olivia walked through Pike Place Market dressed in an oversized denim poet shirt, a pair of old, badly faded jeans, and a shapeless, wide-brimmed hat pulled down very low over her ears and eyes. She entered an espresso bar in Post Alley and purchased a triple-shot latte.

Cup in hand, she chose a tiny table and hunkered down to wait.

The windowed walls of the espresso bar were open so that the customers could enjoy the sights and sounds of the colorful alley. From her vantage point, Olivia surveyed the terrain through a pair of darkly tinted sunglasses crafted with her regular prescription.

She was not completely satisfied with her disguise, but she told herself it would have to do. There had been little time to come up with anything really clever. Less than an hour, in fact. The blackmailer's note had been very specific. A missed payment meant that the price would double next time.

The Market swarmed with the usual mix of tourists in search of souvenirs and cold-smoked salmon, office workers in search of quick lunches, and street musicians in search of an audience. In addition to the customary assortment of characters, Olivia thought, there was also one extremely amateur sleuth in search of a blackmailer.

The project seemed simple enough. Optimism rose within her. How hard could it be to keep an eye on the small yellow paper bag Zara had left on the edge of the large planter?

The planter, itself, was about thirty feet away on the opposite side of a busy courtyard. It stood near the entrance to a small arcade filled with craft and food shops.

Olivia slouched lower in her chair, trying to appear invisible as she pretended to sip her latte. Her goal today was to identify whoever picked up the yellow sack. The conversation with Zara had convinced her that the blackmailer had to be someone that her aunt knew well. If that was true, Olivia reasoned, she might recognize him, or her. Over the years she had met most of her aunt's friends and acquaintances.

Even if she did not know whoever it was who retrieved the bag, she could at least get a description that would identify the blackmailer to Zara.

Once they knew who the bastard was, Olivia thought, she would decide what to do next. Zara was adamant about not going to the police, but there were alternatives.

A scruffy-looking man with a beard and a guitar wandered past the front of the espresso bar. Olivia watched to see if he headed toward the planter. When he walked straight past it into the arcade, she turned her attention to two stylishly dressed women pushing strollers. The little vehicles were laden with sleepy toddlers and bags full of fresh-cut flowers. Camouflage for a team of blackmailers?

I'm going off the deep end here, Olivia thought.

For a few seconds the women with the strollers came between Olivia and the yellow sack. She leaned to one side to keep the paper bag in sight.

A large shadow fell across the tiny table.

Olivia barely managed to swallow a startled shriek. *"Jasper."*

"I got your message." Jasper took the chair across from her. He put a cup of coffee down on the table. "This had better be good."

Olivia jerked herself back to an upright position. "What are you doing here?"

"You tell me. It's not like I didn't have anything else to do this afternoon. What was so damn important that it couldn't wait until tonight?"

She stared at him in amazement. He was not in a good mood. That made two of them, she thought.

"You're blocking my view."

"Sorry." He did not sound sorry. He picked up his cup and took a swallow. Above the rim his eyes gleamed with irritation. "I probably ought to mention that I'm not a real spontaneous kind of guy. I don't like being summoned out of an important meeting on a whim."

"Get out of my way," she hissed, straining to see around his broad shoulders.

"Get out of your way or what?" He lowered the cup. "Did you call me here to issue threats? You could have done that in my office."

"It's not *your* office. It's *our* office. Oh, damn." She slammed down her coffee cup and leaped to her feet.

A cluster of young Japanese tourists surged through the busy courtyard. They passed in a blur of black and white clothing emblazoned with New York designer logos.

Olivia started around the table, intent on keeping the yellow sack in sight. When she went past Jasper he reached out in a casual, almost absent way and snagged her wrist.

"Let me go." She tugged furiously to free herself.

"I think I deserve an explanation. I left three department heads cooling their heels in the conference room to meet you here."

"Go back to your stupid conference."

The last of the young tourists disappeared into the shopping arcade. Olivia gazed anxiously at the planter.

"Oh, damn," she whispered. "Damn, damn, *damn*."

The yellow bag was gone.

She scanned the courtyard in vain. The small crowd had dwindled. Whoever had retrieved the yellow bag had chosen his or her moment well.

Furious, she turned on Jasper. "Now see what you've done."

He released her wrist and searched her face with enigmatic eyes. "What, exactly, have I done?"

She threw up her hands. "You've ruined everything."

"Everything?"

"Yes, everything. Thanks to your lousy timing, I never even got a look at him."

"Maybe," Jasper said slowly, "you ought to tell me what's going on here."

"It's none of your business." She took one last look around the courtyard. "Nothing to do with you whatsoever."

"Now there is where you've got it all wrong," he said softly.

"What are you talking about?" She frowned as a thought struck her. "In fact, what in the world are you doing here in the first place?"

"I'm here because someone, presumably yourself, sent word that you had to talk to me immediately."

"About what, for crying out loud?"

"About, and I quote, *an extremely urgent matter involving the future of Glow.* The message said that you were waiting for me here at this espresso café in the Market."

"Good lord." She stared at him, momentarily distracted. "You broke off an important meeting to rush down here just because you got some weird message telling you to do that?"

"The message implied there was a serious situation." Jasper paused meaningfully. "And we're partners in the business. Not equal partners," he elaborated carefully, "but partners, nevertheless. If I left a message for you telling you that something was wrong at Glow and that I had to see you immediately, I'm sure you'd come running, too."

"I wouldn't put that theory to the test, if I were you. For your information, I sent no message to your office." The light breeze fluttered the brim of her slouchy hat. She reached up to steady it. "How did you recognize me, anyway?"

"No offense, but the disguise, assuming it was meant to be one, isn't that great."

"Oh." She could hardly argue that one.

"Who was he?"

Annoyed with the failure of her project, Olivia yanked the hat off her head and attempted to stuff it into the pocket of her voluminous shirt. It did not fit, so she jammed it back on her head.

"Who was who?" she muttered.

"The man you planned to meet here today?"

Careful, Olivia thought. He's smarter than the average bear, to say nothing of the average CEO. "What are you talking about?"

"I assumed that the hat and the shades were meant to conceal your identity while you met with someone," Jasper said with grim patience.

It was on the tip of her tongue to inform him that he had assumed wrong. But it occurred to her that it might be better for him to leap to the conclusion that she had a secret lover than to guess that she had been spying on a blackmailer.

She smiled coldly. "As I said, it's really none of your business. This whole thing has been a complete waste of time, thanks to you. I'm going back to the office."

She rose quickly from the table and started to turn away.

Jasper got to his feet. "Olivia."

Something in his voice, perhaps the very softness of it, made her stop. She glanced back over her shoulder.

"Now what?" she said ungraciously.

"I don't have any idea yet what was going down here, but I do know that I'm at this particular place, at this particular time today because someone wanted me to be here. Between now and seven o'clock this evening when we're scheduled to do take-out, why don't you think about just what that might mean?"

She stared at him, open-mouthed, as the implications finally hit her. Jasper had no idea just how terribly ominous this turn of events was.

Of course. The blackmailer had known she was here. He or she had spotted her despite the disguise and devised a quick, simple, highly effective plan to distract her for a couple of crucial minutes.

Someone knew a great deal about both her and Jasper.

By the time Olivia got her mouth closed, Jasper was gone.

At ten minutes after seven, warm paper sack in one hand, briefcase in the other, Jasper came to a halt on the sidewalk. He surveyed the heavy glass doors that marked the entrance to the lobby of Olivia's condominium.

Fortunately, he had made it ahead of the storm that was preparing to swoop down over Elliott Bay.

He was ten minutes late because that was how long it had taken him to get here after discovering that the offices of Light Fantastic were closed for the day.

He had been torn between quiet anger and an uneasy sense that something was very wrong, when he finally spotted the note someone had left in the door. It had been brief.

Plans have changed. My place.

It was unsigned, but he recognized Olivia's handwriting. There had been plenty of samples of it on the papers he had seen on her desk that first day. The style of her penmanship echoed her own personal style. Bold, feminine, and intriguing.

A formally attired doorman, with buzz-cut blond hair, and a discreet ring in his ear, admitted Jasper with a polite smile.

"May I help you?"

"Jasper Sloan. Ms. Chantry is expecting me."

"I'll let her know you're here." The doorman picked up a phone and punched out a number. There was a brief pause before he spoke into the receiver. "Mr. Sloan is down here in the lobby, Ms. Chantry."

There was another pause. A longer one this time. The doorman's covertly curious gaze went to Jasper. "Yes, of course. I'll send him right up."

A short while later Jasper stepped off the elevator on the eleventh floor. The gray carpet and walls of the hushed hallway were accented with a gleaming black credenza and a mirror. An elegant black vase filled with white silk flowers stood in front of the mirror. Jasper counted four suites.

He turned left and stopped in front of the door in the northeast corner. She'd have a view of Lake Union and the Space Needle, he thought. Morning sun. An early riser like himself.

If the corridor was any indication of the tastes of the occupants on this floor, he was pretty sure he knew what to expect inside Olivia's condo. He envisioned a lot of black leather and chrome furniture and tiny, twisty European lamps.

The door opened just as he reached toward the bell. Olivia stood in the entrance. She was still clad in the jeans and the oversized denim shirt she'd worn to the Market earlier that afternoon.

Clearly the prospect of having dinner with him had not inspired her to put on something silky and sexy. Well, what did you expect? he thought. You told her this was going to be a working dinner.

Her hair was caught up in a loose twist at the back of her head. A few tendrils had come free. Jasper felt his insides tighten. When all was said and done, he was a simple man, he thought. He didn't need to see her in slinky lounging pajamas. The jeans and those little tendrils of hair drifting down around her ears were all he needed to give him an erection.

She looked at him with somber, shadowed eyes.

"How bad is this?" he asked.

"You'd better come into the living room and have a seat. I'll pour you a glass of wine."

Her grim, subdued tone worried him as nothing else had in a long time.

"Am I going to need the wine?" he asked.

"You might not, but I certainly do."

Maybe he would finally get the whole story now. Jasper waited for her to close the door. He noticed that she set the dead bolt.

He followed her through a small hall tiled with terra-cotta and into an open living and dining room lined with windows. He was oddly relieved to see that he'd been wrong about the black-and-chrome furniture and the trendy little lamps.

His first thought was that he had walked into a sun-baked Mediterranean villa. Even the metallic gray sky outside could not dim the warm, golden glow inside the condo.

The rustic-looking, rough-plastered walls were painted with the richly faded yellows, reds, and browns one associated with the stucco and stone of an Italian palazzo. Jasper saw that the terra-cotta flooring extended throughout the suite.

A rug striped in dark, cloudy hues of green, blue, rust, and ochre framed a sitting area furnished with a low, wooden sofa. There were dull gold cushions on the sofa and the chairs across from it.

The wide coffee table was covered with colorful mosaic tiles. Large, painted pottery containers filled with leafy foliage were scattered about on the floor. There were more pots filled with flowering plants on the tiled window seat.

The effect was sultry, vibrant, and compellingly sensual in a way Jasper could not explain. Interior design had never ranked high on his list of interests. Straightforward comfort and clean functionality were his chief requirements in his personal environments. But Olivia's sunny little villa on the eleventh floor made him see new possibilities.

He held out the paper bag. "Dinner. It was a lot warmer ten minutes ago when I got to your office."

"Thanks." She took the bag, but she did not bother to peek inside.

Maybe she wasn't hungry, Jasper thought. Another bad sign.

"Have a seat." She waved him to a low chair. "I'll get the wine."

She went around the corner into a kitchen that looked as if it had been ripped out of an old farmhouse in the south of France. Through the opening above the counter that divided the two rooms, Jasper could see a lot of gleaming pans suspended from iron hooks. Not the kitchen of a woman who lived on take-out and microwave, he thought.

He set his briefcase down on the striped rug beside one of the low chairs. He took off his jacket, slung it over the sofa, and tugged at the knot of his tie.

"Nice place," he said.

Olivia caught his eye as she removed the cork from a bottle of chardonnay. "Surprised?"

"By your condo? A little. But it suits you." He paused. "I was more surprised by the note in the door at Light Fantastic."

"Something came up." She tossed the cork into the waste basket and poured two glasses. "We need to talk."

"I thought we were going to do that at your office."

"I didn't feel like staying there alone until you

arrived." She picked up the glasses and walked around the corner into the living area. "It's been what you might call a difficult day."

Jasper studied the wine in the glass she handed to him. It was almost the same buttery shade of yellow-gold as the art glass bowl that sat in the center of the coffee table.

Olivia sank down in the chair across from him and tucked one leg under her thigh. She took a sip of wine and then nodded toward an envelope that lay on the mosaic table.

"Take a look at that," she said quietly.

"I'm not really into the mysterious approach." He did not pick up the envelope. Instead he took a swallow of the chardonnay. It was good, just as he'd anticipated. Lush and mouth-filling. It made him wonder what it would be like to kiss Olivia. "I like to do things in a logical progression."

"All right, we'll do it your way. Where do you want to start?"

"Why don't you begin by telling me why you were trying to hide behind an old hat and a pair of shades at the Market this afternoon? Then I'll open the envelope."

She shrugged. "I was trying to identify the person who is blackmailing my aunt."

Jasper stilled. He realized he had been braced for a completely different kind of admission. He had expected to be told that she had gone to the Market to meet someone, a married lover, perhaps, who had been scared off by Jasper's appearance on the scene.

The relief that surged through him was totally

inappropriate to the situation, he told himself. But it sure felt good.

He did not take his eyes off Olivia's face. "Explain."

"When I returned from your office this morning I found Zara, in tears. She told me she'd found a black-mail note on the front seat of her car that morning. The instructions ordered her to leave five hundred dollars in a paper bag on a planter in the Pike Place Market."

"This is for real?"

"You think I'd make up something as nasty as this?"

Jasper went cold to the bone as he put the rest of the tale together. "You went to the Market to see if you could spot the blackmailer when he picked up the money." He shut his eyes. "Shit."

"It seemed like a perfectly reasonable move to me." She sounded offended.

He opened his eyes and stared at her. "You and I obviously have two different definitions of the word *reasonable*. Let's go back to the beginning. Why is your aunt being blackmailed?"

Olivia's mouth tightened. "It's a personal matter."

"Of course it is." He forced himself to exert some patience. "Blackmail is always a personal matter. If it wasn't personal, there would be no threat. I need to know why your aunt was willing to pay for someone's silence."

She frowned warily. "Why do you need to know the details?"

"I always gather as much information as possible before I act. It's the way I work."

"You sound just like Uncle Rollie," she muttered. "I

suppose your basement is full of file cabinets, too?"

He had a brief, mental image of the row of black metal cabinets that lined one wall of his Bainbridge Island basement. He told himself he would rise above the goad.

"Olivia, the fact that you've gone so far as to say the word *blackmail* means that, for some reason, you now consider me to be involved in this."

She groaned. "Unfortunately, you are. Sort of."

"If I'm in it, I have a right to all the details."

She contemplated him for a moment. He thought at first that she would continue to be stubborn for a while longer. But she proved to be as smart as he had believed she was.

"Okay." She exhaled slowly. "I guess you've got a point."

"I'm listening."

"What I'm about to tell you was news to me, too. I was aware of Aunt Zara's long career in television soaps, of course. But today I found out for the first time that before she got the role of Sybil on *Crystal Cove*, she, uh, had another job in the industry."

"X-rated films?"

Olivia's eyes widened. "How on earth did you know that?"

"It seemed sort of obvious, given the direction you were already going."

"I see." She frowned. "You're right. Given her career and the blackmail threat, the conclusion is rather obvious, isn't it? I'll cut to the chase. Someone has learned about Zara's past and has threatened to expose it."

"Why the hell does she care? She's retired."

Olivia glared at him. "You don't understand. Zara is very proud of her career in the soaps. In her day, she was quite popular. She still gets fan mail asking for autographs. The tabloids call once in a while to interview her for their what-are-they-doing-now columns."

Jasper put down his glass. "Let me get this straight. Your aunt, the ex-soap queen, is afraid she'll be humiliated if word gets out that she once did porno flicks?"

"She's very conscious of the fact that her old fans still identify her with the character she played on *Crystal Cove*. Sybil was a heroine, not a villainess."

"Olivia, she was just a character in a soap opera."

Olivia's delicate jaw went rigid. "I was afraid of this."

"Of what?"

"That you would not be the least bit sympathetic or understanding."

"No offense," Jasper said, "but I would have thought that a retired soap star would kill for a little splash of gossip in the tabloids."

"You don't know my aunt. Zara would be much more likely to kill to keep her character's reputation from being tarnished."

Jasper shook his head, amazed. "She's actually willing to pay off a blackmailer to preserve the rep of a TV character?"

"You have to understand, Zara is very upset. She's kept the secret of her X-rated film career a secret for years. She's afraid that all the rest of the Chantrys will be humiliated and embarrassed if the truth comes out."

Jasper raised one brow. "Is that true?"

Olivia hesitated. "I have to tell you that, speaking as her niece, it's a little mind-boggling to think of Aunt Zara as an X-rated actress. But I can't say I'm overcome with shock and horror."

"I didn't think so."

"Zara's worried about the others, though. My brother, for example, is involved not only professionally, but personally, with Eleanor Lancaster."

"Are you serious? Your brother has fallen for a politician?"

Olivia nodded unhappily. "Uh-huh. Aunt Zara's afraid that if the Lancaster campaign gets wind of Todd's connection to a former porn star, it could hurt his career as well as his relationship with Eleanor Lancaster."

Jasper considered that angle for a few seconds and dismissed it. "It's an old story that might be worth a couple of inches of newsprint, but that's about it. Nothing that would endanger Lancaster's run for the governor's chair."

"I tend to agree with you, but Zara is convinced that if she doesn't pay off the blackmailer, she might inadvertently ruin Todd's career and personal life. And then there are all of the relatives in Zara's generation. The Chantrys are a large family. There's no denying that some of them are on the prissy side."

"So you tried to identify the blackmailer today."

"Yes." She narrowed her eyes. "Unfortunately, you screwed things up at the last minute."

He held up one hand, palm out. "Don't blame me, lady. Whoever sent that message telling me that you wanted to see me ASAP is the one who screwed things up for you."

She sighed. "You're right. I thought about it a lot after I left you this afternoon. The snafu at the market was my fault. The blackmailer spotted me and called your office. I guess it really wasn't a very good disguise."

"No, it wasn't." He had recognized her instantly. The graceful curve of her spine, the tilt of her head, the shape of her hand as she gripped the coffee cup. Hell, he would have known her in a darkened room.

"The bad news," Olivia continued in very distinct tones, "is that because I messed up today, you are now involved in this problem."

He let a beat of silence go past before he said, very carefully, "I'm flattered as hell, of course, that you've seen fit to include me in your little adventure."

"You won't be so thrilled once you open that envelope and find out what an active role you've got."

Her entire mood had changed since he had seen her at the Market, he reflected.

He picked up the envelope and slowly raised the flap. There was a single sheet of letter-sized paper inside. It was the kind of ubiquitous, anonymous paper that was used in laser printers in offices and homes everywhere.

He withdrew the note and read the computer-generated message.

I do not tolerate interference in my business affairs. Now you and Sloan must be taught a lesson.

9

~

"**Y**ou do realize," Jasper said quietly, "that it's time to go to the police."

"*No.* At least not yet." Olivia uncurled herself very quickly and sat forward in her chair. She pressed her knees tensely together. "I know that there's an implied threat to you in that note. That's why I told you the whole story."

"The threat is to both of us," he pointed out dryly.

"Yes, but it's probably meaningless."

"Meaningless?"

"The blackmailer is lashing out in anger," she said. "He must know that you and I are not the kind who would ever pay blackmail. He's just trying to scare us off so that he can prey on Zara."

Her airy dismissal of the threat to herself irritated Jasper. "I take it you've had a lot of experience with blackmailers?"

"Don't be ridiculous. I'm just telling you that I don't think you're in any real danger."

"Thanks. I can't tell you how much better that makes me feel."

She gave him an annoyed glare. "There's no call for sarcasm."

"Sorry, don't know what came over me."

"My only concern here is for Aunt Zara. I promised her that we'd make another attempt to identify the blackmailer."

"We?" he repeated cautiously.

"If the next attempt fails," she continued briskly, "I think I can talk her into hiring a private investigator. She has a rather romantic view of PIs because of her years in television."

Jasper dropped the blackmail letter onto the table. "Just how do you propose to catch this guy? You didn't have much luck this afternoon."

"I didn't have time to put together a really good plan today. The disguise was a spur-of-the-moment thing."

"I see."

"But surely between the two of us we should be able to come up with a way to nail him." Olivia paused. "Or her."

"The quickest way to end this is to turn it over to the authorities."

"The quickest, *quietest* way to end it is to identify the blackmailer."

He contemplated the fresh enthusiasm and determination in her eyes. Apparently now that she had got past the awkward part, namely informing him that he was involved, her goal-oriented nature had reasserted itself. She was ready to move forward on the project.

"What do you plan to do with this blackmailer if you do make an identification?" he asked.

"Zara believes it's someone from her past," Olivia said. "She says it has to be someone who once knew her very well. Maybe someone who actually worked with her on those X-rated films. She's convinced it's an old rival who's now down on his or her luck and looking for a way to make some quick cash."

"I see."

"She thinks that once we know the identity of the blackmailer, she can confront the person and warn him or her to leave her alone."

"What makes her think that will work?" Jasper asked.

"She believes that the blackmailer won't want to be exposed as someone who once worked in the porn industry any more than she, herself, does."

"In other words, she thinks she can neutralize the threat by making her own threats."

"Right." Olivia looked pleased by his quick grasp of the concept.

"Hmm."

She pursed her lips. "You don't sound convinced."

"I probably don't sound convinced because I'm not convinced."

"Look, if it's any consolation, I happen to agree with you. I think we should turn the matter over to the authorities. But I promised Aunt Zara that we'd try to identify the blackmailer first and let her decide whether or not to handle it on a personal basis."

Jasper said nothing.

Olivia's brows came together in a tight line above the frames of her designer glasses. "You know as well as I do that Zara's approach to this is no different than the way most businesses handle employees who commit fraud or embezzlement. It's all hushed up."

"This is not quite the same thing."

"Yes, it is," she said urgently. "Companies rarely go to the authorities when they suspect embezzlement because they don't want their clients and customers to find out that their internal security was lousy. They prefer to handle the matter privately. Zara wants to deal with this the same way."

"And you promised her we'd help."

"Yes."

"Tell me something," he said quietly. "Do you always rush to the aid of any member of the Chantry or Glow family who comes to you for help?"

She scowled. "What kind of a question is that?"

He exhaled slowly. "Forget it. You're right. It's a stupid question." One to which he already knew the answer.

My niece is a lot like me, Rollie Chantry had said at one point during the contract negotiations. *She understands her responsibilities to the family. When I'm gone, she'll watch out for Chantry interests.*

"Jasper, I'm very sorry about what happened this afternoon. I know that it's my fault that you're involved now."

The apology annoyed him. "It was the blackmailer's fault, not yours."

"If my disguise hadn't been so crummy, he or she would never have recognized me and called your office to send you rushing down to the Market."

"That kind of logic makes me hungry. When do we eat?"

She blinked a couple of times at the abrupt change of topic. "What about Zara? We need to make some plans."

"I think better on a full stomach." He got to his feet and started toward the kitchen. "I hope you've got a microwave. We're going to need to reheat dinner. Got any lettuce?"

She glared at him through the opening above the counter. "Lettuce?"

"As long as there's a kitchen available, I might as well make a salad to go with the spinach lasagna I brought." He opened the refrigerator. "Good. You've got some romaine."

"Hang on, that's my kitchen." Olivia bounced to her feet and hurried around the corner to join him. "Give me that lettuce."

"Whatever you say." He handed her the plastic sack full of romaine.

She shot him another scowling glance as she reached up to remove a stainless steel colander from a hook. There was an easy competency in her movements that told him she was comfortable in a kitchen.

Satisfied that she was going to proceed with the salad, he opened the paper bag. He removed the containers of lukewarm lasagna and the loaf of crusty, rustic-style bread.

Olivia grudgingly pointed toward a cupboard. "The olive oil is in there." She tipped her head slightly in the opposite direction. "Bread knife is in that drawer."

"Thanks."

For a few minutes they worked side-by-side without speaking. Jasper was aware that Olivia kept glancing at him out of the corner of her eye.

"Do you like to cook?" she finally asked. "I mean, something more than just slicing bread and sticking take-out in a microwave?"

"I got used to kitchens after my nephews came to live with me a few years ago. It was either feed Kirby and Paul at home or watch them grow up addicted to hamburgers and pizza. All the books I read on the subject emphasized the importance of kids eating at home in a family environment."

She looked intrigued. "You read books on how to raise kids?"

"As many as I could find." He stuck the lasagna into the microwave and closed the door. "Like I said, my approach to most things is to collect as much information as possible before I take action."

"Why did your nephews move in with you?"

"My stepbrother and his wife were killed on a skiing trip in Europe." Jasper selected the cooking time on the face of the microwave. "There wasn't anyone else for Kirby and Paul."

"I see." Her eyes were suddenly unreadable. "No kids of your own?"

"No." There was something about working with

someone in a kitchen that broke down the usual social barriers, Jasper reflected. Or maybe it was having a blackmailer threaten both of you in the same note that induced a certain artificial sense of togetherness. "My wife left a few months after Kirby and Paul moved in with me. I never found the time to remarry."

"I know what you mean." Her voice was quiet and cool. "I was in the process of filing for divorce when my husband died. Afterward I lost interest in the whole concept of marriage. Then I got very busy with Light Fantastic." She shrugged.

Jasper recalled the Crawford Lee Wilder piece in *West Coast Neo*. The article had hinted, darkly, that it was his wife's threat to leave him that had caused Logan Dane to risk his neck running with the bulls in Pamplona. Wilder had also implied that the net result of Dane's death had been to leave Olivia holding a fortune in art.

From what he had seen of her private world, Jasper doubted that last bit. There was not a single painting hanging on the wall. She gave every appearance of being successful, but not wealthy. Everything he had seen thus far, including the Light Fantastic studio and this condo, could be explained by her own hard work and maybe a little assistance from her uncle.

"Where are your nephews now?" she asked.

"Both are at the university. They're taking summer sessions so that they can graduate sooner. Paul's headed for engineering, I think. But I can see Kirby in the academic world."

She flashed him an impulsive smile. "Like my brother, Todd."

Jasper glanced at her. "I thought you said he was a political consultant and a speechwriter."

She wrinkled her nose. "He is now, but I'm hoping it's just a phase."

"What happens if Lancaster wins in November?"

"I'm a little worried, if you want to know the truth."

"About Lancaster winning?"

"No, of course not. She'll make a good governor. Maybe a great one. What concerns me is that Todd is falling for her."

"Ah," Jasper said softly. "And you'd rather he didn't?"

She leaned back against the counter, crossed her arms, and rolled her eyes. "How would you feel about having a politician in the family?"

He grinned. "Point taken. Personal sentiments toward politicians aside, what really worries you about the possibility that your brother is involved in a relationship with Lancaster?"

She hesitated, gazing thoughtfully into the middle distance. "Right now Eleanor's on a political roll, thanks in large part to Todd's skill as a political theorist. I guess I'm worried about what will happen to the relationship if Eleanor loses the election."

"In other words, you're afraid Lancaster's feelings toward your brother have more to do with the fact that she needs him as a consultant than with true love?"

"And, to be fair, vice-versa. I'm afraid that Todd is attracted to her, at least in part, because she's given wings to all his policy theories and ideas. He sees her as a sort of modern-day warrior queen, Boadicea leading the Britons against the invading Romans."

"Got it."

"But what do I know?" She unfolded her arms and pushed herself away from the counter. "I'm the first to admit that I'm not the world's best judge of what makes a relationship work."

"Neither am I." Jasper was startled by the sound of his own words. He did not know where they had come from. He had not intended to say them. But there they were, hovering in the air alongside hers, stark admissions of past failures.

There was a short silence. And then Olivia got very busy taking plates down from a cupboard. The microwave pinged. Jasper jerked open the door and took out the steaming containers. He winced when his fingers came into contact with hot spots on the plastic. He grabbed a towel.

Sharing a kitchen and being threatened by a black-mailer could promote only so much togetherness between two people who had very separate agendas, he reminded himself.

Five minutes later, dinner was on the table. Olivia managed to wait until she had finished her lasagna and salad before she swept her plate aside and fixed Jasper with a steely gaze.

"Well?" she said. "You've been fed, and you've had a chance to think. Got any ideas about how to handle Zara's problem?"

He took his time savoring the last of the lasagna. Then he put down his fork. "First we need a list."

"A list of what, for heaven's sake?"

"Of all the people Zara knew in the good old days."

Olivia's eyes narrowed thoughtfully. "That would

111

probably be a very long list." She gave the subject a few more seconds of reflection. "It could take ages to check out every person who worked with Zara and then try to figure out which one might be the blackmailer."

"It won't take long for an experienced private investigator to figure out which ones are here in Seattle at the moment," Jasper said bluntly.

"Of course." She stared at him, understanding flashing across her animated face. "Jasper, that's brilliant."

"It's a CEO's job to be brilliant. That's why I get the corner office with the big windows."

She ignored him. "I should have considered that approach right off. Whoever is blackmailing Zara has to be here on the scene. He could hardly pick up a blackmail payment from L.A., could he? Besides, he obviously knows too much about all of us and the layout of the Market."

"Right."

"The threat is definitely local. There can't be that many people who both knew Zara in the old days and who also happen to be here in Seattle."

"It's a place to start." Jasper told himself not to get too excited about the look of glowing admiration in her eyes. "It means Zara has to be convinced to bring in a PI, however."

Olivia waved that problem aside with a flick of her wrist. "Don't worry. I can talk her into it."

"Get the list from her first. When you have it, I'll call someone I know at a firm I use for background checks on potential business clients."

"I'll have Zara start working on the list first thing in the morning." Olivia jumped to her feet and began clearing the table. "You know, I feel much better about this whole thing now that we have a plan."

"Nothing like a plan." He wished he felt as buoyed as she apparently did. He rose, picked up his dishes, and followed her into the kitchen. "Promise me you won't do anything else about this blackmail thing without talking to me first."

"Okay," she said a little too easily. She set the dishes in the sink. "Speaking of consulting with each other, that reminds me. We have to talk about Melwood Gill. What with this blackmail mess, I almost forgot about him."

Jasper came up behind her to put his plate and silverware into the sink. He was so close he could smell the warm, womanly scent of her body mixed with something herbal from the soap and shampoo she used. He wondered what she would do if he put his arms around her and kissed her. *Bad timing.*

"If you want to see the reasons I shifted Gill to another position," he said, "I'll be happy to open my briefcase and show them to you." He ought to move back, put some distance between them. He was too close for his own good. He was getting hard again.

She took care of his dilemma by stepping adroitly to the side. He watched her turn and lead the way back out of the kitchen.

"You can bet your corner office with the window that I want to see those reports," she said.

He stifled a groan. It was better this way. Even someone with bad timing in this kind of thing could see that.

Reluctantly he followed her out into the living room.

Lightning crackled in the distance just as he reached down to open his briefcase. Real lightning, not his libido-driven imagination this time, he thought. It was followed by a distant roll of thunder.

Great. The rain would hit soon. Just about the time he was ready to walk back to the ferry dock. He'd get drenched.

Distracted, Olivia swung around to stare out the windows. A look of anticipation crossed her face. "We're in for a genuine summer thunderstorm. We don't get too many. I love to watch from here."

She opened the sliding glass doors and stepped outside onto her small corner balcony.

Jasper took his hand off the briefcase latch. He watched Olivia go to the railing. She stood there studying the dark, roiling clouds as if something she saw in them fascinated her.

He followed her out onto the balcony. She did not turn around.

"Olivia." He was intensely aware of the energy-charged air. He tried to think of something intelligent to say. "About Gill—"

"It's not that I don't think you know what you're doing," she assured him without turning around. "It's just that I feel a certain sense of responsibility toward the longtime employees of Glow."

"I understand." He closed the distance between them until he was once more standing directly behind her. "It was because of his long years of service that I did not let Gill go."

"But it's humiliating for a man in his position to be moved aside."

"It would be considerably more embarrassing for him if I fired him."

She turned around very quickly, her eyes huge and shadowed in the strange storm light. "Are you absolutely certain that there is no better way to handle the situation?"

"Absolutely certain. Give me a little credit here. A few minutes ago you called me brilliant, remember?"

She smiled wryly. "I remember."

He watched her face. "It may interest you to learn that when it comes to business, I'm known for having a really great sense of timing."

"Is that a fact?"

"So they tell me. I am not, however, known for my good timing when it comes to other things."

"Such as?"

"Such as this kind of stuff." Need overrode logic. He bent his head and kissed her full on the mouth.

She went very still, but she did not pull away. Jasper put his hands out on either side of her and gripped the balcony railing with so much force that he wondered it did not fracture.

He felt the tremor that went through Olivia. It made everything in him very hard and tight. He heard a small, muffled sound, and then she pulled her mouth an inch or so away from his. She looked at him with deep, unreadable eyes.

"I don't have the best timing in the world when it comes to this kind of thing, either," she whispered.

"Maybe we both need practice."

He took his hands off the railing and wrapped her in his arms. This time her mouth opened beneath his. Some of the wild energy in the air pulsed in him. He felt her palms settle tentatively on his waist, not clinging, but not pushing him away, either. She touched him cautiously, as if testing the waters of a very deep, very dark pool.

He could feel the thrust of her breasts beneath her loosely fitted denim shirt. The warmth of her body was a sharp contrast to the cool breeze that heralded the onrushing storm. He wanted to lose himself in that soft, feminine heat.

He deepened the kiss. Her arms went all the way around his waist. He eased one hand down the length of her spine to the graceful curve above her buttocks. He urged her hips against his thighs, seeking to ease the straining tension of his heavily aroused body.

She was invitingly firm in all the right places, enticingly soft in others. And she wasn't wearing a bra beneath the poet shirt. He could feel the tight buds of her nipples.

He slid his leg between hers.

The rain struck without warning. The balcony overhang provided little protection against the chill, wind-driven blast, and Jasper was suddenly drenched. The cold, wet fabric of his shirt clung to his skin. Olivia flinched in his arms.

"Good grief." She stepped back quickly, pushing a tendril of wet hair out of her sultry eyes. Her kiss-softened mouth curved in with laughter. "I'm soaked. So are you."

"You see what I mean about my lousy timing."

10

She was still laughing a few minutes later when she handed him his jacket and his briefcase and ushered him out of her cozy little villa.

"Hurry." She leaned out into the hall to watch him get on the elevator. "The cab will be downstairs by now. You don't want to miss your ferry."

Jasper was still smiling to himself when he got out of the elevator eleven floors below. He should have been feeling at least a little let down, given the abrupt ending to what had promised to be an interesting evening. But for some reason he was in a surprisingly good mood.

There was a new, unfamiliar sense of anticipation humming inside him, a feeling of possibilities.

Or maybe it had just been so long since he'd gotten laid that he'd forgotten what the prospect could do for his mood.

He nodded to the doorman who had summoned the taxi and walked out onto the sidewalk. The wind gusted, sending another sheet of rain across his shoulders.

The cab was not directly out front. It waited on the far side of the street. It figured.

Jasper jogged through the rain to where the taxi was parked. He opened the door of the cab and got inside.

"Ferry dock," he said.

"You got it."

Jasper looked back as the car pulled away from the curb. His eyes went straight to the eleventh floor. It was easy to spot because Olivia was standing at the railing, watching him leave.

The Mediterranean warmth of the sunny palazzo glowed behind her. She had put on a hooded raincoat for the second venture outside. It gave her a romantic, old-fashioned glamour. Juliet on a high-rise balcony.

As he watched, she raised her arm in a farewell wave.

He returned the salute and then settled back against the seat. A mistake. The movement plastered his damp shirt against his back. Still, he felt good.

Very, very good.

The rain was still coming down steadily forty-five minutes later when he walked off the ferry on Bainbridge Island. But he was still feeling good. He found his Jeep in the parking lot, climbed inside, and drove to the big house overlooking the waters of Puget Sound.

The mildly intoxicated sensation lasted until he walked into the darkened kitchen.

Three steps past the door, he came to a halt, keys in hand. For a moment he listened to the silence. There had been a lot of it since Kirby and Paul had left for college. He was slowly growing accustomed to it.

But for some reason the sense of deep quiet was disturbingly intense tonight. It felt wrong.

Awareness flickered through him. He reached out and pushed the control panel button that turned on the lights in every room in the house at once. When the place was fully illuminated from top to bottom, he listened hard.

No panicked, fleeing footsteps. No squeak of floorboards.

But the sense of wrongness persisted.

Jasper walked slowly from room to room. Nothing was missing. There was no evidence of a break-in. No shattered windows. No one leaped out of a closet.

The heavy door to the basement was still safely locked. Jasper had had it specially designed. It would have taken a great deal of effort to open it. Any attempt to do so would have left obvious signs.

The average burglar probably did not expect to find anything of value in a basement, Jasper thought. And given that most prowlers were after items that could be fenced quickly and anonymously, the assumption would have been correct.

He worked the sophisticated code to unlock the door. Then he opened it and went slowly down the steps. In the light of the overhead fixtures he surveyed his row of gleaming metal file cabinets.

They were solidly made, built more like safes than standard cabinets. They housed and protected the kind of information that he did not trust to computers.

There was a *lot* that he did not trust to computers. He liked to think of himself as a modern business-man, but he could not deny that he had an atavistic distrust of the new information storage and retrieval technology. He was keenly aware of the risks and vul-nerabilities.

Inside the file cabinets were the confidential back-ground information on clients, tax records, and personal financial data that he had accumulated during the years he had been in business.

There were other things in the cabinets. Pho-tographs and personal effects that had once belonged to Fletcher and his wife. Jasper intended to give them to Kirby and Paul when they graduated from college.

He walked down the row of cabinets, checking each drawer. When he was satisfied that none had been touched, he went back upstairs and locked the base-ment door again.

There was no proof that anyone had been inside the house. Still, he could not shake the sensation that someone had prowled through it tonight.

This paranoia thing may be getting worse, he warned himself. He wondered if he should be worried. This was the second time in less than two weeks that he'd imagined that someone had deliberately targeted him. For sure he would not mention his little problem to Kirby.

Jasper paused at the doorway of his study and glanced inside.

He had already checked this room once to make certain none of the computer equipment had been stolen, but something made him go back into it a second time.

He stopped in the center and tried to figure out what seemed different or out of place.

It took him a few seconds to realize what was wrong. The pen that he habitually left on top of the closed laptop was now sitting beside the computer.

A cold feeling that had nothing to do with his damp shirt drifted through him. He reached across the arm of his chair, raised the lid of the computer, and switched on the machine. It hummed happily to itself as it went through its opening sequence. A moment later his files were neatly arrayed on the screen.

No one had wiped his hard disk. Of course, there would be no way of telling if someone had downloaded his files onto floppy disks, he reminded himself. But he had no confidential client data or business records on this machine at the moment. He could not think of anything he had stored in the computer that was worth stealing.

He crossed the study to the file drawers and opened them one by one. He never bothered to lock this cabinet. The truly valuable documents were all downstairs in the basement.

Nothing appeared to be out of place in the first three drawers. He was about to close the fourth when he noticed the yellow file folder in front of the red one.

He looked at it for a long time before he removed it and glanced inside to be certain that all of the papers were there. When he was satisfied, he dropped it back into its proper place behind the red folder.

It was very likely that anyone who chanced to glance into his filing cabinet would assume that the system he used was governed by date and the alphabet, which it was. But within that system, it was also color-coded.

Kirby and Paul had often teased him about his elaborate, many-tiered personal filing system. Jasper had developed it on his own years ago. It worked. He had never seen any reason to alter or simplify it.

It was just barely possible that he, himself, had misfiled the red folder at some point in the past, he told himself. But given his precise filing habits, it was far more probable that someone else had removed the file and then returned it to the wrong place tonight.

Hell, maybe I really am getting paranoid.

Maybe he needed another vacation.

But what if he wasn't going over the edge? What if someone had searched his study tonight?

If that was true, he would have to reconsider a few of the evening's events in a slightly different light. Whoever had entered his house must have known that he would be delayed getting home tonight.

That observation gave rise to other, more troubling questions. After Olivia agreed to a working dinner with him, had she plotted to keep him busy while someone searched his house?

He sat down at his desk to think. After a while he realized what it was that bothered him the most.

He could deal with the possibility that Olivia did not trust him. He could even handle the concept that, in her zeal to protect Glow, Inc., interests, she might have sent someone to go through his private files to see if he had a secret agenda for the company.

What he did not want to believe was that she had lured him out onto her windswept balcony for a flaming-hot, incredibly sexy kiss that meant absolutely nothing to her.

11

The chess player looked down at the pieces on the board The motive behind the opponent's strategy was not clear. Once again, lack of sufficient information complicated the situation.

But in the end the most focused player would win.

The chess player was very, very focused.

12

"It was very kind of you to take time out from your busy schedule to have breakfast with me, Olivia." Eleanor Lancaster smiled across the expanse of snowy white tablecloth.

"*My* busy schedule?" Olivia chuckled. "Yours must be even more hectic than mine. Campaigning is exhausting. I don't know how you do it."

"A lot of caffeine and a great deal of help from my close supporters."

Olivia smiled. "I can identify with that."

"Yes, I imagine you can." Eleanor paused as the waiter poured more coffee from a gleaming silver pot. "I have also learned a useful trick. I make myself take time for a quiet breakfast every morning. Not only does it compose me and center my thoughts for the day, but I find that I can do a great deal of business over breakfast."

"I'll have to try it," Olivia said. She glanced around at the opulent hotel restaurant. She and Eleanor were seated in a velvet-cushioned booth that gave them both privacy and a view of the posh room. "Of course, it helps when you do breakfast in a place like this."

Eleanor laughed softly. "I eat here every morning. Management has been most accommodating. I'm always given this table."

Holy cow, Olivia thought. She told herself not to be dazzled, but who wouldn't get a kick out of the situation? Not only was she on a first-name basis with the future governor, possibly the future president, but she was doing a power breakfast with her. The invitation had come in the form of an early morning phone call from Eleanor, herself.

This kind of thing was bound to be great for business.

If Todd married Eleanor, there would be more breakfasts in the future, Olivia thought. Some day she might find herself dining at the White House.

Holy cow.

Maybe she should go straight home and jot it all down in a journal. She would want to tell this story to her children and grandchildren.

Of course, she reflected, that scenario could only occur if she actually got around to having some kids. Logan had not had any interest in becoming a father.

Unfortunately, he had not thought to mention that fact to her when he proposed marriage.

But Olivia blamed herself for not having understood right from the start that he was too focused on his art ever to be a parent. There was no room in his heart for anything except his painting and occasional, short-term obsessions. She had been a fool not to see that.

"I asked you to meet me here this morning," Eleanor said, "because I thought it was time that you and I got to know each other better. I'm sure you're aware that Todd and I have more than just a, shall we say, business relationship?"

Olivia picked up the thin china cup in front of her. "Todd has mentioned something about it," she said vaguely.

A knowing look appeared in Eleanor's eyes. "I realize you probably have some qualms. After all, you are his older sister." She smiled wryly. "And I am a politician."

Olivia was mortified. She put her cup down too quickly. It clanged in its delicate saucer. "I don't have anything against politicians. Really."

Eleanor chuckled. "It's okay. If I were in your shoes, I'd be a little concerned, too. Politics is an incredibly demanding lifestyle." Her expression turned serious. "You know, you and I have a great deal in common, Olivia."

"I doubt it. They're talking about you as a future president. I can't envision myself in the White House, but I can see you there."

"Thank you. That is exactly where I hope to be eventually. I feel that the country needs me."

"Yes, well . . ."

"I know that sounds less than modest." Eleanor held her cup poised between the fingers of both hands. "But believe me, the first thing you have to learn when you get into politics is that modesty is not a virtue."

"I see."

"As I said, you and I are alike in many ways. We're both strong women. We've earned our places in the world. We're smart, and in our separate ways, we're both ambitious."

Olivia shrugged. "That's pretty much where the comparison stops, I'm afraid. I don't have your presence. People look at you and see a leader."

"You underestimate yourself. From what Todd has told me, your family and the people who work for Glow, Inc., view you as a leader."

"It's not exactly my company," Olivia mumbled. "I only own half of it." Forty-nine percent, but who, besides Jasper Sloan, is counting, she thought.

Eleanor eyed her shrewdly. "Nevertheless, I got the impression from your brother that everyone at Glow looks to you to ensure their future."

"My, uh, new partner and I intend to work together to take care of Glow," Olivia said. A united front, she reminded herself.

"Todd is a little concerned about Sloan."

"People always get nervous during a transition. But everything will settle down soon."

Eleanor nodded with understanding. "That's the way it is in politics, too. Nothing stands still in life, does it? We must go forward."

"It's not like there are too many options."

"Very true. I learned that lesson after Richard was killed." Eleanor smiled wistfully. "I had no choice. My first election campaign was an antidote for my grief. Fighting for stronger criminal laws gave me a purpose, a reason to go on."

Olivia read the papers. She knew the story of Eleanor Lancaster's first campaign. Her husband, Richard Lancaster, a wealthy businessman, had been shot dead when he interrupted a burglary in progress. The killer had never been caught but was believed to have been a career criminal, someone who should have been incarcerated long before he murdered Lancaster.

Eleanor had run for the state legislature on a law-and-order platform. The campaign had been fueled by her fervent ambition to make certain that the kind of violent person who had killed her husband was taken off the streets. Once in office, she had quickly demonstrated the full range of her abilities as a leader.

"I understand," Olivia said.

Eleanor's immaculately shaped brows rose. "I told you that in my business, modesty is not a virtue. I will be honest with you. I am running for the governor's office because I believe that I have something important to offer to this state and, ultimately, to this country."

The passion that flickered in Eleanor's eyes was real, Olivia thought. She was a committed woman.

"I believe you," Olivia said.

"Your brother has done a great deal to help me shape and define my message and my agenda. I need him. I'm grateful to him. He's important to me. I realize that you are probably afraid that what I feel for him is tied to those things."

"Well . . ."

"I can't deny that I recognize how much he contributes to my campaign." Eleanor put down her cup. "But I want you to know that I'm smart enough not to get my personal emotions mixed up with what I know is good for my future in politics."

"I see."

"I was very fortunate," Eleanor said softly. "My marriage to Richard was based on love and commitment. Because of Richard, I understand those feelings. I want to assure you that those emotions are at the heart of what I feel for Todd."

"I appreciate your telling me that, Eleanor."

Holy cow. One day she might find herself dining in the White House.

It was a delightful fantasy, Olivia thought. But it didn't change anything. She still did not want Todd to marry Eleanor Lancaster.

"Mr. Sloan is going to hire a real private eye to check out a list of the people I knew in the early days of my career?" Zara's eyes lit up with excitement. "What a brilliant idea."

"I'm glad you approve," Olivia said.

"Approve? I don't know why I didn't think of it, myself. It's just the sort of thing Sybil would have done. I'll get started on my list of names immediately." Zara paused. "It will take a while. I had so many friends and rivals in those days."

Olivia's chair squeaked as she leaned back in it. She tapped the tip of a cheap ballpoint pen on the arm. Todd had once given her an outrageously expensive fountain pen, but she did not dare use it here at the office. She knew it would get lost amid the clutter.

"You're not upset because I told Sloan about the situation?" she asked.

Zara paused, one hand on the doorknob. "I'm sure we can trust him to be discreet. After all, Rollie trusted him with the future of Glow."

She sailed out through the door. The trailing end of the long fuchsia silk scarf she wore around her throat floated in her wake.

The towering spires of papers and documents stacked on Olivia's desk fluttered in the draft created by the closing door.

Ting, ting, ting. The small, repetitive sound of the ballpoint striking the arm of the chair became irritating after a while. Olivia tossed the pen onto a heap of invoices.

It was amazing what a plan could do for a person's attitude, she reflected. Zara's mood had undergone a sea change this morning after she learned that Jasper had concocted a scheme worthy of a television private eye.

Olivia had to admit that she was also feeling a lot more confident about resolving the blackmail problem today than she had felt yesterday. Last night's chat with Jasper had been oddly reassuring, even fortifying.

There were not many men who would have taken the news that they had been dragged into the middle of an extortion scheme with such stoic aplomb. In fact, she could not think of a single person of her acquaintance, male or female, who would have handled the situation as calmly and matter-of-factly as Jasper had.

There was steel at the core of Jasper Sloan. She had felt it in his kiss.

131

There had been another part of him that had been equally rigid last night, too. She felt a pleasant heat rise in her cheeks at the memory. It had taken her a long time to get to sleep, and it had not been thoughts of a blackmailer that had kept her awake.

Maybe she should try to get out more. She had been so busy lately she had forgotten what a normal social life looked like.

She rubbed her hands briskly up and down her arms, gave herself a mental shake, and turned to her computer. She stabbed the on-off switch. She had more important things to do than view mental reruns of the sexy look in Jasper's eyes when she had gently pushed him out into the corridor.

Bolivar stuck his head around the corner of her office door.

"Cindy at the *Private Island* office is on the phone." He made a face. "Says she doesn't want our people on board the boat until two in the afternoon."

Olivia glanced up from a preliminary schedule for the Camelot Blue event displayed on her computer screen. "That's impossible. We need every hour we can get before sailing time. Cindy knows that."

"You want to tell her?"

Olivia picked up the receiver. "Cindy? What's the problem here? I told you weeks ago that I need to get my crew on board first thing tomorrow morning. It's going to take all day to get the *Private Island* ready for the Silver Galaxy Foods Night event."

"Sorry about this, Olivia." On the other end of the line Cindy Meadows sounded frazzled even though it was not yet eight-thirty. "My boss scheduled a last-minute dinner cruise for tonight. The boat won't return to the dock until two A.M. I can't get it cleaned up until tomorrow morning."

"You have to find a way to get your cleaning people out of there by eight A.M."

"How about noon?"

"How about eight, just like your boss agreed in the contract we signed," Olivia said grimly.

Cindy sighed. "Bill's right here. Why don't you talk to him?"

"Fine." Olivia drummed her fingers on the desk until the manager of Private Island Cruises, Bill Cranshaw, came on the line.

"Hi, Olivia. Got a problem?"

"No, you do, Bill. We've got a contract that says Light Fantastic can have access to the boat for decorating and preparation purposes by eight o'clock on the sailing date. I need every minute I can get."

"I don't see why you can't wait until noon."

"I can't stand it when you whine, Bill."

"Give me a break. I can't cancel the dinner cruise."

"Don't cancel it. Pay your cleaning people a little overtime and have them come in late tonight after you finish the cruise."

"Have you got any idea what that will cost?"

"Whatever it is, it won't cost nearly as much as you'll lose if Silver Galaxy Foods takes Silver Galaxy Foods Night to another charter boat operator," Olivia said sweetly.

Bill groaned. "Okay, you win. Your people can come on board at eight."

"Great. See you first thing in the morning." Olivia

hung up the phone and looked for the final version of the Silver Galaxy Foods Night schedule. She knew she had left it on one of the stacks on her desk. Her organizational scheme was a simple one. Hot items were always placed on top.

When she could not locate the schedule atop any of the towers of papers, she turned to the pile of documents arrayed on the floor behind her desk.

It was not there, either.

She got up, went around the desk, and opened the door. "Zara?"

Zara looked up from her drafting table. "Yes, dear?"

"Have you got a copy of the Silver Galaxy Foods Night schedule? I can't find mine."

"I saw it on your desk yesterday afternoon."

"I know, but it's gone now. Someone must have borrowed it."

Bolivar emerged from the entrance of Merlin's Cave. Blue vapor drifted out in his wake. "There's a copy on my desk."

"Thanks."

Olivia crossed the studio to Bolivar's realm and retrieved the schedule.

She walked back into her office, absently closing the door behind herself. The papers on her desk rustled softly as the small draft caught them. A fax containing a price quote from a catering company wafted off the top of a pile and floated gently to the floor.

Olivia bent down to pick up the wayward fax. When she reached for it, she saw the corner of another sheet of paper lying on the floor beneath the computer station. The words *Silver Galaxy* were clearly visible.

There was also a small page that had been ripped off a telephone message pad. A note in Bernie's flowing handwriting was scrawled across it.

Your cousin Nina called again. She wants you to call her back.

Olivia sighed. Uncle Rollie had been right. One of these days she was going to have to get organized.

It was when she crawled beneath the computer station to pick up the stray schedule that she saw the outline of a dried, muddy footprint on the floor. It was only a partial impression, but she could see enough of it to make out the outline of a man's shoe.

The print was in the precise spot that one would expect to find it if a person had sat down in her chair to use her computer.

"*Bolivar.*"

The door opened a few seconds later. Bolivar put his head inside the office. "Now what?"

"Did you use my computer last night?"

"No, I went home at five, remember? Besides, you know I wouldn't touch that relic unless I was absolutely desperate. Why?"

"I think someone touched it. There's a muddy footprint on the floor."

"How do you know it's from last night?"

Olivia thought of the damp gust of wind that had interrupted the scorching scene on her balcony. "It didn't start raining until sometime after eight last night."

"Oh, yeah. I guess that's right."

Olivia crawled out from under the computer station. "Think the janitors changed their schedule without telling us?"

"Doubt it. Far as I know they're still coming in twice a week. That means they would have skipped last night."

Olivia glanced at her wastebasket. It was overflowing. No one had emptied it last night. "I wonder who used my computer?"

Bolivar shrugged. "I'll check with Bernie and Matty, but I don't think either of them would have used it without checking with you."

"No." Olivia sat down. "Don't worry about it. No big deal. I just don't like the thought that someone might have come into my office and used my computer without my knowing about it."

"Don't blame you," Bolivar said. "But why would anyone do that?"

"I can't imagine."

Olivia automatically flattened a palm on a stack of papers to hold them steady when Bolivar closed the door behind himself.

If she had not been coping with a blackmailer, she thought, she probably would not have thought twice about the muddy print under her desk. But extortion threats, she discovered, had a way of making someone a little paranoid.

The good news was that if a blackmailer had accessed her computer with a view to finding damning information, he had wasted his time. She used the machine only for Light Fantastic business data and correspondence. She could not imagine any of it being of much use to an extortionist.

She glanced at her overstuffed file cabinets. It would be impossible to tell whether or not someone had rummaged around in them last night.

Take it easy. Don't go off the deep end here.

There was only one real secret in her past, Olivia reminded herself. And she had destroyed the evidence of it three years ago on the night of Logan's funeral.

She glanced down at the partial print of a man's foot and tried to marshal some logic. She had a couple of pieces of information to work with, she thought. First, whoever had entered her office had done so after the rain had started to fall.

Second, the person who had left the print must have known that she was not working late as she often did during a busy period.

It occurred to her that there was at least one man of her acquaintance who would have been aware of the fact that she was occupied at home last night.

Jasper Sloan.

She had sent him off in a cab to catch the ferry. He could easily have stopped off at the Light Fantastic studio first.

She had spent a lot of time wondering if she could trust him. She hadn't considered the possibility that he did not trust her.

13

$\approx$

Jasper walked out of the busy, brightly lit test lab through the swinging doors at the far end. He had a copy of the engineers' revised report on Glow's latest electroluminescent technology applications in his hand.

He scanned the highlighted sections as he went down the hall to his office. Rollie had done a fine job when it came to hiring innovative thinkers in the applications area, he concluded. The atmosphere in the engineering labs was open and freewheeling. No one wore suits.

The people who worked at Glow brainstormed readily and easily without fear of being shot down by an old-fashioned management style. Above all, Jasper thought, he wanted to retain that essential element of the Glow corporate culture.

As he went through his office doorway he was studying a paragraph describing the way in which thread-fine fibers of light powered by very tiny batteries could be woven into wallpaper or fabric.

Rose looked up, excitement bubbling in her face. "Oh, there you are, Mr. Sloan. I was just going to page you. Andy Andrews is on line one."

Jasper frowned. "Andy Andrews?"

"You know, the editor of *Hard Currency*," Rose said breathlessly. "It's a very influential business newsletter."

"I'm familiar with it."

Hard Currency was a hot regional investment newsletter. It was faxed two or three times a week to a subscription list that included CEOs, board members, stockbrokers, and bond traders throughout the Northwest. Jasper occasionally found it useful, although in his opinion Andy Andrews frequently walked the fine line between breaking financial news and wild rumor.

Unfortunately, *Hard Currency* was the first thing most local executives read when they arrived in their offices in the mornings.

"Rollie had a subscription," Rose confided. "But he never got called for an interview."

That was because in Rollie's day nothing even remotely resembling gossip of the kind that would be of interest to the business community had ever occurred at Glow, Jasper thought. Glow's image had always been on the staid side.

But things had changed.

He rapidly assessed the situation. Talking to journalists, especially Andrews, was not one of his favorite activities. In his previous career as a venture capitalist, it had been relatively simple to avoid the media.

But he was operating in a different sphere now, one in which rumors were tools that had to be well managed. The wrong sort of speculation could be extremely damaging to a company in Glow's position.

The fact that the editor of the region's most influential investment newsletter was on the phone meant that gossip was already swirling in the Northwest business community.

"I'll take the call in my office, Rose. When I'm through, send Morrison in, will you?"

"Yes, Mr. Sloan." Rose gave him an expectant look. "Does this mean that Glow will be featured in *Hard Currency?*"

"Not if I can help it."

Ignoring Rose's obvious disappointment, Jasper walked into the inner suite and closed the door. He reached across the desk to pick up the phone.

"Sloan here." He lounged on the edge of the neat, polished surface.

"Andy Andrews with *Hard Currency.*" The voice was artificially warm and hearty, the voice of a journalist who made his living on the phone. "We met a year ago when I stopped by Sloan & Associates to get a quote from you regarding the Hatcher merger."

"I remember. What can I do for you, Andrews?"

"I'm putting together a short feature on the recent changes there at Glow. I'd like to ask you a few questions, if I may."

"What questions?"

"A lot of my readers have heard about you, of course. Sloan & Associates has backed some of the most successful young entrepreneurs in the region as well as a lot of expansions like the one at Glow. But it's my understanding that you don't generally get involved in the management of your clients' firms."

"Glow is no longer one of my clients. I own it."

"Fifty-one percent, according to my information."

"Fifty-one percent is enough."

"I'll cut to the chase. Why did you take control of the company?"

"Glow is a change of direction for me," Jasper said evenly. "I've been looking for a situation that would allow me to take on the challenge of dealing with all aspects of a growing and diversified business."

Andy cleared his throat. "There is some speculation that you took it over because the recent death of Glow's owner and CEO may have put the company in jeopardy."

"That speculation is absolutely false."

"The firm is, after all, at a very delicate point in its expansion process, isn't it? Is that why you felt you had to step in and take command at this juncture?"

Time to squelch that rumor, Jasper thought. "Glow has always been a well-run company. In keeping with his usual far-sighted management philosophy, Rollie Chantry made appropriate provision for the present scenario."

"Uh-huh." Andy did not sound convinced. "I'm told that forty-nine percent of the company is now owned by Rollie Chantry's niece, Olivia Chantry."

"Right."

"Ms. Chantry obviously represents the interests of the rest of the Chantry family. How would you describe your relationship with her?"

"Close," Jasper said. "Very close."

"That's not what I've heard," Andy said with the deliberately vague air of someone who's a little uncertain of his facts and a little slow to put those facts together.

Oh, shit. Jasper allowed only the most casual curiosity into his own voice. "What have you heard, Andy?"

"There's a rumor in certain circles that the Chantrys don't like having an outsider at the helm. Care to comment?"

"I don't know what you've heard. I can, however, assure you that I have Olivia Chantry's complete trust and cooperation. We've both got the long-term interests of Glow at heart."

There was a short, heavy pause. "Are you officially denying that you're there to fatten up Glow for a possible sale or merger?"

"Categorically," Jasper said. "Glow is my company, and it will stay that way."

He brought the interview to a close five minutes later and immediately hit the Light Fantastic office number on his phone.

"This is Olivia." She sounded distracted.

"I just had a call from Andy Andrews of *Hard Currency,*" Jasper said without preamble.

"Congratulations," she said dryly. There was a short silence during which Jasper heard a small slurping sound. It sounded like Olivia was taking a sip of coffee.

"Andy Andrews must think you're interesting. He never pays any attention to us small-time entrepreneurs."

"That," Jasper said, "is about to change."

"What do you mean?"

"Andrews called me because he wanted information about our relationship."

There was a half-strangled exclamation followed by a gasp, a choking sound, and a couple of small coughs.

"You okay?" he asked.

"Uh-huh. Coffee went down the wrong way," she wheezed. "What about our relationship?"

"Our business relationship."

"Oh." There was another pause. Another slurp. "Well? What did you tell him?"

"That the two owners of Glow enjoy a very close working partnership."

"I see." Her voice was elaborately neutral.

"That we share an identical vision for Glow's future."

"Uh-huh."

"And that you," Jasper said very deliberately, "as the representative of the Chantry family, had absolute confidence in my ability to manage the growth and expansion of Glow, Inc."

"Absolute confidence?"

"Yes. Absolute confidence." Jasper carried the phone to his office window and looked down at the street six floors below. "Andrews said he'd heard rumors, Olivia."

"What sort of rumors?"

"The kind that could spell trouble." He hesitated.

143

"Someone is either feeding him gossip or else he's just fishing. Either way, we've got to squelch this before it blows up in our faces."

"How do you suggest we do that?"

"Andrews will probably call you next to get your side of the story. Remember what I said about presenting a united front."

"Oh, yeah. Right. A united front."

"I hope I've got your attention here, Olivia. Rumors of trouble between the two of us could do a lot of damage to Glow. You're a businesswoman. You know what the wrong kind of talk can do to a company."

"Uh-huh."

"We don't want suppliers, vendors, and customers getting nervous. Especially not at this stage."

"Uh-huh." There was another faint slurp.

Exasperated with her apparent lack of interest in the subject, Jasper tightened his grip on the phone. "Think of this as a marriage of convenience."

"I tried marriage once." She sounded thoughtful. "It wasn't very convenient."

"I had a similar experience with the institution. But this time it will be different."

"You're sure?"

"I'm sure. This is business." He watched the traffic on First Avenue. He wondered if it was possible to read the future in the movements of cars the way some people read it in tea leaves. "When it comes to business, I'm always sure."

It was just the personal stuff in life that gave him problems, he thought.

He heard another sip on the other end of the line.

"Nice to be sure about things, isn't it?" Olivia asked eventually.

Something had happened, Jasper realized suddenly. Something serious. This was not the modern-day Juliet who had waved farewell to him from her balcony last night. Olivia was tense. Cautious. Distant.

Was she feeling guilty because she had arranged for his house to be searched while he was at her place?

He decided to try a subtle probe.

"Olivia?"

"What?"

"God knows I'm no nutritionist, but do you think maybe you're drinking a little too much coffee?"

There was a short, startled pause on the other end. "This is only my second cup today. No, wait, I guess it's my third. Or maybe my fourth. Eleanor Lancaster invited me to breakfast. I had some there."

Jasper frowned. "You had breakfast with Lancaster?"

"I'm moving in some pretty exalted circles these days, thanks to my brother. Why did you ask about my coffee consumption?"

"I just wondered. You sound a little uptight."

She went off like Mount St. Helens, without any warning.

"Uptight? Now, why would I be uptight? Just because I've got a major event scheduled for an important client tomorrow night, my aunt is being black-mailed, I've got footprints on my floor—"

"You're worried about footprints? No offense, but I don't see you as the compulsively neat type, Olivia."

"And on top of everything else," she said, overriding the interruption, "I'm about to get a call from a reporter who wants to grill me about my relationship with the new CEO of Glow. No, sir. Nothing going on around here that might make a person a little tense. Nothing at all."

Jasper heard another slurp. A large one this time.

From out of nowhere he was overtaken with a wholly irrational urge to soothe her. "About your aunt's blackmailer . . ."

"What about him?" she demanded.

"Try not to worry too much. Once we get Zara's list, it won't take a professional investigator long to figure out who's behind the extortion."

"I hope you're right. Zara certainly believes in you. She feels much better this morning now that you've taken charge of the situation."

Olivia sounded disgruntled now. Jasper wondered if his assuming the lead on the problem annoyed her. She was accustomed to making the decisions.

"Like I said, blackmail, especially this kind, is almost always a personal thing."

"You may be right," she said. "I would certainly like to personally throttle the jerk who's terrorizing my aunt. Look, I've got to go, Jasper. I've got a lot to do this morning."

"So do I." But he did not hang up the phone.

Neither did she.

Jasper heard her take another swallow of coffee. He sensed that she was steeling herself.

"Jasper?" Her voice was tight.

"Yes?"

"Where did you go last night after you left my place?"

Of all the questions he had been expecting, that was last on the list.

"Home to Bainbridge." He propped one shoulder against the windowsill. "Why?"

"No reason."

Like hell, he thought. So much for the subtle approach. He had nothing to lose by being a little more direct, himself. "Funny, I was wondering about something, too."

"What's that?"

"Did you send someone to search my house last night while we had dinner together?"

There was an unnatural stillness on the other end of the line. Not even a coffee slurp disturbed the crashing silence.

Jasper continued to lean against the edge of the window, but every muscle in his body went taut as he waited for her answer. Not that it would tell him much, he thought. Not if she chose to lie.

"I think," Olivia said very carefully, "that you and I had better talk."

"We are talking."

"Privately. I'll meet you at that Market espresso bar where you found me yesterday. Ten minutes."

"Olivia, what the hell is going on here? I don't have time for any more cloak-and-dagger stuff."

There was no response. Olivia had already hung up the phone.

"Searched your study?" Olivia wrapped her hands around the small cup of supercharged espresso she had just bought. She leaned urgently across the little table. "And your computer files? You're sure?"

Jasper gave her a warning glance as he methodically unwrapped the piece of biscotti he had purchased to go with his coffee. "This is a public place. You might want to keep your voice down."

Olivia did a quick, impatient survey of the handful of occupied tables nearby and lowered her tone. "You really believe someone went into your home and through your personal records last night?"

"I figure I've got two choices. Either someone searched my study or I've gone full-blown paranoid."

That gave her pause. "Is paranoia a meaningful option here?"

He ignored the question. "You're sure about the footprint?"

"Yes." She took a swift sip of the potent espresso and waited hopefully for the jolt. "That is, I'm sure there was a man's footprint on the rug under my computer desk this morning. But in all honesty, I'm not sure what it was doing there. I couldn't tell if someone had actually used my computer."

"What about your hard copy files? The stuff in the drawers? Any evidence that someone went through them?"

"Who knows? How could you tell if someone had rummaged through a filing cabinet?"

"Those of us who take filing and organization seriously are probably better equipped to detect the work of an intruder than those who don't," Jasper said very dryly.

"I can do without the lecture on office management."

"I'll save it for another time." He dunked the

piece of biscotti into his coffee and took a large bite. "So you found a footprint on your floor this morning and leaped to the conclusion that I had been fooling around in your computer files? I'm hurt. Deeply hurt."

Olivia did not understand the sudden change in his mood. Earlier on the phone he had sounded distant, cool, almost grim. But now he seemed downright cheerful, which did not make a lot of sense given the topic of conversation.

It was almost as if he had gotten some good news since she had talked to him on the phone a few minutes earlier.

"Don't pull the offended act with me, Sloan. You went home to Bainbridge and did some conspiracy theory work, yourself. You actually believed that I hired someone to search your study? Thanks a lot."

To her astonishment, Jasper grinned fleetingly. "Great working relationship we've got here, Chantry. Lot of trust."

His unwarranted amusement acted like a goad on her caffeine-strained nerves. "For the record, Sloan, if I had wanted to have your study searched, I might, just possibly, have agreed to have dinner with you while someone else did the dirty work."

"Yeah?"

"But I would never, *not in a million years*, have gone so far as to kiss you."

He gazed at her very thoughtfully for a long moment. Then he inclined his head once in grave acknowledgment. "I'll remember that."

She suddenly felt much too warm. She knew she

was blushing, and the fact infuriated her. She rushed to get the subject back on track.

"It must have been the blackmailer who searched our offices," she said briskly.

"I'd say that's a safe bet." He munched biscotti with apparent unconcern. "Probably looking for something to use to carry out his threats against us."

Olivia heard a soft tapping sound. She glanced down and saw that her fingers were doing a nervous little dance on the rim of her espresso cup. With a monumental act of will she forced herself to cease the nervous staccato.

"One thing's certain," she said. "Whoever he is, he wouldn't have found anything in my office that would make me pay blackmail."

"There was nothing for him to find in mine, either. But in the process he may have told us a little more about himself."

She shot him a swift glance. "Such as?"

"First, if you're right about the footprint, the gender question is resolved. It probably is a man we're after, not a woman."

"Right." Olivia thought about it. "We also know that he's someone who feels very comfortable around computers."

"And," Jasper added quietly, "we know that he must have followed me to your condo last night and figured I'd be there for a while."

A chill zapped the length of Olivia's spine. "Gives me the creeps to think that someone is following us around."

"Yes." Jasper finished his coffee. "And when we

catch the sonofabitch, I'm going to make certain that he pays for that."

The sudden shift to the dangerously neutral tone in Jasper's voice sent an entirely different kind of frisson across Olivia's nerve endings.

She watched with fascination as he finished his coffee and picked up the used napkins, the stirring sticks, and the biscotti wrapper. He folded everything into a tidy bundle and tucked the little package into one of the empty cups. He then stacked the two cups neatly, one inside the other.

When he was finished with the small construction project, he got to his feet and dropped the lot very neatly into a nearby trash can.

He turned his head and saw Olivia watching him. One dark brow rose. "What is it?"

"Have you always had this unnatural tendency toward order and neatness?"

"You'll get used to it."

14

"**Y**es, Nina, I got your messages." Olivia did not look at the wastebasket, where she had tossed the last message shortly after discovering it on the floor. She smiled politely at her cousin. "I'm sorry I haven't been able to give you a call. As you can see, we're going a hundred miles an hour around here today. It's been like this for weeks."

"I understand."

Olivia sighed inwardly. She shouldn't have been surprised to find Nina waiting in her office when she returned from the Market a few minutes ago. She had been ducking Nina's calls for a week. It had been only a matter of time before her cousin confronted her in person.

"What with all the changes going on at Glow," Olivia continued weakly, "I just haven't had a chance to give you a ring."

"I know that Uncle Rollie's death has put a lot of pressure on you." Nina's smile was laced with a knowing look.

Olivia opened her mouth to elaborate on her excuse, but she closed it again very quickly. Damn it, she hated excuses, her own more than anyone else's.

"All right. What did you want to talk to me about?" she asked quietly.

Nina clasped her hands together very tightly in her lap. She had fragile, delicate hands. Everything about Nina appeared fragile and delicate, Olivia thought. The polar opposite of herself.

Nina was five years younger than Olivia, petite and pretty. With her dark hair, big eyes, and ethereal air, she made Olivia think of a Regency-era portrait.

Nina was the sort of woman who brought out the protective instincts, not only in men but in everyone around her.

She regarded Olivia with pleading eyes. "I want you to come to the opening night reception at the Kesgrove Museum."

All the muscles in Olivia's shoulders tightened painfully. Absently she reached up to massage the back of her neck.

She had been afraid of this. The reception to launch the retrospective exhibition of Logan's art was scheduled to be held at the end of the month. Everyone in the Dane family, including Sean, would be there. The last time she had seen any of them, Olivia reflected, was at the funeral.

She had no desire to subject herself to another round of the silent reproach and accusations that had filled their eyes on that occasion.

"I really don't think that would be such a good idea, Nina."

"Please. It would mean so much to Sean and his family."

"I doubt it."

"I know you think they still blame you for what happened to Logan in Pamplona," Nina said. "They were consumed by their grief. That's why they turned on you. But Sean has gotten past it, and I think his parents have, too."

Olivia seriously doubted that. "Even if that's true, it doesn't mean that it would be comfortable for all of us to be in the same room together."

"I'm asking you to come as a favor to me, Olivia. I'm sure you know that Sean and I have been seeing a great deal of each other?"

"Yes."

Nina took a shaky breath. "We've talked about marriage."

"I see."

Nina's hands twisted together. Her eyes misted. "I love him so much, but I just don't know if I can marry him after what happened. It doesn't feel right."

Olivia surged to her feet, grabbed a tissue, and shoved it into Nina's hand. "I've told you before, and I'll tell you again. Forget what happened three years ago. There's no point dredging up the past. If you're sure about your feelings for Sean . . ."

"Very sure." The pain in Nina's eyes disappeared

for a moment. A warm glow took its place. "I've never been more certain of anything in my life."

Must be a nice feeling, Olivia reflected as she sat down. "Then go for it."

Nina's expression turned resolute. "I love him too much to hurt him, and if he finds out about Logan . . ."

Olivia looked at her very steadily. "Sean will never find out. Don't let the past ruin your future. Don't give Logan the final victory."

Nina looked down at her hands. "I owe you so much. I don't know how to thank you."

"You don't owe me a damn thing." Olivia glanced at her watch. "Look, I really do have to get back to work."

"I know." Nina rose from the chair. "Olivia, about the reception. I realize I have no right to ask you to attend. But I promise you that Sean no longer blames you for what happened to Logan. He wants to mend the breach because he loves me."

"Nina . . ."

"Think about it, please," Nina begged. "For Sean's sake, if not for mine."

"Okay, okay. I'll think about it."

The wife of the president and CEO of Silver Galaxy Foods, Madeline Silverthorne, had made one thing very clear to Olivia. She wanted silver to figure predominately in the theme and decor for the firm's annual Silver Galaxy Foods Night event.

Olivia believed in giving the client, or the client's wife, in this case, what she wanted and a bit more. The interior of the dining room of the *Private Island* gleamed, glistened, and glowed with silver.

Deep in the bowels of the vessel the engines throbbed at half speed. The *Private Island* was on a cruise to nowhere, meandering its way through the islands of Puget Sound.

Olivia knew that few of the guests on board intended to sleep tonight, although cabins had been assigned to everyone. The point of Silver Galaxy Night was to eat as much of the host's free food and sample as many fine wines as possible and then party the night away until the free buffet breakfast was served.

It was a grueling contract for an event design and production company, but a lucrative one.

Olivia cast a critical eye across the dazzling scene that her staff had created.

The heavily laden buffet tables displaying Silver Galaxy's gourmet food products were covered with silver-foiled cloths trimmed with tinsel fringe. Guests chose caviar and canapés from silver serving dishes. Silver candles stood tall in elegant silver candelabra.

The walls were covered in shimmering foiled paper. Mirrored spheres reminiscent of those that hung in swing-era ballrooms dangled from the ceiling. Their glittering surfaces reflected the silvery light.

Madeline Silverthorne, her opera diva figure resplendent in a silver lamé gown that accented her silver-gray hair, joined Olivia. Her gaze rested approvingly on the massive silver vase filled with foil flowers in the center of the room.

"Fabulous," she said. "And so elegant. Just right for our company image."

There was nothing like a satisfied client, Olivia thought.

"The event firm I hired last year refused to pay any attention to my requests," Madeline continued. "The person I dealt with actually had the nerve to tell me that so much silver foil and tinsel would be tacky. Can you imagine?"

Olivia suppressed the memory of the day her entire staff had lined up in front of her desk to tell her the same thing.

"It's going to look like the inside of an aluminum foil factory," Matty announced.

Bolivar frowned. "Kinda bright, don't you think? The guests will need shades."

"It will be a bit, er, bright, dear," Zara said.

"I doubt that there's enough aluminum foil in all of Seattle to pull this off," Bernie said. "Probably have to import some from Bellevue."

"I can't imagine why the other firm had a problem with your silver concept," Olivia murmured. "My staff very much enjoyed working on this project. They felt that it allowed them to release their creative energies."

Madeline looked pleased. "I can see that. What a difference between this year's Silver Galaxy Foods Night and last year's. I intend to tell Charlie that we will definitely use Light Fantastic again next year."

It would definitely be tacky to pump one fist in the air and holler *yes* in a very loud voice, Olivia decided. She restrained herself. She gave Madeline a smile that held, she hoped, just the right degree of businesslike warmth.

"I'm glad that you're happy with the final result, Mrs. Silverthorne. Light Fantastic's goal is always a satisfied client."

Madeline studied the array of servers lined up behind the buffet table. "It was a stroke of genius to put all the waiters in silver lamé jackets and ties. Whose idea was that?"

"I believe it was Bolivar who came up with the suggestion." Olivia decided not to mention that Bolivar had intended it as a joke. As soon as Bolivar had said it, however, she had instantly implemented it. "I'll tell him you appreciated it."

"We must remember to do it again next year. I also like what you did in the dance lounge with those intertwining silver ropes—" Madeline broke off to smile at someone who had come up behind Olivia. "Jasper, dear. How good to see you. So glad you could make it."

"Thanks for letting me crash your party at the last minute, Maddy."

"Now, Jasper, you know perfectly well that you're always welcome. I'm delighted you could make it this year."

Olivia whirled around to stare at Jasper. She did not bother to conceal her astonishment.

"I didn't know you would be here tonight." She realized that she sounded less than gracious. She could not help it. She was irritated that he had not mentioned he planned to attend.

She had to admit that he looked remarkably at ease and wonderfully sexy in the classic power suit, a tuxedo. The black jacket hugged the strong line of his shoulders. He looked amused by the frosty expression Olivia knew was in her eyes.

"I told you I had an invitation."

"Yes, but I thought you said—" Belatedly Olivia recalled Madeline's presence. She hurriedly swallowed the rest of her words. No need to let her client know that Jasper had told her only a few days ago that he did not plan to be here this evening. She wondered what had changed his mind. She had a feeling that he did not do anything without a clear-cut reason.

"Thought I'd see what kind of work my new business partner did." Jasper glanced casually around at the sparkling scene. "Very impressive. I'm surprised you didn't issue sunglasses at the door."

The dry amusement in his voice floated straight over the top of Madeline's head without ruffling a single silver hair. But Olivia heard it quite clearly. She raised her brows.

"I'm glad you approve." She gave him a very pointed smile. "Madeline was just telling me how much she likes the silver effect. She feels it underscores the company name in a very elegant way."

"Indeed it does," Madeline said happily. "Jasper, I really am delighted to see you here tonight. I keep telling you that you don't get out enough."

"You aren't the only one who's mentioned that lately." Jasper smiled. "Always good to see an old friend, Maddy."

"Old friends?" Olivia repeated blankly.

Madeline looked at her. "Oh, yes. We've known each other for ages. Jasper's firm supplied financial backing and management expertise for our youngest son several years ago when Charlie Junior went into the software business."

"Oh." Olivia could not think of anything else to say.

159

It occurred to her that after a decade of venture capitalism in the Northwest, Jasper probably had tentacles throughout the local business community.

"Silver Galaxy Foods was having a bit of a cash flow problem at the time," Madeline explained. "We weren't able to help Charlie Junior out much. But Jasper took care of everything."

"I see."

Madeline winked at her and then at Jasper. "So the two of you are partners in Glow, now, eh?"

"That's right," Jasper said evenly.

"Charlie Senior was talking about Glow just the other day." Madeline's musing tone belied the sharp speculation in her eyes. "He said he hoped that it would not be sold or merged now that Rollie is gone."

"Not a chance," Olivia said.

Jasper looked amused again. "You heard the lady."

"That's very good news. We'd hate to see another old family firm put on the block." Madeline smiled at Jasper. "But how on earth will you continue to operate Sloan & Associates now that you've taken the helm at Glow?"

"I'm selling Sloan & Associates," Jasper said.

"How very interesting," Madeline murmured. "Jasper, why don't you and Olivia go on into the lounge and enjoy that very expensive band we hired?"

The fond, almost maternal gleam in Madeline's gray eyes alarmed Olivia. "Mrs. Silverthorne, I'm not a guest. I'm here in my professional capacity this evening."

"Nonsense." Madeline waved a silver-gloved hand. "One dance won't shatter your professional image.

160

Everything is going very smoothly, thanks to all your advance planning. Run along now, I insist."

Olivia was about to protest again when she felt Jasper's hand close very firmly around her arm.

"Good idea, Madeline," he said. He hauled Olivia toward the door. "Haven't danced in years."

Olivia plastered a smile on her face and allowed herself to be steered through the crowds at the buffet tables into the adjoining lounge.

The band, attired in silver lamé jackets similar to those the servers wore, launched into a slow, smooth, easy ballad. Jasper went straight out onto the floor and pulled Olivia into his arms.

"I like the dress," he said before she could demand further explanations of his presence.

For some reason the compliment confused her. Automatically she glanced down at the simple column of heavy black silk she wore. The only touch of silver was the narrow trim on the discreet curve of the neckline and at the wrists of the long, close-fitting sleeves.

"It was the only thing in my closet that had any silver on it," she admitted.

His mouth curved slightly as he took in the glittering decor in the lounge. "I wouldn't have thought that there was this much foil and tinsel to be had in Seattle."

Olivia grinned in spite of herself. "I cleaned out my suppliers. I only hope none of my competitors is trying to do a twenty-fifth silver jubilee wedding anniversary tonight. I can just about guarantee that there is not a single silver candlestick or tray left in town to rent."

"I believe it."

"All right, let's have it." She stopped smiling and pinned him with a severe glare. "What are you doing here tonight? When I talked to you this morning you said nothing about attending."

"That was before I found out that the business press was planning to be here this evening," he said.

"Of course the business press is here. Mrs. Silverthorne invited the business page reporters from the *Banner-Journal,* the *Seattle Times,* and the *Post-Intelligencer,* personally. This is a major business affair. The whole point is to garner publicity for Silver Galaxy Foods."

"I found out late today that she also invited Andy Andrews."

"So?"

"Did he ever get hold of you yesterday?"

"No." She frowned. "I was out of the studio most of the afternoon. Lot of last-minute stuff. He left three or four messages. I didn't return any of them."

"Hmm." Jasper glanced across the room, his expression thoughtful. "Maybe that's why he's still so interested in us tonight."

"What do you mean?" Olivia followed Jasper's glance and saw a short, round man in an ill-fitting dinner jacket. He had a glass of champagne in one hand. In the other he held a large plate piled high with canapés, fancy cheeses, and smoked salmon. He was watching Jasper and Olivia. She could see the shrewd gleam in his pale eyes from halfway across the room. "Is that Andrews? He looks like a teddy bear."

"Don't let the innocent, slow-on-the-uptake look

fool you. I've known Andy for years. He has a sixth sense when it comes to the gossip side of a business story."

Olivia gave Andrews her most charming smile and then turned back to Jasper. "He looks pretty harmless to me. I fail to see the problem here."

"You will if Andrews decides to do a story in *Hard Currency* with a headline like FEUD AT GLOW."

"I think you may be overreacting, Jasper."

His eyes narrowed. "I know what I'm talking about. I've been down this road in the past with other firms."

"Really?" She gave him a politely inquisitive look. "Are you dancing with me to show Andy Andrews that all's well between the two partners of Glow?"

To her surprise a dull red appeared on Jasper's high cheekbones. Irritation gleamed briefly in his eyes. "That's one of the reasons."

His answer tripped a switch somewhere inside her. Anger surged. The memory of the torrid kiss on her balcony flashed through her brain. She wondered if it had been prompted by something other than mutual attraction.

"I see," she said coldly. "Tell me, is pretending to romance potentially difficult business partners a routine technique in your line of work?"

She regretted the reckless words as soon as they left her lips, but it was too late. Jasper gripped her hand so tightly she was surprised he did not mash her fingers. He continued to smile down at her, but she saw that there was a new and rather dangerous expression in his eyes.

163

He bent his head closer, in what no doubt looked like an intimate manner to onlookers. He spoke directly into her ear.

"No," he said very evenly. "*Pretending* to romance difficult business partners is not part of my usual approach. In my professional opinion, it's an inefficient, tiresome, and extremely frustrating method of controlling a company."

"I'm sure it is." Olivia felt heat in her own cheeks. She hoped she was not blushing.

He met her eyes. "If I decide to romance a business partner, you can be sure of one thing."

"What's that?"

"I won't be pretending."

The heat in his eyes kindled the smoldering embers that she had not realized had been left behind by his kiss. Olivia stumbled. She had to clutch wildly at his shoulder to steady herself.

"Sorry," she gasped. "I tripped over my own feet. Haven't danced in quite a while."

"Let's get something to drink." He came to a halt, took her hand, and led her off the floor.

Olivia caught another glimpse of Andy Andrews as they walked toward the silver-spangled bar. The journalist was skulking behind a silver palm and fountain display.

"I don't think we're going to be able to avoid Mr. Andrews," she said.

"I don't intend to avoid him. But I would prefer to make him come to us."

"I can't hang around here very long, in spite of what Mrs. Silverthorne said. I've got a job to do."

"I know." He brought her to a halt at the foiled bar. "Do you have time for one drink?"

She hesitated and then shrugged. "I could use an espresso."

Jasper groaned. "Don't you worry about building up an immunity to caffeine?"

"It's been a long day." For some reason she felt obliged to defend herself. "And it won't end anytime soon."

Jasper shook his head and then turned to the silver-jacketed bartender. "One espresso and one cognac."

"Make that espresso a double," Olivia said.

"Coming right up." The bartender moved off to fill the order.

Jasper leaned one elbow on the gleaming bar and glanced casually across the dance floor. Olivia knew he was watching Andy Andrews slink toward them.

"When do you get off duty?" Jasper asked without shifting his gaze away from Andrews.

"Technically, not until the *Private Island* docks back in Seattle tomorrow morning and the ship is unloaded and cleaned."

Jasper frowned. "You're going to be up all night?"

She grinned wryly. "Part of the job. I've got one of the cabins downstairs. Assuming there are no major disasters, I'll probably try to nap for a couple of hours after the karaoke bar closes down. With any luck, that will be around three this morning."

"A couple of hours? Is that all?"

"I have to be up at five to make sure everything is in place for the farewell breakfast buffet that will be served at eight. And then I have to supervise the disembarkation."

"Is your schedule always like this?"

"I'm sometimes up very late because of an event, but most of them don't go overnight and into the next day the way this one does. The good news is that I get to go home and crash after the guests have disembarked. Bolivar and some of the other members of the Light Fantastic staff are going to come on board to handle the cleanup."

"How long have you been running Light Fantastic?"

"Almost five years."

"What did you do before that?"

"I worked for a couple of different event design and production companies on a freelance basis, learning the ropes."

"It's a strange business," Jasper said reflectively.

"I love it. Never a dull moment. Every event is different. Light Fantastic never repeats a production. Uncle Rollie always said it was the perfect career for me because it allows me to combine my creative side with my business side."

Jasper sipped his cognac thoughtfully. "Rollie told me once that when it came to business, you were as good as he was, just a lot younger."

"Did he really say that?"

"Yes."

"That was sweet of him." Olivia was warmed by the compliment. "I wouldn't go so far as to say that I've got Uncle Rollie's genius for business. But I can make a living with what genes I did get in that department. I'd starve, however, if I had to depend entirely on my creativity genes."

Jasper raised a brow. "Why do you say that?"

She shrugged. "I enjoy creative design, and I love putting together ideas for an event, but I'm not a real artist. For me art is a strong interest but not a great passion."

"What's the difference?"

"Genius. True talent. Fire in the belly. Whatever you want to call it. I don't have it. At least not for art."

Jasper watched her intently. "How can you tell?"

"Because I married someone who did have it." Why was she doing this, she wondered? Had she suddenly developed masochistic tendencies?

But she knew the answer. Incredible though it was, Jasper had not yet mentioned Logan's name in her presence. The failure to do so made him virtually unique. Sooner or later, most people found a way to bring up the legend of Logan Dane shortly after meeting her. Crawford Lee Wilder had seen to that.

Olivia realized that she wanted to get beyond that hurdle with Jasper. She wanted him to know just whom he was kissing. Assuming he ever kissed her again.

"That's right," Jasper snapped his fingers as if suddenly recalling an unimportant scrap of information. "You were married to that artist, weren't you? Logan Dane."

Olivia took a deep breath. She felt blindsided by his monumentally casual reaction. "You, uh, knew that Logan was my husband?"

"I read that stupid mix of fact and fiction in *West Coast Neo*. You should have sued Crawford Lee Wilder."

"It wouldn't have been worth the effort," Olivia said carefully. "The damage had been done."

"You're probably right. Only the lawyers make out in lawsuits, anyway." His mouth twitched. "You must have scared the hell out of Wilder, though."

"I beg your pardon?"

"The guy was obviously intimidated by you. The article was his way of getting even."

"An interesting analysis."

"What the hell did you do to him, anyway?"

"Crawford? Among other things, I dated him for a while when he worked at the *Banner-Journal*."

"No kidding?" Jasper's chuckle was low, rich, and deep. "Wilder had to bring out the garlic and silver crosses to ward you off after only a few dates? This sounds interesting."

She eyed him warily. "Interesting?"

"Very." He met her eyes. "I'm a sucker for interesting."

"I see."

"So, will you go out with me? A real date this time, not take-out?"

She tipped her head to one side and studied him intently. "You're not taking my sordid past real seriously, are you?"

He looked offended. "I didn't take the Crawford Lee Wilder article seriously, but I'm very serious about the date."

"Are you?"

He winced. "So much for the snappy repartee. I've been told that my social skills are a little rusty. Like Madeline said, I don't get out much. I know my timing isn't always the greatest when it comes to this kind of thing, but—"

"Your timing is just fine." She suddenly felt lighter and happier than she had in a very long time. "In fact, it's great."

A curious warmth appeared in his eyes. "You really think so?"

For a moment the silver-studded room seemed to slide away into another dimension. Olivia could still see the silvery decor around her. The mirrored balls continued to glitter. She could hear the music and the laughter of the crowd. But it was all happening in another, unimportant realm.

The only thing that was important at that moment was the look in Jasper's eyes.

The clarion call of the media shattered the spell. Typical, Olivia thought.

"Am I interrupting anything here?" Andy Andrews asked as he shoved a cracker heaped with salmon spread into his mouth.

"Yes," Jasper said without looking away from Olivia. "But since you're here, let me introduce you to Olivia Chantry. Olivia, this is Andy Andrews. He'll be crushed if you tell him that you've never heard of him."

Olivia reluctantly switched her attention to the rumpled-looking man who had come to a halt in front of her. Automatically she went into full business mode.

"Andy Andrews, with *Hard Currency?* How exciting. I always read your newsletter the instant it comes through my fax machine."

Andrews was clearly unprepared for such a cordial greeting. He blinked and then grinned broadly around the mouthful of cracker and salmon. "Glad to hear it. I do my best to keep the info moving through the pipeline."

"I especially enjoyed the piece you did last month on the charitable foundations that have been established by our new wave of local techno-millionaires." Out of the corner of her eye Olivia saw Jasper lift his gaze to the ceiling in silent supplication. She ignored him. He ought to know that a little judicious gushing worked wonders with the press.

"You liked that one?" Andy asked eagerly.

"It was not only extremely interesting, but useful as well," Olivia assured him. "It gave me some background on prospective clients."

"Always glad to be of service to the members of the business community. That's what I'm here for." Andy cleared his throat. "It's a pleasure to meet you, Ms. Chantry."

"Please call me Olivia."

"Sure. Olivia." Andy tossed back the last of the champagne in his glass. "I tried to get hold of you yesterday."

"Unfortunately I was so busy with tonight's event that I didn't get your messages until very late in the day. I intended to return your calls first thing Monday morning. I didn't realize you would be here tonight."

"Between you and me, I wasn't planning to attend." Andy sidled closer to the bar and waved at the attendant. "I did Silver Galaxy Foods Night last year, and it was a dead bore. But when I heard that you were running the event this year, I decided to accept Silverthorne's invitation."

Olivia smiled cautiously. "I'm flattered."

"Big change from last year." Andy surveyed the glittering scene while he waited for the bartender. "A lot more glitz and glamour, y'know?"

"Thank you," Olivia murmured.

Andy eyed Jasper. "Didn't know you'd be on board tonight, Sloan. Got something going with Silver Galaxy Foods?"

"No." Jasper gave Olivia a deliberate, intimate smile. "My interest here tonight is strictly personal."

"Is that a fact?" Andy broke off as the bartender arrived. "S'cuse me a minute. Open bar, you know. Some first-class hooch on board tonight. Don't want to waste the opportunity."

"I understand." Olivia traded glances with Jasper while Andy ordered an expensive single-malt whiskey. "The Silverthornes pull out all the stops on Silver Galaxy Foods Night."

"They sure did this year, I'll give 'em that." Andy got his whiskey from the bartender. He turned and raised the glass in a small toast. Then he chugged a couple of swallows. When he was finished he let out a long, satisfied sigh.

"I'm glad you're enjoying yourself," Olivia said.

Andy gave Olivia a bland smile that did not disguise the shrewd, if slightly inebriated, gleam in his eyes. "So, everything settled down now at Glow?"

"Yes," Jasper said before Olivia could respond. "I told you yesterday that everything was under control."

"Yeah, so you did." Andy kept his attention on Olivia. "Losing Rollie Chantry must have been really rough on the firm."

"It was rough on the family, too," Olivia said pointedly.

"Oh, sure." Andy bobbed his head several times. "Right. Big personal loss, too, of course." He crinkled his brow in a vaguely bewildered fashion. "Sort of an unusual situation, I guess, having an outsider come in and take over the way Sloan is doing."

Olivia widened her eyes. "We don't consider Jasper an outsider. He's part of the Glow team."

"Yeah?" Andy glanced from Olivia to Jasper and back again. "I've heard a few rumors about Glow. Maybe you'd like to confirm or deny them? I'll be happy to set the record straight in print for you."

"What rumors?" Olivia asked.

"Like I told Sloan, yesterday, there's talk about a sale or merger."

Jasper put down his cognac very casually. "And like I told you, Andrews, that's a lot of hot air." He gave Olivia another intimate smile. "I'm looking forward to a very long-term relationship with Glow."

At that moment Olivia would have been willing to believe that Jasper had telepathic powers. She could actually feel him willing her to back him up. There was no need for him to waste all that mental energy, she thought. She obviously had no other option than to go along with his demand for a united front.

"I can assure you, Andy," she said very smoothly, "that the Chantrys are delighted to have an executive as experienced and capable as Jasper Sloan at the helm."

Cool satisfaction gleamed in Jasper's eyes. He reached out and took Olivia's hand with an unmistakably proprietary air. "There's your story, Andrews. Now if you'll excuse us, I'm going to steal another dance before Olivia goes back to work."

Olivia glanced inside the karaoke bar shortly after midnight. The crowd was clearly enjoying the entertainment. Charlie Silverthorne, himself, set the tone. In classic Las Vegas lounge lizard style, he made love to a microphone and crooned the lyrics to a 1940s torch song. His silver-sequined cummerbund and matching bow tie sparkled in the dim lights. His voice, augmented by the latest electronic gadgetry, oozed over the audience like thick, warm syrup.

It was amazing what technology could do, Olivia reflected. Earlier she had heard Charlie sing the Silver Galaxy Foods song without the aid of a karaoke machine. He had the voice of a healthy sea lion.

Things were under control, she concluded, turning away from the karaoke lounge. The late-night dessert buffet had opened a few minutes ago and was attracting an enthusiastic crowd. The dance band was still going strong. There were no serious disasters going on at the moment.

She had time to slip downstairs to her cabin and change her shoes, she decided. She always brought along a second pair when she expected to spend a long evening on her feet.

She went down two flights of stairs and walked along the narrow corridor. Her tiny cabin, together with the others that had been assigned to the crew and staff, was on the lowest passenger deck just above the waterline. The better rooms had all been allocated to guests.

At the end of the hallway she took her key out of the hidden pocket in her black and silver gown and slipped it into the lock.

She saw the envelope on the carpet as soon as she walked into the room. Someone had pushed it under the door.

She scooped up the note and switched on a lamp. She opened the sealed flap and unfolded the single sheet of paper.

Your punishment has been determined. The price for keeping the secret of Logan Dane's real Dark Muse is one thousand dollars. You will receive instructions for the first payment soon.

For a few seconds Olivia could not grasp the meaning. And then the computer-generated message hit her with the force of a blow to the stomach.

Impossible. It could not be true.

She read the note a second time, but the words did not magically disappear. The secret she thought she had shredded three years ago had come back to haunt her.

The blackmailer knew about Nina.

15

He was lounging against the bar, a glass of the spring water he'd switched to an hour ago in his hand, when he saw her in the doorway. For a split second there was no one else in the room. At least, no one else who mattered.

Jasper wondered if he would gradually grow accustomed to the light-headed sensation that came over him whenever he saw her.

She stood there, unconsciously regal in silver and black, the never-ending mystery of her eyes enhanced by the upswept hairstyle. For an instant he simply stared while he absorbed the impact of her presence. She was looking for someone in the crowd. Probably a member of her staff. But he could always indulge the hope that she had come to search for him, he thought. He watched her scan the room with a shadowed, searching gaze.

When she saw him, she started through the crowd. Satisfaction washed through Jasper. She *had* been looking for him. He had seen very little of her since their two dances in the lounge.

And then he saw the simmering fury in her eyes. Beneath the anger was something else. Something that could have been fear.

Something had gone very wrong.

When she came to a halt in front of him, he put the half-finished glass of spring water very carefully down on the bar.

"What is it?" he asked quietly.

"I have to talk to you. Immediately."

He took her arm and escorted her through the darkened lounge toward the doors that opened onto the deck. A moment later they were outside.

The night was clear, the summer moon almost full. The silvery sheen on the black waters of the Sound was a perfect complement to all the glitter inside, Jasper thought. He wondered if the effect had been ordered up by Light Fantastic especially for the Silver Galaxy Foods Night event. If anyone could talk the supplier of moonlight into putting on a show, it would be Olivia.

Lord, he was waxing poetic, he thought, chagrined. Maybe he should have switched to the spring water earlier in the evening.

Only the barest hint of a wake disturbed the water

down below. There was a small background shudder from the engines. The *Private Island* was barely moving. The captain was conserving fuel. It was not as though they had a destination, Jasper thought. A party cruise to nowhere.

He felt the small shiver that went through Olivia's arm. It occurred to him that her gown offered little protection against the chill of the night air. He took off his jacket and draped it around her shoulders.

She looked at him with a small frown. "You'll be cold."

"I'm fine." He put both hands on the teak rail and gazed out at the moonlit water. "You'd better tell me about it."

She stood tensely beside him. "I got another message from the blackmailer."

"Shit." The last vestige of his poetic mood disintegrated. "Where? How?"

"It was shoved under the door of my cabin sometime this evening."

Jasper absorbed the implications of that single statement. "What did it say?"

"Just that the price would be a thousand dollars and that instructions for the first payment would come soon."

He thought quickly. "We won't tell your aunt that there's been another demand. Not yet, at any rate. She'll panic."

"You don't understand, Jasper."

"What do you mean? You just said the blackmailer had contacted you with his new demands."

"He did not contact me to tell me what Zara must

pay for his silence regarding her secret." Olivia's eyes were deep in shadow. "The note I got demands money for keeping *my* secret."

A quiet rage unfurled inside him. He said nothing while he dealt with it.

"Do you realize what this means?" Olivia whispered. "The blackmailer is on board the *Private Island* tonight. He's here, somewhere, walking around on this boat."

He forced himself to think logically. "We can't be certain of that. Someone could have delivered the note before we sailed."

"I just told you, it wasn't in my room earlier when I went downstairs to my cabin to change for the evening."

"What time was that?"

"Shortly after we sailed." She clutched the lapels of his jacket very tightly. "It has to be someone on this boat, Jasper."

"Not necessarily." He put his hands on her shoulders. Gripped her hard to get her attention. "The note could have been delivered to the *Private Island* before we sailed. A crew member might have been tipped to put it under your door."

She turned abruptly to search his face. "There must be a way to find out if that's what happened."

"Let me handle it. You've got work to do. I'll talk to some of the crew. See if anyone knows anything about a note that might have been delivered to the ship before sailing."

She looked briefly stubborn, but in the end the logic of his suggestion overrode her resistance. She nodded once. "All right. Thanks."

He glanced at his watch. "It's nearly two. You said you were going to try to catch a nap between three and five?"

"I'm not likely to get any sleep now."

"Maybe not, but you might as well go on down to your cabin at three, anyway. Put your feet up for a couple of hours, at least. I'll meet you there as soon as I've checked with the crew about the note."

She hesitated again. At that moment the lounge door opened. A couple swept through the opening. They were laughing uproariously at some private joke. Music spilled out behind them.

Jasper watched Olivia pull herself together and smile graciously at the guests. The fury in her eyes disappeared behind a thoroughly professional mask. When the couple moved off toward the aft deck, she looked at Jasper.

"All right, my cabin at three." She went to the lounge door and paused, fingers on the handle. "Thanks, Jasper."

"Sure." He waited until she got the door open. "Just one more thing."

She slanted him a quick, questioning look. "What's that?"

"My jacket. It might look a little strange if you wear it back inside."

She looked startled. Then she hastily removed the coat and tossed it to him. "Three o'clock."

She disappeared back into the warmth and the music of the lounge.

Jasper remained at the railing for a few minutes and absently inhaled the scent of Olivia's perfume that clung to his jacket. She was more than just angry, he thought. She was afraid.

What did the blackmailer know that made him think Olivia would even consider paying blackmail?

At three o'clock Olivia let herself into her cabin. The ship was quieter now. Some of the revelers had retired to their rooms. She had seen nothing of Jasper since she had left him out on deck an hour ago.

She switched on a small lamp, sat down on the bed, and kicked off her shoes. Jasper had been right. She could not sleep, but it would be a good idea to put her feet up for a while. She still had the breakfast buffet and disembarkation to handle.

She lay down on the bunk and propped her heels high against the wall. It was a trick she had learned long ago, one that she found to be remarkably restorative. But the tactic did not work tonight.

Someone knew her secret. She clenched her fists at her sides on the bed. Adrenaline surged through her system.

After a while she took her feet down off the wall, stood, and started to pace the small confines of the cabin.

No one alive now could possibly know about Logan and Nina. She had destroyed the journal, herself, every last damning page.

A soft knock interrupted her thoughts. She hurried across the room and opened the door. Jasper stood there, jacket hooked over one shoulder, black tie hanging loose around his neck. His shirt was unfastened at the throat.

A wholly unwarranted sense of relief shot through her. He looked so incredibly solid and strong and substantial, she thought. The kind of man who controlled his inner demons. Not the sort who would ever be controlled by them. Not the kind who would use them as an excuse for weakness and self-indulgence.

This man was nothing like Logan.

"Well?" she demanded. "What did you find out?"

He glanced meaningfully back along the hallway. "You want to discuss this out here in the corridor or inside where we can have some privacy?"

"Oh. Yes, of course." She stepped back quickly. "Come in. Hurry. The last thing we need is for someone to notice that the event producer is entertaining one of the guests in her cabin."

He quirked a brow as he moved past her, but he said nothing.

She leaned out into the hall to make certain that no one had witnessed Jasper entering her cabin. Satisfied that the coast was clear, she closed the door and leaned back against it. Her hands squeezed around the knob.

"Did you learn anything useful?" she asked.

"Yes and no." He tossed his tuxedo jacket down on the foot of the bed and went to stand looking out through the small porthole. "The note was put under your door by one of the crew."

"Where did he get it?"

"He told me that a cab drove up to the dock just before the *Private Island* sailed. The driver said he'd been paid to deliver the message to a member of the crew with instructions to put it in your room." Jasper glanced at her. "Which the crewman did as soon as he had a free moment."

Her spirits plummeted. "So the blackmailer is not on board after all."

"Doesn't look like it."

"That's unfortunate, isn't it?" She continued to grip the doorknob. "It would have made everything so much easier if he were. At least we would have had a finite number of suspects."

"Yes. But I doubt that the blackmailer would have made things so simple."

"No, of course not." She closed her eyes. "This is so bizarre."

"We'll find him," Jasper said quietly. "But I need more information."

She opened her eyes. "I've told you everything I know. Maybe the crewman could give us a lead on the taxi driver."

"He doesn't even remember what kind of cab it was."

"Damn."

Jasper turned slowly around to face her. His eyes were impossible to read in the dim light. "What does the blackmailer know that makes him think you'll pay him for his silence?"

She had been expecting this, she reminded herself. It was the same question he had asked after he had learned that Zara was being blackmailed. A logical, rational question under the circumstances. A question that she would have asked if their positions had been reversed.

Olivia shook her head slowly. "Please don't ask me that."

"I can't help unless I know what I'm dealing with."

She sighed. "If it was a secret that affected only me, I would tell you, Jasper. I swear it. But this affects other people. People who will be badly hurt if the truth comes out."

"Are we going to play the guessing game again?"

She glared at him. "Don't push me on this."

"Why not? Someone else is already pushing you pretty damn hard."

The soft, lethal edge on his words startled her. She measured him through half-lowered lashes. So much for Mr. Tall, Dark, and Reassuring, she thought. Mr. Tall, Dark, and Dangerous had just materialized in his place.

She released the doorknob and straightened her shoulders. "I've got to think about this."

"You do that." Jasper moved toward her. "Think about the fact that someone knows your secret. Think about all the possibilities."

She had to fight the instinct to step back when he came to a halt directly in front of her. "I will."

"Think about the fact that I'm involved in this, too."

"I know you're involved." She tried to keep her voice steady, but it was not easy. He was so close, almost on top of her. "And I realize it's my fault."

"That's right." He captured her face between his big hands. "I'm in this because of you. Correct me if I'm wrong, but at the moment I seem to be the only ally you've got."

"Well, yes, in a manner of speaking, I guess you could say that."

"That's exactly what I'm saying." He looked into her eyes. "I thought we agreed we'd form a united front."

"That was in regard to business, for heaven's sake. It hardly applies to this mess."

"You're wrong. It does apply to this mess."

She reached up to catch hold of his wrists. "I told you, I need to think."

"You'd better do your thinking in a hurry because we both know you're not going to pay off a blackmailer."

The icy reality of his words struck her like cold winter rain. He was right. She could not, would not pay blackmail.

"Just give me a little time to sort out a few things," she whispered.

"What's the problem here, Olivia? Don't you trust me? Your uncle did."

She'd had enough of feeling cornered. "Stop pressuring me, damn it. I told you, I've got to think about this before I make any decisions."

Lightning crackled in his eyes. "While you're at it, think about this."

Before she realized his intent, his mouth was on hers, hard, demanding, and very, very hungry. Her nerves, already inflamed by an unholy brew of adrenaline, fury, and desperation, exploded on contact.

Desire flooded her veins.

She managed to tear her mouth free for an instant.

"Jasper. This is so crazy."

"Tell me about it. No, on second thought, don't say a damn word." He took off her glasses and set them on the tiny bedside table.

Then he covered her mouth again and tightened his hold on her.

She gave a small, half-choked exclamation, put her arms around his neck, and flung herself headfirst into the kiss.

Jasper made a hoarse, half-strangled, extremely urgent sound and fell back onto the bed. He pulled her down on top of him. She sprawled across his chest and thighs. He caught her legs between his own.

She was shocked by the fierceness of his erection. She could feel the shape and size of him beneath the fabric of his trousers.

His fingers were at the nape of her neck. He found the zipper of her dress and dragged it the length of her spine all the way to where it ended at the small of her back. He slid his hand inside the opening. His palm was warm and heavy on her bare skin.

"You have a great back," he muttered. "A really terrific back."

She raised her head and looked down at him. "You're not going to break this off if it suddenly starts to rain in here tonight the way it did on my balcony, are you?"

His eyes gleamed with wicked amusement. "I don't think I could end it if an entire tsunami came through that porthole."

"Good." Relieved, she went to work on his shirt.

It took her a while to bare his chest, but once she had accomplished the task she could see that it had been well worth the effort.

"Nice." She splayed her fingers across his flat belly and bent her head to kiss his shoulder. He felt warm and powerful and utterly male beneath her hands. "Very, very nice."

"My turn."

He rolled her over onto her back and peeled down the black and silver gown. The front clasp of her black lace bra came apart in his hands. He looked down at her breasts with an expression of stark wonder. Then he cupped her in his fingers and took a nipple very gently between his teeth.

A luscious, liquid heat pooled in her lower body. A deep, tight urgency assailed her. Olivia closed her eyes as the exquisite sensations sizzled through her. Nothing had ever felt like this, she thought. Nothing. But all Jasper had done was kiss one breast. She would surely shatter into a gazillion stars if he did anything else.

She put a hand over her mouth to muffle a tiny shriek.

Jasper paused. "Are you okay?"

"Yes." She could barely get the single word out between her lips. She reached up and clutched at him. Sank her fingers into his shoulders. *"Yes."*

"Glad to hear it." His laugh was low and husky, more of a groan. He eased her dress off and hurled it out of the way. "You had me worried there for a minute. I told you, my timing isn't always the greatest when it comes to this kind of thing."

"You took me by surprise, that's all." She sounded breathless. She could not help it. She *was* breathless. "It's been so long. I'm a little tense, I guess. I mean, I've been busy. You know how it is."

"Yeah." He slid his warm hand slowly down over

her stomach. "I know. You've been too busy, and I don't get out much. We're a real pair, aren't we?"

She blushed, and then she giggled. *Giggled*. She never giggled. Olivia was mortified.

By the time she had recovered, Jasper had his hand inside the waistband of her black lace panties. She shivered when she felt his gently probing finger. The bubbling laughter dissolved in a heartbeat. Excitement flared in its place. She knew she was already soaking wet.

"This," Jasper said in reverent tones, "is the most amazing thing that's happened to me in a very long time."

Olivia buried her face against his shoulder. He stroked her until she was so desperate that she began to nip gently at the muscle in his arm.

Jasper rolled to the side for a moment. When he rolled back he had his pants off. Her mouth went dry as she watched him sheath himself in a condom.

"Oh, my." She could not think of anything else to say.

"Thank you." Jasper's eyes gleamed as he watched her stare at his erection. "It would have been a little disconcerting if you had started to giggle again."

"This," she said, wrapping her fingers around him, "is no laughing matter."

He gave a muffled exclamation and came down on top of her. Before she could even begin to orient her senses or prepare herself, he was easing slowly, deliberately, completely into her.

The rhythm of her breathing altered abruptly as her body adjusted to the indescribable tension. She felt stretched, taut, full to the bursting point.

When he was buried deep inside her, Jasper paused. He held himself unmoving. There was a sheen of dampness on his forehead. Olivia tentatively flexed her hands and realized that his shoulders were also slick with perspiration. He said nothing, but she knew that he was as riveted as she was by the moment.

He started to move, slowly, at first, much too slowly. She could feel something within her trying to snap free. She dug her nails into his sleek back.

"Faster," she urged.

"It feels good this way."

She tried to force the pace. "Hurry."

"Shush." He braced himself on his elbows and brushed his mouth lightly across her parted lips. "Cabin walls and doors are thin on a ship."

She raked his back with her nails.

His teeth flashed in the shadows. "I get the point."

He changed the depth of his strokes, but he refused to quicken them. The unpredictability of his movements made her wild. She wanted to scream. She squeezed every muscle in her body, struggling to get control of the situation. A shudder went through Jasper.

"You're going to make me crazy," he said against her throat.

"What do you think you're doing to me?"

Jasper's shoulder grew slicker beneath her hands. His whole body was hot and wonderfully heavy. She squeezed her eyes shut as the tension of his maddeningly slow, incredibly deep thrusts built. She was almost afraid to breathe for fear the magic would go away and leave her hanging in midair.

But she realized very quickly that she had underestimated the magician. Just when she thought she could not stand the sensual torment another instant, Jasper reached down to find the tightly swollen bud. He pressed it up and back.

Olivia did scream then. All thought of thin cabin walls and the possibility that someone might be walking past outside in the corridor was forgotten in the flash fire of her release.

Jasper sealed her mouth with his, trapping her cries in his own throat.

She returned the favor when he surged against her one last time, every muscle rigid.

"You were wrong," Olivia said a short while later.

Jasper watched the moonlight through the porthole. He felt drowsy and deeply satiated. All he wanted to do at that moment was drift off to sleep with Olivia's derriere nestled against his groin.

He yawned. "What was I wrong about?"

"Your timing is actually very, very good when it comes to this kind of thing." She breathed deeply. "Fantastic, in fact."

Jasper smiled into the darkness.

He opened one eye when he felt Olivia edge out from under his arm. "Where are you going?"

"It's four-thirty." She sat up on the side of the rumpled bed and reached for her glasses. "I want to take a quick shower and change my clothes before I go back to work."

He opened the other eye. He had been right. She

really did have a great back. He liked the elegant way her spine connected to the curve of her buttocks.

"You didn't get any rest," he said.

She went to the small closet to take down some clothes. "I told you, I'll crash when I get home today."

He folded his hands behind his head. "When are we going to talk about the blackmail problem?"

She whirled quickly to face him, gripping her fresh clothing in front of her like a shield. "You don't give up, do you?"

"I'll admit this is the best thing that's happened to me in a very long time." Satisfaction rippled through him again as he breathed in the scents of the bed. "But it did not bring on total amnesia. We've still got a problem."

"I told you, I need to think about things." She stepped through the narrow door of the tiny bath. "I'll call you."

The door closed firmly behind her nicely curved rear. The sound of the shower cut off further conversation.

"Oh, no, you don't, lady," Jasper said very softly.

He got to his feet and crossed the room. He opened the door of the bath and stood in the entrance. Steamy vapor swirled around him.

He could see the outline of Olivia's body behind the white curtain. He forced himself to concentrate on more important things.

"I will call you," he said.

"What?" She stuck her head around the curtain. Her hair was bundled up in a makeshift turban fashioned from a towel. "I didn't hear you."

"I said, I'll give you a call. Tomorrow." He propped

one shoulder against the door and admired the way the towel turban enhanced her regal cheekbones. "There's no use talking to you today. You're running on adrenaline and caffeine."

She blinked. "Your point?"

"My point," he said with grave precision, "is that there's no way that you can think clearly and logically about something as serious as blackmail and extortion until you get some rest. Go home after we dock. Get a good night's sleep tonight."

She smiled a little too brightly. "That's exactly what I plan to do."

"Then we'll talk." He straightened away from the door frame and walked back into the bedroom.

"Jasper—"

He pretended that he could not hear her over the noise of the running water.

Olivia emerged from the bath a few minutes later. She said nothing as she dressed in a flurry of activity.

When she was finished she flung open the door.

"Bye," she said with brittle good cheer.

And then she was gone.

When the cabin door closed behind her, Jasper made use of the facilities. He caught sight of his own face in the steamy mirror and grimaced at the stubble. His razor was in his cabin, together with the change of clothes he had brought with him.

He glanced at his watch. It was barely five A.M. He could probably make it back to his own room without arousing any curiosity. If he did run into a fellow passenger, he could always claim that he had partied all night and had never made it to bed.

He put on the wrinkled white tuxedo shirt and black trousers, grabbed his jacket and tie, and headed for the door.

He saw Andy Andrews as soon as he stepped out into the hall.

Damn. This was no coincidence. The reporter had obviously staked out Olivia's cabin.

"Morning, Sloan." Andy gave Jasper an ingenuous smile. "Didn't know you were such an early riser. Early morning conference with your new business partner?"

Jasper walked deliberately toward him along the narrow hall. "If I see one word of this in your column, I will personally feed you to a shredder, Andrews."

"Hey, I cover regional business issues." Andy put up his hands, palms out. "I'm no gossip columnist."

"The hell you aren't." Jasper kept moving forward, taking up most of the room in the narrow hall.

At the last instant, Andy hastily flattened himself against the wall in order to get out of Jasper's path.

16

"**Y**ou're sure this is what you want to do?" Al asked.

"I'm sure." Jasper opened another drawer in his desk and began removing the items stored there. He stacked them neatly in the carton on the floor.

It was Sunday morning. Al Okamoto had reluctantly agreed to meet him here today to finalize the sale of Sloan & Associates.

It felt strange to be cleaning out his own office after all these years. But it was the right move. He knew it with that same, inexplicable sense of certainty he relied on when it came to making all his business decisions.

"You and your stepbrother built Sloan & Associates from nothing." Al shoved his hands into the pockets of his trousers. "How can you just walk away from it like this?"

"It's time, Al." Jasper placed his collection of expensive pens into the box. "I've got a new company. I'm ready for the change."

Al watched him with troubled eyes. "Maybe it was a mistake to send you off on vacation."

Jasper smiled briefly. "The vacation had nothing to do with it."

"You're certain that you want to go through with this deal?"

"I'm certain."

Jasper glanced around the office that had served him well for over a decade. It was on the thirtieth floor of a downtown highrise. The windows gave a sweeping view of Elliott Bay and the Olympics.

His new offices down the street were considerably less plush, he thought. The decor was more utilitarian. The view was not nearly so panoramic. But he already felt more at home in Glow's executive suite than he ever had here at Sloan & Associates. He did not know how to explain that to Al. He could not even explain it to himself.

Jasper knew that everyone assumed he had a strong sentimental attachment to Sloan & Associates, not only because he had helped found it, but because of its connection to his stepbrother. As far as he was concerned, however, Fletcher was a specter who haunted the offices of the firm that he had once brought to the brink of scandal and ruin.

In the year following Fletcher's death, Jasper had been forced to fight hard, not only to salvage Sloan &

Associates, but to conceal Fletcher's embezzlement and fraud. He had won the battle, but he had never successfully exorcised Fletcher's ghost.

Jasper glanced at his watch. It was nine o'clock. He figured he'd give Olivia another hour or two to catch up on her sleep, and then he'd show up on her doorstep. He did not intend to call ahead to warn her that he was on his way. She might decide not to be at home.

"I've got the papers in my office," Al said.

Jasper closed the drawer he had just emptied. "Let's get them signed. I've got a lot to do today."

"Whatever you say." Al studied him for a moment, dark eyes filled with concern. "What happens if you decide you don't like the daily grind of running a company like Glow? How can you be sure you won't miss the adrenaline of the venture capital game?"

"There's plenty of risk involved in keeping a company like Glow profitable." Jasper thought about how Olivia had shuddered in his arms. He smiled. "Don't worry, I'll find some way to get my daily dose of excitement."

Al gave him an odd look. "Funny you should mention that. I was wondering how to bring up the issue of your continuing dose of excitement."

Jasper peered into the back of a drawer to make certain it was empty. "What the hell are you talking about?"

"Don't get me wrong. I, for one, am happy to see that you're developing a social life, but I've got to admit it came as something of a surprise."

"Damn it, Al—"

Al cleared his throat. "I take it you haven't seen the special edition of *Hard Currency?*"

Jasper went very still. "*Hard Currency* usually gets faxed to the office on Mondays and Thursdays."

"This edition is dated yesterday." Al handed him the single-page newsletter.

Jasper frowned. "Saturday?"

"Yeah. Fresh off the boat, you might say. Looks like Andy Andrews went straight back to his office after he left the *Private Island* and whipped it out. It was in the fax machine when I got here this morning. Every exec in the Northwest who goes into his office this weekend will see it."

Jasper scanned the contents of the newsletter.

"Damn," he said. "The little weasel couldn't resist. I was afraid of this. Olivia's going to explode when she sees it."

Al cleared his throat politely. "So, uh, is it true?"

"Is what true?" Jasper did not look up from the article.

"The not-so-subtle reference to your *cozy relationship* with your business partner."

Jasper finished the article and tossed the newsletter into the waste can. "Oh, sure. It's all true. That's not the point."

Al grinned. "What is the point?"

"Andrews called her event on board the *Private Island* 'Foil Town.' He might as well have come right out and labeled it tacky. If he's smart he'll stay out of her way for a long, long time." He realized Al was chuckling. "What's so damn funny?"

"Was it? Tacky, I mean?"

Jasper scowled. "Olivia believes in satisfying her clients. In this case the client was Madeline Silverthorne."

"Got it. Tacky."

"In a very tasteful sort of way."

"You do realize what the implications are here, don't you, Olivia?" Todd's new, Extremely Important voice sounded even more extremely important over the phone. "It could be awkward for all of us."

"All of us?" Olivia cradled the phone between her ear and her shoulder and reached for the coffeepot. She scowled at the special weekend edition of *Hard Currency* as she poured herself a second cup of coffee. Todd had just faxed the newsletter to her on the machine she kept at home.

She read Andy Andrews's report on Silver Galaxy Foods Night with growing irritation.

Everything glittered on board the *Private Island* last night, including the new partnership between Jasper Sloan and Olivia Chantry. Ms. Chantry is the proprietor of Light Fantastic, the event design and production company responsible for turning the *Private Island* into Foil Town.

Rumors have circulated to the effect that, once in control of Glow, Inc., venture capitalist Sloan would likely sell or merge the firm. Family members and longtime employees alike reportedly feared that he would take the money and run.

But those who witnessed the cozy working relationship between the twosome on Friday report that

Mr. Sloan is not running anywhere. At least, not alone. . . .

"Foil Town?" Olivia sputtered past a mouthful of coffee. "Where does Andrews get off calling my Silver Galaxy Foods Night production Foil Town?"

"Olivia . . ."

"Mrs. Silverthorne wanted a silver motif, and that's exactly what she got. I always give the client what she wants."

"Olivia, I don't give a damn about Andrews calling your event Foil Town," Todd said sharply. "I want to know if it's true?"

"Okay, so maybe Silver Galaxy Foods Night wasn't the most elegant, sophisticated production Light Fantastic has ever done." She pushed the newsletter aside. "It sure as heck didn't deserve to be called Foil Town."

"For the last time, I'm not talking about your event." Exasperation simmered in Todd's voice. "Is the rest of the article true? Do you and Sloan have something personal going?"

Something personal? She took another slug of coffee. Something personal?

Only the best sex she'd ever had.

Granted, she might not be a great judge, she reminded herself. Her experience had been limited to some early minor adventures and a husband who had never loved her.

But she was very sure that the event that she and Jasper had staged in her cabin in the wee hours of Saturday morning rivaled anything Light Fantastic had ever produced.

She was not about to discuss it with her younger brother or anyone else, however.

"Don't worry, Todd," she said in the tone of voice she reserved for difficult suppliers. "Andrews read a bit too much into what he saw. The truth is, Jasper and I have decided that the only way to squelch the rumors of a sale or merger is for the two of us to present a united front."

"It was all for show?"

"Sort of." Mercifully, the call-interrupt beeped in her ear. "Hang on a second, that's my other line." She switched quickly to pick up the incoming call. "This is Olivia."

"Ms. Chantry, this is Hamilton down in the lobby. There's a Mr. Sloan here to see you."

A curious sense of panic swept through her. She hadn't yet made up her mind how much to confide in Jasper. "Tell him—" Her mind blanked. "Tell him I'm not here, Hamilton."

"Sorry, Ms. Chantry," Hamilton said apologetically. "He's already in the elevator. Want me to follow him on up?"

"No, never mind. It's all right, Hamilton. Thanks." She switched back to the other line. "Todd? There's someone at the door. Or there will be in a few seconds I've got to run. I'll see you and Dixon tomorrow at the pier. We'll go over the entire Lancaster fund-raiser program."

"Wait, Olivia, I want to talk to you some more about this situation between you and Sloan."

"Don't worry, everything's under control. I keep telling you, I can handle Jasper Sloan."

The doorbell chimed. Olivia flinched. Now she was jumping at the sound of a simple doorbell, she thought, disgusted. Maybe she had been drinking a little too much coffee.

"Bye, Todd."

The bell bonged again as she hung up the phone.

She took a deep breath, pasted a polite smile on her face, and went to open the door.

Jasper stood in the hall. He had a white paper sack in one hand. The smell of something hot out of an oven wafted through the air.

She realized that she had not yet ingested anything except caffeine since getting out of bed. She eyed the sack and grudgingly held the door open.

"A little early for a Sunday morning, isn't it?" she asked.

"We've got a lot to talk about." He held up the paper bag. "I brought something to sop up the coffee."

"That was very clever of you." She closed the door and led the way down into the living room. "I woke up this morning and realized I had no food in the house. I've got to do some grocery shopping."

Jasper went straight into the kitchen and made himself at home. He opened a cupboard door, found a plate for the scones, and then checked the refrigerator.

"We're in luck," he said. "You've got some butter and marmalade."

"And coffee."

"All the basic food groups." He eyed the copy of *Hard Currency* lying on the counter. "I take it you've read Andy Andrews's report on Silver Galaxy Foods Night?"

"I certainly did." Fresh outrage swept through her. "He had the nerve to say that Light Fantastic turned the *Private Island* into Foil Town. After all that gushing I did over his stupid newsletter, too. Little twit."

"It wasn't the, uh, Foil Town reference that caught my attention," Jasper said dryly. "It was the mention of our cozy relationship."

"Oh, that." She did not look at him as she picked up the coffeepot.

"Yes, that."

"My brother called about it." She busied herself pouring two mugs full of the strong, dark-roast brew. "I told him it was all part of your united front plan."

Jasper gave her an enigmatic look as he opened the marmalade jar. "Very good. That was the right answer."

She focused her attention on the task of getting two knives out of the silverware drawer and onto the counter.

She did not understand the edgy feeling that gripped her. It was just one very short night of sex, she reminded herself, not proof that cold fusion actually worked.

There was something disturbingly intimate about the sight of Jasper moving comfortably around her kitchen. Memories of how it had felt to lie beneath him while she experienced the orgasm of the century did weird things to her concentration this morning. She had to think carefully in order to remember how to arrange the knives beside the plates.

Jasper put the platter of warm scones down on the counter between the coffee cups. He sat down on one of the stools.

Olivia slid onto the stool next to his and picked up a scone. She inhaled with deep appreciation. It really did smell wonderful. She lathered butter on it.

"Ready to talk about the blackmailer?" Jasper asked.

"Yes." She sighed around a mouthful of scone.

There really was no choice, she thought. She had awakened this morning with the knowledge that Jasper was right. Once she had started to think clearly, the necessity of telling him the whole story had been obvious. After all, he was involved in this mess. He had already been threatened once. There was no telling what the blackmailer would do next.

"I'm listening."

"Later," she said. "We'll go to the Kesgrove Museum as soon as it opens. It's easier to talk about Logan when you're standing in front of his art."

He watched her. "This is about your husband?"

"Yes. It's all about Logan. Many of the truly depressing things in my life have been about him."

17

It was early. They had the museum to themselves. Their footsteps echoed on the marble tile floor of the Contemporary Northwest Artists wing. Olivia came to a halt in front of one of the dark, murky canvases.

Jasper studied the picture. "Sort of like standing inside a thunderstorm."

"That was Logan. His work is a good illustration of the forces that were at war inside him. Eventually the storm overwhelmed him."

"You said you were only married for a few months?"

Olivia nodded. "It was a mistake, of course. I think I knew it all along deep inside."

"I see."

"We met when he wandered into my office to ask for part-time work. He needed money to keep himself in paint and supplies. Light Fantastic was a very tiny business in those days, but I was able to give him some freelance assignments."

"What happened?"

She smiled slightly. "I was stunned by his work. And that was just the commercial art that he did for me. When I saw some of his personal work, I knew that I had to introduce him to Wilbur."

"Wilbur Holmes?" Jasper raised his brows. "Your uncle's close friend?"

She nodded. "Wilbur owned and operated one of the most exclusive galleries in Seattle at the time. He took one look at Logan's work and knew it for the brilliant art that it is."

Jasper glanced at her. "So that part of Crawford Lee Wilder's article in *West Coast Neo* was true? You were responsible for launching Logan Dane's career?"

"Wilbur was the one who got it off the ground. All I did was introduce Logan to him." Olivia shrugged. "And I made a couple of suggestions about marketing Logan's art that worked."

"When did marriage come up?"

"Logan and I became friends. Good friends." She hesitated. "Looking back, I think he was grateful to me."

"Looking back," Jasper said, "I think he figured he could use you to further his career."

She shot him a quick, sidelong glance. She wanted to argue, but she knew that he was right. Logan had used her. "For my part, I thought that the friendship between Logan and myself would make a solid foundation for a lasting relationship. I thought I loved him."

"Don't feel bad," Jasper said. "I once made the mistake of thinking that a mutual interest in business would make a good foundation for marriage."

"It only goes to show, I guess."

"What does it show?"

She gave him a rueful smile. "Darned if I know."

"Go on with your story."

"Logan was easy to like. He was charismatic and capable of great charm. He played the role of the passionate, intense artist to the hilt." She hesitated. "Logan's family was thrilled when we got married."

"Because you did so much for his career?"

"No." She sighed. "Because they thought that I could save him from himself."

"Hell of a job, saving someone from himself. Not real do-able."

"No. I realize now that Logan's brother, Sean, and his parents must have understood intuitively that Logan was the kind of person who could easily self-destruct. They hoped my practical, businesslike nature would help stabilize him. But I failed."

"Saving Logan Dane was Logan Dane's job," Jasper said. "Not yours."

She turned her head quickly at that, but Jasper was gazing at the painting on the wall.

"At any rate," she continued after a moment, "it didn't take me long to realize that I had made a horrific mistake in marrying Logan."

"Friendship wasn't enough."

"No." Olivia swept out a hand to indicate the ominous canvases that surrounded them. "I found out too late that the only thing Logan could love was his art. He would do anything for it. He needed recognition and success the way some people need drugs."

"So he turned the business side of his career over to you." Jasper went to stand in front of another bleak canvas. "And you created the legend of Logan Dane."

"Logan created his own legend," she said. "All I did was help market it."

"And you did it brilliantly." Jasper turned to face her. "What does this have to do with blackmail?"

She exhaled deeply. "Unfortunately, while I don't think that Logan ever loved anyone or anything except his own talent, he was quite capable of short-term obsessions. He developed one for the young woman who modeled for him."

"What happened?"

"Logan convinced himself that he was desperately in love at last. A great, tragic, romantic love. He recorded everything in a journal that I found after his death." Olivia grimaced. "Knowing Logan, I'm sure he wanted me to find it. He was obsessed with his own legend, and I'm sure he considered the journal part of it."

"Who was the object of this great, tragic, romantic love?"

"My cousin Nina. She was still in college at the time. Logan was larger-than-life. He was already being hailed as a magnificent talent." Olivia shrugged. "He overwhelmed her for a few weeks."

Jasper's gaze was very steady. "They had an affair?"

"Yes. I found out about it almost immediately, thanks to Uncle Rollie."

Jasper frowned. "How did Rollie find out about it?"

She smiled. "My uncle always seemed to know stuff before anyone else. It was one of the things that made him a good businessman. He always claimed that information was power."

"I see." Jasper's voice was suddenly very neutral in tone.

"When I confronted Logan about his relationship with Nina, he was too arrogant and too obsessed with her to bother to deny it."

"What did you do?"

"It was the last straw. I told him that I intended to file for divorce. I don't think he believed me."

"Is that what made him take off for Pamplona?"

Olivia hesitated. "No. As I said, I don't think it ever occurred to Logan that I might actually leave him. He assumed that I was as invested in his career as he was."

"So what sent him to Pamplona?"

"My cousin Nina came to her senses and ended the affair."

"Ah."

Olivia looked at the canvas in front of her. "Logan was still deep in the throes of his obsession with her. I think he went a little crazy. He said he had to get out of the country for a while."

"So he left for Spain, and the Dane family blamed you."

"That pretty much sums it up," Olivia said. "They were grief-stricken. Logan's brother, Sean, took the news very hard. Logan was his older brother. He had idolized him. They all needed to place the guilt on someone. I was the obvious target."

"And you let them place it squarely on you," Jasper muttered. "For Nina's sake."

He sounded irritated, Olivia thought, surprised. Apparently he did not think highly of her decision. On the other hand, she had the strange feeling that he empathized. It was as if he understood what she had gone through when she made her decision three years ago.

"There's not much else to tell," she continued. "Except that, a few months ago, Nina fell in love, really in love, with Sean. But she feels so guilty about what happened three years ago that she can't let herself be happy. She thinks that if Sean and his family learn that she was Logan's so-called Dark Muse, they'll all turn against her."

"Is that true?"

Olivia recalled the look in the eyes of the Dane family at the funeral. "Probably."

"Hell. The blackmailer threatened to reveal the affair, didn't he?"

"Yes." She reached up to massage the tight muscles at the base of her neck. "That's it in a nutshell."

Jasper pondered that. "But he threatened you, not Nina. He obviously knows that you've kept quiet about the past in order to protect her. Hell, you even let Crawford Lee Wilder print that garbage about you without making a protest. The blackmailer figures you'll be willing to pay to go on maintaining the silence."

"He's probably also concluded that I'm a richer target than Nina. I've got deeper pockets, thanks to my half-ownership in Glow."

"Forty-nine percent," Jasper corrected absently.

Olivia almost smiled, in spite of the mood. "I beg your pardon, my *forty-nine-percent* ownership. Either way, it's obvious that I can afford more blackmail than Nina could."

Jasper's eyes darkened. "Someone knows a great deal about you, Olivia."

"Too much." She stopped rubbing her neck. She folded her arms tightly beneath her breasts instead. "The thing is, until I got that note, I was positive that I was the only other person, besides Nina, who knew about the affair. I just don't understand how the blackmailer could have discovered it."

"Maybe Nina confided in someone?"

Olivia shook her head quickly. "No, I'm sure that she has never told a soul. Her greatest fear is that the secret will come out. It's eating her up inside. She thinks I'm the only one who knows about it."

"Can you think of anyone else besides you and Nina who could possibly have known about the affair at the time it occurred?"

Olivia looked at him. "There was one other person, of course. But he's dead."

Jasper's eyes narrowed. "Your uncle?"

"As I said, Uncle Rollie was the one who told me about it."

Jasper glanced around the echoing exhibition hall. He took Olivia's hand. "Let's get out of here."

He couldn't think of a great place to talk about dead men and blackmail so he took her to the closest place, instead. Myrtle Edwards Park on the waterfront. He chose the path labeled "heels." The one that ran parallel to it was labeled "wheels."

He studied the small, choppy waves of Elliott Bay and put his questions into an orderly pattern. "How do you think your uncle found out about Logan and Nina?"

"In a lot of ways, Uncle Rollie was an old-fashioned patriarch."

Jasper was briefly amused. "*Patriarch* is an odd word to use to describe a man who was happily gay."

"I know." Olivia carefully unsealed the triple-shot latte she had purchased from a sidewalk espresso stand. "But it was the truth. He was the oldest of his generation and the first really successful member of the Chantry clan. He had a very strong sense of family responsibility. He provided jobs for relatives who needed them and summer employment for their kids. He helped finance first homes and first cars. Established college funds. Never forgot birthdays. Etc., etc."

"I get the picture."

"He always seemed to know what was going on in everyone's life. He kept track of things. He was obsessive about his files." She took a quick sip of her latte. "Both verbally and in his will, he gave explicit instructions to me to destroy all of his personal records after his death."

Jasper glanced at her. "Did you carry out those instructions?"

"Didn't have to." She took another sip. "There was a fire in Uncle Rollie's study the day after we got word of his death. It took care of everything."

He came to an abrupt halt. "Arson?"

Olivia nodded. "The police said there had been a rash of trash bin fires in the neighborhood where Uncle Rollie lived. They think the arsonist got especially bold that night and tried to burn down a whole house. He probably chose my uncle's because it was vacant."

"I see." Jasper resumed walking. "Back to my question. How did Rollie learn about the affair?"

Olivia made a face. "If you want to know the truth, I suspect he hired a private investigator. Pretty tacky, huh?"

That brought Jasper to another halt in the middle of the path. "Why in hell would he do that?"

She sighed. "Uncle Rollie never approved of my marrying Logan. He told me that Logan was using me right from the start. He had the decency to shut up about it after the wedding, but I know that he was still worried."

"So he kept tabs on Dane?"

"I wouldn't put it past him," Olivia said. "All I know for sure is that one day Uncle Rollie took me to lunch and asked if I knew that Logan was having an affair with Nina. He was furious, not only on my behalf, but on Nina's. She was young, inexperienced, and out of her league. Logan took advantage of her naïveté and innocence."

"What did you say?"

"I admitted I'd had some suspicions and that I was already considering a divorce. I never asked Uncle Rollie outright how he had learned about the affair, however."

"You just assumed he'd used an investigator?"

"It was a logical assumption. I knew that he hired a firm from time to time to, uh, check out stuff."

"What kind of stuff did good old Uncle Rollie check out?"

She looked at him over the rim of her latte cup. "Potential business partners, for example."

"Me, for instance?"

"Uh-huh."

Jasper whistled softly. "Makes sense. I had Rollie's background investigated before I signed the contract to finance Glow's expansion."

Olivia rolled her eyes. "Sheesh. Lord save me from obsessive-compulsive information types."

Jasper ignored that. "The bottom line here is that Rollie and at least one other person besides yourself knew about the affair."

Olivia looked briefly baffled. Then she nodded. "Oh, sure. Of course. The private investigator—" She broke off. "Hey, do you suppose the investigator is using the information in his files to blackmail people connected to some of his former clients?"

"Unlikely. Too obvious. And too easy to check out. Besides, I'm sure your uncle used a first-class firm." Jasper considered the possibilities. "There's another interesting question here, though."

"What's that?"

"Any chance that Rollie knew about Zara's former career in X-rated films?"

Olivia mulled that over briefly. "Sure. In fact, I'd bet he did know about it although he never mentioned it, of course. Like I said, Uncle Rollie knew just about everything about everyone in the family. Why?"

"It gives us a link. Don't you see? Whoever is blackmailing you and Zara knows information that only Rollie Chantry knew, right?"

"As far as I'm aware, yes."

Jasper paused to connect a few more facts. "You said there was a fire in Rollie's house that destroyed his personal files."

"That's right."

"Did his bank register and credit card statements survive, by any chance?"

She gave him a curious glance. "Where are you going with this?"

"If we assume that the private investigator-turned-blackmailer theory is unlikely, that leaves two other possibilities we need to check."

"And they are?"

"Either someone got into Rollie's personal files before the fire and removed some of them—"

"Oh, my God. I never thought of that." Olivia stared at him. "What if the fire wasn't random vandalism? What if the blackmailer broke in, stole some files, and then set the fire to cover up the theft?"

"Possible, but I think there's another possibility. What if the blackmailer broke in looking for information and found the location of it, instead? He might have still gone ahead and set the fire to cover his tracks."

"What do you mean?" Olivia demanded.

"One of the reasons your uncle and I did business together was because we understood each other. We had a lot in common."

She raised her brows. "Not everything, fortunately."

He smiled fleetingly. "You're right. Not everything. I'm not gay."

"You can say that again."

"But we did have the same approach to information," Jasper continued. "And the same degree of respect for it."

"So?"

"So I think I can almost guarantee that if Rollie possessed information that he knew was potentially damaging to members of his family, he probably stored it somewhere safer than his study."

Olivia's eyes widened. "What in the world made you think of that possibility?"

Jasper thought of the heavy, locked cabinets in his basement. "It's what I'd do."

"I see." Olivia's voice was very dry.

"Did you check the basement of his house?"

"There was only a partial basement. Nothing in it. I looked when I cleaned out the place."

"Nothing in his study survived?"

"Nope. He didn't use fire-proof filing cabinets."

Yet Chantry had apparently treated information with the same kind of respect that he, himself, did, Jasper thought. Which meant that Rollie would have taken pains to protect the most vital and the most potentially dangerous records.

"Safe deposit box?"

"I cleaned it out, too. I was his executor, so I got stuck cleaning out everything. There was nothing unusual in the box."

Jasper went down a mental list of options. "What about a storage locker in a commercial self-storage facility?"

"Uncle Rollie never mentioned one."

"If he had a locker," Jasper said slowly, "there would be a record of it somewhere."

"Probably in his study. Burnt to a crisp."

"To paraphrase an old expression, there ain't no such thing as free storage. Not in this day and age. If Rollie had a locker, he was paying for it. And if someone got into it after his death, there will be a record of that, too."

"Hmm." Olivia pursed her lips. "I've arranged to have his mail forwarded to me so that I can be sure to pay any outstanding bills or credit card statements. I haven't received an invoice from a storage facility of any kind."

"If he had an off-site locker, he probably paid the rent annually or semiannually. You might not see a bill for months."

"In which case, the charge would probably be on one of his credit card statements or buried in his check register."

"Damn." Jasper thought quickly. "We'll have to request copies of the statements and canceled checks from the credit card company and the bank. That's going to take a few days."

"No," Olivia murmured, "it won't."

He glanced sharply at her. "What do you mean? Weren't they destroyed in the fire?"

"Yes, but after the funeral I ordered copies of Uncle Rollie's bank and credit card statements. The lawyer and I needed them to settle the estate."

Jasper allowed himself a cautious flash of optimism. "You've got them stored somewhere very convenient, I hope?"

"In my basement storage locker." She took another swallow of coffee. "I'll dig them out this afternoon and take a look."

"I'll help you."

"Right." Clearly energized, Olivia polished off the latte and tossed the empty cup toward a nearby trash can with a flourish. "You really think we may be on to something here?"

"Maybe." The cup would never make it into the trash can, he thought. Olivia had made no allowance for the gently gusting wind. Both her aim and her timing were off.

He watched the breeze catch the empty latte cup just before it reached the can. The paper vessel was whipped about by the light air currents. It sailed away onto the grass.

"Darn. Hang on a second." Olivia veered off the path to chase down the wind-tossed cup. She scooped it up, dropped it into the can, and trotted back to join Jasper.

He refrained from pointing out that it would have been more efficient to have simply put the cup directly into the trash can in the first place. He had a feeling she would not appreciate the advice.

18

An hour later Jasper helped Olivia pry a large, heavy box out of the condo's basement storage locker. They hauled it to the elevator and took it to her sunny eleventh-floor villa.

Olivia saw the disapproval in his eyes when she lifted the lid off the box to reveal a loose array of documents, envelopes, and mail addressed to Roland Chantry.

"Okay, so I don't subscribe to the anal-retentive system of filing," she said. "At least it's all there."

"How can you be sure?" Jasper rummaged through the contents of the box. "We'll be lucky to find all of the credit card statements, let alone every single check."

"Trust me." She reached into the box for a handful of bills. "Everything is in here."

"I'll believe it when I see it."

It only took fifteen minutes to find the record of payment to the Pri-Con Self-Storage facility. Olivia spotted it first. A jolt of non-caffeine-related energy shot through her.

"You were right. He paid a bill to a storage facility in south Seattle last January."

"Let's see." He reached for the credit card statement and contemplated the payment for a long moment. "It's a place to start. But don't get too excited. We don't know what he kept there. When we open the locker we may find nothing but old fishing gear or his military service memorabilia."

"Let's see if we can get into the locker this afternoon." Olivia reached for the phone book and picked up the phone.

Two minutes later she found herself listening to a recorded message.

Thank you for calling Pri-Con Self-Storage. Pri-Con stands for private and confidential and we guarantee both. Our offices are open from eight to five weekdays and Saturday. On Sunday we close at two P.M. . . .

"Shoot." Olivia glanced at the clock as she dropped the phone into the cradle. "We can't get in today. The place closed half an hour ago. It doesn't open until eight tomorrow morning."

Jasper's mouth tightened. "I've got meetings with two critical path suppliers tomorrow starting at eight-fifteen. I probably won't be finished until eleven at the earliest."

Olivia drummed her fingers on the table. "I've got an appointment with Todd and Dixon Haggard in the morning. We're going to review final plans for the Lancaster fund-raiser."

"Let's shoot for noon. I usually leave my Jeep on Bainbridge, but I'll drive it in to work tomorrow. I'll pick you up at your office."

"All right." She reached back into the file box to heft a small, zippered bag.

"What's in there?"

She smiled, feeling a trifle smug. "All of Uncle Rollie's keys. They survived the fire. With any luck, one of them will fit the lock on the storage locker."

Jasper shrugged. "If we don't find the right key, we can cut off the lock. I'll bring some tools."

Her small burst of euphoria collapsed. "This is an interesting development, but like you said, it might lead nowhere."

"It's a place to start. And it feels right."

"What do you mean, right?"

He hesitated. "I can't explain. All I can tell you is that I think we're on to something here. The fact that your uncle had a storage locker that you didn't know about is very interesting. And if we discover that someone else has gotten into it and if we can figure out who that person was . . ."

"Yes. I see what you mean." She shuddered. "This is weird, Jasper."

"Blackmail is weird."

"True." She eyed the box of papers, restless now that they had an objective. "We're stuck. There's nothing we can do until tomorrow."

Jasper's smile was slow and intimate. "I wouldn't say that. We can always work on our united front project."

A weightless sensation settled into Olivia's stomach. "In the middle of the afternoon?"

"Think it would be tacky?"

"No. No, I don't think it would be tacky at all. But, then, what do I know? I'm the one who brought you Foil Town."

"That's true," Jasper said. "But I sort of liked it."

"Remember that the next time you need an event producer."

"I need one right now." He grinned and reached for her.

She would try very hard not to giggle this time, she promised herself.

Olivia got the call canceling her appointment with Todd and Dixon at twenty minutes after eight the next morning.

"Mr. Haggard and Mr. Chantry need to reschedule for two this afternoon," the secretary said on the other end of the line. "Would that be convenient?"

Not hardly, Olivia thought. There was no way she could get to the Pri-Con Self-Storage facility, go through the contents of Rollie's locker with Jasper, and get back to the office in time for a two o'clock meeting. "How about three?"

"I'm afraid that doesn't work for Mr. Haggard. He and Ms. Lancaster have a rally to attend in eastern Washington this evening. They'll be flying to the Tri-Cities at four."

Damn, damn, damn. The fund-raiser was a very

220

important contract with a wealth of future possibilities. She could not afford to annoy the client. Olivia glanced at her watch and stifled a groan. "Two o'clock will be fine, in that case."

She hung up the phone and gave the problem a moment's consideration. So much for the noon trip to Pri-Con. On the other hand, she now had her morning free. There was no reason she could not go out to the self-storage facility alone and have a look around. If one of the keys in the zippered pouch fit, she would be able to get inside the locker. If not, she would have no choice but to reschedule with Jasper for later in the day.

She picked up the phone again and dialed Jasper's office number. Rose answered.

"I'm sorry, Olivia, Mr. Sloan is out. May I take a message?"

"Yes, please, Aunt Rose. Tell him that my schedule got changed. I'm no longer available for the one o'clock we had planned together. Tell him that I'm going to go out to the facility in south Seattle this morning, instead. He'll know what I'm talking about."

"I'll tell him, Olivia. But I better warn you, Mr. Sloan is not in a good mood today."

Olivia frowned. "Things not going well with the supplier meetings?"

"It's not the suppliers. He was like this when he walked through the door."

"Like what?"

"Sort of icy, if you know what I mean. Like he was getting ready to go into battle or something." Rose's voice dropped to a confidential whisper. "Quincy suggested that maybe you and Sloan quarreled about some of the changes going on around here."

"Nonsense," Olivia said crisply. "Jasper and I are in, uh, perfect accord regarding the transition at Glow."

"If you say so."

"Just give him my message as soon as you can, Aunt Rose."

Olivia hung up the phone and sat quietly, thinking for a moment. Jasper had looked anything but icy when he left her condo shortly after eleven last night.

She got to her feet and grabbed her purse and keys. She would worry about Jasper's mood later.

The Pri-Con Self-Storage company occupied an aging, four-story cinder-block building located on a neglected street in the south end of the city. A vacant warehouse stood adjacent to it. There was no sidewalk in front. Weeds had long since replaced whatever professional landscaping had once existed.

It looked like the No-Tell Motel of storage facilities, Olivia thought, as she drove into the tiny, graveled parking lot. The sort of place where management probably did not ask too many questions so long as the rent got paid on time.

From out of nowhere, she suddenly recalled a story she had read in the papers about a man who had murdered his wife and hidden her body in a self-storage locker. It had been three years before the corpse had been discovered.

"Get a grip, Olivia."

When she got out of her car, she noticed that there was only one other vehicle in the small parking lot.

Either Pri-Con Self-Storage was not a thriving operation, or there were not a lot of people who wanted to move their personal possessions in and out of storage at eight-forty-five on a Monday morning.

She surveyed the building as she walked toward a door marked *Office*. Every window on all four floors had been bricked up. For security purposes, she speculated. Or perhaps to create additional space for lockers inside. It was amazing how forbidding a building without windows looked.

The small office was empty. There was an *Eleanor Lancaster for Governor* poster taped to the window.

Olivia pressed a buzzer. It was a good five minutes before a thickly built man appeared. He was garbed in a pair of well-worn camouflage pants and a black T-shirt. His long gray hair was tied in a ponytail. The word *Privacy* was tattooed on one arm. *Freedom* was spelled out in large, flowery capitals on the other. He did not look pleased at the prospect of having to assist a customer.

"Yeah?"

Olivia decided the occasion required a certain degree of assertiveness. She drew herself up to her full height and gave him a steely smile.

"My name is Olivia Chantry. I'm the executor for the estate of Mr. Roland Chantry, recently deceased. In the process of settling his affairs, I discovered that he maintained a locker in this facility. I'm here to examine the contents. I can, of course, provide proof of my legal authority to do so."

The attendant squinted at her and then shrugged. "Help yerself." He turned to go back through the door from which he had emerged.

"I take it you're not real big on security around here?" Olivia called after him.

The attendant paused. He looked at her over his shoulder, eyes slitted. "What we're real big on around here is privacy."

"Privacy?"

A demonic glint blazed in his squinty eyes. "That's the problem with this country today, y'know. No privacy anymore. The founding fathers went to the wall to secure privacy and confidentiality for the citizens of these here United States. Guys like me fought and died in a lotta wars for the right to privacy."

"Yes, well . . ."

"You'd think people today would have a little respect for all the blood that's been shed to protect the constitutional right to privacy and confidentiality. But, no. Every time you turn around the govmint's chipped away another piece of our personal privacy."

Olivia decided to transition from assertive to soothing-the-client mode. "I understand."

"Pri-Con Self-Storage guarantees absolute privacy and confidentiality to its clients. No questions asked. Long as you pay yer rent, you can store anything you damn well want in yer locker."

"I was simply commenting on your lack of security measures."

"Pri-Con don't guarantee security." The broad face worked furiously. "Can't rightly do that without a coupla grenade launchers and some mortars, which, thanks to the socialist elite that's taken over our govmint, us entrepreneur types can't hardly get hold of, let alone set up in front of our place o' business."

"I see." Olivia cleared her throat. "Could you kindly direct me to Roland Chantry's locker, Mr. Uh— I didn't catch your name."

"Name's Silas." He gave her a suspicious look. "Thought you was an executor."

"I am." She held up the zippered pouch. "I have Mr. Chantry's keys and plenty of identification, but I don't have the number of his locker. Many of his records were lost in a house fire."

"Huh."

"Perhaps you'd like to call the lawyer who handled his estate," Olivia said smoothly. "He'll explain everything."

Alarm flickered in Silas's eyes. "Don't want to talk to no lawyer. Got too many of 'em in this country. We got one rule here at Pri-Con. Whoever pays the rent gets to go inside the locker."

Olivia recognized the opening he had given her and moved briskly to seize it. "It may interest you to know that, as the executor of my uncle's estate, I now pay the rent on Roland Chantry's locker."

"Huh." Silas mulled that over for a long time.

"I will be happy to call my lawyer," Olivia said again.

"Chantry's dead, you say?"

"That's right."

Privacy and *Freedom* rippled on Silas's big arms as he raised his shoulders in a massive shrug. "Guess it'll be okay then. Guy's dead, probly don't care too much about his privacy anymore."

He stalked into the office, sat down at the desk, and reached for a large rotary card file.

"I see you don't use a computer for your office records," Olivia murmured.

"Don't trust 'em." Silas flipped through the cards. "No privacy with computers. Chantry, Chantry, Chantry. Yep, here we go. Locker Number Four-ninety. That's up on the top floor clear to the back."

A rush of excitement swept through Olivia. "Thanks. How do I get up there?"

"Elevator's over there in the corner." Silas scowled. "Gonna need a hand truck or a platform truck to haul out his stuff?"

"Not right away." She smiled brightly at him as she backed out the door. "I'll have to inventory the contents of the locker first to determine the disposition of the items."

"Yeah, sure. Disposition 'em all you want. Light switch for each floor is just to the right of the elevator. Turn out the lights when you leave."

"You bet."

When the elevator door slid open on the fourth floor a short while later, Olivia understood why Silas had mentioned the location of the light switches.

She could barely see her hand in front of her face.

The fourth floor was cloaked in a thick darkness that was relieved only by the eerie green glow of an emergency exit sign above the stairwell.

Olivia felt her way out of the elevator and groped for the light switch. She found it just as the door of the elevator cab slid shut behind her.

Only a few of the fluorescent fixtures overhead stuttered to life. In its endless quest for privacy and confidentiality, the management of Pri-Con Self-Storage was obviously committed to maintaining low light levels.

The floor-to-ceiling lockers were arranged in blocks separated by long, shadowy corridors. Olivia wished she had thought to bring along a flashlight. She would need one if she managed to get inside number four-ninety.

She glanced at the number stenciled on a nearby door. Four-oh-one. Silas had said that Rollie's locker was somewhere in the rear.

She started down the nearest corridor. The heels of her oxfords echoed strangely on the concrete floor.

The fourth level of the facility seemed much larger from the inside than it had looked from outside the building. It also felt very empty. She heard nothing as she made her way deeper into the complex. As far as she could tell she was alone on this floor.

She kept a wary eye out for rats.

It was cold up here, too, she noticed. A chill went through her when she turned down another aisle and started toward the back wall of the building.

She crossed three more intersections before she admitted to herself that what she really felt was a growing unease.

She turned another corner and collided with a large wooden pallet mounted on casters. She yelped in surprise and stepped back very quickly.

The platform truck was nearly as wide as the corridor between the lockers. It effectively blocked her path.

She gripped the steel bar that had been installed at one end and pushed the heavy contraption into another aisle. The casters squeaked and groaned, but the platform moved fairly easily.

When it was out of her way, she checked locker numbers again. Four-eight-seven. She was close.

She found number four-ninety in the very last aisle. The padlock that secured the door looked surprisingly shiny, almost new.

Olivia unzipped the pouch containing the keys and rummaged around inside for one that looked as if it might fit the lock.

She was on her third try when a small scraping sound in the distance caused the hair on the nape of her neck to stand on end.

The elevator door had just opened. Someone else was on the fourth floor. Olivia was suddenly, intensely aware of how very alone she was here at the back of the labyrinth.

Her vivid imagination produced an image of the privacy-crazed Silas stalking female customers through the maze of lockers. He could murder dozens of people and conceal the bodies in their own lockers for years before anyone realized that something strange was going on at Pri-Con Self-Storage.

Stop it, Olivia told herself. *You're acting like an idiot.*

At that moment the weak fluorescent lights overhead winked out. The fourth floor was plunged into unrelenting darkness.

A jolt of fear shafted through Olivia.

Her fingers froze on the padlock. She opened her mouth to call out. It was possible that someone, another attendant perhaps, had turned off the lights on the assumption that the fourth floor was deserted.

But just as she started to shout that there was a paying customer in the last aisle, something made her pause.

A soft, distant thud echoed from the other end of

the room. It sounded remarkably like someone blundering into a locker wall.

In that moment she knew for certain that whoever had turned off the lights had not gone back downstairs in the elevator. He was still here on the fourth floor.

In the dark.

With her.

Olivia no longer tried to talk herself out of the panic that rose like nausea within her. She definitely had a right to be afraid now, she thought.

She considered going back into assertive mode. Perhaps she could bluff her way out of this. The downside to that plan, she realized, was that, if she called out, she would give away her position. If Silas was playing some evil game, that was the last thing she wanted to do.

On the other hand, if Silas was stalking her here in the darkness, he already had a good idea of her location. He worked here, after all. He knew exactly where locker four-ninety was located.

She had to get out of this aisle. She had to put some distance between herself and locker four-ninety.

Olivia realized she was gripping the padlock as if it were a talisman. With an effort of will she pried her icy fingers away from the cold metal.

Flattening one palm against the nearest plywood wall, she prepared to use her sense of touch to guide her back toward the next intersection.

She took one step and heard the faint but unmistakable sound of her own shoe sliding on concrete.

She froze. When she could breathe again she bent down, quickly untied her oxfords, and stepped out of them. She winced when she put her stocking-clad feet on the glacier-cold concrete.

She inched slowly forward. Her eyes had begun to adjust to the darkness. It was still densely shadowed here in the last aisle. But when she ran out of wall at the intersection, she looked down a darkened corridor and saw the green glow of the exit light above the stairwell.

She realized that she could use the exit lamp to guide her back to the elevators. But maybe that was exactly what the stalker expected her to do.

She crossed the intersection and slipped cautiously into another black aisle. At least she was no longer standing next to locker four-ninety.

The thought that she was not quite so much of a sitting duck as she had been a few seconds ago brought a tiny shot of hope. She seized on it as she worked her way along the gloom-filled corridor.

She heard another scraping sound and realized that the stalker was on the move. He was not waiting for her at the elevator. She wondered how he was navigating his way along the cave-dark paths.

The answer came a moment later when she crossed another intersection and glimpsed a narrowly focused beam of light. It vanished almost at once, but she knew now that whoever he was, the stalker had come here better prepared than she had. He had thought to bring a pencil-thin flashlight

She tried frantically to think of a strategy. If she could work her way back to the elevator, she could go down the stairs. But if she turned down the wrong corridor enroute, she would blunder into the stalker.

From out of nowhere she recalled something Silas had said about guns. She did not have access to a grenade launcher or a bazooka, but she had left a very large, extremely heavy platform truck in a nearby aisle. It would have to do.

If she could find it.

She closed her eyes. For some reason it was easier to construct a mental map of the locker complex with her eyes shut. She was certain that she had made only one turn after pushing the platform truck into a side aisle.

Almost certain.

A soft thud made her snap open her eyes. She was out of time. The stalker was getting closer. If she was going to act, she had to do it now.

Slowly, painstakingly, she made her way back to the intersection she had just crossed. When she reached it, she turned and went slowly along another corridor. If she was right, she was only one aisle over from four-ninety. This was where she had left the platform truck.

She must be careful not to stumble into it.

She went down on her hands and knees and began to crawl along the cold concrete.

Her fingers connected with one of the casters on the platform truck a few seconds later. She stopped and took a deep breath. She could not see the outline of the truck, but she found the steel handle bar by touch.

Slowly she got to her feet and gripped the bar.

She did not have long to wait.

The scraping sound drew closer. Olivia held her breath. She was very cold, but rivulets of perspiration dampened her blouse.

The thin beam of the stalker's flashlight crossed the

entrance to the aisle in which she stood poised with the platform truck.

A shadowy figure stepped into the intersection. It swung the flashlight beam down the opposite aisle.

It was now or never. The beam would shine into her aisle next.

With every ounce of strength she possessed, Olivia shoved the platform into motion. She pushed it as fast as possible toward the figure in the intersection.

The creaking and groaning of the heavy truck caused the stalker to whirl around. The narrow beam of the flashlight struck the truck, lifted. It hit Olivia squarely in the eyes, blinding her.

She kept moving, shoving the platform truck in front of her. All she had to do was keep it going forward in a relatively straight line, she thought. She couldn't miss.

There was a choked, angry cry. The stalker staggered back, frantically trying to get out of the path of the heavy cart. He succeeded only partially.

The wheeled platform caught the figure on the thigh at the intersection. The jolt of the impact went through Olivia.

Her victim reeled backward.

There was a hoarse shout. The flashlight flew out of the stalker's hand and rolled on the concrete.

He was down, but Olivia did not know if he was hurt. She did not know if he had a gun.

She did the only thing that made sense at that moment.

She ran toward the glowing green exit sign

19

Jasper planted both hands flat on the desk and leaned forward. He kept his voice very soft because he did not trust himself to speak in a normal tone. The rage that had been swirling inside him all morning made him extremely cautious.

"What do you mean, she left a message about a *facility?*"

On the other side of the desk, Rose flinched. Her mouth worked tremulously. "I . . . I really can't tell you anything else, Mr. Sloan. Olivia called and said to let you know that her appointment schedule for the day had been ch . . . ch . . . changed. She said she was going to check out the facility in south Seattle this morning, since she had time."

"Damn."

Rose swallowed. "I'm sorry, sir, if I didn't get the message right."

"Don't worry about it, Rose." Jasper straightened. "I'll take care of the problem."

"Yes, sir."

He glanced at his watch as he went into the inner office. "I'm going to be out of the office for the rest of the day. Call Tyler. Tell him what's going on. He can handle things until tomorrow."

"Yes, sir."

Jasper grabbed his jacket off the back of the door and walked swiftly through the outer office. He could feel Rose's curious, nervous eyes on him as he went out the door and headed toward the elevator.

He was well aware that his odd reaction to the phone message from Olivia would be all over the office by noon. Rose might not know quite what to make of it, but one thing was for certain. It constituted Chantry family gossip.

He was overreacting, he told himself as he drove into the small lot in front of the Pri-Con Self-Storage company. There was no reason for the chill in his gut. What could possibly happen to Olivia in a storage locker facility?

He parked his Jeep next to Olivia's sleek red Nissan and got out. He walked swiftly toward the battered red, white, and blue sign that pointed to the office.

Relief shot through him when he reached the grimy one-window room and saw Olivia inside. She had cornered a harassed-looking man with tattoos behind a battered metal desk. Her angry, outraged voice floated through the open door.

"I'm telling you there's some idiot on the fourth floor with a flashlight. He's stalking people up there. Don't you care?"

"Look, lady, the lights up there are a little tricky, y'know? They're always goin' out."

"He deliberately turned them off, I tell you."

"Calm down, ma'am. There ain't no other customers here."

"Someone is upstairs playing vicious games."

The attendant put up his hands as if to ward her off. "I'll take a look if it will make you feel any better."

"Don't you dare speak to me as if I'm hysterical. There is a person up there who stalked me through the aisles."

"But I'm tellin' you there's no other customers around—" The attendant broke off as he caught sight of Jasper standing in the doorway. "Leastways, there wasn't until now."

"What's going on here?" Jasper asked.

Olivia spun around. *"Jasper."*

The relief in her face had an unexpectedly warming effect. He glanced down and saw that she was barefoot. Her nylons were shredded.

"What the hell happened?" he asked.

"I found Uncle Rollie's locker, but before I could get it open someone turned out the lights upstairs, and then, I swear to God, he came through the aisles with a flashlight. It was as if he was hunting me. I knocked him down with a platform truck and—"

"Is he still up there?" Jasper interrupted.

She frowned. "Well, yes. I think so. At least I haven't seen anyone else come down the stairs or use the elevator since I got back to the office. But, Silas, here, just told me that there's an emergency exit door on the other side of the building. He might have escaped through it."

Jasper looked at the hapless Silas. "Let's go take a look."

"Sure, sure. Whatever you say."

Silas came out from behind the barricade of his desk with alacrity. Jasper got the impression he was grateful for the excuse to flee the office.

Jasper looked at Olivia. "Wait here."

"Not a chance." She was already in motion, striding crisply toward the door. "I'm coming with you."

There was no time to argue. Besides, Jasper consoled himself, if there was a stalker prowling the grounds, Olivia was safer in a crowd than she was on her own down here in the office. "Stay close."

She did not bother to respond to that. She went past him out the door.

Silas reached the elevator first and punched the button.

"Let's take the stairs," Jasper said. "If he's looking for a way out, he'll probably use them rather than the elevator."

"What if he hears us in the stairwell and decides to use the elevator?" Olivia asked.

"Lock it out," Jasper told Silas.

"Okay, okay. Take it easy." When the elevator opened, Silas reached inside and pulled out a red knob "There. It ain't goin nowhere."

Jasper opened the stairwell door and listened for a few seconds. No footsteps echoed on the concrete. He moved inside and started up the first flight, taking the steps two at a time.

Olivia followed, silent on her bare feet. Silas brought up the rear. He was panting heavily by the time they hit the second floor. He wheezed on the third.

Jasper opened the door on the fourth level and looked at the blocks of storage lockers.

"He turned the lights back on." Olivia peered past Jasper's shoulder. "I wonder why he did that?"

"Maybe he never turned 'em off," Silas gasped behind her.

She glared at him. "What's that supposed to mean?"

"Nothin', honest."

She narrowed her eyes. "You think I made it all up, don't you?"

"Look, lady, the lights are on, that's all I'm sayin' . . ."

"Quiet," Jasper said. He glanced at Silas. "Stay here to make certain that he doesn't try to use the stairs. I'll check the aisles."

"Sure." Silas looked relieved to have someone else take command. He sagged against the wall to catch his breath. "Right."

Olivia stepped out of the stairwell. "I'll come with you, Jasper."

"All right. But stay close, understand?"

"Yeah, sure."

He did not like the sound of that, but he could not think of anything else to do except conduct a meticulous search.

There was a pattern to the way the blocks of lockers had been laid out. Jasper quickly identified the main aisles and walked through them, checking each cross aisle whenever he came to an intersection. Olivia paced at his side, her eyes flicking back and forth. He was acutely aware of the tension in her.

"The place feels empty now," she said when they paused in an intersection three aisles from the rear wall. "But he was here. I swear it, Jasper."

"I believe you."

"The platform truck should be in the next aisle." Olivia hurried forward.

"Damn it, I told you to stay close." He caught up with her just as she came to a sudden halt and stood staring down a corridor.

"There it is," she whispered. "I told you."

Jasper studied the platform truck parked innocuously in the middle of the aisle. There was no sign that it had recently been used to mow down a stalker. There was no evidence that anything at all out of the ordinary had occurred.

"Hang on while I check the last two aisles," Jasper said.

Both were empty.

Olivia watched him with somber eyes as he walked back to join her. "He's gone."

"Looks like it." Jasper glanced down the long center aisle to where Silas stood guard at the stairwell door. "Are there any empty lockers on this floor?" he called.

"Nope." Silas shouted back. "Rented the last one about a month ago. Only open lockers are down on the first floor."

"So much for the possibility that he's hiding in an empty locker," Jasper said.

"He must have escaped down the stairs and out the emergency exit while I was in the office with Silas."

"Maybe." Jasper walked into the aisle occupied by the platform truck.

Olivia followed slowly. "This is spooky, Jasper. Silas thinks I got scared when the lights went out and made up the whole story. Now I can't prove that I didn't."

"I believe you." He edged past the platform truck. "You said you thought you knocked him down with this thing?"

"Yes. But I didn't hang around to see if he was hurt. I ran for the stairs."

"Smart."

Jasper crouched to study the front edge of the wooden platform. It was scarred and nicked from years of heavy use. There was no way to tell if it had collided with a man's leg during the past half hour.

Then he saw the crushable khaki canvas hat lying beneath the front right caster just as he started to rise. "I think you may have managed to score yourself a souvenir of today's events, after all."

She followed his glance to the mashed hat. "Do you suppose he dropped it when the truck hit him?"

"Maybe." He picked up the hat and took a closer look. It was a soft, wide-brimmed affair studded with metal grommets for ventilation. It was designed so that it could be rolled up and stuffed conveniently into a back pocket. "Could have fallen out of his pants or his shirt when he fell."

Olivia grimaced. "I don't think Silas will see that hat as proof that there was someone besides me up here this morning. It could have been dropped on the floor days ago."

Jasper glanced up. "Kind of a coincidence that it ended up beneath the casters on that platform truck."

"Yes, it is."

"Hey, down there," Silas yelled. "You folks about finished? I gotta get back to work."

"We're through," Jasper called. "You can go downstairs now."

"About time."

The stairwell door opened and closed. Silence descended.

Olivia's eyes widened. "I never got a chance to open Uncle Rollie's locker."

"We'll do it now."

"It's in the last aisle. Number four-ninety." Olivia looked down at her side. "Oh, damn."

"What?"

She whirled and dashed around the corner. "I just realized I dropped my purse and the pouch full of keys back there."

Jasper went after her. He found her in the last aisle, bending over to pick up a shoulder bag and the key pouch. She straightened and turned toward him, a relieved expression on her face.

"They're both still here."

Jasper looked at the shiny padlock on locker four-ninety. "Doesn't look like it's been there very long."

"I know. Maybe Uncle Rollie installed a new one before he left on his trip."

In the end none of the keys in Olivia's pouch fit. Jasper went back downstairs to the Jeep and got his tools.

It did not take long to cut off the small padlock on locker four-ninety.

Olivia looked inside when the door swung open. Dismay replaced the anticipation that had gleamed in her eyes.

"It's empty," she said.

"I don't understand it." Olivia paced back across her living room, arms crossed, shoulders hunched. "Why keep an empty locker?"

"Who knows?" Jasper lounged against the sofa and watched her pace. He could feel the cold anger moving through him. "Maybe Rollie cleaned it out before he left on vacation."

She turned and started back across the room. "Why keep the locker, in that case?"

"He may have planned to move something else into it when he returned. After all, he'd paid for a year's rent."

Olivia threw up her hands. "It makes no sense."

He looked at her. "You shouldn't have gone to the storage facility without me today."

That brought her to an abrupt halt. She turned, frowning. "What on earth are you going on about that for?"

"You had no business trying to get into that locker alone," he said very evenly.

"What's the big deal?" She waved her hands. "My morning was clear, yours wasn't. Then my afternoon got crowded. I knew I wouldn't be able to get away later. It made perfect sense for me to run down to Pri-Con to take a quick look."

"You call that an example of good sense?" Jasper got to his feet. He walked toward her. "What if that jerk who turned out the lights was doing more than playing games with you? What if you hadn't gotten lucky with the platform truck?"

Her eyes narrowed. "You've got no right to lose your temper with me. I made a perfectly reasonable executive decision under the circumstances."

"Reasonable?" He stopped directly in front of her and lowered his voice still further. "Who knows what that guy intended?"

Olivia's head came up swiftly. "Don't you dare use that tone with me. Let me remind you that this black-mailer has targeted my family. When you get right down to it, this is my problem, not yours."

"No."

She gave him a ferocious glare. "What do you mean by that?"

"I mean," he said very quietly, "that this is no longer just your problem."

"What are you saying?"

"I found a blackmail note waiting for me this morning on the front seat of my Jeep."

For a few beats she did not seem to comprehend. Then understanding flashed in her eyes.

"Oh, my God," she whispered. "But what—?"

Jasper said nothing. He watched her intelligent face as she made the connections.

"I see." She turned away and sank down slowly onto

the tiled window seat. She pressed her knees together and clasped her hands on top of them.

"There goes our theory that the blackmailer is using information from Uncle Rollie's files," she said eventually.

"Not necessarily."

She glanced sharply at him. "Why do you say that?"

Jasper went to stand at the bank of windows that looked out over the Space Needle. "Rollie and I had similar approaches to business. I told you, I had him thoroughly checked out before I did the deal. He probably did some serious checking into my background before he signed that contract with me."

"So?"

"It's just barely possible," Jasper said, "that he stumbled across something."

"Whatever it was, he obviously didn't think it was very important," Olivia said. "After all, he went ahead and signed that contract with you."

"Probably because what he found was not directly related to me." Jasper gazed intently at the Needle. "It involved someone else. Someone who died over eight years ago."

"I don't understand. If it didn't involve you, why would a blackmailer come after you with threats?"

"For the same reason that he targeted you with threats that would hurt people in your family."

She sighed. "He knows that you'll want to protect someone who would be hurt if the information were made public?"

"Yes." He turned to find her watching him with her clear, perceptive eyes. "Eight years ago I went to great lengths to conceal some information about my step-brother, Fletcher. I thought I had been successful. But obviously I was not."

She watched him very steadily. "Now what?"

He smiled humorlessly. "Now, I will have to tell you what I have told no one else in eight years."

She tensed. "Jasper, maybe I don't need to know this. If you'd rather not . . ."

"You need to know," he said. "You told me your secrets. Now I'll tell you mine. We're in this together."

She was silent for a moment. Then she nodded. "I'm listening."

He sorted through the facts, searching for a place to start. It was strange, he thought. He had buried the information in the farthest corner of his mind, but when he went looking, he found it all too easily.

"Fletcher was several years older than I was. I idolized him when I was a kid. He spent time with me. Showed me things."

"What kind of things?"

Jasper shrugged. "All the things my father never had the time to show me. How to fish. How to play basketball. How to wear a tux."

"I see."

"He was a natural salesman. People responded to him. He had a way of making the world seem like a more exciting place."

"I know the type. Larger-than-life. Logan was like that."

"Fletch moved from one job to another. He worked for Dad for a while. Then he went on to some broker-age and investment houses. He loved the adrenaline rush that goes with the financial markets. He was always chasing the next big deal. But adrenaline is like any other drug. Once you get addicted to it, you need more and more of it."

"What happened?"

Jasper went back to the window. "What happened was that when I got out of college, Fletcher suggested we go into business together. We formed Sloan & Associates. We were a good team. I had an instinct for selecting the right projects to back. Fletcher had a gift for talking investors into putting their money into the companies I selected."

"Go on."

"Things went well for a while. Fletcher married a woman named Brenda. They had two sons, Kirby and Paul. I married Rachel Sands. She was a vice-president in the firm."

"That was the marriage based on business interests that you once mentioned?" Olivia asked.

"Yes. It fell apart when Kirby and Paul came to live with me after Fletcher and Brenda were killed in a skiing accident. Rachel wasn't into motherhood, especially not with two young boys who were not even related to her."

"How did you take to fatherhood?"

He turned slightly toward her and propped one shoulder against the steel frame of the window. "It was a little rocky at times, but we all made it."

She gave him a quick smile. "Know what? I'll bet you made a pretty terrific father."

The comment startled him. "Why do you say that?"

She hesitated, as if she had to search for the right

words. "Because you're the type who sticks to things once you've made a commitment. Sticking to the job is most of what parenting is all about."

He frowned. "There's a lot more to being a good father than just sticking to the job."

"No," she said. "There isn't. I can't think of anything more important than just being there, day in and day out, come hell or high water."

The directness of her gaze made him uncomfortable. Jasper was aware of an awkward heat in his face. He hoped he was not doing anything really dumb like turning red.

He cleared his throat. "A few months after Kirby and Paul came to live with me, one of the investment projects for which Fletcher had had primary responsibility and which had been sold to a consortium of investors began to unravel."

"What went wrong?"

"It took me a while to find out," Jasper said softly. "Things nearly blew up in my face before I realized that Fletcher had scammed everyone, including me."

"Oh, Jasper."

"Yes." Absently, he rubbed the back of his neck. "I won't bore you with the details. It took me nearly three months to work through them, myself. But the bottom line was that the investment was a total fraud. The equivalent of a very complicated pyramid scheme. God only knows how Fletcher intended to pull it off. He must have figured he could keep it going like a game of three-card monte."

"What did you do?"

"It cost me a bundle, and I nearly went bankrupt

246

before it was over, but in the end I managed to cancel the deal and pay off the consortium's investment. The clients weren't happy when I told them some mistakes had been made in the original projections, but at least they hadn't been defrauded."

"And after you had cleaned up the mess, you destroyed the evidence of Fletcher's involvement, didn't you?"

"Yes."

She got to her feet and came toward him. Her eyes were deep and knowing. "Because you didn't want Kirby and Paul ever to know that their father had been a swindler and a thief."

"Hell, I had a hard enough time facing the truth, myself. Fletcher was my big brother. I trusted him. Kirby and Paul loved him. I did not want his memory tarnished in their eyes. He was, after all, their father."

She smiled tremulously. "Believe me, I understand."

Something eased slightly inside him. He thought about her desire to protect Nina and Zara and everyone else around her. "Yes, you do, don't you?"

"Tell me, was it after you cleaned up the mess Fletcher left behind that you began doing serious background checks on potential clients?"

He smiled humorlessly. "You could say the incident taught me a lesson. I learned a lot about the importance of information. If you can't trust your big brother, who can you trust?"

She touched his arm, but she said nothing.

"That's it. I burned all of the records I could locate that related to Fletcher's scheme. Until I found that blackmail note in my Jeep this morning, I thought I had erased all the evidence."

"But Uncle Rollie may have found something and filed it."

"Yes." Jasper thought about the cabinets in his basement. "I guess I can't blame him. I've got the same bad habits."

Olivia studied his face. "What's done is done. We'll both be hearing from the blackmailer again soon. We need a new plan."

"True." He brushed his fingers lightly against hers. "We've got a lot of information to work with, and I think I know where I can get some more."

"Where?"

"From Silas at Pri-Con Self-Storage."

She frowned. "You're going back there to talk to him?"

"Yes. Right now, in fact." Jasper shifted her gently out of his path. He went across the room to where his jacket lay on the back of the sofa. "That padlock on Rollie's locker looked new, didn't it?"

"Yes."

"What if the blackmailer broke in, took out whatever was inside, and then installed another lock to make it look as though no one had opened the locker?"

Her eyes widened. "Good thought. If someone removed the entire contents of a locker during the past month, Silas would have been aware of it. Whoever did it would have had to use the elevator to bring everything downstairs and put it into a car or a truck."

"Right. With any luck, Silas will have some kind of

record of the move-ins and move-outs. His office looked fairly well organized. All I need is a name."

Olivia frowned. "Silas didn't mention anyone else asking him about locker four-ninety, though."

"If the blackmailer already knew about Rollie's locker, he wouldn't have had to ask Silas about it. You saw how the system worked. If you know your locker number, you get inside without too many questions."

She glanced at the clock. "I wish I could go with you, but I've got a meeting with Todd and Dixon Haggard."

Jasper walked to the front door. "I'll let you know what I find out from Silas."

"All right." She grabbed her purse, slung it over her shoulder, and hurried after him.

"By the way," Jasper said as they went out into the hall. "I'm going to fire Melwood Gill this afternoon."

Olivia gave a half-strangled yelp of outrage and spun around. Behind the lenses of her sleek glasses Jasper saw green flames leap in her eyes.

"What are you talking about?" She blocked the path to the elevator. "You can't fire poor Mel. I won't allow it."

Jasper reached past her to push the elevator call button. "Olivia, Gill is guilty of more than bad management. He's embezzled over a hundred and fifty thousand dollars from Glow in the past four months. What do you want me to do? Give him a medal?"

She was still staring at him, open-mouthed, when he gently hauled her into the elevator.

20

The chess player considered the new positions the opponent had taken. The unpredictable element in the other's strategy had become more evident. And more difficult to anticipate. It was time to remove one of the pieces on the board.

21

Twenty-four hours. Olivia was still fuming forty-five minutes later as she stood with Todd and Dixon in the old pier warehouse. The two men were poring over the plans for the huge, glowing flag that was to unfurl down from the ceiling behind the speaker's platform.

The argument with Jasper had lasted for the duration of the very brisk walk from her condo to the Light Fantastic studio. She had fought every inch of the way and had at last managed to buy Melwood Gill a twenty-four-hour reprieve.

Fat lot of good it would do, she thought. It was clear that Jasper had already made up his mind.

A hundred and fifty thousand dollars? Melwood

Gill? It was a staggering thought. Jasper had to be wrong.

"Love the lit flag concept, Olivia." Dixon looked up at the heavily timbered ceiling. "I can see it now, unfurling behind Eleanor just as she finishes her speech. The flag is large enough to provide strong visual impact, I hope?"

"It's a really big flag," Olivia assured him. "When it's released, it will fall full length, all the way from that rafter to the floor of the stage behind Ms. Lancaster."

Todd looked dubious. "A glowing flag?"

"Wait'll you see it," Olivia said. "Very dramatic."

He mulled that over. "Won't it look a little tacky?"

She glared at him. "No, it will look patriotic."

"I like it," Dixon said. He shot Todd a cold look. "You don't understand the importance of visuals." He looked at Olivia. "How do the lights work? Will they shine on it?"

"No, this is very high-tech. We've used some of the latest and greatest gadgetry from Glow, Inc. The red, white, and blue electroluminescent fibers are woven right into the fabric of the flag. The audience will see glowing red and white stripes and a lighted blue background behind the stars."

"Fantastic." Dixon looked impressed. "At the finale of the speech, all the lights in the room go out simultaneously. Then the lighted flag descends full length behind Eleanor."

"That's the idea," Olivia agreed. "The effect will be accented with music. A single flip of the switch on the control panel behind the curtain makes it all happen."

"She'll be framed in the red, white, and blue glow

of the American flag." Dixon nodded, pleased. "Perfect."

"She's running for governor, not president," Todd said mildly.

Dixon scowled. "Stick to writing her speeches, Chantry. I'll handle her image."

Todd shrugged. "A politician who looks overly ambitious can turn off voters."

"We want to establish the feeling that Eleanor is a future leader for this country," Dixon snapped. "It will be a great photo op for the press."

Todd's jaw tightened. "This flag-and-music thing sounds a little gimmicky to me."

Dixon gave him a scornful look. "Welcome to the wonderful world of the modern media campaign. No such thing as too many special effects."

"I just don't want the bells and whistles to detract from the message," Todd said.

"She can't implement her agenda if we don't get her elected, now, can she?" Dixon turned back to Olivia. His eyes still smoldered with anger, but his voice did not betray it. "I like it. We'll go with your plans."

Todd said nothing, but he did not argue.

Olivia cleared her throat politely. "If you're satisfied, I'd like to conclude this meeting. I've got a big event scheduled for tomorrow night. We're rather busy back at the studio."

Dixon nodded. "That would be the Camelot Blue launch?"

"Right."

He glanced at his watch. "We'll see you there. Eleanor cleared her schedule so that she could attend."

I'll just bet she did, Olivia thought. And so would her rivals, if they could get invitations. That many monied people in one place at one time would be an irresistible lure to all of the candidates.

She got back to her office fifteen minutes later. The seat of her chair was heaped with faxes and phone messages. She had barely started through them when Zara put her head around the door.

"I've finished my list."

Olivia looked up. "What list?" Then it all came back in a flash. She managed a smile. "Oh, yes. Of course. Your list."

Zara walked into the office. Her eyes shone with satisfaction. "I had to pull out my old press clippings to get some of these names. Brought back a lot of old memories, I can tell you. But I think I've got everyone."

Olivia decided not to inform Zara that the list-making endeavor had probably been a total waste of time because the focus of the investigation had shifted. She made an effort to appear enthusiastic.

"Great," she said. "Give it to me, and I'll pass it along to Jasper. He'll contact his private investigator."

"My money is on Beatrice Hanford." Zara handed Olivia a thick sheaf of neatly typed pages that had been stapled together at the corner. "She was always insanely jealous of me. It got worse after I got the part of Sybil on *Crystal Cove*."

"I'll tell Jasper to put Beatrice Hanford at the top of the list." She hesitated. "You haven't had any more messages from the blackmailer, have you?"

"No, thank heavens. But I'm sure it's only a matter of time."

It was more likely that the extortionist had turned his attention to his juicier prey, Olivia thought. But she said nothing. She had a feeling that Zara would be disappointed if she found out that the blackmailer had lost interest in her.

Olivia dropped Zara's list into her satchel. "Everything set for our staff to start work first thing in the morning at the Enfield Mansion?"

"Yes. I've also talked to the manager of the catering company to make certain that there were no glitches there."

"Thanks. Send Bolivar in here, will you? I want to go over the lighting plans one more time."

"Right away." Zara paused in the doorway. "Did I tell you that your mother called last night?"

"No." Olivia went back to her pile of messages.

"We had a lovely chat. She wanted to know how things were going at Glow."

Olivia looked up, frowning. "Why didn't she call me, in that case?"

"Because," Zara said pointedly, "she wanted to know, specifically, what was going on between you and Jasper Sloan, and she was pretty sure she wouldn't get the whole truth out of you."

Olivia drummed her fingers on the desktop. "Someone blabbed. Aunt Rose, probably."

"Could have been any number of people, knowing this family." Zara gave her a commiserating smile. "Don't worry, dear. I downplayed the gossip as much as I could. Told her not to worry."

Olivia sighed. "Everything okay down in Tucson?"

"Oh, yes. Candace was a trifle annoyed with your father because he played golf yesterday without his hat. She says she's always having to remind him to wear sunscreen and a hat when he goes out on the course."

"His hat." Olivia heard a crackling sound.

She looked down and saw that she had just crumpled a yellow sticky note in one hand. She did not see the message that was scrawled on it.

What she saw was a sudden, sharp mental image of the crushable, wide-brimmed hat her mother had given to her father to carry in his back pocket. She had bought it for him after the dermatologist had removed some rough patches of skin caused by exposure to the sun. The diagnosis was an extremely common one, actinic keratoses. Not dangerous, but left untreated such patches could eventually change into skin cancers.

Melwood Gill had been badly shaken by a recent brush with skin cancer.

Melwood Gill, blackmailer? *Impossible*. Not Melwood. She was leaping to wild conclusions. Intuition was all well and good, but you couldn't rely on it for something as vitally important as this.

Logic was needed here.

Jasper's words echoed in her ears. *Blackmail is always personal.*

The blackmailer knew a lot about both her schedule and Jasper's. He had information that had probably been known only to Rollie. Melwood had worked at Glow for more than twenty years. Rollie had relied on him. Given his position in the accounting department, it was likely that Melwood knew more about Rollie and Glow, Inc., than anyone else in the company. If he *had* been embezzling funds for several months, there was no telling how much snooping he had done.

Anyone who was capable of embezzling from an employer who trusted him was capable of going through a dead man's files.

Capable of blackmail?

"Olivia?" Zara looked concerned. "Something wrong, dear?"

"No." Olivia forced a quick, reassuring smile. "Nothing. I was just thinking about tomorrow night."

"Don't worry. The Camelot Blue event will be a smashing success. You'll see." Zara wafted out through the door, silk scarf trailing behind her.

Olivia waited until she was alone. Then she snatched up the phone.

"Mr. Sloan's office."

"Aunt Rose, it's me, Olivia. This is going to seem like a bizarre question, but I was wondering if you've ever noticed Melwood Gill wearing a hat since he had his skin cancer surgery?"

"A hat? Well, yes, of course. The surgery gave him quite a scare, you know. He told me that he's extremely careful these days. He never goes outside without first putting on sunscreen and a hat."

"Have you ever actually *seen* him in a hat?"

"Heavens yes. He has a couple of those soft, crushable types in his office. You, know, the kind people sometimes wear on boats. I've noticed that he generally puts one in his back pocket when he's getting ready to leave the building. Why do you ask?"

Olivia's mouth went dry. One step at a time here, she thought. Keep the logic straight. "I found a hat matching that description on my way out of Glow the other day. I remembered that Dad wears one a lot down in Tucson because of the sun. It crossed my mind that Melwood would have gotten the same advice and that the hat I found might belong to him."

Weak, Olivia, very weak.

Fortunately Rose did not appear to notice.

"I can ask him, if you like."

"No." Olivia closed her eyes and forced herself to sound calm and casual. "No need to do that. I'll drop it off in the accounting department next time I'm in the building. Thanks, Aunt Rose."

Olivia hung up the phone and sprawled back in her chair, thinking furiously. She was making too many wild assumptions. She was probably going off the deep end here. Jasper was already convinced that Gill was an embezzler. She definitely did not want to provide further ammunition to be used against Melwood unless she was absolutely certain that he was guilty.

There was one more thing she could easily check, she realized. If it was Melwood she had run down with the platform truck this morning then he would have been out of the office at the same time that she was at Pri-Con Self-Storage.

She picked up the phone and tapped out the number of the Glow accounting department. A crisp, precise voice answered on the other end of the line.

"Accounting. Barry Chantry here."

"Cousin Barry? It's Olivia."

"Hi, cuz. What's up?"

"Pretty busy here at Light Fantastic. Listen, I've got a quick question. This is going to seem a little weird, but I was wondering if you noticed if Melwood Gill was out of the office for a while this morning."

"Gill? Yeah, I think he said something about having a doctor's appointment. Why?"

"Nothing." Olivia forced herself to breathe. "I'm just a little worried about him, that's all. The transfer and all, you know."

"Gill's always been a little on the tense side," Barry said conversationally. "Got worse after that brush with skin cancer. But the transfer really agitated him."

"Thanks, Barry. Give my love to Millie and the twins."

"Will do. Say, anything to the gossip about you and Sloan?"

"You know better than to listen to gossip, Barry."

"Sure would make things simpler."

She did not like the fake innocence in his voice. "What would make things simpler?"

"If you and Sloan, uh, you know . . ."

"No, I don't know, Barry. If Sloan and I did what?"

"Got serious. And, like, maybe even got married."

"Barry."

"Well, you know, it would sorta fulfill Uncle Rollie's dream of keeping Glow a family-owned company."

"Good-bye, Barry." Olivia hung up before Barry could make further suggestions on the subject of keeping Glow in the family.

She sat for a while, thinking. After a few minutes she got up to prepare another infusion of caffeine.

There were a lot of questions that had to be answered before she made a move, she decided, as she spooned dark French roast coffee into the filter cone. The biggest one of all, assuming Melwood was the blackmailer, was how had he gotten hold of Rollie's files and what had he done with them?

She thought about the fire in her uncle's study. It had occurred only a day after news of Rollie's death had reached Seattle. Melwood Gill? He had been among the first to know that his employer was dead.

Icy adrenaline shot through her. Everyone said that poor Melwood was just not himself these days.

The phone rang again before she could finish her ruminations. She picked up the receiver.

"Light Fantastic. This is Olivia."

"Hi, Olivia. Andy Andrews of *Hard Currency* here."

"Andrews?" Olivia pulled herself out of the morbid maze of speculation that swirled in her brain. "You've got a lot of nerve calling me after that Foil Town crack in your newsletter."

"Where's your sense of humor, Olivia?" Andy chuckled. "I thought you'd appreciate the mention."

"I'm supposed to appreciate Foil Town? Give me a break."

"Sorry," Andy said casually. "Just trying to add a little punch to the article. But Foil Town, as we say in the business, is yesterday's news. I'm calling about tomorrow's."

"Which is?" Olivia asked cautiously.

"Talk to me about what happened to Logan Dane's

paintings after his death, and I promise that when I do the piece on the Camelot Blue launch party I'll make it sound like the event was staged by Disney."

Olivia tightened her hand around the phone. "I'll give you the same answer I give everyone else. When it comes to the subject of Logan Dane, I have absolutely no comment."

"Is it true that you've got his pictures stored someplace and you're selling them off real slow so as not to flood the market and drive down the prices?"

"Good-bye, Andy." Olivia tossed the phone back into the cradle.

She wondered if Crawford Lee Wilder's version of the legend of Logan Dane was going to haunt her for the rest of her life.

Jasper looked at Todd. "Don't get me wrong. I'm glad you came by the office to introduce yourself. I was just wondering if the reason you're here is because you're worried about the future of Glow, Inc., or because you're concerned about your sister?"

"What do you think?" Todd did not take the seat that Jasper had offered. He went to stand at the office window, instead. "Just because most of the Chantrys you've met so far seem more concerned about their jobs and their Glow pensions, doesn't mean everyone is."

"I'm glad to hear that." Jasper leaned back in his chair. "Makes a change."

Todd shot him a quick, annoyed glance before turning back to the window. "It's not that they don't care about her, you know. It's just that they all think she can take care of herself. They expect her to look after them, not vice-versa."

"I got that impression," Jasper said dryly.

"A lot of it is Uncle's Rollie's fault. He always said that she inherited his head for business." Todd's jaw tightened. "He was right. But Olivia never wanted to take over Glow. She loves Light Fantastic."

"It suits her."

"Uncle Rollie knew that. But from the time she was little he drilled it into her that, after he was gone, she was supposed to make certain that Glow stayed in the family. It was a big burden to put on a kid's shoulders."

"Have you considered the possibility that in the end he decided not to stick her with the full responsibility for Glow, after all?" Jasper asked quietly. "Maybe that's why he did the deal with me. Maybe it was a way of letting her off the hook."

Todd's eyes narrowed. "That doesn't make any sense. Uncle Rollie intended to pay off the financing you arranged for him. He never intended for you to inherit half of Glow."

"Fifty-one percent," Jasper corrected softly. "And bear in mind, Rollie was eighty-three years old. Who knows what he intended? I can tell you one thing, though."

"What's that?"

"Rollie was in no hurry to get out from under the loan I made him. By the terms of our contract, the first payments on the principal were not even scheduled to begin for another two years. All the payments he made before he died were interest only."

"Why did you agree to that?"

Jasper shrugged. "Felt like it. I've always had a good sense of timing when it comes to business."

"Your timing was pretty damn good in this case, wasn't it?" Todd watched him warily. "You wound up owning half of a company that's set to make a lot of money in the years ahead."

"Fifty-one percent," Jasper said. "I own a little more than half of the company. Why do I have to keep reminding everyone?"

At seven that evening Jasper walked into the Light Fantastic studio with a pile of take-out boxes in his hands.

Bolivar intercepted him within ten feet of the door.

"Please tell me there's a pizza in one of those boxes," he said.

"Bottom container. Help yourself."

Bernie and Matty loomed in his path. Both gazed at the stack in his arms with longing eyes. He handed them each a take-out box. "Focaccia sandwiches."

"Great." Bernie tore into his container with relish.

"Mr. Sloan." Zara gave him her Sybil smile. "How lovely to see you this evening. I don't suppose—?"

"Phad Thai. Medium spicy."

"One of my favorites," she murmured, relieving him of another box.

By the time he walked through the door of Olivia's office, he was down to one box of chilled buckwheat noodles with sea vegetables, wasabi, and dipping sauce.

She peered at him through her designer glasses as he cleared a place on the corner of her desk. He put down the box and raised the lid.

"What are you doing here?" she asked as he placed two packets of chopsticks and some napkins on the desk.

"Feeding you. Have you noticed that I do that a lot these days?"

"Why?"

"It's dinnertime."

She glanced at her watch and frowned. "Good grief. I didn't realize. We've been swamped getting ready for tomorrow night. I'd better tell the others to take a break."

"They are on break even as we speak." He pulled up a chair.

"Oh." she examined the contents of the box with deep interest. "What have you got there?"

"Noodles and seaweed." He handed her a set of chopsticks.

"Thanks." She put down the papers she had been working on and dug in with the chopsticks. "Where have you been all afternoon?"

"Long story." He picked up his own chopsticks. "We need to talk."

"So talk," she said around a mouthful of noodles dipped in sauce and hot green wasabi paste. "Did you have any luck with the Pri-Con Self-Storage attendant?"

"Silas was very informative in his own way." Jasper dipped some of the noodles into the tamari-laced sauce. "He said there have been no move-outs from the fourth floor in at least two months. And he was pretty adamant about the fact that no one could have removed the entire contents of a locker without his knowing about it."

"So what happened to the stuff Uncle Rollie stashed in locker number four-ninety?"

Jasper shook his head. "We don't even know for certain that he had anything stored in that damned locker."

"Why pay rent on a locker he never used?"

"He may have had plans to put something in there and never got around to doing it."

Silence fell.

"Jasper?"

Something in her tone of voice made him look at her very sharply. She was watching him with enigmatic eyes. "What is it?"

"I had a wild thought this afternoon. I did a little checking. I'm still not sure, and I've got absolutely no proof, but . . ."

"Talk fast."

"Two words. Melwood Gill."

Jasper hesitated while he assimilated that. "Correct me if I'm wrong, but I was under the impression that it was your stated goal in life to protect poor Melwood."

She shifted uncomfortably. "I admit he seems a little pathetic. And he hasn't been himself for the past few months."

"He's an embezzler. What makes you think he's also into blackmail?"

"His hat."

22

Olivia gazed unhappily out the rain-spattered windshield as Jasper drove her car through the quiet streets of Queen Anne. The comfortable, well-established homes and dignified brick-faced apartment buildings climbed the hillside overlooking downtown and Elliott Bay. It was not the richest neighborhood in the city, but Olivia knew that there was a fair amount of wealth tucked away here and there in the cul-de-sacs and lanes of Queen Anne.

"Melwood has lived here for as long as I can remember," Olivia said. "He once told me that the house belonged to his parents. He inherited it." She was chattering, she thought. A sure sign of nervousness. She clenched her back teeth together.

Jasper did not look at her as he navigated the winding street. "You okay?"

"Yes. Sort of." The truth was, the prospect of confronting Melwood Gill was proving to be far more disturbing than she had anticipated. "How do you look a person you've known for years in the eye and ask him if he's blackmailing you?"

"Simple. Start by telling him that we can prove he's been embezzling from Glow for months. While he's still dealing with the shock of knowing that he's been found out, we'll hit him with the blackmail questions. My guess is Gill will crumple fast."

Jasper's words were imbued with a calm ruthlessness that stunned her. She turned her head quickly to stare at him. His face was hard and unyielding in the last light of the dying day.

Why was she so shocked? she wondered. Her intuition had warned her about this side of his nature. She had caught glimpses of it from time to time. She could not let a couple of nights of great sex blind her to his basic nature. She crossed her arms and hugged herself.

"You've done this kind of thing before, I take it?" she asked.

"It happens in business."

She shivered. "It's never happened to me in my business."

"It has now," Jasper said softly.

She could not think of anything to say to that. "Next right."

Jasper turned the corner. And drove immediately into a space at the curb.

"Oh, my God." Olivia stared at the scene through the windshield.

The flashing lights of the ambulance and the police cruiser were reflected on the rain-slick street. People stood in small clusters, some with umbrellas, watching the activity with the morbid fascination reserved for crime and accident scenes.

Olivia saw a medic close the door of the aid car and get into the driver's seat. A terrible sense of certainty settled into her stomach.

"Melwood's house is that narrow, two-story one on the left. You don't suppose . . . ?" She could not finish the question.

"Be a hell of a coincidence, wouldn't it?" Jasper switched off the engine, pocketed the keys, and got out of the car. "I'll be right back."

With his usual air of quiet authority, he started toward the nearest uniformed officer.

Olivia shoved open her own door and started after him. She paused when she overheard a nearby conversation among two onlookers.

". . . wasn't paying attention. Never even saw the car. Hasn't been himself lately, you know."

Olivia stopped. Jasper was already talking to the cops. She might as well see what the neighbors had to say.

"What happened?" she asked a middle-aged woman.

"Hit-and-run," the woman said. "No one saw it, but we heard the most ghastly thud. My husband is the one who called nine-one-one."

"Who was hit?"

"Melwood Gill." The woman pointed at the unlit windows of the narrow house in the middle of the block. "Lived over there. He always takes his walk at this time of night in the summer months. Regular as clockwork."

Olivia tightened her grasp on the strap of her shoulder bag. Jasper had finished his conversation with the officer. He was walking back toward her.

"*Lived?*" Olivia repeated carefully. "Past tense?"

The woman looked at her. "I heard someone say poor Melwood was killed instantly."

Forty minutes later, Jasper parked Olivia's car in her slot in the condominium building garage. The deeply troubled look on her face made him uneasy. She had said very little since learning of Melwood Gill's death. He knew she was going over the various possibilities and coming to the same unpleasant conclusions that he had reached.

They walked to the elevator in silence. A short while later they stepped out of the cab into the hall. He took the key from her hand and shoved it into the lock.

"I think we both need a drink," he said.

He went into the kitchen to rummage through her cupboards. He knew he had seen a small bottle of cognac in one of them.

Olivia stood watching him from the other side of the counter. "I still can't believe it. Hit-and-run."

"Yes." He found the cognac and opened it. "There will be an investigation. But if the driver doesn't turn himself or herself in, it could be a long time, if ever, before the cops locate the owner of the car."

"You're thinking what I'm thinking, aren't you?"

"Probably." He finished pouring the cognac into

two small glasses and turned to face her. He met her shadowed eyes through the opening above the kitchen counter. "But we could both be wrong. It really could have been an accident."

She nodded slowly. "There's a general consensus of opinion that Melwood hadn't been himself for a while. He might not have been paying attention when he took his evening walk tonight. A drunk driver might have hit him and then fled the scene. Accidents happen."

"So do coincidences," Jasper said quietly. "But I don't trust them. Gill was an embezzler and possibly a blackmailer. He could have been deliberately run down by someone who had a reason to want him dead."

Olivia took the glass of cognac from him. It trembled ever so slightly in her hand. "Someone like you or me or Aunt Zara, you mean."

"Not you and not me." He leaned back against the counter. "We have each other for an alibi."

"Not Zara, either," Olivia said with absolute conviction. "I know it wasn't her. She didn't have a clue that we suspected Melwood. She's still hoping that the blackmailer is one of her old rivals."

"What we don't know is how many other people might have been on Melwood's list of blackmail victims."

"True." She took a sip of the cognac and looked at him very steadily. "But if he was getting the damaging information from Uncle Rollie's files, then we have to assume that, if there were any more victims, they're either family or closely tied to Glow, Inc."

"Could be a long list."

Olivia put down her glass and propped her elbows on the counter. "I realize I'm biased, but I honestly cannot imagine anyone in my family resorting to murder to stop someone like Melwood Gill."

"It doesn't have to be a family member. As you said, it could be someone who is somehow tied to Glow, Inc. Someone with whom Rollie did business, perhaps."

She met his eyes. "What are we going to do now?"

"The first step," Jasper said, "is to take a look at Melwood Gill's personal files."

She frowned. "His office files? I doubt that Melwood would have kept any incriminating evidence at Glow."

"Not his office files," Jasper said deliberately. "The ones he kept in his house."

"What makes you think there are any?"

Jasper finished the cognac and set the glass down on the counter. "I know a fellow obsessive-compulsive filer when I meet one."

Shortly after one o'clock in the morning Olivia stood, shivering, on Melwood Gill's back step and watched as Jasper put a gloved fist through the window he had just finished taping.

There was a soft, muffled crunch and a few tinkling sounds, but no telltale crash of breaking glass. The tape held most of the shards in place.

"I sure hope you're right about Melwood never having installed an alarm system," Olivia muttered.

"If he had he would have plastered those little stickers the security companies give you on every door and window."

"How do you know that?"

"Because the stickers warning the crooks that there's an alarm system are the first line of defense,"

Jasper said patiently. "In fact, some people don't go any farther than putting on the stickers."

"Yes, but—" She broke off when he opened the door and moved quietly into the kitchen.

This was a very bad idea. She knew it in her bones.

But she also knew that there was nothing else she could do except follow Jasper inside. It had not been easy convincing him to allow her to accompany him on this jaunt. If she got cold feet now, he would probably spend the rest of the night saying *I-told-you-so*.

Ahead of her in the gloom, Jasper was a large, dark shadow. He was already moving silently through the kitchen into the front room. She followed quickly, wincing when her rubber-soled shoes made tiny squeaking sounds on the vinyl tile floor.

Jasper halted briefly in the living room. Olivia stopped just behind him and surveyed the surroundings. The curtains had been left open. Enough light filtered in from the street to reveal a sofa, two armchairs, and a television set. There was a shabby, out-of-date feel to the room, as if no one had bothered to redecorate in a very long time.

"Melwood's wife died a few years ago," Olivia said. "He never remarried. Aunt Rose said he asked a couple of the women who work at Glow out to dinner, but it was always a disaster."

"Why?"

"Aunt Rose said the women claimed it was like dating a robot. I gathered Melwood was not exactly the spontaneous type."

She saw Jasper turn his head to look at her in the shadows, but he said nothing. He led the way down a thinly carpeted hall. They passed a bathroom. At the end of the corridor they found a small room cloaked in darkness. The curtains had been drawn across the windows, cutting off the street light.

There was a small *snick*. An instant later the pencil-thin beam from Jasper's flashlight pierced the shadows. For a moment Olivia could only stare, uncomprehending, at the scene of chaos.

Then she realized that she was looking at a home office that had been turned upside down. File cabinets stood open. Folders full of papers littered the floor. The drawers of the desk had been emptied. The contents were strewn across the rug.

"Damn," Jasper said softly. "Looks like someone got here ahead of us."

Olivia heard a small squeak.

"Your shoes?" Jasper whispered.

"No." Her mouth went dry. "The ceiling, I think."

"I was afraid of that." He flicked off the flashlight and went to stand, motionless, in the doorway.

The squeak sounded again. Olivia stopped breathing for a few seconds.

Whoever had ransacked Melwood's office was still in the house.

Jasper shifted slightly in the dark opening. He glanced back at her and hesitated. Olivia read his intentions as surely as if he had sent her a telepathic message. He wanted to go after whoever was prowling around upstairs, but he was afraid to leave her alone down here.

Anger surged through her. She was not about to let him risk his neck in such a foolish stunt. She grabbed his arm and shook her head emphatically, mouthing two words. "No way."

He glanced back out into the darkened hall. She detected a hint of something that bordered on a predatory eagerness in him. But he finally nodded reluctantly. She let out a small sigh of relief, aware that her presence had been the deciding factor. Jasper did not want to take any chances with her safety.

He reached for her hand. She gave it to him. He tugged her very close and put his mouth on her ear.

"Out. The way we came in."

She gave a quick, jerky nod to indicate that she understood.

Together they eased back down the hall. The dark, jagged outline of the staircase loomed to the right.

Olivia caught the shadowy movement midway up the steps out of the corner of her eye. The light from the stairwell window revealed a figure hovering there. He held a large, heavy-looking object in his upraised hands.

"Jasper."

He was already in motion, shoving her hard to the side. She fetched up against the wall with enough force to make her gasp.

She watched helplessly as Jasper launched himself at the figure on the stairs. The two collided with a heavy, dull thud halfway up the steps.

There was a solid crunch as the object in the prowler's hands flew over the side of the banister and struck the floor.

Olivia scrambled out of the way as Jasper and the prowler tumbled down the steps. She caught a glimpse of a face with distorted, deformed features. Muttered grunts were followed by a muffled gasp.

Frantically she looked around, searching for something, anything that could be used as a weapon. The large object the prowler had attempted to smash into Jasper's head lay on the floor.

She seized it in both hands and discovered that she was holding a heavy brass planter. She hefted it and then realized to her horror that it was not going to be a simple matter to get a clear shot at the prowler.

Jasper and his opponent shifted positions in the blink of an eye, rolling together across the floor and into the living room. Olivia followed, planter held on high.

It was obvious that Jasper's opponent was bent only on escape. He heaved himself upward, struggling to free himself. Jasper made a wild grab for the back of the man's jacket. The prowler wrenched first one arm and then the other free of the garment and lurched toward the kitchen.

Footsteps pounded on the vinyl floor.

Jasper rolled to his feet, the windbreaker still clutched in his hand. He flung it aside and started toward the kitchen at a dead run. The light from the street gleamed briefly on his face. Olivia saw the mask of intent ferocity etched there.

She ran after him. "Jasper, forget it. You'll never catch him now."

She collided with him on the back step, where he had come to an abrupt halt. There was a jolting thud. Jasper staggered and nearly went down.

"What the hell?" He caught his balance and put a hand to his ribs. He turned to peer at the heavy brass planter she clutched. "I hope the plan was to use that thing on the other guy."

"Of course it was. But you kept getting in the way." Chagrined, Olivia took two steps back into the kitchen and put the planter down on the nearest counter. "Are you all right?"

"Yeah. I think so."

She saw him touch the corner of his mouth with an absentminded gesture as he surveyed the darkened backyard. She was about to pin him down on the subject of personal injury when she heard the first bark.

It was followed by several more in quick succession. She had a sudden vision of the prowler arousing every golden retriever and shih tzu in the neighborhood as he escaped through a series of backyards.

"We'd better get out of here," she said.

"Hang on." He went past her up the steps and into the kitchen.

"Hurry," she whispered when she saw him disappear into the living room.

She cringed when she heard him go swiftly up the stairs. She knew he was checking the rooms above.

After what seemed forever but was probably no more than a couple of minutes, he returned. He had the prowler's windbreaker in his hand. He used it to wipe off the planter. She realized he was removing her fingerprints.

"Let's go," he said when he finished.

He followed her back out onto the step and closed the kitchen door quietly. They went cautiously around to the front of the house. Olivia was relieved to see that no lights had appeared in any of the windows in the neighboring houses. The dog had stopped barking.

When they reached the sidewalk, she had to fight the impulse to break into a run. She made herself match Jasper's sedate but purposeful pace. They clung to the shadows of the trees that lined the street.

She did not draw a deep breath until they rounded the corner and saw her car sitting right where they had left it earlier.

She did not see the blood on Jasper's mouth until she slid into the passenger seat.

"You're hurt." She was suddenly incensed. "You told me you were okay."

"Take it easy." Jasper closed the door, cutting off the light and her view of the blood. "I just sliced the inside of my mouth up a little. It won't show in the morning."

She could have sworn that she saw him wince when he switched on the ignition.

"I'm not worried about how it will look," she said crisply. "I'm concerned about how much damage has been done."

He glanced at her as he pulled away from the curb. "I appreciate that."

His blasé attitude fueled her ire. She opened the glove box, found the small pack of tissues she kept inside, and yanked one out. She handed it to Jasper without a word.

"Thank you."

There was a short silence as he wiped the blood off his chin.

"He could have had a gun," Olivia said finally.

"Yeah."

"You could have been killed."

"I don't think he was any more of an expert at that kind of thing than we are."

She recalled the quick glimpse she'd had of distorted features. "He was enough of an expert to wear a mask made out of half a pair of pantyhose."

"He could have picked up that handy burglary tip by watching television," Jasper said. "I don't think it qualifies him as a pro."

A beat of silence passed.

"He could have been the hit-and-run driver who killed Melwood," Olivia said.

"Could have been." Jasper sounded thoughtful now. "Hit-and-run doesn't seem like a real professional way to murder someone. Too uncertain. The victim might survive."

"Even if he did, he would be seriously injured," Olivia said. "And very likely confined to a hospital for a few days, which would give whoever had tried to murder him some breathing room."

"Good point. But either way, I think we can assume we're not dealing with a professional hit man."

"I guess a real pro wouldn't have left his windbreaker behind." She picked up the black microfiber jacket that Jasper had tossed down onto the seat.

Jasper gave it a sidelong look. "I don't suppose there's anything useful in the pockets?"

"No. They're empty." She leaned forward and held the inside of the collar in the dash lights. The label was decorated with the logo of a familiar New York designer. "Whoever he is, he likes expensive clothes." She sat back. "So what was he doing there?"

"Two options spring to mind," Jasper said. "Either we

ran into the local neighborhood prowler looking for a stereo and a VCR he could fence for drug money or—"

"Or else he was there for the same reason we were," she concluded unhappily. "Looking for a blackmailer's files."

"That about sums it up as far as I can see."

"Good grief. I wonder how many people Melwood Gill was blackmailing?"

"We won't know the answer to that until we find those damned files of Rollie's." Jasper slowed for a red light. "But I think we can assume one thing."

She looked at him. "What's that?"

"The other guy had more time to look around inside Gill's house than we did. The upstairs was torn apart. But whoever I tangled with on those stairs wasn't carrying anything except that brass planter. I don't think he found whatever it was he was looking for."

"In other words, Uncle Rollie's files are still missing."

"Yes."

"But the blackmailer is dead. Surely that takes some of the pressure off all of us."

Jasper shook his head once. "This thing won't be over until we find those files."

Fifteen minutes later, stripped to the waist, Jasper leaned over the sink in Olivia's tiled bath. He splashed more cold water on his face, rinsing off the last traces of blood.

When he was finished, he raised his head and studied his reflection in the mirror. His mouth was not a pretty sight, and he knew he would have a few bruises on his ribs from the stairs, but all in all, not too bad.

With luck, the swollen lip would return to its normal size and shape by morning. He would have to be careful about what he ate for a couple of days, but he would not cause any undue comment in the office.

"What's the verdict?" Olivia asked as she walked back into the bathroom with the roll of paper towels he had ordered.

"The good news is, no black eye in the morning. With luck, I won't have any explaining to do." He ripped off one of the towels and used it to dry his face. "And I didn't even get any blood on your nice white towels."

"I told you not to worry about the towels." She put the roll of paper towels down on the counter. "Are you sure you're all right?"

"Yeah." He wadded up the used towel and tossed it into the waste can. "I'm okay."

She opened the mirrored medicine cabinet and took out a small bottle. "Let me put some of this on your lip."

He eyed the bottle warily. "What is it?"

"Antiseptic." She already had a small ball of cotton in hand and was dampening it with the contents of the bottle.

He grimaced when she dabbed his lip. He was proud of the fact that he managed not to say ouch.

Olivia stepped back and recapped the bottle. She eyed his chest and ribs with an expression of deep concern. Then she made a twirling motion with her hand.

"Turn around."

"Why?"

"I want to see if I did any serious damage with that planter."

He started to grin and then winced when the burning sensation lanced his lower lip. "Don't worry about it. You didn't hit me that hard. I may have a few bruises on my ribs tomorrow, but not because of that damned planter." He reached for his shirt. "It's only a few minutes after one. If I hurry, I can still make the last ferry."

"No."

He paused, one arm in one sleeve. "What?"

She watched him with her deep, luminous eyes. Then she gently touched the side of his face. "You were in a fight tonight. There may have been more damage than you realize."

He raised his brows. "I doubt it. Like I said, a few bruises . . ."

"I don't think you should go all the way back to Bainbridge tonight." Her gaze was very steady. "You could be suffering from shock and not realize it yet."

"Trust me, I'm not in shock."

"I really wish you would stay here where I can keep an eye on you."

He realized that something very important, something that could well turn out to be momentous, was happening. Don't read too much into the situation, he warned himself. Don't say too much, you'll screw it up.

He cleared his throat cautiously. "You could be right. I, uh, think maybe I am in shock."

Her brows knit together above the frames of her glasses. "Do you think you should go to the emergency room?"

"No." He eased his arm very carefully back out of the sleeve. "I think I should go to bed. And so should you. You're the one who has to spend all day tomorrow preparing for the Camelot Blue event."

"Don't remind me." She smiled, apparently satisfied with his decision. "I'll let you finish here in the bathroom. Take your time."

He held his breath as she quietly closed the door behind her. Then he turned to his reflection in the mirror. Don't get the wrong idea just because her nurturing instincts got the better of her tonight, he told himself.

But when he climbed into the pale mint-green sheets a short time later he was still focused on a lot of wrong ideas. Or were they the right ones? he wondered.

He listened to Olivia moving about in the bathroom. After a while she turned off the lights and walked into the darkened bedroom. A white cotton gown drifted around her thighs. He decided that she looked sexier in it than a centerfold model looked in lingerie from Fredericks of Hollywood.

She went to the windows and pulled the curtains open. The jeweled lights of the city glowed behind her as she came to the bed.

Jasper was violently aware of his erection. What the hell was his problem tonight, he thought. It was not as if they had not already made love on more than one occasion. So what if he would be spending the night this time?

But he could not escape the feeling that what was happening between himself and Olivia this evening was fraught with meaning.

He just wished very badly that he knew what that meaning was.

Her scent clouded his brain when she climbed into bed beside him. She leaned over him and brushed her mouth across his.

"You're sure you're all right?" she asked.

"Yeah." He ignored the dull ache in his ribs and reached for her.

"We both need our sleep." She eased gently away and settled herself on her side, giving him her back. "Wake me if you get worried about your ribs."

"I'll do that."

Between his erection, his bruises, and the fraught-with-meaning thing, he knew he could look forward to a very long night.

He savored the warm pleasure of having Olivia's body close to his and forced himself to concentrate on the problem of the missing blackmail files.

But for some unfathomable reason, it was the memory of his close call on the Pelapili cliffs that tugged at him. He had been luckier than Gill, he reflected. He had managed to evade the vehicle that had tried to run him off the road.

It was only a coincidence that the weapon of choice in both instances was a car. It had to be a coincidence. What possible link could there be between the two events?

The search for an answer kept him awake for a long time. Eventually he fell into a restless sleep

Somewhere in his dreams he found himself walking down endless corridors of self-storage lockers.

23

At eight o'clock the following evening Jasper got gingerly out of the cab in front of the Enfield Mansion. He had been right about the bruises on his ribs. They had not improved in the course of what had proved to be a very long day.

"Looks like the Mansion's been taken over by space aliens or somethin'." The cab driver squinted up at Jasper. "Some kinda weird gig goin' on here tonight, huh?"

Jasper glanced at the old Capital Hill house as he removed some cash from his wallet. Every window of the stately two-story mansion glowed with an eerie blue light. "Just your typical software launch party."

The driver examined the surreal scene with an expression of bemused wonder. "Looks kinda like a giant arcade game."

"Perceptive of you to notice." Jasper slipped his wallet back into the inside pocket of his evening jacket.

He walked up a brick path that wound through a garden stuffed with rhododendron bushes to the graceful, colonnaded veranda.

A young man garbed in blue chain mail and a blue tunic emblazoned with the Camelot Blue logo inclined his shaved head. He held an electronic notebook computer in one hand.

"Welcome to the festivities, Sir Knight. May I please have your name?"

"Sloan. Jasper Sloan."

"Ah, yes." The gatekeeper clicked a name. Then he bowed deeply from the waist and swept out an arm. "I bid you enter the world of Camelot Blue, Sir Knight."

"Thanks."

Walking into the wide hall was akin to sinking into the deep end of a bottomless swimming pool. Jasper was enveloped immediately in an unearthly realm.

He was amused, in spite of his sore ribs and generally frustrating day. He had made a bet with himself that Olivia would not be able to top her Silver Galaxy Foods Night event, but he had been wrong.

The entire interior of the mansion was illuminated in the odd, dark turquoise hue that was the Camelot Blue trademark color. A forest of deep azure banners hung from the ceiling. The walls were draped in yards of iridescent blue fabric. Tables were covered in faux blue stone. Even the cushions of the chairs were blue.

Although the unrelenting blue furnishings created a bizarre impression, Jasper realized that the other-worldly sensation was achieved primarily with special effects lighting. He suspected that most of the high-tech fixtures had been "borrowed" from the test labs of Glow, Inc.

Great advertising, he reminded himself. At least, that's what Olivia claimed.

A waiter dressed in a Camelot Blue medieval page costume held out a blue tray. "Hors d'oeuvres, Sir Knight?"

"Thanks. I didn't get dinner." Jasper was relieved to see that the food was not blue.

He piled several canapés onto a napkin and wandered into a ballroom suffused in a hazy blue light.

He recognized the centerpiece of the room. It was the large sword-in-the-stone model he had seen in the Light Fantastic studio. Tonight only the blue gem-stone-studded hilt of the sword was visible. The blade portion was sunk deep into the fake blue stone. The entire assembly pulsed and glowed neon blue.

Computer stations were set up in a circle around the model. Heads were bent intently over screens that flickered with Camelot Blue software products.

Guests, some in futuristic medieval fantasy costume, others in evening dress, swirled around him. Musicians garbed in gleaming blue tunics played on a stage illuminated in a foggy turquoise light. The decibel level of laughter and conversation indicated that the crowd was enjoying itself.

"It's a mock-up of Camelot Blue's new game," said a familiar voice. "The idea is to find the secret code that allows you to pull the sword out of the stone."

Jasper glanced at Todd, who had come up beside him.

Todd was dressed as conservatively as himself in a black evening jacket and tie.

"Bolivar explained the game to me." Jasper selected the canapé on top of his small pile and took a large bite. "Looks like it will be another hit for Camelot Blue."

"Probably. They haven't had a failure yet."

"I know," Jasper said. "That's why Sloan & Associates financed their new product line research four years ago."

Todd shook his head. "I should have guessed. Have you been upstairs?"

"No."

"If you think this is weird, wait until you see what Olivia did on the floor above."

"I'll check it out."

The gold rims of Todd's serious glasses winked in the blue light. "I didn't know you planned to be here tonight."

"I had to see if Olivia could outdo Foil Town."

Todd winced. "Whatever you do, don't call the Silver Galaxy Foods Night event Foil Town in her presence."

"What do you think I am?" Jasper munched down on a cracker. "Stupid?"

Todd did not smile. He appeared to take the question seriously, as if Jasper had asked about a campaign policy issue.

"No. Whatever else you are, Sloan, you aren't stupid."

Jasper decided to change the subject. "Does the fact that you're here tonight mean that Eleanor Lancaster is somewhere in the vicinity?"

Todd studied the crowd with a neutral expression. "Lot of money in this room. It's an ideal venue for Eleanor."

Something cool and distant in his voice caught Jasper's attention. He wondered if there had been a few ripples on the seas of the perfect political relationship. He downed the rest of his cracker. "Campaign looks like it's going well. Picking up a lot of momentum."

"And money." Todd took a swallow from the glass in his hand. "Eleanor is going straight to the governor's office in November. And after that there's no reason she shouldn't eventually take a look at running for the White House."

Jasper whistled soundlessly. "Big plans."

"Very big."

"Takes a lot of money to get all the way to Washington, D.C."

"She can pull it in." Todd's jaw hardened. He took another swallow from his glass. "She's very, very focused."

"Guess that's what it requires to be president."

"Yes. If you're going to be a winner like Eleanor, everything else in your life has to take a back seat."

He wasn't the most intuitive person on the planet, Jasper told himself, but even he could feel the undercurrents here.

"Something wrong, Todd?"

"No." Todd smiled without a trace of amusement. "Everything's right on schedule. Including me."

Jasper was wondering how far to push, when another man shouldered his way through a nearby knot of guests. It was obvious from the slow, careful way he moved and the hot, glittery look in his eyes that he had started drinking before he had arrived at the party.

"Hello, Dixon." Todd glanced quickly at Jasper. "Have you met Dixon Haggard? Eleanor Lancaster's campaign manager. Dixon, this is Jasper Sloan. The co-owner of Glow, Inc."

"Haggard." Jasper nodded slightly.

"Sloan." The single word was slightly slurred. "Didn't know you'd be here tonight. Quite a production, isn't it?"

"It's definitely got the Light Fantastic stamp all over it," Jasper agreed. "Where's the candidate?"

"Over there." Dixon waved the glass in his hand in a vague manner to indicate a spot on the other side of the room. "Talking to some VIPs from Camelot Blue. Can't waste a golden opportunity like this to raise a few bucks."

There was no quiet, melancholic resignation in Dixon's voice as there had been in Todd's, just a willing, eager acceptance of the facts. Politics was fueled with money. Everyone knew that. But maybe, Jasper reflected, it took idealists such as Todd a little longer to realize exactly what that fact meant in the real world.

He looked across the heads of the crowd and saw a ring of people gathered around the statuesque figure of Eleanor Lancaster. His first thought surprised him. *She looks just like she does on TV.*

Her black hair gleamed a metallic blue in the eerie lights. The air around her seemed to shimmer with energy. It was obvious even from where Jasper stood that everyone in the small group clustered near her was hanging on every word.

Dixon shoved a hand into the pocket of his evening trousers and slurped blue-tinted champagne. "Been upstairs yet?"

"No. I hear it's interesting up there."

Dixon made a face. "Light Fantastic turned the entire floor into a neon arcade. Not exactly the height of sophistication."

"Olivia has a policy of giving her clients exactly what they want," Jasper said quietly. "It's good business. Sort of like a politician getting herself invited to a shindig like this so that she can troll for financial donors."

Todd gave him a sharp, slightly startled look but said nothing.

Dixon's eyes narrowed. "Okay, I get your point. Business is business. I notice that Sean Dane and his family are not here tonight. I know for a fact that they were invited. Guess it's no surprise they stayed away, given their history with Olivia."

Todd stiffened visibly. He looked at Dixon with ill-concealed annoyance. "The Danes owe my sister a hell of a lot."

"No shit?" Dixon gave him a mockingly innocent look of inquiry. "Thought they held her responsible for driving Logan Dane to his death."

"Dane got drunk and did something stupid. He was responsible for his own death," Todd said.

Dixon shrugged as if the matter were supremely

unimportant. "Sorry. Didn't mean to step on any toes."

"Bullshit," Todd said very softly.

Dixon ignored him. Perhaps he had not heard the succinct comment.

Jasper looked at Todd. "Why do you say the Danes owe Olivia?"

Todd's jaw jerked slightly. "If it hadn't been for her, they wouldn't have been able to cash in on Logan Dane's reputation during the past three years."

Dixon looked briefly interested in the conversation again. Money, Jasper noticed, had a way of grabbing his attention.

"What do you mean?" Dixon demanded.

"One of the little details that Crawford Lee Wilder conveniently left out of his piece on Olivia," Todd said, "is the fact that right after Dane's funeral she gave every single one of his paintings in her possession to the Dane family. Sean and the others have been selling off Logan's pictures very quietly ever since. They've made a fortune."

Dixon scowled. "That's not the way I heard it."

"Like everyone else, you bought the Crawford Lee Wilder version of the Logan Dane legend." Todd looked Dixon up and down with unmistakable disgust. "Wilder was right on one point. Dane did have a will. He left everything to Olivia, including his unsold paintings. At the time of his death, his work had just begun to escalate in value. Nobody knew better than Olivia did how much his stuff would be worth in a few years."

Dixon's features twisted in disbelief. "You're telling me she gave every damn one of those pictures to Dane's relatives?"

"Yes. Olivia likes money as much as anyone else, but unlike some people, there are a lot of things she won't do to get it." Todd turned on his heel and walked away into the crowd.

"Sonofabitch." Dixon sounded genuinely awed. "We must be talking about a couple of million bucks worth of art."

"That might have been the value of the pictures at the time of Dane's death." Jasper watched Todd's rigidly set shoulders. "But they would be worth four or five times that amount now. Even more in the future."

"Nobody gives away that kind of cash." Dixon shook his head. "Nobody. I can't believe Olivia would have been fool enough to do it."

"Olivia is no fool." Jasper felt anger coil deep inside. "But she does make her decisions on the basis of values rather than money."

Dixon's brow furrowed in confusion. "What the hell are you talking about?"

"Forget it. The subject of values is probably a little too high-concept for you, Haggard. Especially after a few drinks."

In his inebriated state, Dixon was having difficulty following the thread of the conversation. Jasper waited patiently until a belligerent expression belatedly dawned in the other man's eyes.

"Are you insulting me, you bastard?" Dixon finally managed.

"If you can't figure that out, you've definitely had one too many, Dixon."

Jasper turned and made his way out into the hall to hunt for Olivia. He did not look back.

At the foot of the wide blue-lit staircase he paused to contemplate the murky azure glow that emanated from the next level. A steady stream of animated guests moved between the two floors. He wondered which room housed Merlin's Cave.

He had a special attachment to that cave, he thought. He would never forget his first sight of Olivia floating toward him through eerily lit vapor.

He went down the hall behind the staircase, glancing into various rooms. Some glowed blue and were in use as smaller, quieter spaces for guests to gather. Others were closed to the public.

The door of one of the closed rooms opened just as Jasper walked past. Olivia, dressed in a long, Camelot Blue, off-the-shoulder gown, stepped out of a pantry closet. She had what looked to be a stack of blue tunics in one hand. She did not see him until she collided with him.

"Jasper."

He caught her arm and gently steadied her. "Congratulations on another big success."

She ignored that to glare at him as she pushed her glasses more firmly back on her nose. "It's about time you got here. I tried to call you every time I had a free second this afternoon. Aunt Rose always said you were either out of the office or couldn't be disturbed."

"I was a little busy today."

She gave him a knowing look. "Because of Melwood's death?"

"Among other things. I spent most of the morning going through Gill's desk and his computer files."

Her eyes widened eagerly. "Find anything?"

"No. But I'm not what anyone could call an expert hacker. If Gill hid something deep in his computer files, I probably wouldn't be able to find it."

"We can't exactly call in a real hacker, can we?"

"No. We'd have to tell him what we're looking for, and that means one more person would know what was going on."

"This is so complicated," she muttered.

"It gets worse. I also talked to the police."

She searched his face. "Did they tell you anything?"

"I pulled the concerned employer routine. One of the detectives bought it. I was told that the car that killed Gill had been found. An old Cadillac."

"What a break." Olivia brightened. "I don't suppose they told you who owns it?"

"An elderly couple in Ballard."

"An elderly couple?" Olivia's face fell. "But that doesn't make any sense. Why would—"

"The car was stolen," Jasper explained. "And abandoned after the crime. Everything inside had been wiped clean. No prints. No evidence."

"That must have aroused the cops' suspicions."

"At the moment they're working on the theory that whoever stole the Cadillac was probably drunk or high on drugs. When the driver realized he had accidentally hit someone, he ditched the car and ran. Unless he sobers up and turns himself in, odds of finding him are not real good."

She groaned. "And probably even worse if he deliberately set out to kill Melwood."

"Which we don't know for certain yet," Jasper said carefully.

Her hand clenched tightly around the blue tunics. "We must locate Uncle Rollie's missing files. Whoever killed Melwood is obviously looking for them, too. We can't let him find them first."

"We'll find them," Jasper said quietly. "Between the two of us we've got more information on both Gill and Rollie than the blackmailer could possibly have. That gives us an edge."

"What do you mean?"

Jasper shrugged. "In the end the guy with the most information usually wins. Provided he uses it properly."

She eyed him narrowly. "Is that a bit of Sloan management theory?"

"You could say that."

"Do you obsessive-compulsive filers go to special schools? Is there a degree in information hoarding?"

He stopped smiling and flattened his hand against the wall behind her head. "Olivia, I did a lot of thinking today while I went through Gill's desk. There is one tiny scrap of information that we've been ignoring."

"What's that?"

"Silas at Pri-Con told us that he rented the last empty locker on the fourth floor about a month ago, remember?"

She nodded. "So?"

"Rollie died about a month ago."

She stared at him. "Oh, my God, you don't think—?"

"What if," Jasper said slowly, "whoever took those files rented that last locker? What if those files were never removed from the building? What if the blackmailer transferred them into another locker?"

"It would certainly explain why Silas never saw anyone empty out an entire locker." Her eyes lit with excitement. "Jasper, it's a brilliant thought. But there are a lot of *what ifs* involved."

"Yes. But they can be checked out fairly easily."

"Am I interrupting anything here?" Todd asked dryly.

Olivia looked around Jasper's shoulder. "Hi, Todd."

Jasper turned to look at Todd. "Your sister and I were just having a short business meeting about what to do in the accounting department now that Melwood Gill is gone."

"Don't let me stop you." Todd took a swallow from his glass. "Too bad about poor old Gill. Quincy and Percy said he hadn't been himself for several months."

"That's true." Olivia frowned. "Todd, how much have you had to drink tonight?"

"Don't worry about it, big sister." Todd smiled grimly. "I'm not driving."

Olivia's eyes filled with growing concern. "You never have more than a couple of glasses of anything. What's wrong?"

"Special occasion." Todd hoisted his glass in a mocking salute. "You may as well be the first to know. There won't be an engagement announcement after the election, after all."

"Oh, Todd." Olivia sighed. "I'm sorry."

"Hate to admit it, but you were right all along." Todd grimaced. "The only thing Eleanor and I have in common is a mutual interest in getting her elected."

"Oh, *Todd.*"

Todd glared at her. "You think maybe you could skip the *Oh, Todds?*"

Jasper saw Olivia open her mouth. He could tell that she was about to say *Oh, Todd* again.

"Your sister has a lot to do this evening," Jasper said smoothly. "What do you say we leave her to it? Come on, I'll buy you a drink."

Todd frowned at the glass in his hand. "The drinks are free."

"Hell of a deal." Jasper clapped him on the shoulder. "Let's go."

Todd shrugged and fell into step beside him. Jasper glanced back once and saw Olivia watching them with a worried expression.

"I don't really want another drink," Todd confided. "But thanks for giving me an excuse to avoid any more explanations."

"No problem."

"It isn't always easy having an older sister who thinks she's right most of the time."

"I understand." Jasper reached the elegant staircase and started up the steps. "Let's take a look at Merlin's Cave. I want to see what Bolivar did with a couple of thousand dollars' worth of Glow equipment."

Todd smiled briefly. "Cousin Bolivar missed his calling. He should be studying to go work for a firm that designs carnival attractions. Of course, some folks would say that working for Light Fantastic was not far off the mark."

"I won't tell Olivia you said that."

"Thanks. I appreciate that."

At the second-floor landing, they went down a hazy

blue hall. Flashing lights pulsed in quick, strobelike intervals. Miniature lightning bolts arced overhead.

The entrance to Merlin's Cave was easy to find. The crowd waiting to get inside wound out the door of the upstairs ballroom and halfway down the corridor.

Jasper came to a halt. "Guess it's a big hit."

"Yeah." Todd grimaced. "Forget trying to get inside for another hour."

"What do you say we go out onto the veranda for some fresh air, instead? I've had enough blue fog for a while."

Todd shrugged again. He accompanied Jasper out onto the second-floor balcony.

The cool evening and a measure of quiet greeted them.

Jasper made no move to force a conversation. He gripped the railing and watched a handful of guests mill about below in the blue floodlit gardens.

Todd leaned against the nearest pillar. "She was right, you know. Should have listened to her in the first place."

"Olivia?"

"Yeah. She warned me not to make the same mistake she made when she married Logan Dane."

"What mistake was that?"

"Olivia always refers to her marriage as a marriage of convenience. A business arrangement based on everything but love. She figured it was solid because they had so much in common, you see. But she was wrong. I got suckered by the same logic."

"What made you decide that you and Eleanor Lancaster didn't have so much in common, after all?"

"The problems have been building for a while." Todd grimaced. "But tonight they came to a head. Eleanor and I quarreled about some of her fund-raising techniques."

"You didn't go along with her plans?"

"She made some promises to some people in exchange for contributions. Promises I knew she wouldn't be able to keep if she stuck to our agenda after the election."

"What did she say when you confronted her?" Jasper asked.

"Can't you guess? She called me naïve. Reminded me that there won't be any agenda to fulfill unless she gets elected, and to do that, she needs money. She told me I'd better get used to politics as usual if I want the two of us to go all the way to the White House."

Jasper glanced at him. "What did you say?"

"I told her that I had decided that I don't want to be the First Husband, after all." Todd smiled ruefully. "I'm going back to my nice ivory tower. Olivia was right about that, too. I wasn't cut out for the real world of politics. I was born for the academic side of things."

"You're leaving the campaign?"

Todd nodded. "The news will be kept low-key, of course. I've stayed in the background all along so as not to distract the media's attention from Eleanor and her message. If we handle it right, I doubt that anyone will even notice that I've eased out of the picture."

Jasper started to respond. He stopped, sensing a new presence on the scene. He turned his head and saw Dixon standing in the doorway.

"Use 'em and lose 'em, is that the Chantry family motto?" Dixon asked thickly. "Hey, maybe someone should call up old Crawford Lee Wilder and tell him there's another story here in Seattle. He could call it Dark Muse II, the sequel."

"Go to hell," Todd said wearily. "You've got what you want."

"What's that supposed to mean?" Dixon demanded.

"You've resented my relationship with Eleanor from the start. I should think you'd be glad that I'm out of the picture."

"You've left her high-and-dry, you bastard." Dixon took two steps forward and flung the contents of his glass straight into Todd's face. "You're so fucking stupid, you don't even know how much damage you've caused."

Before Todd could react, Jasper moved. He grasped Dixon's shoulder and spun him around.

"This has gone far enough," Jasper said quietly. "You're drunk, Haggard. It's time you left the party."

Dixon's enraged eyes widened in the darkness. "You stupid sonofabitch. I figured you were screwing Olivia because you intended to screw her out of Glow, Inc. But I had it backward, didn't I?"

"I'm warning you, Haggard."

Dixon uttered a shrill bark of laughter. "She's the one screwing you, isn't she? That's what this is all about. She's setting you up the same way she set up Logan Dane. Be careful you don't get a sudden urge to run with the bulls in Pamplona. Or maybe take a dive off a tall building?"

Jasper slammed Dixon up against the wall with

enough force to make the boards shudder. He pinned him there and lowered his voice to a whisper.

"One more word out of you, Haggard, and I will throw you off the edge of this balcony. It's not a real tall building, and you're drunk, which means you'll probably land softly. I bet you'll only break a leg or two."

Dixon scowled, eyes bleary with alcohol and rage. "Let me go. I'll have you arrested."

Jasper smiled slowly. "That will look great in the papers, won't it? I can see it now. LANCASTER CAMPAIGN MANAGER IN DRUNKEN BRAWL."

Dixon blinked rapidly and seemed to sag. Jasper thought he saw a flicker of common sense surface somewhere in the blurred gaze. Or was it fear?

Olivia appeared in the doorway. The light in the hallway behind her enveloped her in an ethereal blue glow. But there was nothing otherworldly about the expression that snapped in her eyes.

Jasper wondered what had brought her out onto the veranda. Unerring instincts for avoiding potential disaster at Light Fantastic productions, no doubt.

She glanced at Todd and then peered into the shadows where Jasper still held Dixon against the wall.

"Is there a problem?" she asked crisply.

"No, ma'am." Jasper gave her a bland smile and took a firm grip on Dixon. "Haggard, here, was just leaving. Had a little too much champagne. Todd and I are going to help him into a cab. Isn't that right, Todd?"

"Right." Todd moved with gratifying speed. He took Dixon's other arm and gave Jasper a knowing, appreciative, man-to-man look.

Jasper wondered if he and Todd had suddenly developed one of those male bonds he'd heard about.

Together they got the silent, subdued Dixon down the back stairs and out to the sweeping drive, where a line of cabs waited.

Haggard did not protest when they stuffed him into a taxi. Jasper slammed the door and stepped back. He stood with Todd and watched the vehicle's taillights disappear down the driveway.

"I think, in his own weird way, he loves her," Todd said eventually.

Jasper looked at him. "What about you? Did you love her?"

"I guess not. I can't say I'm really torn up or anything. Mostly what I feel is a sense of relief, if you want to know the truth. Hell, I should have gotten out weeks ago."

"You mean when Olivia first warned you not to get personally involved with Lancaster?"

"No." Todd frowned in surprise. "When Uncle Rollie told me that I ought to steer clear of the Lancaster campaign."

Jasper went cold. "Rollie told you to stay away from the Lancaster campaign?"

"It was the last piece of advice he ever gave me. The very next day he and Wilbur left on that photo safari."

Jasper could have sworn that somewhere in the distance he could hear the ominous grinding sound of a steel trap closing.

"Damn," he said very softly. "I should have thought of that."

24

Olivia waited until the elevator door closed behind Jasper and Silas. When they were safely on their way to the fourth floor of the storage facility to check out Jasper's phony complaint about a water leak near locker four-ninety, she went into action.

She slipped into the small office and hurried to the rotary file that contained the names of people who had rented lockers at Pri-Con Self-Storage. She flipped through the cards until she hit the G's.

Melwood Gill had to be in the file, she thought. If she could not find a locker registered in his name, the search was at a dead end.

It was only five minutes after eight. Her car was the

only one parked in the tiny lot. She was still surprised by how swiftly Jasper had agreed to the scheme she had concocted to search Silas's files. She had expected him to argue that it was too risky.

It was another measure of the heightened urgency she sensed in him, she thought. She had first noticed it after the Camelot Blue event had ended. It was as if whatever had happened between him and Dixon and Todd had ratcheted up the stakes.

She still had a lot of questions about what had taken place out there on the upper veranda at the Enfield Mansion. The answers she had pried out of both Todd and Jasper had been extremely vague. All she really knew was that when she had outlined her plan to search Silas's office, Jasper had accepted it without much argument.

Her scheme was the essence of simplicity. Jasper's job was to distract Silas by inventing a problem on the fourth level. While both men went upstairs to contemplate the magical appearance of water on the floor near Rollie's locker, she would go through the files. It was Jasper who had suggested pouring a quart of real water on the floor so that Silas would have something to look at once he was conveniently out of the way.

Simple. Except that there was no card for Melwood Gill in the rotary file.

Her hand hovered in midair above the cards.

She had been so sure she would discover that Melwood Gill had rented that last locker on the fourth floor.

Frantic, she went through the G's a second time. Gamberling, Geyser, Gonerly. No Gill.

Damn. Despair swept through her. Jasper's logical deduction, so obvious on the surface, had been wrong. Maybe Melwood had managed to remove all of Rollie's files from Pri-Con Self-Storage without Silas seeing him, after all.

But how had he gotten inside the facility in the first place if he had not had the excuse of having rented one of the lockers?

She glanced toward the elevator. Jasper could not keep Silas occupied up there on the fourth floor forever. She whirled to look at the file cabinet in the corner. She forced herself to think.

If she had been in Melwood's place, what would she have done? For starters, she would probably try to muddy the waters a bit, just in case someone else came looking for the files.

She would have rented the locker under a fictitious name.

She groaned. If Melwood had used an alias, she would never find him in the rotary file. It did not contain any billing addresses, just names and locker numbers.

But if Gill had rented a locker here at Pri-Con, the transaction would have taken place during the past few weeks. What kind of records got filed according to date?

Invoices.

She scanned the labels on the file drawers and saw the one she wanted immediately.

She jerked open the drawer, half afraid that Silas's filing system would be exotic or indecipherable.

But it was not. It was very straightforward and

extremely neat. The numbered, dated invoices were arrayed before her in an orderly fashion.

Maybe there was something to be said for good filing habits, after all, she thought as she started through the most recent invoices.

Her automatic reflex was to look for a name that Melwood might have used. She remembered reading somewhere that people who changed their names tended to choose new ones that began with the same initials as the old ones. Martin Gore or Melvin Gantry, perhaps.

But she could not count on that logic, she decided. Better to look for a familiar address.

It was suddenly there, right in front of her, an invoice in the name of Mr. John Jones at Melwood's Queen Anne address. Locker four-sixty-three, rented three days after news of Rollie's death had reached Seattle.

So much for the quaint theory that people selecting aliases went with identical initials.

A squeak followed by a sighing groan warned her that the elevator was in motion.

She slammed the file cabinet drawer shut and rushed out of the office.

She was lounging against a brick wall, trying to look bored, when the elevator doors opened a few seconds later. She hoped she did not look as flushed and excited as she felt.

"I tell you there's no way that water could be from a plumbing pipe," Silas grumbled as he stalked out of the elevator. "I know every pipe in this place, and there ain't any up there in that corner."

306

"Must have been from the last rain." Jasper's shuttered gaze went straight to Olivia.

She gave him her best business-as-usual smile. "Find the source of the leak?"

Silas bristled. "Ain't never had any rain leaks up there in that corner. But hell, this is Seattle. Just about every building in town leaks. If you think I'm gonna refund Mr. Chantry's rent just because of a little water that didn't do any damage, forget it."

"Take it easy," Jasper shot Olivia another quick glance. "We'll keep the locker until Ms. Chantry winds up the estate. Isn't that right, Olivia?"

"Absolutely. It's a very convenient solution to our storage problem." She tried not to grin in triumph as she straightened away from the wall. "In fact, if you two have finished diagnosing the leak, I'd like to get busy upstairs. We've got a lot to do today."

"Nice work." Jasper walked out of the elevator and started down a gloomy corridor on the fourth floor. He had a large box cradled under one arm. The box was very light. The only things inside were the tools he anticipated he might need to cut through padlocks or pry open steel filing cabinets.

"I thought so." Olivia followed him off the elevator. "Of course, I couldn't have pulled it off if you hadn't come up with the idea that Uncle Rollie's files had never left the building."

"I keep telling you, that's why guys like me get the corner office and the—"

"Okay, okay, enough with the mysterious act. Your theory about Melwood having a locker up here has been proven true. Tell me why you're acting as if this situation is a lot worse today than it was yesterday?"

"Last night your brother and I had a short man-to-man talk about his relationship with Eleanor Lancaster."

"What about it?"

Jasper glanced at the locker numbers on his left as he went down the aisle. Four-fifteen, four-seventeen, four-nineteen. Four-sixty-three would be in the rear of the building.

"He told me that you weren't the only one who had warned him not to get involved with Lancaster," he said.

"Someone else gave him the same advice? Who was it?"

"Good old Uncle Rollie."

There was a short, terse silence behind him. And then the full implications of what he had just said hit her.

"Good grief." She paused briefly and then hurried after him. Her footsteps echoed on the concrete floor. "You mean . . . ?"

"That Rollie may have launched one of his now-famous inquiries into the private lives of his relatives before he left on that photo safari trip?" Jasper turned down another aisle. "And found something he didn't like in the background of Eleanor Lancaster? Something that made him think Todd should steer clear? Yeah, I think it's a real possibility."

"Jasper, that would mean that Melwood could have found that information, whatever it was, and tried to blackmail Eleanor Lancaster with it." Olivia sounded thunderstruck. "My God. He may have been blackmailing the next governor of this state."

"We don't know that for certain yet. But I'd say it's a real possibility."

"Oh, my lord," Olivia said. "Eleanor would not brush aside any kind of threat that jeopardized her future in politics. Something tells me she would be very dangerous if cornered."

"I got the same impression."

"Why didn't you say something last night?"

"I wanted to find the missing files before I went any farther with the theory." Jasper paused in front of a locker. 463 was painted on the plywood door. A new padlock gleamed in the shadows. "But thanks to you, I think we may have accomplished that."

He set down his box, lifted the lid, and removed a pair of bolt cutters. Olivia hung over his shoulder, watching intently.

It only took a moment to sever the padlock.

"Don't get too excited." Jasper dropped the broken lock into his pocket. "We may find only another empty locker."

"I don't think so." Olivia pulled the door open.

The weak glow of the flickering fluorescent fixture overhead spilled partway into the dark locker.

Jasper whistled softly. "I told you that your uncle and I had a lot in common when it came to filing."

"Apparently Melwood did, too," Olivia whispered.

Rows of sturdy cardboard file boxes were stacked halfway to the ceiling on freestanding, bolt-together metal shelving. Each box was neatly labeled. A small desk and a stool had been set up at the rear of the locker. A flashlight sat on top of the desk. A single file box stood on the floor near the stool.

"All the comforts of home." Jasper moved past Olivia into the shadowed locker. He picked up the flashlight. "I'm surprised there isn't a hot plate and a mattress."

"Uncle Rollie's secret files." Olivia looked stunned. She bent down to get a better look at one of the labels. "This is incredible. Some of these boxes go back forty years."

"Gill broke into Rollie's locker, moved everything, including the metal shelving, into this one, and then went through the boxes looking for information he could use in his extortion scheme."

"Poor Melwood. He just wasn't—"

"Please," Jasper interrupted. "Don't say it."

"Sorry. It's gotten to be kind of a habit." Olivia lifted the lid off one of the boxes and peered inside. "We'll have to go through these one by one to find the same damaging information that Melwood found."

"Not necessarily." Jasper studied the box on the floor beside the stool. "When I went through Gill's desk yesterday, I noticed that he had a habit of keeping the papers he was working on at any given moment in a convenient hot file."

Olivia watched him crouch in front of the box and raise the lid. "You think he may have had one for his special blackmail stuff?"

Jasper aimed the flashlight at the neatly arranged folders inside the box. *Chantry, Dane, Lancaster, Sloan.*

"He had a hot file, all right. This box is it."

He plucked the Sloan file out of the box and opened it. The single page inside bore the name of a very exclusive, very high-priced agency that specialized in discreet corporate investigations.

"Damn," he muttered. "Rollie, old buddy, you've taught me a good lesson. Maybe it is possible to be a little too obsessive about files and information. As God is my witness, when this is all over, I'm going to destroy everything in my records that could possibly come back to haunt anyone."

"Good idea," Olivia murmured.

Jasper dropped his own file back into the box. He set Gill's flashlight on the desk, picked up the hot file box, and turned toward the door. "Go grab that platform truck. I want to get this stuff out of here. I think we can fit most of them into your car."

"What's the rush?" Olivia asked. "We know where they are now."

He met her eyes. "If we found these files, someone else might be able to find them, too."

Her mouth tightened. "Good point." She turned and went out the door.

Jasper put the hot files box near the door, turned and started dragging more boxes off the top shelf. He stacked them on the floor, one on top of the other. In the distance he heard the low rumble of the heavy casters on the platform truck.

Olivia parked the cart in the aisle and started stacking boxes on it.

It took a surprisingly short amount of time to load half the file boxes onto the cart.

"It's going to take two trips," Olivia observed.

"Let's get this load downstairs."

Jasper took hold of the metal steering bar and pushed the load toward the elevator. Olivia went ahead to press the call button.

The elevator cab had not arrived by the time Jasper got the platform truck past the last row of lockers. He saw Olivia frown and punch the call button again.

"Wouldn't you know it?" She glanced at him. "Another customer must have arrived. Whoever he is, he's commandeered the elevator. We'll have to wait until he's finished loading or unloading his stuff."

A whisper of premonition raised the hair on the nape of Jasper's neck. "The parking lot was empty when we got here."

"I know." She shrugged and punched the call button a few more times. "But the elevator has definitely been locked out."

Jasper looked at the glowing green exit sign over the stairwell door. "I'll go downstairs and see what's going on. Stay here with the files."

"Okay."

Jasper pushed the loaded platform truck into a nearby aisle and went to the door beneath the exit sign. For some reason he could not explain but that he did not question, he opened it quite gently.

Footsteps echoed hollowly on the concrete stairwell. Deliberate, steady, footsteps. Making their way up the stairs.

Silas, perhaps, come to tell them that the elevator was out of commission.

Or someone else. Someone who had followed them to Pri-Con Self-Storage this morning.

Jasper closed the door even more carefully than he had opened it. He turned to look at Olivia. She was watching him with a questioning expression

"What's wrong?" She spoke very softly.

"I'm not sure. Someone's coming up the stairs."

"Probably because the elevator isn't working."

"Probably." Jasper made a quick assessment of the terrain. "I could be overreacting here, but it strikes me that to date we have made some dumb moves in this mess. Let's try doing something smart for a change."

"Such as?"

He took her arm and steered her swiftly back down the central aisle. "Such as not stand here like a couple of Thanksgiving turkeys just in case it turns out that whoever is coming up those steps is also after Rollie's files."

"Jasper."

"Shush. Sound carries in this place."

She lowered her voice. "Do we have a plan?"

"Of course." He yanked her down another corridor. "What kind of CEO would I be if I didn't have a plan?"

"Just thought I'd ask."

"The way I see it, there are not a lot of options when it comes to hiding in a place like this. We've got two."

"Two?" She looked at him sharply as they turned another corner. "Surely you don't mean one of the empty lockers?"

"That's exactly what I mean. Silas told us all the

313

lockers on this floor were rented. But we have access to two of them. I'm going to stash you in the one Rollie leased."

"What about you?"

"I'm going to wait this out in Gill's locker. With any luck, whoever is coming up that staircase won't have a clue which lockers belonged to Rollie or Gill. With the doors closed and the broken locks hanging in place, our lockers will look just like all the others."

Her eyes narrowed in suspicion. "Why are you separating us?"

"Common sense. Increases our odds in case I am not being unduly paranoid."

"Our odds? What are you saying? Jasper, wait, let's discuss this—"

"No time." He stopped in front of Rollie's locker, opened the door, and pushed Olivia inside. He dug the slim flashlight he had brought with him out of his pocket and handed it to her. "Here. Just in case."

"In case what? Jasper, I don't like this."

"If you hear a disturbance, make a break for the stairwell, understand?"

"Jasper."

"Just do it. I want your word."

"Yeah, sure."

He closed the door gently and adjusted the broken padlock so that it looked like all the others. It would take close examination to see that it had been cut.

He prayed that there would be no such examination.

He went quickly back through the complex of intersecting corridors and halted at Melwood Gill's locker.

He heard the sighing rasp of the stairwell door being opened just as he stepped into the shadowed interior. An instant later the sputtering fluorescents overhead flickered and went out.

Not Silas. The attendant knew that Jasper and Olivia were still on the fourth floor.

Someone else.

Jasper closed the door of the locker with great care. Then he waited for what he knew would happen next.

Footsteps. The rattle of a lock being shaken at the far end of the aisle. More footsteps. A pause and then another padlock clattered briefly.

Whoever had turned out the lights was making his way systematically through the aisles checking each locker door as he went.

Jasper hoped that Olivia would not realize he had lied to her when he told her that the reason he was putting her in a different locker was because it made sense to separate.

The real reason he had stashed her in Rollie's old locker was because it was in the very last aisle. It was only logical that whoever had followed them would be forced to do exactly what he was doing: Search every aisle and try every locker on the floor to find the one in which his quarry was hiding.

Such a methodical approach meant that whoever was prowling the darkened corridors would find the broken lock on Melwood Gill's locker long before he or she got anywhere near Olivia's hiding place.

He or she? There weren't too many possibilities, Jasper thought. Rollie's information, whatever it was, pertained to Eleanor Lancaster. The future governor looked like the type who could take care of herself.

"Come out, come out, wherever you are," Dixon Haggard called as he tried another locker. "I know you're both here somewhere. Things will be a little different this time. I came prepared, you see. Brought along my gun."

25

Well, hell, Jasper thought. He'd had a fifty-fifty chance, and he'd guessed wrong. He had been almost positive that it was Eleanor Lancaster who had followed them here today.

Why had he been so certain? he wondered. After all, he'd known that it was a man he'd battled with on the stairs in Gill's dark house.

"No point hiding up here in hopes that the attendant will come rescue you," Dixon sang out cheerfully. "He's having a little nap downstairs under his desk. I locked out the elevator and put a sign on the office door telling everyone that the facility was closed due to an emergency."

Footsteps. Another padlock clattered.

Jasper eased to the rear of the locker. He crouched at the end of one of the freestanding metal shelves. With luck, the boxes left on the shelves would block Haggard's view for a few crucial seconds.

"An emergency in a self-storage facility. Pretty funny, isn't it? But this situation definitely qualifies, I'd say."

Dixon's voice was loud enough to carry across the fourth floor. He sounded keyed-up, edgy, excited. He also sounded sure of himself. It was the voice of a man who is certain he has the upper hand.

"Gill wasn't too bright, was he? I set a trap for him when I left the first blackmail payment. Saw him pick up the cash. Followed him back to his house. He never had a clue."

Jasper wrapped his hands around the metal uprights of the shelving. He would only get one chance.

"Getting rid of Gill was no problem. You owe me for that hit-and-run, by the way. I did us all a favor when I offed the little bastard."

Another padlock clattered.

"But I made a real unfortunate assumption," Dixon continued. "I figured that since he wasn't a very clever blackmailer, he would have been dumb enough to stash his files somewhere in his house. To tell you the truth, I had a bad moment or two when I realized they weren't there."

A padlock clanged. Much closer this time.

"But when I ran into you two there, I realized that the sonofabitch had been blackmailing other people, as well. Imagine my surprise when I recognized

Olivia that night. I knew it was you with her, Sloan. Had to be."

A lock rattled. Jasper estimated that Dixon was no more than half a dozen doors away.

"I figured right off that you two would have a much better chance of finding Gill's files than I would. After all, you were his employers. You had access to all kinds of information about him that I couldn't get."

The leading edge of a flashlight beam flickered under the locker door.

"So I decided to sit back and wait for you folks to do the legwork. I knew when you came here today that there had to be a good reason."

Jasper tightened his grip on the uprights. With the overhead lights out, Dixon had only his flashlight for illumination. He would have to move at least a couple of feet into the locker to make certain that his quarry was not hiding inside behind the ranks of boxes.

"Got to admit, I was pretty amazed when the first blackmail note arrived." Dixon chuckled. "Who the hell would have thought that some dipshit little accountant could have dug up that old information? I was so damn careful."

Another padlock rattled in the darkness.

"Even the police bought the story six years ago. They conducted a very thorough investigation. Concluded that poor Richard Lancaster had just been in the wrong place at the wrong time. Walked in on a burglary in progress and got himself shot to death. Hey, shit happens, y'know?"

That answered one of those nagging questions of

history, Jasper thought. It was Dixon who had murdered Eleanor Lancaster's husband.

He listened as Haggard tried the lock on the locker next door.

"Had to get rid of good old Richard, you see. He was standing in her way. He didn't approve of her going into politics. And he was rich. Eleanor needed the money to run her first campaign. As her campaign manager, it was my job to make sure she got what she needed."

The flashlight gleamed beneath the edge of the door. It jerked sharply.

"Hey, hey, hey. What have we here? A broken padlock?" Dixon's laughter held a razor-sharp edge of tension and anticipation.

Jasper waited, motionless. Timing was everything.

"I think we've played hide-and-seek long enough," Dixon said. "I'm sorry about what has to happen here. But I know you'll understand when I tell you that the future of the country depends on getting Eleanor elected. And that might not happen if the media finds out that her campaign manager killed her husband. Public's kinda fickle."

Jasper heard him yank the broken lock off the door. It clattered onto the concrete floor.

The door slammed open. The flashlight beam roared into the darkness like the light of an oncoming train.

Jasper kept his eyes fixed steadily on the side wall of the locker. He could not afford to be blinded by Dixon's flashlight.

"Sloan, you bastard, I know you and Olivia are in

there. You might as well come out and get it over with. I'll make it quick and clean."

The flashlight flickered wildly as Dixon played it over the boxes.

"Goddamn it, come out. This has to end. It's my job to end it. I've got to protect Eleanor's future. This country needs her, you see."

Jasper used his peripheral vision to track the dark figure behind the flashlight. Dixon took one cautious step into the locker.

"Shit," he muttered.

Jasper knew that it had just occurred to Dixon that he might have opened the wrong locker.

Dixon took another step into the darkness. And then another. The light flared as it arced across the shelving. It danced across the toe of Jasper's shoe.

"I knew you were in here." Dixon's voice rose in ghastly triumph. "I knew—"

Jasper yanked hard and fast on the steel uprights. There was a high squeak of metal. And then the entire structure toppled suddenly, abruptly, as though an earthquake had struck.

The boxes that remained on the shelves rained down on Dixon. The flashlight was knocked from his hand. It rolled on the concrete floor. The beam ricocheted wildly and finally came to rest aiming uselessly at the wall.

The top of the steel shelves fell against the opposite wall and lodged there. Several heavy boxes slid to the floor, striking Dixon.

He screamed in rage and pain.

Jasper switched on his own flashlight and aimed the beam straight into Dixon's eyes.

Dixon was on his knees, trapped in a cage formed by the metal shelves and uprights. Tumbled boxes hemmed him in on all sides. Papers and file folders littered the floor.

Dixon was trying to raise his right arm. The light caught a glint of metal. He still had his gun.

Jasper threw the flashlight straight into his face. Dixon dodged reflexively, but his movements were limited by the shelving and the boxes.

Jasper leaped onto the steel skeleton of the shelving. It groaned beneath his weight, but it did not give way. He balanced on an angled upright and kicked Dixon's right shoulder.

Dixon yelled again. The gun clattered onto the concrete. There was enough light bouncing off the locker walls for Jasper to see that the weapon had slid out of Haggard's reach.

"Jasper."

A flashlight beam flared in the aisle outside the locker. He put up his hand to shield his eyes.

"It's okay." He bounded from one steel section to the next and jumped down on the far side near the open door. He scooped up the gun. "It's okay."

Olivia appeared in the doorway. "Are you all right? Are you hurt?"

"I'm fine." He looked at her. "I told you to make a run for it when you heard a disturbance."

"My God. This was your big plan, wasn't it?" Outrage rose in her voice. "Jasper, you could have been killed."

There was no point yelling at her. She was not in a mood to listen. He gently pried the flashlight from her hand and used it to survey the toppled shelving and the array of fallen boxes that imprisoned Dixon.

"Like I always say, there is no substitute for a good filing system."

"This is no time for dumb jokes," she said tightly.

"No," Jasper agreed. "It's not. We've got some work to do."

"What do you mean?" she demanded. "We've got to call the police."

"We're going to make certain that the files in Gill's hot box are all safely out of the way before we call the cops." He paused. "Except, of course, for the Lancaster file."

"The hot box is on the platform truck."

An odd, rasping sound caught Jasper's attention. He aimed the flashlight at Dixon.

Haggard was still on his knees. His face was wet with tears.

"I did it all for her," Dixon whispered. "I did it for Eleanor. The country needs her."

26

That night they burned the contents of Melwood
Gill's hot box in Jasper's big river-stone fireplace. The
flames devoured decades of facts and rumors and
grainy photographs shot through long camera lenses.
They consumed yellowed, hand-typed pages from a
private investigation agency that had gone out of business twenty years earlier. They ate new reports produced by the computer printers of a modern, more
sophisticated agency.

The police had taken the Lancaster file into evidence, but not before Jasper and Olivia had scanned
the contents.

Rollie's private investigator had tracked down an

unnamed retired police detective who had been involved with the Richard Lancaster murder investigation.

The former detective had retired to a beachfront house in Mexico. He had confided to the investigator that he had been convinced from the beginning that Richard Lancaster was not the victim of an unknown burglar who was never caught.

Lancaster had known his killer, the retired detective claimed. He also said that he would have bet his pension that the murderer was Dixon Haggard. But there had never been any proof to take to a prosecutor. The case had gone into a cold file.

Dixon took full responsibility for the murder. He was apparently proud of the fact that he had acted alone. Eleanor Lancaster had no inkling of the truth.

"I talked to Todd this afternoon." Olivia fed another sheet to the flames. "He said he feels an obligation to stay on with the Lancaster campaign for a while. He's going to do whatever he can in the way of damage control. But he told me privately that he's not sure that Eleanor's candidacy can survive the scandal."

"No big surprise there." Jasper picked up his glass of scotch. "The police said that Haggard confessed to the crime. He also made it clear that he acted on his own initiative. He's obsessed with Eleanor Lancaster."

"She's innocent, but she'll be tainted no matter how much spin control her people do. It's going to be hard to explain why she inadvertently hired a campaign manager who committed murder to help her launch her political career. Doesn't exactly demonstrate astute judgment."

Jasper's mouth curved faintly as he tossed another sheet into the fire. "The public doesn't expect a lot of sound judgment from politicians, but it may feel that Lancaster pushed the envelope of stupidity in this instance."

"You're sure Dixon won't tell the police that some of the files were removed?" she asked again.

"He didn't see us take the one box downstairs to the car. Besides, all he could think about was that he had screwed up. He was oblivious to what was going on around him."

Olivia knew that Dixon Haggard had slipped into a world of his own, one in which he was Eleanor Lancaster's failed knight in shining armor. He was still weeping when the police took him into custody.

Silas had recovered consciousness shortly after Olivia and Jasper had arrived downstairs, but he had remained stretched out on the floor of his office, dazed, until the aid car got there.

Olivia raised her brows. "I trust you really have learned your lesson from all of this. An obsession with filing is not a healthy thing."

Jasper grinned briefly. "I knew you wouldn't be able to resist rubbing it in. Don't worry. Like I said, I've already made plans to clean out some of my old records."

"I should hope so." She contemplated the flames. "I suppose we'll never know for certain how Melwood Gill discovered Uncle Rollie's secret files."

"The information about the storage locker at Pri-Con Self-Storage was probably in Rollie's home office files. You would have come across it when you cleaned them out, if Gill hadn't gotten there first and set the fire to cover his tracks."

Olivia nodded and tossed another page to the ravenous flames. "We'll never be able to prove it, but that's the only scenario that makes sense. No wonder Rollie told me that if anything ever happened to him I was to destroy all of his personal files. He knew there was some potentially lethal stuff in them."

"Rollie trusted you." Jasper met her eyes. "He must have known that you'd figure out what to do when you came across the Lancaster information."

"I wonder why he didn't tell Todd the whole story before he left on that safari trip?"

"Not enough hard data to make accusations," Jasper said. "And none of it implicated Eleanor Lancaster, herself, just her campaign manager. But it was enough to make Rollie uneasy about Todd's involvement with the campaign. He tried to warn him."

Olivia nodded. "Uncle Rollie may not have been unduly concerned at that point. As far as he knew, Todd was only serving as a temporary consultant to the campaign. He hadn't realized that the relationship between Eleanor and Todd was getting personal and serious."

"He would have been a lot more worried if he had known that your brother was getting sucked deeper into Lancaster's intimate circle. After all, the closer he got to Eleanor, the more a nutcase like Haggard was likely to resent him."

Olivia shivered. "At some point Dixon's twisted brain might have concluded that Todd was a rival and a threat. I think he was already heading in that direction."

"Yes."

"My God. Dixon might have eventually worked himself up to the notion that Todd had to be removed the same way Eleanor's husband had been removed. He might have murdered my brother."

"It's over now," Jasper said quietly.

There was a short silence broken only by the crackle of the flames.

"Yes," Olivia whispered. "It's over."

"Jasper." Olivia came out of the nightmare with his name on her lips. Her pulse pounded. She gasped for breath.

"It's all right." Jasper's warm arms closed tightly around her. "Only a dream."

"No." She refused to be comforted. She pried herself out of his arms and sat up, clutching the sheet to her breasts. She stared down at his shadowed face. "No, it wasn't a dream. It really happened. You almost got killed in that locker."

She trembled as fragments of the nightmare wafted through her mind. She relived the ominous rattle and clatter of padlocks as Dixon made his way through the aisles. Closer and closer until she had realized too late that his search would bring him first to Jasper's hiding place.

Jasper had *known* that would happen when he left her in Rollie's locker.

"Don't ever do that again," she whispered.

"Don't ever do what again?"

"Don't ever leave me behind while you go off to deal with things the way you did today. We're supposed to be partners, remember?"

His eyes were enigmatic pools of night. "I made an executive decision. I thought it would be easier to handle Haggard alone."

"You should have discussed it with me first."

His mouth quirked, but he said nothing.

Olivia flushed. She was grateful for the shadows that enveloped the bed. "Okay, okay, forget the preplanning discussion idea. Obviously there wasn't time. But promise me you won't do anything like that ever again."

"I promise you that I have absolutely no intention of repeating today's exercise. In fact, I may never even rent a self-storage locker again."

She sensed the amusement he was trying to suppress and groaned. "I suppose neither of us could have predicted what would happen when we went to find those files this morning."

"You're wrong." The humor vanished from Jasper's voice as if it had never existed. It left behind a grim edge. "I should have considered the possibility that whoever else was after those files would follow us."

"Stop it." She put her fingers over his mouth to silence him. "It was eight o'clock in the morning in a commercial establishment. We should have been perfectly safe."

He caught hold of her wrist and dragged her fingers away from his lips. "A commercial establishment in which there had already been another dangerous incident between you and Gill. I was an idiot to take you back to that place."

"There was no one else who could have gone with you. This affair has involved only the two of us right from the start."

"I could have gone alone. I should have gone alone."

She smiled. "What are we going to do, spend the rest of the night telling each other that we should have done things differently? Even a couple of brilliant executives like us can mess up once in a while. The bottom line is that we both got out of it in one piece."

Jasper curled a strand of her hair around his fingers. "About this affair."

She stilled. Even without her glasses she could see the intensity of the look in his eyes. She knew that he was no longer talking about blackmail.

"What about it?"

"You keep saying we're partners."

"Yes," she whispered. "I do say that a lot."

"When it comes to Glow, I'm the senior partner."

"Jasper, this is not a good time to discuss your fifty-one percent."

"I need to know how you really feel about the fact that I control the company."

She smiled. "You want the truth? I feel relieved to know that it's in good hands and that I can concentrate on Light Fantastic. I've dreaded the day when I would have to be responsible for Glow. But Uncle Rollie kept reminding me that there wasn't anyone else in the family who could handle it."

"You trust me to run Glow?"

She touched the severe line of his jaw. "I trust you with my life."

He smiled slowly. Then he turned his head just far enough so that he could kiss her fingers. "About the other aspects of this partnership . . ."

"What about them?"

"I'm aware that any kind of personal arrangement based on mutual business interests makes you uneasy. But I would like to take this opportunity to point out that we've got a few other things going for us, too."

Everything in her went on hold, poised on some invisible ledge, straining to hear his next words.

"Do we?" she prompted gently.

His eyes narrowed. "You want me to list them?"

"Just a couple will do."

He frowned. "All right, let's start with the fact that we've been through a traumatic, dangerous experience together."

"A relationship based on that kind of thing is no more secure than one based on business interests. Once the artificially enhanced emotional edge wears off . . ."

He pushed her back down onto the pillows and rose on one elbow to lean over her. "We were both willing to break into a house, steal some papers, and lie by omission to the cops in order to protect some people who are important to us. I'd say that gives us a hell of a lot in common."

She curved her hands around his sleek shoulders and looked up into his shadowed face.

"In the event the question ever arises, let's set the record straight here," she said. "Melwood was run down and killed by a car. He had no next of kin in Seattle. Acting in our capacity as his concerned employers, we entered his house with a key that he had provided to the company for emergency purposes."

"Oh, yeah, right. I keep forgetting."

"Regarding today's activities," she continued briskly, "we did our civic duty. We gave the police everything they needed to arrest Dixon Haggard. The stuff we didn't tell them about had nothing to do with either Melwood's death or Richard Lancaster's murder."

Jasper grinned. "I love it when you talk like a big-time corporate CEO."

She clung to the word *love* and let the rest of it go. Wrapping her arms around his neck, she pulled him down so that she could kiss him.

She wondered why he had brought up the subject of their relationship in such a roundabout way. She wanted to ask him what his point was, but something told her he'd have to come to it in his own time. If ever.

Jasper was as skittish around the subject of marriage as she was.

Now, what had put marriage into her head?

"I forgot one other thing on my list of stuff we have in common besides our business interests," Jasper muttered against her mouth.

"What's that?"

He curved his hand around her hip. "The sex is great."

"There is that."

27

≈

"The good news is that Glow and Light Fantastic got some great publicity out of this thing." Bolivar opened the newspaper and spread it out across the Café Mantra lunch counter. "But the Lancaster people will be doing some very heavy spin work for a while. Wait'll you see the headlines."

Olivia leaned over his shoulder to look. Zara, perched on a stool beside him, did the same.

LANCASTER CAMPAIGN REELING
FROM ARREST OF MANAGER

Dixon Haggard, manager of gubernatorial hopeful Eleanor Lancaster's political campaign, was arrested yesterday and booked on charges of murder and attempted murder.

Jasper Sloan, CEO of Glow, Inc., and Olivia Chantry, proprietor of Light Fantastic, a Seattle event design and production firm, were instrumental in apprehending Haggard. "We were in the wrong place at the wrong time," Mr. Sloan said. "But we got lucky."

Sloan and Chantry, who share ownership of Glow, Inc., had gone to a south-end self-storage facility to retrieve some documents from lockers rented by the former head of Glow, Roland Chantry, and Melwood Gill, a Glow employee. Both men are recently deceased.

While at the facility, Sloan and Ms. Chantry were surprised by Haggard, who had followed them to the facility.

Police say Haggard believed that Gill had been blackmailing him with information stolen from the files of Roland Chantry. After allegedly murdering Gill in a hit-and-run incident, Haggard conducted a search for the information that Gill had allegedly used in his extortion efforts.

Haggard allegedly followed Gill's employers to the storage facility, assuming that they would lead him to the information stored in Roland Chantry's private files.

"We had reason to believe that Gill had taken some files from Mr. Chantry's locker and stored them in his own locker," Sloan explained. "We were looking into the situation when Dixon Haggard arrived and threatened to kill us."

Police state that Haggard has confessed not only to the murder of Melwood Gill, but to the killing six years ago of Richard Lancaster. The effect on the Lancaster campaign is difficult to predict.

Todd Chantry, a spokesperson for the campaign, issued a statement saying that Lancaster is stunned by the news that she had unwittingly hired her husband's alleged killer.

"We believe Haggard may have been a kind of stalker," Chantry said. "He apparently developed a sick obsession with Ms. Lancaster and—"

"Whew." Bolivar shook his head. "Todd's good, but I'm not sure anyone is good enough to pull Lancaster's bacon out of the fire this time."

"But Eleanor Lancaster is just an innocent victim," Zara protested. "Surely the public will understand. She's in the same terrible situation Sybil was in when she hired Burt, the gardener, never knowing that he was a stalker. She can't help it if some sicko murdered her husband and then insinuated himself into her campaign so that he could be near her."

Olivia rolled her eyes. "The woman hired her husband's murderer. Don't you see the problem here? It makes Lancaster look something other than brilliant, to say the least. At best, she comes across as a naïve victim."

"Not exactly leadership material," Bolivar concluded. He opened the second section of the paper. "Maybe if this had happened earlier in the campaign she could have put it behind her before the primary. But now? Who knows."

"You can bet that the Stryker people are going to have a field day," Olivia said.

Bolivar looked up. "What about the fund-raiser?"

Olivia shrugged. "No one has called me yet to cancel it. The only thing we can do is keep going forward with the preparations until we get word to the contrary."

"We're scheduled to hang the flag this afternoon," Bolivar reminded her.

Olivia thought about it. "I'll give Todd a call and see if he thinks there's likely to be a last-minute cancellation. If not, we'll keep to our schedule."

Zara pursed her lips. "Seems to me Eleanor Lancaster will need a fund-raiser and a big rally more than ever now."

"Good point," Bolivar said. "Everyone says she's a fighter. If she's determined to overcome this, she'll want to go ahead with a big, splashy show."

"So it's business as usual, folks." Olivia spun around on her stool and got to her feet. "Let's get to work."

Bolivar refolded the paper. "I'll get the flag ready to take down to the pier. Matty and Bernie can help me."

"Thanks." Olivia looked at her aunt. "Zara, I need to discuss something with you."

Zara gave her a conspiratorial look that was laced with just a touch of melodramatic dread. "Of course, dear."

They all trooped upstairs together. Olivia led Zara into the office and closed the door.

"Melwood Gill was your blackmailer, Aunt Zara."

"*Melwood?*" Zara stared at her, dumbfounded. "But that's not possible. How could he have known about those films I made?"

"He knew about them because Uncle Rollie knew about them." Olivia went around behind her desk and sat down. A rush of sympathy went through her. Poor Zara. Bad enough to be the victim of blackmail. To have the extortionist turn out to be someone as unexciting as Melwood Gill was adding insult to injury.

"Rollie knew about my past?" Zara frowned. "But he never said anything."

"That's because it didn't matter to him," Olivia assured her. "Unfortunately he kept the information in a file. After he was killed, Melwood went through Uncle Rollie's personal records. He found the folder on you when he discovered the one on Dixon Haggard."

"Good lord." Zara absorbed that information. "So it wasn't one of my old rivals?"

"I'm afraid not. I destroyed the file last night."

"I see." Zara paused. "You destroyed the entire file?"

"It wasn't very big." Olivia recalled the short document she had fed to the flames. "Only a couple of pages."

"No, uh, photos?"

"Nope."

"I see."

"It's all gone, Aunt Zara. Just as though it had never existed."

Zara sighed dolefully. "Very kind of you, dear."

"There is nothing to worry about now."

"Wonderful," Zara said sadly. She raised her chin so that the light from the desk lamp accented her cheekbones the way it had the day Sybil had decided she would survive Nick's infidelity. "I will be forever grateful."

Olivia groped for some way to cheer her up. "Of course, there are probably a few copies of your early films still floating around somewhere in the old files of the studio that made them."

Zara brightened. "Yes, that's true, isn't it?"

"One never knows when one of them might fall into the wrong hands."

"My God, you're right." Zara rose to her feet, her hand on her breast. "I shall never be entirely free of the threat of exposure."

"Probably not."

"I will live the rest of my days with a sword of Damocles hanging over my head."

"Yep." Olivia smiled. "But life must go on. And so must business. Can you finish the sketches for the Simmons-Cameron charity auction for me by three?"

"I'll get right on it." Zara opened the door and wafted happily out of the office.

"You saved her life." Todd shoved his hands into the pockets of his trousers. He studied the cloudy sky outside the office window as if he saw arcane runes there. "I don't know what to say, except thank you."

"It was my fault that she was in danger." Jasper lounged back in his chair and contemplated Todd's intent, serious profile. "You don't thank someone for screwing up the way I did."

Todd glanced over his shoulder. Sunlight glinted on the rims of his glasses. "Too bad folks like you don't run for public office. What this country needs is more people in leadership positions who will take responsibility for their actions."

"I'm happy here at Glow, thanks. I'd never make it as a politician."

"Why not?"

Jasper shrugged. "Politics is all about compromise. I'm not good at compromise."

Todd gave him a knowing look. "You like to be in charge, is that it?"

"Yeah. Speaking of politicians, how are things at Lancaster campaign headquarters?"

Small, troubled furrows appeared on Todd's intelligent forehead. "Dicey, to say the least. This morning's polls were not good. People feel sympathy for Eleanor, but they've lost respect for her judgment."

"Any way you cut it, she's a politician who ran for office on the money she inherited after her husband was killed by one of her most trusted campaign aides."

"Unfortunately, that's the way the public sees it." Todd frowned. "We're off-message while we try to explain things to the media. It's too late in the campaign to be off-message. Still, with a little luck, we may survive the primary. If that happens, we'll have several weeks to regain our position before the election."

"Good luck. The public has a short attention span. You've got that much in your favor."

Todd grimaced. "True."

"Still planning to get out of active politics when this election is over?"

"Definitely. I'm only staying on with the Lancaster campaign because I feel I owe Eleanor that much. I can't abandon her at this juncture. After all, if it hadn't been for her, I might never have had an opportunity to see some of my theories and policy ideas launched in the real world."

"I understand."

"Whatever happens to Eleanor and her campaign, I think some of my ideas will stick. Other candidates are already picking up some of them. The newspaper columnists debate them on a regular basis these days. That's how change happens in politics."

Jasper smiled briefly. "You've had an impact. Not many people can say that."

Todd turned fully around to face him. "You've had an impact, too. On my sister."

Jasper said nothing.

"You know," Todd said slowly, "Eleanor told me that she believes she and Olivia are a lot alike. I think she sees my sister as a sort of kindred spirit. A reflection of herself in some ways. Two strong, independent women who have carved out their own destinies."

"I won't argue with the destiny bit, but I think the rest of her assumption is garbage. Eleanor Lancaster and Olivia are very different in one essential respect."

"You're right," Todd said. "When push comes to shove, Eleanor will sacrifice everything for her future in politics. She truly believes the country needs her."

"Whereas Olivia would sacrifice anything for her family."

Todd shot him a considering look. "You know her very well, already, don't you?"

Jasper shrugged. "We have some things in common."

Todd's gaze did not waver. "I want to know what happens next between the two of you."

"Are you, by any chance, asking me if my intentions are honorable?"

Todd thought about it. "Yes. I guess that's what I want to know."

"Why don't you ask Olivia that question?" Jasper suggested quietly. "She's an equal partner in this thing."

"She's not an equal partner in Glow." Todd watched him steadily. "But Uncle Rollie dumped the responsibility for protecting the company and the people who work here on her shoulders."

"What are you afraid of? That she'll do something over-the-top like marry me because she thinks she can protect Glow and her Chantry relatives that way?"

Small brackets appeared on either side of Todd's mouth. "That's a little blunt, but yes, that's exactly what I'm afraid she might do. Olivia deserves better than that. I don't want her to feel that she has to marry you in order to fulfill her responsibilities to the family."

Jasper felt the icy, empty sensation coalesce inside him. "The subject of marriage has not come up. But if it does, I can tell you this much, Chantry. I'd rather Olivia didn't marry me for that particular reason, either."

Todd hesitated. Then he nodded once. Without a word, he turned and walked out of the office.

Jasper waited until the door had closed behind him before he got slowly to his feet.

He walked to the window and looked out at the summer storm that was sweeping in across Elliott Bay. It looked like one of Logan Dane's paintings.

What did he want? he wondered.

The answer was etched in the lightning that flashed in the distance. He had not been entirely honest with Todd. It was true that he would rather Olivia did not marry him because she thought she could control the fate of Glow that way.

But the bottom line was that he wanted Olivia. Any way he could get her.

He was in very dangerous territory without a map.

Olivia did not get an opportunity to glance at the special edition of *Hard Currency* until nearly noon. When she finished reading it, she slapped it down on her desk and snatched up the telephone. Seething, she dialed the number on the bottom of the newsletter.

"Andy Andrews here."

Olivia drummed her fingers on the arm of her chair. "Where do you get off calling my Camelot Blue event a glow-in-the-dark arcade game?"

"Come on, Olivia, where's your sense of humor?"

"You ask me that after the way you stabbed me in the back?"

"Readers remember the name of your firm better when it's in a humorous context," Andy assured her.

"You've got absolutely no scientific proof of that." Olivia scanned the article a second time. "And what's this stuff at the end about Seattle's own Mr. and Ms. Sleuth?"

"You can't blame me for working that into the piece. After all, you and Sloan were all over the front page because you nearly got yourselves murdered in that storage facility."

"You're on thin ice here, Andy."

"Well, as long as I haven't yet fallen through, I've got a favor to ask. In fact, I was just about to call you."

"Don't hold your breath."

"This is serious." Andy dropped his hearty, cajoling tone. "Any chance you can get me into the Dane Retrospective reception at the Kesgrove Museum tomorrow night?"

"Give me one good reason."

"I'll give you two reasons. I've given you two great mentions in *Hard Currency* recently."

"This may come as a shock, Andy, but I haven't been real thrilled with having my events called Foil Town and a glow-in-the-dark arcade game."

"You're a businesswoman. How about we do a deal?"

"What kind of deal?" she asked suspiciously.

"I'll give you advance notice of some information that I think you'll find interesting. In return, you get me into the reception."

"What's your information?"

"Word is, Crawford Lee Wilder is flying in to cover the Logan Dane Retrospective. He'll be at the reception."

"Damn. Now my day is just perfect."

"Have we got a bargain?" Andy asked.

"Yeah, sure. Why not? I'll get you a ticket to the

reception. After all, Light Fantastic isn't producing the event. You'll have to insult some other event firm in your next issue."

It wasn't until after she hung up the phone that she realized she had just made her own decision to attend the reception.

28

If the event had been anything other than a reception to launch the Logan Dane Retrospective, Olivia thought, she probably would have enjoyed herself. It was not often these days that she got an opportunity to be a guest at an affair staged by one of her competitors.

A glossy crowd in formal black-tie attire filled the Northwest wing of the Kesgrove Museum. The marble floors echoed with the patter of a hundred pairs of high heels.

Olivia conceded privately that Out of Sight Productions had done a fine job. The event firm had had the great good sense to let Logan's disturbing paintings provide the focal points of the evening.

There was no glitter, no sparkle, no garish colors to compete with the dark brainstorms that splashed across the canvases. The only lighting in the room was that which focused on the pictures looming on the walls.

The buffet tables were draped in stark black-and-white bunting. The serving staff wore severe white jackets and black trousers. Most of the guests had instinctively worn black and white.

"Tasteful," Jasper said dryly.

"In a word." Olivia smiled in spite of her edgy mood. "Not exactly a Light Fantastic type of event, is it?"

"We all have our niches in the great ecosystem of the business world."

"Very philosophical."

"We CEOs are supposed to be able to grasp the big picture."

"I try to bear that in mind, but for some reason I keep forgetting." She turned to him on impulse. "Thanks for coming with me tonight. I haven't exactly been looking forward to this. I appreciate the support."

"Forget it." Jasper's eyes gleamed. "That's what partners are for."

It occurred to Olivia that the word *partner* was beginning to grate on her nerves. But, then, everything grated on her nerves tonight. She would not be able to relax until the reception was over.

"Take it easy," Jasper said, as if he could read her mind. "We can leave anytime you want."

"Unfortunately, we just got here," Olivia muttered.

"Olivia, you came."

Olivia turned at the sound of her name and saw Nina. Her cousin was glowing. The happiness in her eyes was more than enough, Olivia decided, to repay her for coming to the reception.

"I'm so glad you're here." Nina squeezed her hand briefly. "You don't know how much your presence will mean to Sean." She gave Jasper a warm smile. "You must be Jasper Sloan. I'm Nina Chantry."

He smiled. "How do you do?"

Nina glanced at Olivia and then turned her attention back to Jasper. "The two of you gave us all quite a scare. What an incredible story."

Jasper shrugged that aside. "Congratulations on the turnout. Looks like the exhibition will be a big success."

Sean, his handsome, sensitive features lightened with a warm smile, emerged from the crowd. He came to stand beside Nina.

"Olivia, I'm glad you're here tonight," Sean said. "It means a lot."

"Thanks." This time Olivia remembered her manners. She made introductions quickly.

Jasper and Sean shook hands.

Nina smiled at Sean. "I think I'd better circulate a bit."

"Go ahead," Sean said. "I'll catch up with you later."

Olivia saw the warm affection in his eyes as he watched Nina disappear into the crowd.

Sean gave Jasper a speculative look. Then he turned back to Olivia. "I want you to know, Olivia, that none of us who were close to Logan will ever forget what you did for his career."

"I wasn't the one who launched him. It was Uncle Rollie's friend, Wilbur. All I did was introduce the two of them."

"You did more than introduce Logan to one of the most influential gallery owners on the West Coast," Sean said deliberately. "You steadied him for a while."

She smiled wistfully. "A very short time, I'm afraid."

"He was a stick of dynamite with a lit fuse," Sean said. "Sooner or later, he was doomed to explode. No one could have saved Logan from himself. It took some of us a while to understand that."

Olivia realized he was trying to tell her something important. "It's all right, Sean."

"No." Sean glanced fleetingly at Jasper before turning back to her. "There are things that need to be said. One of the reasons I wanted you to be here tonight was because I think it's time that the arts community knows that Logan's family has finally gotten things back into proper perspective."

"You mean you've finally stopped blaming her for Dane's death?" Jasper asked coolly.

Olivia, already tense, felt herself go rigid. "Jasper, please."

"He's right," Sean said grimly. "Three years ago we were all mired in our own private world of grief. But I think we knew the truth, even then."

"But a legend is always a lot more interesting than the truth, isn't it?" Jasper murmured.

"Jasper." Olivia glared at him.

He did not look at her. His attention was fixed on Sean, who had flushed a dull red.

"Yes," Sean said very steadily. "There is a seductive sort of comfort in a legend. Those of us who loved Logan needed comfort. So we allowed ourselves to be seduced."

Olivia felt Jasper shift his balance very slightly, just enough to bring him unmistakably closer to her. It was like having a very well-dressed bodyguard, she thought. When the sleeve of his evening jacket brushed against her arm, she was acutely aware of the strength in him.

"You never bothered to correct the legend," Jasper pointed out.

"A legend tends to take on a life of its own," Sean admitted.

"And it can be extremely profitable."

Olivia planted the heel of her shoe on Jasper's toe. It was the only thing she could think of that might make him stop goading Sean.

Jasper gave her a sardonic look and extricated his foot.

"I can't argue with that." Sean's jaw tightened. He glanced meaningfully around at the paintings on the walls. "But I like to think that at least some of the recognition Logan's work is getting tonight is due to his talent, not just a well-orchestrated legend."

"*All* of the recognition his painting is getting is due to his talent," Olivia said firmly.

Sean flashed another, unreadable glance at Jasper who somehow managed to loom even larger.

"I wonder if I might talk to you alone for a few minutes," Sean said to Olivia.

"Don't mind me," Jasper said. "Olivia and I are partners. We share just about everything."

Enough was enough, Olivia decided. Jasper was getting unpredictable. If things continued on in this vein there might well be an embarrassing scene before the evening ended.

"Would you mind getting me something to eat from the buffet?" she asked bluntly.

Jasper's eyes narrowed. It was clear that he did not like being dismissed. For a few seconds she was afraid he would refuse to leave. She beetled her brows at him.

"Sure." With a slight shrug, he turned and waded into the throng.

Sean watched Jasper's broad back disappear into the sea of well-dressed guests. "Sloan is very protective of you, isn't he?"

"We're both still getting over what happened with Dixon Haggard in that storage facility."

Sean looked thoughtful. "I think it goes a little deeper than that."

"Jasper and I do have business interests in common," she allowed. "That sort of thing does tend to create a certain bond."

Sean's fine mouth curved briefly. "I saw the look in his eyes. Trust me, whatever he's feeling toward you goes way beyond a mutual interest in Glow."

"What was it you wanted to say to me, Sean?"

He seemed to brace himself. "I think you should know that I'm aware of everything that happened three years ago."

What was this all about? Olivia wondered. The urge to automatically search the crowd for Nina's face in order to get a clue was almost overwhelming. She resisted with an effort.

"I see," she said, careful to sound noncommittal.

"Nina told me about her affair with Logan."

Olivia went very still. The laughter and conversation around her seemed to recede into the distance.

"I see," she said again, unable to think of anything more intelligent.

"She also told me that you knew about it at the time. She said it was typical of you to protect her by staying silent."

"Sean, there is nothing to be gained from going over this ground."

"You could have thrown her to the wolves three years ago. You could have told Crawford Lee Wilder that Logan's Dark Muse was his young, innocent model. Wilder could have stuck Nina into his damned Dane legend instead of you."

"You don't know Crawford. He would have used whatever he thought worked best in his story."

"She was very young. Very naïve. She never stood a chance against Logan. But she was terrified of what I would think of her if I knew the truth."

"Sean, I really do not want to discuss this."

"Neither do I," Sean said. "But it's time we did talk about it. There isn't much more to say, really. I just wanted you to know that I know."

"When did Nina tell you?"

"Three days ago when I asked her to marry me. She suddenly burst into tears and told me everything.

She said she couldn't marry me unless I knew that she was Logan's Dark Muse. She was terrified that I would blame her for driving him to his death."

Olivia watched him closely. "But you don't blame her, do you?"

"Hell, no. I don't blame anyone anymore. Logan was his own worst enemy, and in the end he killed himself." Sean hesitated. "We haven't told my parents, though."

Olivia stiffened. "I understand."

"I'm not sure my mother could ever accept Nina into the family if she was forced to substitute her for you in the legend of Logan Dane."

Olivia smiled wanly. "There's no need to tell anyone else. With any luck, the legend will fade with time. Only Logan's art will remain. That's as it should be."

Relief and gratitude lit Sean's eyes. "Thanks, Olivia. And thank you for coming here this evening."

"My pleasure," she lied softly.

With a nod, Sean drifted away into the crowd. She watched him until he was no longer in sight. So much for breaking the bonds between the Chantrys and the Danes, she thought. Nina and Sean would no doubt have children. The two families were going to be linked forever.

From out of nowhere, another one of Rollie's pithy remarks came back to her. *Trying to sever a family tie is sort of like trying to pretend that there is no such thing as gravity. You can get away with it for a while, but sooner or later you realize you're stuck.*

Olivia looked at the huge painting hanging on the

wall in front of her. Everything Logan had ever done had been larger than life, most especially his art, she thought. He would have taken enormous satisfaction out of knowing that he had become a legend. She contemplated the roiling darkness that boiled and churned on the canvas.

"If it hadn't been for you, no one here would even know his name," drawled a familiar voice.

She stifled a groan. She really did owe Andy Andrews for giving her advance warning that Crawford would be here tonight, she thought.

"Hello, Crawford."

She studied his trademark black turtleneck, expensive black Italian-cut jacket, and black jeans. It was the look that had inflamed the dreams of countless would-be freelance writers, she reflected. His shoulder-length hair, tied in a ponytail with a silver thong, looked a little too black. She realized that he had resorted to coloring it.

"Very L.A." she said. "I thought there was a dress code for this evening."

He gave her his lazy, white-toothed grin. "They made an exception for me."

"I'll bet they did." The publicity Crawford could give the museum was worth more than enough for someone at the door to overlook a pair of black jeans.

"Saw your name in the paper." Crawford watched her the way a cheerful, hungry shark would watch a school of plump little fish. "You've been busy lately. What's all this about catching the guy who killed Lancaster's husband?"

She smiled sweetly. "No comment."

"I hear the campaign is in turmoil."

"No comment."

Crawford sipped champagne. "Just friendly curiosity."

"Friendly curiosity, my foot. If you want a story, call Lancaster's headquarters."

"The story is hardly an exclusive at this point. It's even been in the *Banner-Journal*, for chrissakes. I'm not interested unless there's a new angle."

"There isn't," she assured him.

His eyes glittered. "My instincts tell me there's more going on here than what got into that *Banner-Journal* piece."

Whatever else you could say about Crawford, Olivia thought, you had to admire his instinct for a story. For a terrible moment she wondered if he had somehow learned about the full extent of Melwood Gill's blackmail efforts.

There was no telling what kind of mischief Crawford could stir up if he suspected that Dixon Haggard had not been Melwood's only extortion victim.

"Forget it, Crawford. There is no story except what was in the local papers. The only question remaining is whether or not the Lancaster campaign can survive the scandal. Your guess is as good as mine."

Crawford cocked his head in a considering fashion. "Eleanor Lancaster might just pull out of this. She's a born fighter. She's also got your brother to guide her. It'll be interesting to see what happens."

"So, how's tricks in L.A.?"

Crawford's smile was laced with satisfaction. "You

may as well be among the first to know. I've been offered a regular spot on a network TV exposé series that will premiere in the spring. Not sure yet what it'll be called, but the show will be hot. I'm seriously considering it."

"You're going to leave print journalism?"

"The new paradigm for the modern journalist is a multi-media career."

"I see. Congratulations, Crawford. You were born for television."

"Thanks." He flicked a meaningful glance at Jasper, who was working his way back through the crowd. "Must have been a shock when you found out your uncle had left fifty-one percent of Glow to a stranger."

"No comment."

Crawford chuckled. "Just trying to make a little cocktail chatter."

"No, you aren't. You're fishing for information, as usual." She smiled at Jasper as he came to a halt beside her. "Jasper, this is Crawford Lee Wilder. Crawford, Jasper Sloan."

"Pleased to meet you, Sloan." Crawford put out his hand.

Jasper looked pointedly down at his own hands. He had a small plate loaded with canapés balanced on each palm. He made no attempt to give one to Olivia so that he could shake Crawford's hand.

"I've heard of you," Jasper said without inflection.

Crawford shrugged with patently false modesty. "I get around a bit."

"Yeah. You're the hotshot journalist whose career Olivia launched, aren't you?"

Crawford dropped his hand back to his side as if he had just touched a red-hot stove. His eyes glittered with annoyance. "Olivia didn't exactly launch me."

"Sure she did." Jasper gave him a suspiciously bland smile. "My secretary happened to mention that Olivia was the one who suggested you do that series on the motivational seminar company. She got the idea after the firm put on a series of motivation talks at Glow. Hell, I guess if it hadn't been for Olivia, you'd never have gotten that Pulitzer prize."

Olivia cringed. "Now, Jasper, Crawford was the one who investigated and wrote the series."

Crawford scowled. "Damn right."

"But he got the idea from you." Jasper's smile turned dangerous. "The way I see it, Olivia pretty much made you what you are today, Wilder. It wasn't real nice of you to repay her by putting her into that piece of fiction on Logan Dane that you wrote last year."

"Now just a goddamned minute," Crawford began.

"Come to think of it," Jasper said a little too pleasantly, "you owe your two biggest stories to Olivia, don't you? Tell me, have you ever come up with an original idea on your own?"

"I've had just about enough out of you, Sloan," Crawford said through set teeth.

"Is that why you're back here in Seattle?" Jasper's eyes glinted. "Are you hoping that Olivia can give your career another shot in the arm?"

Jasper was out of control. Olivia could do nothing but hold her breath. She could see the seething frustration in Crawford's eyes. But she could also tell that he realized he was not going to win the undeclared war.

He drew himself up and gave Jasper a fulminating look. Then he turned on his heel and stalked away without a word.

Olivia released her breath very cautiously. She gazed intently at the nearest painting, afraid that if she was not extremely careful, she would laugh out loud.

Silently, Jasper handed her one of the plates he had brought back from the buffet table. She accepted it, plucked a little bit of crab-stuffed pastry off the top, and took a bite.

Beside her Jasper sampled a small, triangular-shaped sandwich that looked as though it was filled with an olive mixture. He chewed with evident satisfaction, and then he swallowed.

"Actually," Olivia said after a while, "you overlooked the one really important contribution I made to Crawford Lee Wilder's career."

"No kidding? What was that?"

"I'm the one who suggested he start using his middle name in his byline. Before me, he used to go by plain old Crawford Wilder."

Jasper thought about that. "Brilliant piece of advice. Doesn't have the same ring without the Lee."

"Thank you. I was always rather proud of the idea. Did wonders for his career."

"I want you to promise me something," he said after a while.

She did not dare look at him. Very carefully she selected another cracker and took a bite. "What?"

"Promise me that if you ever ask me to marry you, it won't be because you think my career needs a boost."

29

Eleanor Lancaster's decision to throw in the towel broke the following evening on the six-thirty news. Jasper was with Olivia in her kitchen. He had just poured two glasses of zinfandel, and was anticipating a quiet, uninterrupted evening alone with Olivia, when the anchor launched into the lead-in.

"We go live now to Lancaster campaign headquarters. Our sources tell us that Ms. Lancaster will make her announcement momentarily . . ."

"Oh, no. I was afraid of this." Olivia rushed out into the living room to watch the broadcast.

Carrying the wine, Jasper followed at a more leisurely pace. He arrived in front of the television set in time to see Eleanor ascend the podium. She was dressed in a khaki-green silk suit that had a subtle military air. She was not crying, but her eyes looked ever so slightly moist.

"Amazing how she can manage to look both tragic and heroic at the same time," Jasper said.

"Shush." Olivia flapped her hand at him. "I'm trying to listen."

"*—This is the most difficult decision I have ever made. My loyal staff has urged me to stay in the race. But it is incumbent on me to take a pragmatic view of the situation. The truth is, this campaign cannot regain the momentum that has been lost. Were I to continue, I would be wasting the money and energy of those who have worked so hard—*"

"Well, darn." Olivia planted her hands on her hips and glowered at the television. "I guess this means the fund-raiser is off."

"Looks like it."

"You know, I'm surprised that Eleanor is ending the campaign." Olivia shook her head thoughtfully. "I really thought she'd ride out the scandal."

"I know. Lancaster doesn't seem like the type to give up so easily. But the money is probably drying up very fast. Nothing disappears quicker than donations to a troubled political campaign."

Alarm widened Olivia's eyes. "You're right. Money will be tight. I'd better fax my last bill to Lancaster campaign headquarters first thing in the morning."

"I have a hunch there will be a lot of bills being faxed to Lancaster headquarters tomorrow. Everyone who did business with the campaign will be scrambling to get paid."

"You can say that again." Olivia took one of the glasses from his hand. "Poor Cousin Bolivar and Aunt Zara. They're going to be crushed when they find out that their glowing flag won't be on the evening news, after all."

"There must be another use for a twenty-foot-high lighted flag."

A speculative gleam appeared in Olivia's eyes. "We could always unfurl it at the annual Glow picnic."

"Be my guest. Just don't try sending me a bill. That flag was made with Glow technology and Glow products. Hell, I ought to charge you for it."

"Now, Jasper, I've explained my little arrangement with Glow, Inc. Light Fantastic events give you the best advertising you could possibly get."

"You keep telling me that."

"It's true." She started back toward the kitchen. "Come on, let's get dinner on the table. I'm starving."

He watched her walk around the corner. Through the opening above the counter, he could see her moving a little too quickly between the refrigerator and the stove.

There was a nervous quality about all of her movements today, he reflected. He could not attribute it to her caffeine intake. She appeared to have cut back on her coffee consumption lately.

He thought that she had been acting a little strange ever since he had made that maybe not-so-subtle reference to marriage last night at the museum reception.

Maybe his timing had been off again as it usually was in this kind of thing. Or maybe he hadn't been quite so clever after all. He wondered if she was panicking, and if so, what he should do about it.

The truth was, he had been as stunned as she was when he had heard himself make the crack about not marrying him to boost his career. But the instant the words were out of his mouth, he had realized that there was a deep truth imbedded in them.

Now that truth lay between them, a white-hot incandescent lamp that neither of them dared to pick up and handle with bare hands.

"How far did your staff get with the preparations for the Lancaster fund-raiser?" he asked, keeping his voice deliberately casual.

"Bolivar's team got the flag into position on the ceiling beam and completed the electrical connections this afternoon. They also installed the speakers and set up the sound equipment. Everything's ready to go." Olivia opened a drawer. "Just flip a switch, and you get the twenty feet of glowing flag unfurling to the glorious strains of a military marching band and chorus."

He lounged in the doorway. "Sounds impressive."

"It would have been." She went to work slicing hothouse tomatoes. "Now it will all have to be taken down and stored someplace until I can talk someone else into using it. I wonder if the Stryker campaign would be interested."

Jasper raised one brow. "You could always rent a locker at Pri-Con Self-Storage."

"Bite your tongue." She put down the knife and reached for the bottle of balsamic vinegar. "I never want to hear the word *self-storage* again as long as I live."

"How about the word *marriage?*" he asked quietly. "Do you think you might want to hear it again one of these days?"

Her fingers clenched convulsively around the vinegar bottle. Very carefully she released it. "That's the second time you've mentioned marriage in the past twenty-four hours. Can I assume this is not a coincidence?"

"I promised myself I wouldn't bring it up again for at least another week, but I can't seem to help it. You know me, I've got a thing about neatness and order. A place for everything and everything in its place."

"Things seem to be going along quite well the way they are."

He nodded thoughtfully. "We could probably go on like this for a long time. But it feels—" He broke off, searching for the right word. He did not find it. "Like one of the file drawers in your office at Light Fantastic."

"Messy?"

He smiled, pleased that she had grasped the point. "Yes. Messy."

"What makes you think marriage would be neater?"

He met her eyes. "I think that in spite of our cluttered, untidy pasts, you and I both know how to make commitments and keep them."

"We've both made mistakes in the commitment department," she reminded him.

"I've thought about that. I've decided that our previous mistakes can be attributed to the fact that we made commitments to the wrong people. People who didn't have the same understanding of the word *commitment* that we have."

"I see." She looked down at the vinegar bottle as though it were a lit firecracker.

"I figure that two people who have a mutual, shared definition of the concept of commitment have a much better chance of making a marriage work."

"You once said something about a marriage of convenience. If you're under the impression that things might be simpler all the way around at Glow if we got married—"

"Don't get me wrong," Jasper said quickly. "I don't think that a marriage between us would be all that convenient. I have a nasty feeling that there will be times when we drive each other crazy."

She smiled slowly. "We might make it if neither one of us brings any filing home."

The look in her eyes made him think that he ought to invest in a red cape and blue tights. He had the feeling he could leap over tall buildings and catch bullets in his teeth.

"It's a deal," he said. "We leave the filing in the office."

Olivia opened her eyes and looked at the glowing numerals on the bedside clock. Two in the morning.

She sat straight up in bed. "Good grief, Jasper, I just realized we *can't* possibly get married."

Beside her, Jasper groaned into his pillow. He did not turn over.

She looked at him. The city lights showed her that he was sprawled on his stomach. She could see his sleek, bare shoulders above the tide line of the sheet. His dark hair was rumpled from sleep.

"Jasper? Did you hear me?"

"Uh-huh."

"Say something."

There was a short pause before he finally mumbled more words into the pillow. "Okay. Why can't we get married?"

She frowned. "Everyone will think I'm marrying you because of Glow."

"You already own forty-nine percent of the company," he muttered with what sounded like weary patience.

"Forty-nine percent is not a controlling interest. People will naturally assume that I'm marrying you in order to exert more control over the company."

There was another brief silence, as if Jasper was trying to work through the logic of her statement.

"By controlling me?" he finally asked on a yawn.

"Yes. Exactly."

"Is that why you agreed to marry me?"

"Of course not."

"Good." He sounded as if he was about to slide back into sleep. " 'Cause it would be kind of a bad idea."

That gave her pause.

"Are you implying that, as your wife, I won't be able to exert a little influence over you?" she asked very sweetly.

"You'll be able to exert all kinds of influence over me," he mumbled. "I can't wait to be influenced by you. I fantasize about being influenced by you. I yearn to be influenced by you. My secret goal since the day we met is to be influenced by you."

"Hmm."

"Can I go back to sleep now?"

"You're not taking this problem very seriously, are you?"

"No," he admitted into the pillow. "Probably because I don't see a problem here."

"Spoken like a real CEO."

"Hey, that's why I get the corner office and the big—"

"Oh, no, you don't." She pounced, leaping astride his back and seizing his shoulders. "If you say one more word about big offices, big bucks, or corner windows, I swear I will—"

"Squeeze me a little tighter with your thighs?" he asked hopefully. "You could really exert a lot of influence if you did that."

She dissolved into helpless giggles.

Jasper surged up off the bed, dislodging her and sending her tumbling back onto the pillows. He leaned over her, eyes gleaming in the shadows.

"I thought you wanted to go back to sleep."

"For some reason," he said as he lowered his head, "I'm wide awake now."

A last flicker of unease went through her. She braced her hands on his shoulders to hold him off for a moment while she made one last attempt to get him to see reason.

"Jasper, we really should talk about how a marriage between us will affect the business side of things."

"Screw the business side of things." He kissed her throat. "You know what your problem is?"

She gasped when she felt his hand slide between her legs. "No. What is my problem?"

"You lack a certain sense of spontaneity."

"Is that so?" She clenched her fingers in his hair.

"Yeah, but don't worry about it. I've got enough for both of us."

"Yes," she whispered a moment later when he eased himself into her body. "You certainly do."

She woke up again at three-thirty. This time she did not rouse Jasper for a discussion of their future relationship. She had the impression he was not interested in another conversation on the subject so she conducted the argument silently in her own head.

All that stuff about not being able to marry him because people would think you're doing it to secure Glow's future was garbage, wasn't it?

Yes.

An excuse. Not the reason you just woke up in a cold sweat again.

True.

What's the real issue here?

I'm scared.

Why? You said you didn't want another marriage of convenience. Neither does Jasper. Both of you know what a marriage based on mutual business interests looks like from the inside. Whatever else this would be, it wouldn't be the kind of relationship you had with Logan.

So, why does Jasper want to get married?

He told you, he likes a well-organized life. An affair seems messy and disorganized to him.

You can't marry a man just because he thinks marriage is more tidy than an affair.

Why not?

It's not a good reason for marriage, that's all.
How do you know? You've never tried it.
I just know.
What is a good reason for marriage?
Love.
Do you love him?
Yes. Oh, lord, yes, yes, yes.
Then, what's the problem here?
The problem is that I don't know if he loves me. Maybe he's got his passion for order mixed up with his passion for me. Maybe that's what he calls love.
Ask him.

Olivia turned on her side and propped herself on her elbow. She gripped Jasper's shoulder and shook him gently.

"Jasper?"

"Now what?" he growled, in the voice of a bear that has been awakened in the middle of hibernation.

"Are you awake?"

"No."

"I have to ask you a question."

"Can't it wait until morning?"

"No. Do you want to marry me just because you've got your obsessive need to practice good filing habits mixed up with a physical attraction?"

There was a long silence.

"Jasper?"

He opened one eye. "Are there going to be a lot more questions in this vein?"

"Just this one."

"No." He closed his eye.

"No, what?" she asked. "No, you haven't got your

filing impulse mixed up with your sexual impulse? Or, no, you don't want to answer the question?"

"No, I haven't got my desire to organize things mixed up with my desire to make love to you. Believe it or not, I can tell the difference between both basic instincts."

"Oh, good." She waited. He said nothing else. "Is that all?"

There was no response. She realized he had fallen back into the depths of sleep.

30

Olivia was nervous. Nothing strange about that, Jasper thought the following morning as he parked the Jeep in a space on Second Avenue. After all, she'd already made one mistake with marriage. She was keenly aware of the risks involved. So was he, for that matter. Just one more thing they had in common.

She wouldn't panic on him just because she'd had a few qualms about accepting his proposal, he assured himself as he got out of the Jeep. At least, he didn't think she would panic.

But deep down he was afraid that he had rushed things. He wished he had the same instinct for timing in his personal affairs that he had in business. It would make life so much more orderly and predictable.

At least she had not spent breakfast grilling him with more of the strange questions she had asked in the middle of the night. He hoped that meant that his answers had satisfied her.

But deep down he was afraid he had not told her whatever it was she wanted to hear.

Of course, she had not told him what he had hoped to hear, either, he thought. He had not realized until this morning that there had been something missing last night.

He tried to convince himself that he had achieved his goal. Olivia had agreed to marry him. Theirs, clearly, would not be a marriage of convenience. What more could he want?

The answer had eluded him, so he had done what he always did when his personal life got fuzzy. He focused on other things.

There was still one loose end remaining to be tied off in the Dixon Haggard affair.

He walked along the sidewalk toward the storefront office that had served as Lancaster campaign headquarters. No one had bothered to take down the cheerful red, white, and blue pennants that fluttered from the awning. When he reached the front door, he glanced through the window.

From the outside there was nothing to indicate that Eleanor Lancaster's run for governor had collapsed last night. People sat at their desks. *Lancaster for Governor* signs were still plastered across the windows.

He opened the door and went inside.

It was like walking into the viewing room of a funeral parlor.

The subdued atmosphere and hushed conversations told the real tale of disappointment and despair.

A young woman with long blond hair sat at the front desk sniffling into a tissue. When she looked up, Jasper could see that her eyes were wet with tears. He resisted the urge to say something callous like, *hey, it's only politics*. He had a feeling that she would not appreciate his lack of empathy.

"If you're from the media," the receptionist whispered, "I'm afraid Ms. Lancaster is still not available for interviews."

"I'm looking for Todd Chantry."

"Oh." She glanced over her shoulder. "He's in the office at the back. But he's rather busy . . ."

"Thanks."

Jasper walked down an aisle formed by desks, toward the glass-walled office at the rear of the room. The people who sat at the desks did not look up from their somber conversations. Nobody appeared to be doing any work. They were all engaged in rehashing the bad news.

When he reached the closed door of the small office, Jasper saw that he had been wrong. One person was clearly working and working hard.

Todd had his shirtsleeves rolled up to the elbows. There was a five o'clock shadow on his face, even though it was only eight-thirty in the morning. He had a rumpled, harried look, as if he had been up most of the night.

Papers were spread across the desk in front of him.

There were two phones in the office. He was using both of them. One was cradled on his left shoulder. The other was pinned to his right ear. There was an ominous expression on his face as he spoke into the phone.

Jasper opened the door and went into the office.

". . . I don't give a damn what your computer says. I'm telling you that there was over two hundred thousand dollars in that account yesterday. . . ."

Jasper closed the door very quietly.

"I want to talk to your supervisor," Todd snapped. "No, not the computer room supervisor. I'll get back to you later if I need you." He hung up one of the phones and continued talking into the other. "Get me someone who knows what's going on there. Yes, I'll hold."

Jasper waited.

Todd glanced at him. His frown deepened. "Something wrong?"

"Got a couple of questions I thought you could help me with," Jasper said. He raised a brow to acknowledge the phone Todd still had plastered to one ear. "If you've got time, that is."

Todd started to respond, but someone on the other end of the line said something that distracted him.

"What do you mean he's out of the building?" Todd paused. "All right, all right. Have him call me the minute he returns. In the meantime, see if you can find someone else who can help me. You've got my number. If I don't hear from you in the next ten minutes I'll call you back."

He slammed down the phone and glared at Jasper. "This is not my thing, you know."

"What isn't your thing?"

"Straightening out the business side of this mess. Hell, I'm a policy and theory man, not an accountant. But as you can see, everything is a little crazy today. And with Haggard in jail—"

"Dixon Haggard is the reason I'm here today."

"Yeah?" Todd took off his glasses and began to polish them absently with a handkerchief. "Sit down. Want some coffee?"

"No, thanks. I had some before I left—" Jasper broke off. He had been about to say, *before I left your sister's place this morning*, but he decided against it. Todd was well aware that he was involved in an affair with Olivia, but somehow it seemed a trifle undiplomatic to flaunt it. "I had some with breakfast."

"Suit yourself. I need another cup." Todd got to his feet and crossed the small office to pour a thick, foul-looking dark brew from a pot. "I'm going through this stuff the way Olivia did after we got word about Uncle Rollie and she suddenly found herself in charge of both Glow and Light Fantastic."

This was probably as good a time as any, Jasper thought. "Speaking of Olivia . . ."

"What about her?" Todd raised the mug to his mouth and took a long swallow.

"I'm going to marry her."

Coffee spewed from between Todd's teeth. "Jesus H. Christ."

"I assume that means we have your blessing?"

Todd put down his mug and reached for a napkin. He eyed Jasper as he wiped his mouth. "Is this some kind of joke? Because if so, your timing is really lousy. This is not one of my better days."

"My timing is not always great, except in business, but I can promise you, I'm not joking."

Todd sat down heavily. He regarded Jasper with wary eyes. "Has Olivia accepted your, uh, proposal?"

"Yes."

"Huh." Todd leaned back in his chair. He looked dazed. "Sonofagun."

"You know, for an academic think-tank type, you don't seem to have what anyone would call an expansive vocabulary this morning."

"I'm not at my best at the moment." Todd gripped the wooden arms of his chair and shook his head. "Kind of sudden, isn't it?"

"We haven't set the date, if that's any consolation."

Todd sat forward abruptly. "Look, this isn't any of my business . . . Hell, yes, it is. She's my sister." He narrowed his eyes. "Are you real sure you know what you're doing here?"

"Yes."

"Whose idea was this, anyhow?"

"You could say we held talks on the subject and came to a mutually agreed-upon decision."

Todd folded his hands on the desk. "You're positive the idea did not originate with Olivia?"

"What makes you think it did?"

"Damn it, Sloan, you know what's bothering me here. I mean, in addition to the speed with which it's all happening, that is."

"Why don't you just come out and say it?"

"All right, I will." Todd gave him a very direct look. "Let's go to the bottom line, as you business types like to say. Uncle Rollie always treated her as his second-in-command. My sister has been known to go above and beyond the call of duty when it comes to what she feels are her responsibilities to the family."

"I'm aware of that."

"Is there any possibility that she may have put the idea of marriage into your head because she's convinced that she can protect Glow and Chantry family interests by marrying you?"

"No."

Todd blinked owlishly. "You're, uh, sure of that?"

"Positive."

Todd cleared his throat. "What makes you so certain?"

"A couple of reasons. First, I asked her if she was marrying me in hopes of controlling Glow through me."

Todd looked flabbergasted. "You *asked* her that straight out?"

"Well, she raised the issue first. I could tell that it was worrying her that everyone would think Glow was the reason she had agreed to marry me. So we discussed it." And when she had stopped laughing, he had made love to her until all she could say was his name over and over again as she convulsed in his arms.

"I see. What's the second reason you're so sure she didn't agree to marry you on account of Glow?"

"Olivia and I have a working arrangement. She knows that, whenever possible, I will consult with her before I carry out crucial decisions at Glow. But she understands that as long as I own fifty-one percent of the company, I will make the decisions that affect it."

"Huh," Todd muttered again. He unclasped his hands and began to massage the back of his neck. "There's probably something more I should say here, but I can't seem to think of it."

"Maybe it will come to you later."

"Where is Olivia, anyway? At Light Fantastic?"

"No. She's on her way down to the waterfront pier warehouse where the Lancaster fund-raiser was going to be held. She told Bolivar and a couple of her staff to meet her there so that they can start taking apart the stage and the decorations."

Todd nodded wearily. "She probably wants to get that big lighted flag and the sound system equipment out of there as quickly as possible."

"I think she has visions of trying to sell one of the other candidates on the idea of using them for a rally."

"That's my sister." Todd smiled slightly. "Always got an eye on the bottom line."

"Yes. Mind if I ask some questions about Dixon Haggard?"

"What?" Todd scowled. "Oh, sure. What about him?"

Jasper glanced at the calendar on the wall. "I'd like to know where he was on the twenty-sixth of last month."

Todd followed his gaze to the calendar and frowned. "Why?"

"Because I'm trying to tie up a few loose ends. Olivia can tell you that I tend to be a little obsessive about details."

"I'm not sure where he was." Todd squinted slightly, concentrating. "As I recall, he was out of town on campaign business for a couple of days around that time."

"Do you know where he went?"

"No. I just remember him saying something about accepting a check from a big out-of-state donor. Some VIP he had to deal with personally." Todd sighed. "A lot of important people had their eye on Eleanor as a future candidate for Congress or even the White House."

"Any way of finding out exactly where he went?"

Todd thought about it. "I guess we could check the travel records."

"I'd appreciate it."

"This is important?"

"Yes," Jasper said.

"Hell, why not. It isn't as if I've got anything else to do today except deal with the bank, the media, and a bunch of sobbing campaign volunteers."

Todd got to his feet and went to a tall black file cabinet that stood against the wall. He opened a drawer and started rummaging through the files.

Jasper rose and crossed the room to join him. "How's Eleanor handling things?"

"She's in seclusion." Todd did not look up from the files. "Won't talk to the press. Won't even answer the phone."

"You don't sound too empathetic."

"I'm pretty disgusted, if you want to know the truth. The least she could have done was come down here to say thanks to her faithful troops." He nodded toward the small group in the other room. "They worked their tails off for her, and she just walked out on them the minute things got rough."

"You really think she could have overcome the setback caused by Haggard's arrest?"

"I don't know. What makes me angry is that she didn't even try. I always thought she was a fighter, but I guess I was wrong." Todd removed a folder from the drawer. "Here's the travel file. The campaign booked all flights and hotel reservations through an outside agency."

It took Jasper less than three minutes to determine that there was no record of air travel for anyone connected to the Lancaster Campaign during the period when he, himself, had been rusticating on Pelapili Island.

Obviously he had been paranoid, after all.

"That's strange." Todd scanned the travel sheets. "I know Haggard was out of town for a couple of days. And I'm damn sure he wouldn't have paid for his own airfare. He was too cheap. Hang on, I'll ask Sally if she remembers how that trip was handled."

Sally proved to be the blond receptionist. She, too, recalled that Haggard had been out of town on a business trip.

"He didn't ask me to make the arrangements with the travel agency the way he usually did, though," she said. "I assumed he made them himself."

Todd glanced at the clock. "If it's that important, I can call the agency. It opens early."

"I'd really like to get some answers," Jasper said.

"I would, too." Todd picked up the phone. "Looks like I'm going to be spending my whole day on financial matters."

Ten minutes later Todd hung up the phone again.

He looked at Jasper with a troubled expression.

"The agency has no record of any bookings for Dixon Haggard or anyone else connected to the campaign around that time. Any other ideas?"

"Dixon could have made his own reservations. Let's try another angle. Do you have a record of which VIP donor he went to see?"

"Of course." Todd grimaced. "At least, we sure as hell better have a record. Eleanor was scrupulous about the records of all campaign finances, but after what's happened at the bank this morning, I don't know—" He broke off. "Forget it. That's another problem. Let me get the info on big donors out of the computer."

A few minutes later Todd conceded defeat. There was no record of any major donation to the Lancaster campaign during the entire week following the twenty-sixth.

"I don't understand this," Todd said. "I know Haggard was out of town, and he told me, himself, he was off to take care of a big donor."

"The phrase *take care of* has a variety of different meanings."

Todd frowned. "What are you getting at here?"

"I'll tell you after we check a couple of other things."

"Why don't you tell me now?"

"Because I'm going to marry your sister," Jasper said dryly. "I'd like to make a good impression on the family. I don't want the Chantrys thinking that I've got an acute paranoia disorder."

"The Chantrys are a many and varied clan. In the

grand scheme of things, paranoia would probably be viewed as a relatively minor affliction."

"I appreciate that." Jasper glanced at the glowing computer screen. "Can you access the campaign bank account?"

"Sure. I've been working on that damned account all morning." Todd swung around in his chair and punched in some letters and numbers.

A moment later the record of transactions appeared.

"Go back to the period around the twenty-sixth," Jasper said.

A list of deposits received and checks issued by the campaign arrayed itself neatly on the screen. Jasper studied the numbers for a few minutes.

"See anything interesting?" Todd asked.

"That two thousand dollars on the twenty-fourth," Jasper said slowly. "It was not a check issued to pay a bill."

"No." Todd eyed the screen more closely. "The money was transferred into another account." He pointed to a string of numbers that followed the record of the transaction. "That one."

"I don't suppose you recognize the number of that account?"

"No, but it shouldn't be too hard to get the name on it."

"Let's start with Dixon Haggard," Jasper said.

Todd looked thoughtful. "Easy enough to do. Dixon was usually too busy to go to the bank. He often sent Sally. She probably has some of his deposit slips in her desk drawer."

The fog that had clouded portions of the scene was

finally beginning to clear. Soon, Jasper thought, he would have the whole picture. He was suddenly in a great hurry to get the answers. An unpleasant sense of urgency slid through him.

He should have come here sooner, he thought. He had the uneasy feeling that his timing was a little off this morning.

"Get Sally in here," he said. "Now."

31

Olivia glanced at her watch as she walked across the old, scarred timbers that formed the floor of the cavernous warehouse.

Bolivar, Bernie, and Matty were late. She had phoned the studio just before leaving the condo and left a message instructing them to meet her here. They were probably still enjoying their morning hit of caffeine and news at Café Mantra, she thought.

If they didn't show up in the next few minutes, she would call the coffee shop and tell someone to send the Light Fantastic staff off to work.

She walked toward the bunting-draped stage and podium. The shadowed warehouse was so quiet that she could hear the creak of pilings and the muffled slap of water beneath the pier.

She walked up the steps and across the stage to the red, white, and blue curtains that concealed the sound system and the control panel. She glanced up at the heavy, carefully rolled flag overhead.

Her staff had outdone themselves. It really would have been a spectacular production, she thought. Maybe it wasn't too late to interest the Stryker campaign. She wondered if she should delay the teardown until she got hold of a Stryker publicist. If she could talk someone into coming down here to the pier for a demonstration . . .

The squeak of aging timbers broke into her thoughts. The hair stirred on the nape of her neck. She glanced toward the entrance of the warehouse. A figure stood in the gloom.

"Bolivar? About time you got my message. But maybe it's just as well you're a little late. I'm thinking it might be a good idea to call the folks at Stryker headquarters. I might be able to talk them into using this entire setup."

"That's one of the things I've always admired about you, Olivia." Eleanor Lancaster walked through the shadows toward the stage. "You've got your priorities straight. The corpse of my campaign isn't even cold yet, but you're already planning to turn a profit on the remains."

"Eleanor." A sizzle of guilt shot through Olivia. Her words had no doubt sounded extremely callous to a woman who had to be very depressed this morning. "I wasn't expecting you. What are you doing here?"

"I came to say good-bye."

Eleanor stopped at the foot of the short flight of steps that led up to the podium. She gripped the strap of her elegant leather shoulder bag very tightly. Dressed in a fitted red jacket, white blouse, and navy blue trousers, her hair bound sleekly at the nape of her neck, she looked as polished and purposeful as ever.

The tragic heroine air that had come through so powerfully on television last night no longer radiated from her. In its place was the familiar aura of cool-headed determination and charismatic energy that had made her such a standout in the field of campaigners.

"I know this has been a very difficult time for you," Olivia said quietly.

Eleanor's smile was devoid of any real warmth. "You have no idea."

Olivia was suddenly aware of a hot-cold sensation. An uneasy awareness hummed through her. The energy that always vibrated in the air around Eleanor seemed darker, more intense this morning.

Instinctively Olivia edged back a step. The movement brought her up against the curtain at the rear of the stage.

Don't get paranoid here, she told herself. Stay calm. Eleanor's a little upset. Perfectly natural.

She took hold of the edge of the curtain to steady herself. "You know, Eleanor, I have to say I'm a little surprised at how quickly you threw in the towel. I thought you'd stay in the race and fight."

"You haven't got a clue, have you?" Eleanor opened her purse and reached inside. "You have no concept of the damage you did."

"What are you talking about?"

"You're quite right. I could have won the election if I'd stayed in it." Eleanor removed an object from her shoulder bag. "But you made that impossible. You screwed up everything, Olivia. Every single plan I had so painstakingly made. And now I have no choice but to disappear."

Light glinted dully on the pistol in her hand.

Olivia stared, unable to believe what she was seeing. She swallowed and tightened her grip on the curtain.

"I don't know what you're talking about," she whispered. Bolivar and the others would be here any minute, she thought. All she had to do was keep Eleanor occupied until they got here. "You could have been the next governor of this state. You might have been president in a few years."

"Yes." Eleanor smiled again and started up the steps. "Yes, I most certainly would have been the next governor, and I could have gone all the way to the White House. But that is no longer possible, thanks to you."

"Why do you keep blaming me for your problems?"

"There are others who deserve blame, of course. But no matter how I look at the situation, I realize that you are at the heart of it. And so it is you who will pay." Eleanor sighed. "Unfortunately, I don't have time today to take my revenge on Sloan, although, perhaps, at some point in the future, I may get an opportunity to do so."

"Revenge for what, Eleanor?"

"Where to begin?" Eleanor pursed her lips. "Shall we start with the fact that your uncle left only forty-nine percent of Glow to you instead of the entire business?"

"What does that have to do with anything?"

"I thought you were smarter than this, Olivia. Use your head. I had a choice of several highly experienced campaign consultants. Why do you think I chose one who lacked a track record?"

"Todd?"

"It wasn't just his policy ideas that interested me, you know." She chuckled. "It was the fact that, through you, he was connected to Glow, Inc. A company that stood to make a great deal of money during the next decade."

Understanding hit Olivia in a sickening wave. "And you're going to need a lot of money if you go for the White House, aren't you? For God's sake, don't tell me you somehow arranged for Uncle Rollie to die in that balloon accident?"

"No." Eleanor's laugh was deep and throaty. "I saw no need to take that risk. After all, he was a very old man. He was bound to drop dead or retire soon. Either way the company was supposed to come to you. I didn't know about his arrangements with Jasper Sloan until after his death."

"None of us did. Are you telling me that you expected me to finance your political career?"

Eleanor shrugged. "You have a reputation for seeing the possibilities when it comes to other people's futures. Look at what you did for Logan Dane and Crawford Lee Wilder. And you do have a thing about taking care of family."

Olivia was incredulous. "You figured that if you

married Todd, I'd feel obliged to help finance your political aspirations? For his sake?"

"Why not? You would be ensuring Todd's future, not just mine. Your brother would have been famous. The Chantry family would have been connected to the White House, to power. What sister wouldn't have financed that kind of career?"

Olivia stared at her. "Eleanor, for a smart woman, you amaze me. That is some of the craziest logic I have ever heard."

"No, it wasn't crazy. But if the plan had failed, I had a fallback position." Eleanor came to a halt next to the podium. "If you had not proven cooperative, I would have arranged to get rid of you. In which case control of Glow, Inc., would have gone to Todd."

Olivia could not catch her breath. Eleanor was right. Todd was the only other person in the Chantry family who could have handled Glow, and everyone knew it. Even if she had arranged for shares in the company to go to every member of the Chantry clan, she knew her relatives would have left the running of the business to Todd.

"But it didn't happen that way," Olivia pointed out desperately. "My uncle took on a partner. Sloan now owns controlling interest in Glow."

"Yes. That was a shock. I tried a quick, surgical strike to get rid of Sloan while he was out of the country. I thought that any investigation of a deadly accident involving a tourist would be superficial at best on that backwater island."

"You tried to murder Jasper?"

Eleanor smiled grimly. "Unfortunately, Dixon failed

me on that occasion. I did not want to risk another attempt here in Seattle during the campaign. There was too much media attention focused on all of us. I decided to wait until after the election before making another move to get rid of Sloan. But things got complicated. First Gill tried to blackmail Dixon—"

"And then Todd decided he didn't want to marry you after all."

"Thanks to you." Eleanor's fingers tightened on the gun. "You talked him out of it, didn't you?"

"He made his own decision."

"Bullshit. You ruined that plan, too, just like you ruined everything else."

"Why do you keep blaming everything on me?"

"Because other than myself, you were the most powerful piece on this damned chessboard." Sudden rage infused Eleanor's voice. *"You were the only one I worried about. Everyone else could be managed."*

"The way you managed Dixon Haggard? You used him all along, didn't you?" Olivia whispered. "You took advantage of his obsession with you. I'll bet you convinced him to murder your husband, didn't you?"

"Dixon is a fool, but he has one great attribute. He is blindly devoted to me." Eleanor smiled tightly. She had the rage back under control. "Unfortunately, now that he has been arrested, I can no longer depend on that devotion. His lawyer has advised him to stop talking, of course, but sooner or later, Dixon will say something to implicate me. He won't be able to help himself."

Olivia clenched the curtain. "That's the real reason you terminated your campaign, isn't it? You're going to disappear because you're afraid that Dixon will break down soon and tell the cops that you used him as a hit man."

"There is absolutely no proof that I had Dixon get rid of Richard or that I sent him to Pelapili to try to take out Sloan, but once he starts talking, I will be ruined."

"So you're on your way out of town, is that it?"

"Yes. I cleaned out the campaign bank account late yesterday afternoon before the press conference. My flight to the Caribbean leaves in an hour and a half. I doubt if anyone will find your body until this afternoon. By that time I will be safely out of the country."

Olivia took another step back. "My staff is due here at any minute."

"When I saw you leave your condominium building this morning and walk toward the waterfront, I assumed you would be coming here to dismantle the stage and props for the fund-raiser. So I called the Light Fantastic studio."

"What did you tell my staff?"

"I said that I was the receptionist at the Lancaster campaign headquarters. I told the young man who answered the phone that you were there at headquarters talking to your brother and that something had come up. I said you had asked me to call your office to cancel all of your morning appointments."

"But Bolivar will know to go ahead with the teardown," Olivia warned.

"Whoever took the message was very helpful. He asked if he and the others were to go ahead with the project here at the pier. I told him you said to wait until later today."

Olivia took one last small step back and came up hard against the control panel. She put out a hand to steady herself.

Eleanor raised the pistol and aimed it at her heart.

"It's Dixon Haggard's account, all right." Todd's jaw tightened angrily. He studied the deposit slip he held. "I can't think of a single good reason why two thousand dollars from the campaign fund would have been transferred into his personal account."

"I can." Jasper gazed at the glowing computer screen. "Two thousand dollars would have covered the cost of a flight out to Pelapili, a rental car, and a couple of days in a hotel."

"What are you talking about?"

"I'll explain later." Jasper reached for the phone and started to dial the number of the Light Fantastic studio. "Get on the other line. Call Lancaster. Make certain she's still at home."

"She won't pick up the phone. She's screening her calls."

"Tell her it's urgent." Jasper listened to the ringing on the other end of the line. "Tell her a big donor just called and promised to arrange for a new infusion of cash. That should get her attention, if she's there."

"Are you nuts? What's going on here?" Nevertheless, Todd reached for the phone. He dialed quickly, listened impatiently for a few seconds, and then spoke. "Eleanor, if you're there, pick up. You won't believe what just happened. Money is flowing into the campaign."

There was still no answer at Light Fantastic. Was that good news or bad news? Jasper wondered. Maybe the entire staff was with Olivia, in which case she would be safe.

Or maybe she was alone. His insides fused.

A familiar, slightly breathless voice answered. "Light Fantastic. This is Zara. Can I help you?"

"Zara, it's Jasper. Did Bolivar and the team go down to the warehouse to meet Olivia?"

"No, Olivia sent a message telling us to delay the teardown."

"Damn." Jasper tossed the phone aside and started for the door.

"Eleanor's still not picking up." Todd dropped the phone into the cradle. "Hey, where are you going?"

"The warehouse." Jasper zigzagged through the crowded outer office, ignoring the startled looks from the staff.

"Why?" Todd hurried after him. "What the hell is going on here?"

Jasper slammed through the front door and out onto the sidewalk. "You told me yourself that any check or transfer of an amount over two hundred dollars in that account had to have Eleanor Lancaster's written approval, right?"

"Right." Todd followed Jasper to the Jeep. "What about it?"

Jasper yanked open the door on the driver's side, slid behind the wheel, and shoved the keys into the ignition. "So if I'm right about Dixon having used that money to fly out to Pelapili, then we have to assume that Lancaster sent him out there. She would have been the one who authorized the transfer of funds that enabled him to go."

"Why would she do that?" Todd closed the passenger door as the Jeep leaped away from the curb.

"I'll tell you on the way down to the waterfront." Jasper ran the red light at the intersection.

A litany started up in his brain. It pounded through his veins. *I won't be too late. I can't be too late.*

But his timing was off. He could feel it in his bones.

Olivia abandoned the frail hope that Bolivar, Bernie, and Matty would burst through the door to unwittingly rescue her. The pistol in Eleanor's hand did not waver.

"You know, Eleanor, you really would have made an interesting governor."

"I would have made a great governor." Rage leaped in Eleanor's eyes. "And an even greater president. This state needed me. This country needed me. But now, because of you, everything is finished."

Olivia gathered herself. "I always say, give the client what she wants. Eleanor, I want you to know that we at Light Fantastic had planned a really spectacular finale for the fund-raiser. I'd hate for you to leave town without seeing that you got what you paid for."

She swept out a hand and hit a row of switches on the control panel.

Martial music swelled suddenly, surging through the speakers on either side of the stage. Drums thundered. Horns blared. The exhilarating strains of a hundred-voice chorus filled the warehouse.

—Sweet land of liberty

The roaring music shattered Eleanor's focused determination for an instant. She flinched.

"Shut that off." Her gaze shifted wildly toward the nearest speaker.

Olivia dove off the back of the stage. She landed heavily on a tangle of electrical cords.

"Damn you, this country needed me," Eleanor screamed.

Red, white, and blue light blazed in the cavernous gloom of the warehouse. Sprawled on the nest of cords, Olivia looked up and saw the huge flag unfurl in all its glowing majesty.

—Land of the pilgrims' pride

Eleanor came to stand at the edge of the stage. She peered down, searching the gloom for her target.

Olivia rolled off the pile of cords and threw herself headlong beneath the stage. The lights of the flag created a dazzling glare that cast her hiding place into dense shadow. She could crawl out on the opposite side near the steps.

She paused when her hand touched a length of metal on the floor. One of the structural pieces left over from the construction of the some-assembly-required platform overhead. She picked it up.

Another scream, this one of fear rather than rage echoed through the warehouse. Eleanor must have finally looked up and seen the descending flag, Olivia thought.

But it was too late. There was a shuddering crash

on the floor of the stage as Eleanor, scrambling to get out of the way, lost her balance and fell.

Olivia crawled out from under the stage, metal bar in hand. This would be her only chance to try to get the gun away from Eleanor.

But when she stood upright and whirled around to survey the situation she saw that there was no great need to grab the pistol.

Eleanor was trapped unmoving beneath the heavy flag. She had dropped the gun when she put out her hands to break her fall.

The blazing flag lit up the warehouse, and the majestic strains of the music continued to blare forth a moment later when the warehouse door slammed open.

Olivia stood in front of the glowing flag and watched Jasper and Todd rush toward her. She was trembling so violently that when Jasper reached her, she fell into his arms.

"It's about time you got here, partner," she whispered.

His arms tightened around her so violently that she could not say anything else for a long while.

32

It took some doing, but Jasper made certain that they caught the six-fifteen ferry to Bainbridge that evening. They both needed the tranquillity of the island after the endless interviews with the police, phone calls, and demands for interviews. He was certain that the phone in Olivia's condo would be ringing all evening.

As far as he knew, neither the media nor any of Olivia's relatives had his unlisted island number.

They walked on board and stood at the rail as the ferry pulled away from the dock. The summer sun was still high in the evening sky. A warm, golden light glinted on the windows of the downtown highrises.

Jasper put his arm around Olivia and pinned her close against his side.

"She sent him to kill you." Olivia gripped the rail very tightly. "She thought that if she got rid of you in a sort of preemptive strike, it would be easier to control Glow."

Jasper felt the shudder that went through her. "What did she plan to do after Todd told her he did not want to marry her?"

"She expected Todd to stay with the campaign. She probably thought that he wouldn't be able to resist the chance to influence the national political agenda for the next few years. She thought she could manage and control everyone."

"She was living in a fantasy world."

"Yes." Olivia looked at him with huge eyes. "She intended to make another attempt to kill you. She was only biding her time until after the election. She was nervous about risking a second murder attempt while the campaign was under such intense media scrutiny."

He pulled her into his arms. "And when it all fell apart with Dixon's arrest, she came after you for revenge. You don't know what I went through this morning when I finally realized that it had to be Eleanor who had sent Haggard to Pelapili Island. It meant she was probably behind everything."

"How did you know she would try to kill me before she left town?"

"I knew she would be furious because all of her plans had gone down the toilet. She was a very driven woman. I was afraid that she would not be able to walk away without striking out at the one person she could blame for all that had gone wrong. Todd told me that she admired you, saw you as a kindred spirit. A reflection of herself. It was logical that she would turn on you when she, herself, failed."

Olivia smiled tremulously. "For a corporate type, you did a pretty good job of analyzing the psychology of her motivations."

"Trust me, there wasn't anything real deep about Eleanor's motivations."

"Very goal-oriented, would you say?"

He shook his head. "She was more than goal-oriented. She was a predator. And also nuttier than a fruitcake."

Olivia leaned her head against his shoulder. "I can't believe we actually got through the whole thing without anyone finding out that Melwood Gill was blackmailing us as well as Dixon Haggard."

"Just goes to show the value of good teamwork."

"Uh-huh. So what happens if the information leaks out again sometime in the future?"

"I doubt if it will, but if it does, we'll handle it. Hell, we can handle anything together."

"You may, just possibly, be right about that."

The snapping breeze loosened her hair. A few tendrils curled around his neck. He savored the silky feel of it as he watched the glowing city recede across the waters of Elliott Bay.

"You scared the living hell out of me today." He kept his voice very even, very flat, because there was no other way to control the anger and fear that still stormed inside him. "If you hadn't saved yourself by distracting her with the music and that business with the flag . . ."

"You would have saved me, instead. You and Todd."

"We were about two minutes too late." He heard

her suck in her breath and realized that he squeezed her a little too tightly. "Two damned minutes."

She put her arms around his waist and hugged him back hard enough to remind him of the ribs that had gotten bruised in the fight with Dixon. "I'll make a deal with you. If you promise not to dwell on those two minutes, I'll try not to have nightmares about what almost happened on Pelapili Island."

He thought about that. He didn't think he could keep his end of the bargain. The memory of how he had very nearly lost her might fade a little with time, but he would never entirely forget that surge of panic that had sent him running from Lancaster headquarters.

But he also knew that neither he nor Olivia had any choice but to try to put the close brushes with death behind them. Businesspeople are natural optimists. They look to the future, not the past.

"Deal," he said finally.

She raised her head. Her eyes were brilliant in the long, gentle light. "Look at it this way. From now on, if either of us wakes up from a nightmare about what nearly happened to the other person, we'll have each other to hold on to until we go back to sleep."

Something tight within him was eased by that thought. "Good point."

They stayed that way, wrapped in each others' arms, for a while. And then Jasper kissed her.

Two days later the door to Olivia's office opened. She looked up from the stack of invoices spread out on her desk and watched a half dozen of her relatives march into the room. Bolivar was in the lead. Rose,

Zara, Percy, Quincy, and Barry trailed after him with obvious reluctance. No one smiled.

She sighed, put down her pen, and leaned back in her chair. "Is this about the Glow picnic? Because if it is, I promise you that it will be the best one yet. We're talking a live band, a new caterer, and fireworks."

Rose stepped forward. "This is not about the picnic. We're here to ask you if the rumors are true."

"Would those be the rumors concerning my secret dinosaur-cloning experiments or the ones regarding my decision to go into the astronaut training program?"

Bolivar planted his hands on the desk. "This is not a joke, cuz. Todd says you and Jasper Sloan are going to announce your engagement at the Glow annual picnic. True or false?"

"True."

Zara gave a small shriek. "Oh, my God, you're doing it for the sake of the family, aren't you? You're planning to sacrifice yourself to protect Glow. How incredibly noble of you, dear. I understand perfectly, of course. It's just the sort of thing Sybil would have done on *Crystal Cove*."

Quincy stirred uneasily. He exchanged a glance with Percy and straightened his shoulders.

"We're here to tell you that you don't have to do it, Olivia." He paused hopefully. "Unless you really want to, that is."

Bolivar threw him a glare and then switched his attention back to Olivia. "What Quincy means is, we don't want you to do it for us. Isn't that right, everyone?"

Percy cleared his throat and shuffled uncomfortably. "Yeah. Right. You don't have to marry the guy unless you want to."

Quincy brightened. "Right. But, like, if you love Sloan, or think he's really good in bed or something, it's fine by us."

"We wouldn't want to stand in the way of true love, of course," Zara said smoothly.

"Yeah, right," Barry added on a rising note of optimism. "Nothing like true love."

Bolivar quelled them all with another glowering look. "But we definitely do not want Olivia to marry Sloan for our sakes. Right, everyone?"

"Uh-huh," Quincy muttered.

"We don't want you to feel pressured," Bolivar elaborated firmly.

"Yeah, sure." Percy grimaced. "Right. No pressure."

Rose coughed slightly. "We certainly don't want you to endure another unhappy marriage. However, I would like to point out that there's something to be said for a relationship based on mutual interests, and there's nothing like sharing ownership of a large company such as Glow to provide a strong bond of mutual—"

"You do seem rather attracted to him, dear." Zara beamed at her. "And if that's the case, of course, then you must follow your heart."

"Thank you." Olivia gave everyone in the small group a benign smile. "I appreciate your concern for my happiness."

"On the other hand," Percy said quickly, "a sense of family responsibility is a wonderful thing."

"Sure is," Quincy added. "Uncle Rollie would have been real proud of you."

Olivia smiled blandly. "I can't tell you what it means to me to have the full support of my family in this matter."

"Hey, that's what family's for," Quincy assured her.

Olivia got to her feet and narrowed her eyes. "Let's get something clear here. I am not going to marry Jasper Sloan for the sake of my beloved family. Nor am I marrying him because Uncle Rollie would have wanted me to do it. I am not marrying him to protect Glow, Inc."

The crowd in front of the desk stared at her, fascinated.

Rose blinked. "But you do intend to marry him?"

"Yes, I do."

Barry looked at her blankly. "How come?"

"Good question." Jasper materialized in the doorway. He regarded Olivia across the heads of the gathered Chantrys. "Why are you going to marry him?"

An acute silence fell. Like a small school of fish, the members of the Chantry delegation turned to stare at Jasper. Then, without a word, they all swiveled back to Olivia.

She smiled at Jasper. "I'm going to marry him because I love him."

The jaws of the various and assorted Chantrys standing in front of her dropped simultaneously as if on cue.

Jasper ignored them. He did not take his gaze off Olivia. The unfathomable expression in his eyes vanished. A steady heat burned there.

"Nice to hear that," he said. "Because I'm marrying you for a very similar reason. I love you."

33

"About time you got married again, Uncle Jasper." Paul glanced across the top of the crowd to where Olivia stood chatting with Andy Andrews. "I like her."

"Glad to hear it." Jasper followed Paul's gaze. He felt a curious warmth infuse him. He was slowly growing accustomed to this sensation of happiness and satisfaction, he realized. He would never take it for granted, but he had reached the point where he could trust the feeling. With Olivia by his side, it would last.

The annual Glow, Inc., picnic was a success. The smell of broiled salmon and roasted corn on the cob wafted across the crowded park. Pennants snapped from the colorful tents. Children dashed back and forth. Most were playing with samples of the newest product line from Glow's toy division: miniature instant-glow vehicles that looked as if they had been designed on another planet.

On a stage decorated with hundreds of brightly lit Glow products, musicians dressed in jeans and boots pounded out lively country music.

"It was kind of a relief to hear that you're going to marry Olivia, if you want to know the truth." Kirby looked at Jasper with serious eyes. "Paul and I have been a little worried about you lately."

Jasper raised his brows. "Worried?"

"It's not normal for a man your age to live alone," Kirby explained in knowledgeable tones. "And when you sold Sloan & Associates to Al, we were afraid that you might be having something more than a midlife crisis."

Paul wrinkled his nose. "Kirby thought you were sinking into depression. I told him you were just bored. All you needed was a new goal in life. Looks like you found it."

"Yes," Jasper said dryly, "I certainly did."

Al Okamoto wandered over. He had two paper cups in his hands, one of which he offered to Jasper.

"Thanks." Jasper took the cup. He looked down and saw that it held iced tea. "Having a good time?"

"Great party," Al said. "Wouldn't have missed it for the world. So, when are you and Olivia going to get busy having kids?"

Jasper looked at him. "Kids?"

"Yeah, you know." Al held one hand out to indicate

a low level on his leg. "Short little people who get bigger."

"Al's right," Paul nodded soberly. "You'd make a great father. Just ask me or Kirby."

"Yeah," Kirby said. "Think about it."

Paul grinned. "You've probably got all those books you used that first year with me and Kirby still stored in the basement."

Amusement gleamed in Al's eyes. "Don't take too long to make up your mind. After all, it's not like you're getting any younger, you know."

"Thanks for pointing that out to me, Al."

But when he looked at Olivia again, Jasper had a sudden vision of her holding an infant to her breast while she orchestrated a Light Fantastic production. He smiled to himself as he felt the rightness of it all envelope him.

He and Olivia could do kids, he thought. Hell, they could do anything together.

"When's the big announcement going to take place?" Al asked.

Jasper glanced at his watch. "I believe Olivia has us scheduled to go on in about five minutes. We're part of the entertainment."

"Come on, Olivia, give me something I can use," Andy urged. "I'm going to give you another great mention in *Hard Currency*."

"I don't know what else I can tell you," Olivia said. "You got the press release."

"All it said was that the two owners of Glow, Inc., would announce their engagement today at the annual company picnic. Big deal. I'm looking for the business angle. Is this a classic marriage of convenience made to strengthen the image of Glow, Inc., in the eyes of potential buyers or investors?"

"No," Olivia said patiently. "This is not a business marriage. Glow, Inc., will remain a family-held company."

"How do we know that?"

Olivia glared at him. "You know, Andrews, I'm getting a little tired of your interest in my private life."

Jasper came up behind her. He gave Andy a smile that held an unmistakable hint of warning. "No more questions from the press. This is supposed to be a party." He looked at Olivia. "I think it's time for our announcement."

She made a show of glancing at the stage where the musicians had just ended a song. "It certainly is." She flashed a dismissing smile at Andy. "I'm afraid you'll have to excuse us."

She allowed Jasper to take her arm and steer her toward the lighted stage.

"Nice going," she said. "Your timing, as always, was excellent. I was just about to pour my iced tea over Andy."

"I know. And although it's a tempting thought, I don't think it would have done the company image any good."

"I suppose you're right," she said regretfully.

"I'm always right when it comes to corporate matters. Heck, that's why I get the corner—"

Olivia clapped her hands over her ears. "No, don't say it. I can't stand it."

"The corner office with the big windows," he concluded as he guided her up the stage steps. "By the way, in line with our agreement to discuss major business decisions whenever possible before I finalize them, I have an issue I would like to bring up."

Warily she took her hands away from her ears. "What issue is that?"

He did not answer immediately. Instead, he brought her to a halt in front of the podium. Olivia looked out at the sea of faces made up of friends, family, and employees of Glow, Inc. She was conscious of how very good she felt today. Uncle Rollie would have been pleased, she thought, as an expectant hush fell over the crowd.

"I was wondering," Jasper said loudly enough that the microphone picked up the words, "what you thought about having a couple of kids?"

The words boomed out from the speakers on either side of the stage. For an instant, everyone, including Olivia, was too startled to react.

Olivia recovered first. She put her arms around Jasper's neck. "I think that sounds like a terrific idea."

Jasper grinned. Instead of making the formal announcement of their engagement to the crowd, he pulled Olivia into his arms and kissed her.

A loud cheer erupted from the throng gathered in front of the stage.

Out of the corner of her eye, Olivia caught a glimpse of the company slogan spelled out in flashing lights overhead. She decided it said it all.

TOWARD A GLOWING FUTURE

Pocket Books
Proudly Presents

Eye of the Beholder

Jayne Ann Krentz

Available in paperback
from
Pocket Books

Turn the page for a preview of
Eye of the Beholder. . . .

Avalon, Arizona
Twelve years earlier

He swept into the house out of the hot desert night, an avenging warlock from the dark canyons carrying thunder and lightning in his fists.

Alexa froze at the top of the stairs when she heard his voice in the hall. Her sudden stillness was instinctive, the immediate, elemental reaction of any creature to the presence of a potential predator.

"I don't know whether it was you or Guthrie who killed my father, Kenyon," he said. "Hell, for all I know, the two of you planned it together."

The night was warm but Alexa shivered in the shadows above the hall. John Laird Trask was young, somewhere in his early twenties, but the taut control he exerted over his icy rage would have done credit to a man twice his age.

"You listen to me, son, and you listen good." Lloyd Kenyon spoke with a calm authority that reverberated with an underlying sympathy. "No one murdered your father. Once you've had a chance to cool down and think about it you'll accept the facts. It was a tragic accident."

"Bullshit. Dad was a good driver and he knew that road. He didn't go off Avalon Point by accident. One of you forced him over the edge."

Alexa felt suddenly light-headed. A strange, unfamiliar panic left her fighting for breath. *Trask was threatening Lloyd.* He was not only a much younger man, he was even bigger than Lloyd, who still had plenty of bulk and muscle left over from the days when he had run construction crews.

Her anxiety for Lloyd's safety took her by surprise. Until tonight she would have sworn that she had no strong, personal attachment to him. She and her mother had moved in with him eighteen months ago following her parents' divorce. She had been careful to keep a cool distance between herself and this very large, unexciting, rock-steady businessman

Vivien had married; careful to make sure Lloyd understood that he could never take the place of the charismatic hero who had been her real father.

It had been a year since Crawford Chambers had been killed by a sniper's bullet. He had been halfway around the world at the time, photographing the latest in the long list of small, brutal civil wars that had made him a legend in journalism circles.

Crawford had been everything that Lloyd was not, a rakish, dashing, larger-than-life figure who lived life on the edge.

Her father would have been able to deal with Trask, Alexa thought. But staid, steady, unflappable Lloyd probably didn't stand a chance.

Trask's accusations were nothing but crazy talk, Alexa thought. Lloyd would never harm anyone.

She had to get to the phone.

The nearest extension was at the foot of the stairs. With an enormous effort of will, she fought through the temporary paralysis. She went silently, cautiously, down the stairs.

"It was raining that night." Lloyd's voice was calm, infused with reason. "This is what we call our monsoon season. Downpours are common. That stretch of the road is treacherous. Everyone around here knows that. I've always said that portion of Cliff Drive should be closed during a storm."

"The rain had passed by the time Dad got into the car," Trask said. "I checked with the cops."

"The roads were still wet. Even the best driver can make a mistake."

"This was no mistake," Trask said. "I know all about the partnership between the three of you. And I know about the offer from that hotel chain. Dad was murdered because someone wanted him out of the way."

Alexa realized he believed every word he said. She knew that he was wrong, at least about Lloyd. But Trask was clearly convinced that his father had been murdered.

She sensed her mother's presence on the steps behind her. She glanced over her shoulder. Vivien's fine-boned, ascetic face was taut with anxiety as she listened to the two men quarrel.

"You think I was involved in some kind of bizarre conspiracy to kill your father?" Lloyd's voice rose in disbelief. "That's outrageous."

"I looked through some of Dad's papers this afternoon. I heard about the quarrel at the country club the night he died. It didn't take me long to put it together."

"Business partners sometimes disagree. It's a fact of life, son."

"That argument was more than a disagreement. I talked to the bartender at the club. He said the three of you nearly came to blows."

"Guthrie gets a little hot-headed when he drinks," Lloyd admitted. "But I restrained him. There was no physical stuff."

"Maybe not then. But you and Guthrie knew that Dad would never agree to sell the Avalon Mansion property to that chain. So one of you found a way to get rid of him."

"Damn it, I've had enough." Lloyd's voice hardened. "I'm trying to be patient. I know you've had a hellish few days and I know you've got a lot of responsibility to shoulder. But you're going too far here."

"Believe me, Kenyon, I haven't even started."

"You're going to have to get your priorities straight, Trask. You've got your brother to think about. He's only seventeen and you're all the family that boy has left in the world."

"Thanks to you or Guthrie."

"That's a damn lie. When you come to your senses and calm down, you'll see that. Meanwhile, you'd better start thinking about the future. You've got your work cut out."

"Don't talk to me about my *work*, you sonofabitch."

"Someone better talk to you about it. You're going to have to get through the fallout from your father's bankruptcy and take care of your brother at the same time. That's a man-sized job. You need to get focused and stay that way. You can't afford to waste your energy chasing a wild conspiracy fantasy."

"I don't need you to tell me what I have to do, Kenyon. I'll take care of Nathan and I'll take care of myself. But one day I'll find out what really happened at Avalon Point the night Dad died."

Alexa reached the bottom of the stairs. Neither man noticed her. They were intent only on each other. Lloyd had his back to her as he confronted Trask.

This was the first time she had seen John Laird Trask in person. She knew from what Lloyd had said that his family came from Seattle. It was Harry Trask's plan to restore the old Avalon Mansion and turn it into a destination resort that had brought him to Arizona on a frequent and regular basis during the past year. His two sons had remained in Seattle.

Alexa paid little attention to Lloyd's business affairs even though he managed the inheritance she had received from her grandmother. As a result, she knew almost nothing about Harry Trask and even less about his sons.

But after tonight she knew that she would never forget John Laird Trask.

From where she stood she could see him looming in the hall, taking up far too much space. The warm glow of the overhead fixture did nothing to soften the sinister angles of his face and jaw. She could feel the energy waves of his fury.

She was only a step away from the phone now. She took a deep breath, stretched out her hand and picked up the receiver.

"If you don't go away right now, Mr. Trask, I'm going to call the police," she said with a fierceness that startled her as much as it did everyone else.

Both men swung around to stare at her, but it was Trask's relentless green-gold gaze that riveted her. For an instant she could not move. Her hand clenched around the phone.

"It's all right, Alexa." Lloyd's face gentled as he looked at her standing there with the phone clutched in her hand. "Everything is under control. Trask is leaving now. Isn't that right, Trask?"

Trask continued to watch Alexa for another

second or two, as if assessing both her and her threat. Abruptly he turned away, dismissing her with a cold disdain that sent another chill through her.

"Yeah, I'm going now, Kenyon," he said. "But one day I'll come back for the truth. And when I do, someone will pay. Count on it."

Without another word, he walked out into the night.

Twelve Years Later

She saw the Jeep first. A layer of desert grit dulled the dark green paint, evidence of a long drive. The vehicle was parked on the side of the road above Avalon Point. The sight of it brought her to a halt on the path.

It was not unusual to see a tourist stopped here at the Point. The sun was about to set and the view of the stark, red-rock landscape with its towers and canyons was magnificent at this time of day.

Alexa glanced around, searching for the Jeep's driver.

It took her a moment to find him. He stood deep in the long shadow cast by a stone outcropping.

The first thing that struck her was that he

was on the wrong side of the waist-high metal rail that had been erected a few years ago to protect sightseers. Alarm shot through her. He was much too close to the edge of the Point.

He seemed oblivious to the vibrant beauty of the spectacular terrain set afire by the dying light. As Alexa watched he gazed broodingly down into the brush-choked canyon. There was a dark intensity about him, as though he was engaged in reading omens and portents.

Sometimes an overly ambitious amateur photographer took one too many risks in an attempt to get the perfect sunset shot.

"Excuse me," she said loudly. "That guardrail is there for a good reason. It's dangerous to stand on the wrong side."

The man in the shadows turned unhurriedly to look at her.

Her first thought was that he could have stepped straight out of a Tamara de Lempicka painting.

The artist who had become known as the quintessential Art Deco portraitist would have loved him, Alexa thought. De Lempicka had excelled at creating a dark, sinister, edgy energy around her subjects. She had been able to endow them with a highly charged sensuality and an icy, enigmatic aura.

But in this man's case, Alexa thought, de Lempicka would not have had to invent the ominous illusion. The painter's only task would have been to capture the unsettling reality of it.

The jolt of recognition hit Alexa with such force she froze in mid-step.

Trask.

Twelve years older, harder, more dangerous, but unmistakably Trask. He looked even bigger than he had the last time she saw him. Lean and broad-shouldered, he still took up a lot of space. It was a wonder light did not bend to get around him.

He contemplated her for a moment.

"Thanks for the warning," he said.

He made no move to get back behind the guardrail. It figured, Alexa thought. This man was accustomed to standing on the edge of cliffs. She could tell that just by looking at him.

She realized she was holding her breath, waiting for him to recognize her. But he gave no indication that he remembered her from that long-ago scene in Lloyd's hall. She told herself she should be enormously relieved.

She released the breath she had been holding.

A gust of wind broke the peculiar little trance that had gripped her. She managed to keep her polite-to-the-tourist smile firmly fixed in place.

"You really should move back to the right side of that railing." She was horrified by the slightly breathless quality she heard in her own words. Get a grip, Alexa. "Didn't you see the sign?"

"Yeah, I saw it."

His voice was low and resonant. The voice of a man who did not have to speak loudly in order to get the attention of others. The voice of a man who was accustomed to giving orders and having them obeyed.

She had pushed her luck far enough. Time to make her exit before he recalled her face. No sense taking chances. She searched for a suitable exit line.

"Are you lost? Can I give you directions?" she asked.

He looked amused. "I know where I am."

"Well, in that case," she said briskly, "I'll be on my way. It's getting late."

He watched the breeze tangle her hair. "Can I give you a lift?"

"What? *No.*" Startled, she took a hasty step back, although he had made no move toward her. "I mean, thanks, but I live near here. I use this path for exercise." Lord, now she was babbling.

His brows rose. "It's all right. I'm not a serial killer."

She kept smiling. "Yeah, sure, that's what they all say."

"I take it you're the type who doesn't take lifts from strangers?"

"No intelligent person accepts rides from strangers in this day and age."

"Maybe I'd better introduce myself. My name is Trask. My company owns the new resort here in Avalon."

Stay cool, Alexa. "Nice to meet you, Mr. Trask."

"Just Trask."

"Yes, well, best of luck with the new resort." She retreated another step. "Everyone in town is very excited about it."

"Is that so?"

"Yes, it is."

"I'm glad to hear that."

She did not trust the cool amusement she saw in his eyes. She dropped her own polite smile.

"Welcome to Avalon, Trask."

She turned quickly and walked swiftly away from him.

"Better hurry," he said much too softly behind her. "I hear that night falls fast in the desert. It'll be dark soon."

She resisted the sudden urge to break into a run. With grim determination she kept moving, listening intently for the sound of the Jeep's engine.

She finally heard it come to life with a low, throaty growl. She did not look back but neither did she take a deep breath until the sound receded into the distance.

Then and only then did she allow herself to quicken her step.

Adrenaline rushed through her, creating a tingling in her hands and feet. She was both hot and cold. It was the sort of feeling one got after having had a very close call.

The other shoe had finally dropped. Trask was back in Avalon.